He wa...to...er.

...he looked up at... ...seductive ...ook as they walked... ...m, and he gruffly ...ordered her to go to bed and get some sleep.

Hurt flickered in her eyes, but he assured himself it was for the best. She didn't argue. She hurried to ...er bedroom, making him feel like a heel.

Exhaustion tugged at his limbs, and even though ...e didn't think he could sleep, he stretched out on Megan's sofa. He laid his gun by his side just in ...ase of trouble, then closed his eyes.

...le could practically hear her whisper his name as ...f she wanted him to come to her.

...urious with himself, he rolled to his side to face ...e door, a reminder of the reason he couldn't ...ave. Megan was in danger, and he wouldn't let ...nything happen to her.

...f anyone tried, they'd have to kill him first.

E... ...nted to make love to her.

Sweat beaded on his brow, and he silently cursed.

He couldn't do any of those things because as hard as he'd tried not to care about her, he was starting to have feelings for her.

WARRIOR SON

BY
RITA HERRON

MILLS & BOON

First Published in Great Britain 2016
By Mills & Boon, an imprint of HarperCollins*Publishers*
1 London Bridge Street, London, SE1 9GF

© 2016 Rita B. Herron

ISBN: 978-0-263-91907-3

46-0616

Our policy is to use papers that are natural, renewable and recyclable products and made from wood grown in sustainable forests. The logging and manufacturing processes conform to the legal environmental regulations of the country of origin.

Printed and bound in Spain
by CPI, Barcelona

USA TODAY bestselling author **Rita Herron** wrote her first book when she was twelve but didn't think real people grew up to be writers. Now she writes so she doesn't have to get a real job. A former nursery school teacher and workshop leader, she traded storytelling to kids for writing romance, and now she writes romantic comedies and romantic suspense. Rita lives in Georgia with her family. She loves to hear from readers, so please visit her website, www.ritaherron.com.

For Sue, a cowboy lover!

Chapter One

Deputy Roan Whitefeather didn't belong on McCullen land.

Yet here he stood at the edge of the party celebrating Ray McCullen's marriage to Scarlet Lovett like the outsider he was.

Even though he was blood related to the McMullen men. Even though Joe McCullen was also his father.

He was alone. And he would keep it that way.

Maddox, Brett and Ray had no idea that he was their half brother. Hell, he hadn't known until a few months ago when his mother died and he'd found that damn birth certificate.

And after the trouble the McCullens had this past week—two fires on the ranch—and the bombshell that Joe had a son named Bobby with his mistress, Barbara, Roan would keep the truth about his paternity quiet.

A noise sounded from the hill to the right, and he pivoted, senses honed. Since they still hadn't apprehended the person responsible for the fires, he had to keep an eye out for trouble. With the entire family in celebratory mode, their guards were down. Which would give anyone with a grudge against the McCullens the perfect opportunity to attack.

Maddox, the town sheriff and Roan's boss, stepped in front of the group gathered on the lawn by the creek and raised his champagne glass to toast the happy couple.

For a moment envy mushroomed inside him as he watched Ray kiss Scarlet, and the other brothers and their wives congratulating and hugging one another.

They had weathered some storms, but they were one big happy family now.

The only family he'd ever known was his mother and the people on the res.

He didn't need family or anyone else, he reminded himself.

Still, he'd protect the McCullens because it was his job. And his job was all that mattered to him.

Although questions nagged at him. If Joe McCullen had known about Roan, would he have spent time with him? Would he have brought him to Horseshoe Creek and introduced him to his half brothers?

Or would he have hidden him away like he had his other illegitimate son Bobby Lowman?

The wind blew the trees rustling the leaves, and he scanned the horizon again. The ranch spread for hundreds of miles, livestock and horses roaming the pastures. Joe McCullen had definitely built a legacy here for his sons. And although Ray and Brett had been gone for years, they'd recently returned and planned to help Maddox run the ranch.

Someone didn't want the McCullens to thrive, though. Someone who might have a grudge against Joe besides his mistress and son, Bobby. For all he knew, the problems could be about the land or the way Joe did business.

Hell, if Maddox, Brett or Ray knew Roan was blood related, they might accuse *him* of sabotage.

All the more reason to keep quiet about who he was.

And all the more reason to keep his questions about Joe's death to himself until he found out if there was any substance to his suspicions.

DR. MEGAN LAIL finished her autopsy report on a man named Morty Burns, a ranch hand who'd been shot and left dead outside Pistol Whip, Wyoming. So far, the police had no idea who'd shot him, but she'd done her job—established time and cause of death and recovered the bullet that had taken the man's life.

She had been infatuated with dead bodies since her sister's murder. Not that she enjoyed the morbid side of death, but the bodies told the story.

Just as she'd been driven to know who killed Shelly, family members deserved to know the answers about their loved ones. And it was comforting to know she could help give them closure.

Still, her father had been disappointed in her. He'd raved about Shelly and her beauty, constantly reminding Megan that she hadn't been graced with extraordinary looks, that she had to use her brain to get anywhere in life. She hadn't minded that at all. Science had always interested her.

When Shelly had been killed and investigators had converged, she'd realized that the medical examiner was the one who'd discovered the clue that led to the culprit. Sitting at the trial with her father, she'd decided she wanted to be an ME.

She removed her gloves, filed her report, then clicked to the news and studied the story about the recent arrest of Bobby and Barbara Lowman made by Deputy Roan Whitefeather and the sheriff. The arrests had hit big in Pistol Whip because they centered around the McCullens of Horseshoe Creek and revealed that the patriarch of the family, Joe, who had recently died, had another family on the side.

A mistress named Barbara and an illegitimate son, Bobby.

Bobby had resented Joe for years, and his mother Barbara felt betrayed because Joe never married her. They'd also been upset over the stipulations Joe placed on the will regarding Bobby's inheritance, that Bobby would have to work under the tutelage of Maddox.

They'd pulled a gun on Scarlet and threatened the family, and both were in prison. But neither admitted to setting the two fires on the ranch, one of which had ruined the family's long-standing home.

More details followed in the article.

Former rodeo star Brett McCullen has offered a $10,000 reward for information leading to the arrest of the arsonist.

Megan massaged her temple as her mind took a leap. Something had been bothering her about Joe McCullen's autopsy.

Her curious nature, the attribute that helped her most in her job, pummeled her with what-ifs. What if Joe's death hadn't been due to his illness?

She'd detected something odd about the tox screen and relayed her concerns to Dr. Cumberland, the McCullens' family doctor and Joe's lifelong friend.

The conversation replayed in her head.

"You're young and new to this, Megan. You obviously made a mistake," Dr. Cumberland had said. "I took care of Joe during his illness. He had emphysema. Just look at his X-rays and scans."

She'd looked at them and Joe had in fact had emphysema. "But there are slight traces of a toxin indicating he was poisoned. It appears to be cyanide."

Dr. Cumberland had scanned her notes and scowled. "Run the tests again. This can't be right."

Megan had gone to the lab, extracted another sample and sent it to be tested. An hour later, Dr. Cumberland had hand delivered the report to her.

"See, there is no sign of poison. The lab tech mixed up the reports. The result you first received was for another case."

Yet the fact that someone was trying to hurt the Mc-Cullens bothered her. She was meticulous in her work and never made mistakes.

And she couldn't let this go without one more look. Adrenaline pumping, she accessed the autopsy file. Guilt nagged at her for questioning Dr. Cumberland, though.

The family physician had worked in Pistol Whip for years. Everyone in town adored him. For goodness' sake, he'd delivered half the town's babies, including the McCullen boys, Maddox, Brett and Ray.

And he had been distraught over Joe's death.

He wouldn't have had any reason to lie to her or cover up a tox report.

But...something just didn't feel right. She didn't think she'd made a mistake...

She picked up the phone and called the lab tech, a young guy named Howard, then explained about the two different results.

"I guess it's possible that I mixed them up," Howard said. "But I double-check everything. I'm OCD that way."

So was she. In their line of work, details were important.

Howard cleared his throat. "If you still have a sample I can retest."

Megan's pulse hammered. "As a matter of fact, I do. I'll send it over right now, Howard. But please keep this between you and me."

"Sure, Megan. What's going on?"

"I just want to double-check for myself."

He agreed to call her when he was done, and she decided she'd talk to Deputy Whitefeather while she waited on the results. He would know if Joe had any enemies.

She didn't want to bother Joe's sons unless she had something concrete.

The thought of seeing the deputy again stirred a hot sensation deep in her belly. She'd met Roan when he worked on the res on the tribal council.

When his mother died, she'd performed the autopsy. Roan had been devastated. His mother was all the family he had.

She'd hated to see the big, strong man in pain. A comforting hug had led to a kiss. A kiss filled with such loneliness that she hadn't been able to resist. They'd made love for hours.

Sometimes at night when she was alone, she closed her eyes and could still feel his big, strong hands touching her, stroking her, loving her. She'd never felt anything so intense.

But the next morning, he'd walked away from her and hadn't spoken to her since.

What would he say if she showed up with questions about Joe McCullen's death?

ROAN CONGRATULATED THE happy couple before he drove back to the cabin he'd rented on the river. He missed the res, but working for the sheriff's department meant he worked for all the people in Pistol Whip and the county it encompassed, so living in a neutral, more central location seemed wisest.

"Did you see anything suspicious tonight?" Maddox asked as they watched Scarlet toss the bouquet.

"No. I'll ride across the property on my way home and take a look around, though."

"Thanks." Maddox shook his hand. "I appreciate you covering the office while Rose and I were gone. Brett said he was going to hire extra security for the ranch for a while, at least until we find out who set those fires. He's rebuilding the barns and the main house is already done."

"Extra security is not a bad idea," Roan said. Maddox,

Brett and Ray couldn't keep up the ranch and do surveillance around the clock by themselves.

After all, on a spread this size, there were dozens of places for someone to hide.

Some blonde caught the bouquet, prompting squeals from the guests, and Maddox joined his wife on the dance floor.

Roan leaned against the edge of the makeshift bar they'd set up for the reception, his mouth watering for a cold beer. But he didn't drink on the job.

The McCullen men danced and swayed with their wives, and for some odd reason, a pang hit him. They looked so damn happy.

They were family.

Something he didn't have anymore.

Yet…they were his blood kin.

It doesn't matter. You're not going to tell them.

Hell, they'd probably think he was like Bobby Lowman, that he wanted something from them.

He wanted nothing but to live in peace. Caring about folks meant pain when they went away.

His mother's face flashed in his mind. Truth be known, she was the only person in the world he'd ever loved.

His phone buzzed, and he checked the number, surprised to see Dr. Megan Lail's name appear. Damn, he hadn't seen her since last year, the night his mother died.

Since the night they'd…gotten hot and sweaty between the sheets.

Perspiration broke out on his brow and he swiped at it. It was the most erotic sex he'd ever had. For months he'd dreamed about it, woken up to an image of Megan's breasts swaying above him as she impaled herself on his shaft. Of him pumping inside her, of her ivory skin blushing with passion and her soft moans of ecstasy filling the air.

The phone jarred him again, and he cursed and stepped

aside, away from the festivities so he could hear. She was the ME, after all. She might have news about a case.

"Deputy Whitefeather."

"Roan, it's Dr. Lail. Megan."

The sound of her husky voice triggered more memories of their lovemaking and made his body go rock hard.

He kept his reply short, afraid he'd give away the yearning in his voice if he said too much. "Yeah?"

"I need to see you."

His breath stalled in his chest. She *needed* him? Instantly his thoughts turned to worry. What if the damn condoms hadn't worked that night? They'd made love—how many times?

"Megan, what's wrong? Are you okay?"

"I'm fine," she said softly, arousing tender feelings inside him. Feelings he didn't want to have.

"Then why did you call?"

Her sharp intake indicated he'd been brusque.

"I'm sorry, if this is a bad time, I can call back."

Now he *had* to know the reason for her call. "No, it's fine. I'm standing guard at Ray McCullen's wedding in case that arsonist strikes again."

"That's sort of the reason I called."

He frowned, his gaze piercing the night as he pivoted to scan the pastures. "Do you have information that could help?"

"I'm not sure," she said. "But I had some questions about Joe McCullen's autopsy."

Roan went completely still. "What kind of questions?"

"I don't feel comfortable discussing it over the phone. Can we meet?"

An image of her unruly, long wavy hair surfaced. Although she usually wore it in a tight bun, the moment he'd yanked that bun free, he'd unleashed some kind of sexual animal that she kept hidden from the world.

Seeing her was not a good idea.

"Please," she said. "It's important. And…you're the only one I trust."

Damn, did she have to put it that way?

"All right. Where are you?"

"I'm still at the morgue. But I'd prefer to meet you somewhere else."

He could go to her place. But that would be too personal. Too tempting.

"I'll be done soon. How about we meet at The Silver Bullet in an hour?"

She agreed and hung up. For the next hour, Roan watched the celebration wind down. The happy couple kissed and said goodbye as they rushed to the limo Ray had rented. They were headed to the airport to fly to Mexico for their honeymoon.

He left the security team Brett had hired to watch over the ranch, took a quick drive across the property, looking for any stray vehicle or a fire, but all seemed quiet.

By the time he reached The Silver Bullet, he was sweating just thinking about seeing Megan again. He spotted her in a booth to the side when he entered. Country music blared from the speakers, smoke clogged the room and footsteps pounded from the line dance on the dance floor.

Megan looked up at him, one hand clenching a wineglass, her eyes worried. He ordered a beer and joined her. She'd secured her hair in that bun again, she wore no makeup and her clothes were nondescript. Once again it struck him that she downplayed her looks. He wondered why.

She could wear a damn feed sack and she'd still be the prettiest girl he'd ever met. And he knew what she looked like with that hair down, her body naked, her lips trailing kisses down his chest.

"Megan," he said as he slipped into the booth across from her.

"Thank you for coming." She licked her lips, drawing his eyes to her mouth. He took a sip of beer to stall and wrangle his libido.

"You said it was important." *Please spit it out so I can go home and forget about you.*

Not that he ever had. But he was trying.

"Roan, I may be jumping the gun, but I had to talk to someone about this."

The worry in her voice sounded serious. He straightened. "What is it?"

She looked down in her glass. "When I performed Joe McCullen's autopsy the first time, I…thought I saw something suspicious in his tox report."

Roan's heart jumped.

"With all that's happened at Horseshoe Creek recently," Megan continued, "and with that Lowman woman and her son, and those fires…it made me think of that report."

"I don't understand," Roan said. "What was it that bothered you?"

She inhaled a deep breath, then glanced around the room warily, as if she didn't want anyone to hear their conversation. His instincts roared to life. She'd said she didn't feel comfortable talking on the phone.

"Megan, tell me," he said.

"I don't think Joe McCullen died of natural causes." She leaned closer, her voice low. "I think he was murdered."

Chapter Two

Megan's words reverberated in Roan's ears. *Joe McCullen was murdered.*

"How?"

"Poison. Cyanide."

"Are you sure?"

Megan winced. "Not exactly, but—"

"But what?" He leaned across the table, speaking in a hushed tone. "Why did you come to me if you don't know?"

She fiddled with a strand of hair, tucking it back in that bun. He wanted to unknot it and run his fingers through it.

But he had to focus.

"I know what I saw in that initial report. But Dr. Cumberland made me question my results and ran it again. That's when it came back normal."

"So you have one bad test and one normal one?"

"Yes."

"Go on."

She fidgeted with her little round glasses, pushing them up on her nose. "I talked to the lab tech and he's meticulous with details. He didn't think he mixed up the reports like Dr. Cumberland said."

"Everyone makes mistakes," Roan said.

"I know." Megan took a sip of her wine. "But I've seen this guy's work. He's OCD. He checks things at least three times."

Roan didn't know how to respond.

If Megan was right, that meant Joe had been murdered.

But they couldn't make accusations without something more concrete. That would only cause more trouble for the McCullens.

If she was right, though, then someone had gotten away with killing Joe—his father. And he couldn't let that happen.

"Anyway, I talked to the lab tech," Megan said. "I preserved a sample and he's going to retest it."

Roan gave a clipped nod. "When will you have the results?"

"Probably tomorrow. I asked him to keep it quiet."

"Good." His gaze met hers. "Don't tell anyone else about this, Megan. You don't want to create panic if there's nothing to it."

A wary look flashed in those dark brown eyes. "Of course I won't say anything. But if it's true, someone needs to find out who poisoned Joe McCullen."

"And how they did it," Roan muttered. "It would have been difficult with Dr. Cumberland monitoring his health." And there was no way he could accuse the good doctor of foul play. Roan knew Cumberland personally. He was the most compassionate man Roan had ever met. He'd donated time to the res when they needed a Western doctor.

He'd even treated Roan's mother. For God's sake, he'd held her hand and comforted her before she passed.

But Joe could have had visitors. Someone could have slipped something to him when nobody was watching.

"What if Barbara or her son, Bobby, did it?" Megan said. "You know Barbara got tired of waiting on Joe to marry her. Maybe she decided to kill him and get what was owed her."

Roan frowned. "True. But if he was sick anyway, why kill him? Why not wait until the disease got the best of him?"

MEGAN CONSIDERED ROAN'S STATEMENT. Why *would* some-one go to the trouble to kill a man who was already dying?

"Megan?"

His gruff voice always turned her inside out. When she looked up at him, he was watching her with an intensity that sent a tingle through her.

"I don't know." Barbara and Bobby resented the fact that Joe kept them a secret. Part of her understood their animosity. "Maybe Barbara knew that Joe had included her in the will. But what if he'd decided to change it recently? Maybe he was going to cut them out for some reason."

"And one or both of them decided to kill him before he could," Roan finished.

She nodded. "That would make sense."

Roan's wide jaw snapped tight. "If that's the case, I need proof. I doubt either one of the Lowmans are going to cop to murder."

She doubted that, too. "What's our next move?"

Roan's gaze met hers. "*We* don't have a next move, Megan. If you go around making accusations, you could get hurt."

Megan drummed her fingers on the table. She noticed Roan watching and realized how desperately she needed a manicure—the chemicals she worked with at the morgue were hell on her nails and skin—so she curled her fingers into her palms.

Still the questions she'd had since she'd first suspected poison in Joe's tox report nagged at her. She wasn't some delicate princess type who ran from trouble. When she had questions, she sought answers. It was the nature of being a scientist and doctor. "But I can't let this go, Roan."

Roan laid one big hand on top of both of hers. "Listen to me. I'm the lawman. First things first. Get that report, then call me with the results. If you confirm poison, I'll investigate."

Memories of him intimately touching her flooded her as she stared at their fingers. She wanted to relive that night. At least one more time.

But Roan quickly pulled his hand away, his jaw set hard again, his high cheekbones accentuated by the way his hair was pulled back in a leather tie. The only time he'd ever let down his guard was the night his mother died.

He obviously regretted doing it then.

But at least he hadn't thought she was crazy. If that report confirmed what she suspected, he'd investigate.

She'd have to be satisfied with that for now.

ROAN TRIED TO shake off the ridiculous need to fold Megan in his arms and ask her to go home with him. He could use the sweet release of a hot night in bed with her again.

But one look into that vulnerable face and he knew that would be a mistake. Megan was not a one night stand kind of girl.

Which made it even more awkward that he'd used her for comfort the night his mother died and never contacted her again.

She knew what she was getting into. She's a big girl.

Only she wasn't like the other women he knew. She was smart, curious, a problem solver.

And she had no idea how beautiful she was.

But her words disturbed him. She thought Joe was murdered. And she hadn't just offered some harebrained reason. She had offered a believable motive.

One he would investigate. On his own.

He didn't want her near him. She was too damn tempting.

Worse, asking questions could be dangerous.

He tossed some bills on the table to pay for the drink. "Like I said, call me when you get the results of that tox screen."

He stood, tipped his Stetson and strode through the busy bar. Music rocked the establishment, laughter and chatter filling the air. Men and women came here to unwind and hook up.

But he ignored the interested females and strode outside. His mind was already ticking away what he needed to do.

He and Maddox were still trying to figure out who set those fires. Could the same person have murdered Joe?

And then there was Barbara and Bobby Lowman...

Megan's comment about the will made him reach for his phone. He climbed in his SUV and punched Darren Bush's number, but received the lawyer's voice mail. "It's Deputy Whitefeather," he said. "Please call me as soon as possible."

He might be jumping the gun, but he'd drive out to the Lowmans' house tonight and take a look around.

MEGAN WATCHED ROAN leave with mixed emotions. She was relieved he'd taken her concerns seriously.

But disappointed that he didn't hint at wanting a personal relationship.

She blinked back tears. Good grief. She wasn't a crier. She'd learned long ago not to let rejection destroy her. Like her father said, she had brains and she'd use them to survive.

In fact, it was better she wasn't gorgeous like her sister. The cops suspected Shelly was targeted by the man who'd killed her because of her looks. Even their mother had been model pretty.

But she'd never gotten over Shelly's death and had eventually committed suicide as if Megan wasn't enough to fill the void Shelly had left.

As if she was the daughter who should have died instead of Shelly.

Bile rose to her throat at the memories, and she pushed her wine aside, then headed to the door. She elbowed her way through the crowd, ignoring catcalls from drunk cowboys as she stepped outside.

One beefy man in a big black hat grabbed her arm. "What's your hurry? Let your hair down and we could have a lot of fun."

She glared at him with her best "get lost" look. "Sorry, mister. Not interested."

His fingers tightened around her arm. "Hey, don't I know you? You're that medical examiner who sent my brother to jail."

She arched a brow, struggling to recall the details. "I'm sorry, I don't know what you're talking about."

"You don't remember? You said my brother killed this drifter and he's locked up now 'cause of you."

The hair on the back of her neck prickled. His tone reeked of bitterness. "I'm sorry for what happened to your family," she said. "But I was just doing my job."

"Well, you were wrong, lady. My brother didn't kill no one."

Megan forced herself to remain calm. "I file a report based on scientific evidence I find in the autopsy. The rest is up to the law and a jury." She yanked her arm away, then took a deep breath. "Now, good night."

He muttered a profanity as she brushed him out of the way and walked to her car. Gravel crunched beneath her boots, and she glanced over her shoulder to make sure the jerk wasn't following.

Keys already in hand, she pressed the unlock button on the key fob and slid into the driver's seat of her van. She liked driving something with room enough to carry her medical bag and a change of clothes when she worked all night.

The engine chugged to life, and she checked her rearview mirror. The man had followed her outside and was glaring at her as she disappeared.

Nerves knotted her stomach. He'd said she was wrong about his brother. Had she been wrong?

Everyone made mistakes. But she was careful about her reports.

Although sometimes her curiosity got the better of her—like now?

Was she looking for trouble regarding Joe McCullen's death when there hadn't been foul play?

ROAN PULLED INTO the driveway of Barbara's house, noting that most of the lights were off in the neighborhood. Barbara's house was dark, vacant now that she and her son were incarcerated.

He cut the lights, then glanced around the property, hoping not to alert anyone that he was nosing around. Maddox would probably be ticked off if he knew Roan was here, that he hadn't told him about his conversation with Megan.

But there was no need in stirring up Maddox's emotions over questions about his father's death unless he had some concrete evidence that Joe had been murdered.

He grabbed his flashlight and walked around to the rear, then checked the back door. He picked the lock and slipped inside. The house smelled of mildew, stale cigarette smoke and beer.

He shined the light through the kitchen, expecting to see dirty dishes, but the sink was empty and, except for a few empty beer bottles, the counter was free of clutter.

Remembering that he was searching for poison, he opened the refrigerator and scanned the contents. A milk carton, juice, soda, a head of wilted lettuce, carton of eggs, yogurt. He opened the milk and gagged at the sour smell.

But he saw nothing inside that looked like poison.

Next he checked the cabinets, searching below the sink, and found household cleaners, some of which were poisonous, but was it the poison that had allegedly killed Joe?

He quickly cataloged the contents of the cabinet, then searched the living room, the closet, bedrooms and bathrooms. More cleaner in the bathroom, but nothing suspicious per se.

Of course Barbara could easily have had time to dispose of the poison.

Although in light of the fact that no one had questioned Joe's cause of death, she might not have bothered. Some people were cocky enough to think they'd never get caught.

Working on that theory, he checked the bathroom garbage cans, then the kitchen. Beer cans, an empty pizza box, other assorted trash.

Frustrated, he eased out the back door and checked the outside garbage can. Only one bag of garbage, which surprised him, but before he went through it, he noticed the storage shed behind the house.

Sensing he was on to something, he picked the lock on the shed. When he opened it, he shined his flashlight across the interior and noticed several bags of potting soil, planters and gardening tools.

A storage bin sat to the right, and he lifted the lid and illuminated it with the flashlight beam.

Fertilizer.

His pulse hammered as past cases of poisoning played in his head. Fertilizers contained cyanide.

Chapter Three

Roan snapped pictures of the fertilizer bags and other assorted chemicals inside the shed, but he was careful not to touch anything. If they learned that Joe McCullen was murdered, he'd have to go by the book and gather evidence.

But the fact that Barbara had products containing cyanide definitely put her on his suspect list.

He had no idea how she got the poison into Joe, though. Had she laced food or a drink with it? That would be the most common or easiest way.

If so, that meant she had to have had access to him, had to have visited him.

Maddox might know. But Roan wasn't ready to discuss the situation with him.

He noted a pair of gardening gloves, then a box of disposable latex gloves and took a picture of the box. A lot of people bought those disposable gloves for cleaning, but Barbara could have used them when preparing whatever concoction she'd used to hide the cyanide.

He was jumping to conclusions, he realized. Just because Barbara had motive didn't mean she was the only one who wanted Joe dead.

Arlis Bennett at the Circle T was suspected of hiring someone to set the fires on behalf of himself and his cousin, Boyle Gates. Gates had been furious at Maddox for arresting him for cattle rustling.

But the timing was off. Gates hadn't been caught until after Joe's death.

Although, what if Joe had figured out what Gates was doing?

Gates could have poisoned Joe, hoping whatever Joe had on him would die with his death.

Knowing it was too late to question either of them tonight, he mentally filed his questions for the next day.

He locked the shed as he left, once again surveying the yard and property as he walked back to his vehicle. But as he drove away from the house, his mind turned from murder to Megan.

Seeing her tonight had resurrected memories of the one night they'd spent together.

How could the worst day of his life also be one of the best?

Losing his mother had been so painful he'd allowed himself to drown his sorrows in Megan's sweet body. Her erotic touches had assuaged his anguish and helped him forget for a moment that the only person he'd ever loved, the only person who'd ever given a damn about him, was gone.

Forever.

Although, maybe he'd only perceived the night with Megan was so special because he'd been in pain...

That had to be it. If they slept together again, he'd probably be disappointed.

Perspiration rolled down his neck as he crossed through town, then veered down the drive to his cabin and parked. He climbed out, the wind rustling the trees, the sound of a coyote echoing from somewhere nearby.

Shoulders squared, he let himself inside the cabin, the cold empty room a reminder that he was alone.

Sometimes, he imagined walking in and seeing Megan in his kitchen or in his den. But most often he imagined her in his bedroom.

Waking up with Megan in his arms that night had been pure bliss. But when he'd looked at her sweet innocent face, the guilt had overwhelmed him.

Guilt for feeling pleasure when his mother had died. Then guilt for taking advantage of Megan.

Because he'd known that she wasn't the type of woman to hook up on a whim. That she might perceive their night of sex as the beginning of something—maybe a long-term relationship.

And he couldn't go there. Couldn't care about anyone. Losing them hurt too damn much.

Just like he wouldn't allow himself to care about the McCullens. Sure, he'd find Joe's murderer—*if* he was murdered—but then he'd step away.

And the McCullens would never know his secret.

THE NEXT MORNING, Megan couldn't shake her encounter from the night before with the man outside The Silver Bullet. Pistol Whip was a small town, but she worked for the county hospital and medical examiner's office, which covered a much larger territory.

Her boss and the senior medical examiner Frank Mantle had overseen all her cases the first year, but now he pretty much left her alone. He was nearing retirement age, suffered from arthritis and wanted to spend more time with his wife, so Megan shouldered the majority of the autopsies.

She struggled to recall the case the man she'd run into was talking about, then searched through her files. The fifth file she pulled had to be it.

The murdered man's name was Carlton Langer. He was twenty-five, just graduated from college and was traveling across country to sow his oats before he settled into a full-time job.

She rubbed her forehead as she recalled the details of the case. Carlton had been brutally stabbed three times in the chest. The knife had sliced his aorta and he'd bled out immediately.

Judging from the angle of the blade and the fact that the knife was missing, she'd had to rule it a homicide. She turned to her computer and pulled up the news reports that had followed the stabbing and noted that a man named Tad Hummings had been arrested the day after the brutal assault.

According to the officer who arrested him, Hummings had been high on drugs and the murder weapon had been found in his house with his fingerprints on it. Later, when he'd come down off the drugs, he didn't remember anything.

She rubbed her temple. It sounded as if he'd blacked out. She read the drug tox screen. Cocaine.

His brother Dale had hired a lawyer who'd argued that the drugs had caused Hummings's erratic, violent behavior.

But a man was still dead, and Tad Hummings was sent to prison.

She closed the file. Dale Hummings blamed her, but she hadn't made a mistake. His brother had. There was no question about Langer's cause of death, either.

Joe McCullen was a different story. She picked up the phone to call Howard and see if he'd finished that tox screen.

ROAN DROVE TOWARD the prison where Barbara had been incarcerated. He might be jumping the gun, but he'd always suspected she'd lied about setting the fires on Horseshoe Creek.

A cigarette butt had been found in the ashes of the barn fire, the same brand she smoked.

His phone buzzed. Maddox. "Deputy Whitefeather."

"I got a lead on Romley. He was spotted in Cheyenne. I'm on my way to check it out. You're in charge."

Stan Romley worked for Gates and Arlis Bennett and had taken a job at Horseshoe Creek to spy on the McCullens.

"I've got it covered," Roan said, although he was thirty miles from town. But if anything came up, he'd rush back.

"Call me if you need backup," Roan said.

Maddox agreed and hung up. Roan pulled up to the guard's station and identified himself. The guard waved him through and he parked. The wind howled as he waited outside to enter, then it took him another ten minutes to clear security.

Barbara had been placed in a minimum-security prison to serve out her year sentence for aggravated assault against the sheriff and against Scarlet Lovett. She'd cut the brake lines on the woman's car, and Scarlet had nearly been killed when she crashed into the side of the social services building where she worked.

Barbara had pled out to a lesser sentence and had to sign an agreement that she wouldn't file for an appeal in return.

He took a seat at the visitor's station, and a guard escorted Barbara to a chair facing him through a Plexiglas partition. A seed of sympathy for her sprouted inside him— he knew the story. She and Joe McCullen had had an affair when Maddox and his brothers were children, and she'd gotten pregnant with Bobby.

When Joe's wife, Grace, had died in a car accident, Barbara had no doubt expected Joe to marry her. But that hadn't happened. Her bitterness had festered. When Joe died, she'd hoped her son would inherit his share of Horseshoe Creek.

Joe had included him in the will, but neither Barbara nor Bobby were satisfied.

The woman looked pale and angry, her dyed blond hair now mixed with muddy brown. For a moment, she studied him, obviously wondering what his agenda was.

She'd been volatile when she was arrested. Prison had drained the fight from her.

He picked up the phone and waited until she did the same.

"Ms. Lowman," he began. "Thank you for seeing me."

She shrugged, her eyes fixed on him. "Didn't realize I had a choice."

No, she was at the mercy of the justice system now. "How are you?"

She frowned. "What? Like you care?"

She was right. He didn't really care. She'd tried to kill an innocent woman. Scarlet was one of the nicest people he'd ever met.

"Why are you really here, Deputy?" Barbara asked.

Roan narrowed his eyes. "I thought you might be ready to tell the truth about the fires at Horseshoe Creek. I could speak to the judge on your behalf and arrange an early parole if you confess."

Barbara's sarcastic laugh echoed over the line. "Right. I confess to another crime and you'll get me out of here earlier? What kind of fool do you think I am?"

"I don't think you're a fool at all," Roan said. "I think you resented Joe for not marrying you, especially after you waited for him all these years."

"Who said I waited for him?"

"You never married." He leaned closer to the Plexiglass. "Did you even date anyone else, Barbara? Or did you sit at home hoping he'd call?" He lowered his voice, taunting her. "Did you keep thinking that next month or next year he'd finally admit that he loved you and make you his wife?"

Barbara's nostrils flared. "How dare you."

"I understand your anger," Roan continued. "You gave Joe a son just like Grace did, but her sons got to live on the big ranch. They got to have Joe's name and grow up in the house with him. They got a real father. Yet McCullen kept you and Bobby on the side. Made you live in the shadows and take whatever little pieces he had left over from his real family." He paused for effect. "He was ashamed of the two of you."

She lurched up, body shaking with fury. "You bastard. Joe loved me and Bobby."

"If he'd loved you, he would have introduced you to his sons. He would have married you." Roan remained seated, his expression calm, his eyes scrutinizing her. "But he didn't, and every day, every month, every year that went by, your bitterness grew. Then…what happened? Maybe you gave him an ultimatum, that you'd expose him to Maddox and Brett and Ray, if he didn't marry you."

"That's ridiculous," Barbara said, although the guilt that flashed in her eyes indicated he'd hit the nail on the head.

He raised a brow. "But he still refused. That must have torn you up inside."

Barbara sank into the chair again and looked down at the floor, her face wrenched in pain. "He felt guilty about his wife's death. That's why he never married me. Even from the grave she kept her tentacles embedded in him."

"Then you finally snapped, didn't you, Barbara. You decided that if he wouldn't marry you, you'd get rid of him. At least then you and your son could get what he owed you."

"He did owe us," Barbara snapped. "We loved him and kept his secret to protect him, and he still let us down."

"That was the final straw, wasn't it?" Roan said. "He refused to marry you. Maybe he even said he'd never marry you." He arched a brow. "Maybe he threatened to cut you out of the will."

Her chin lifted and tears glittered in her eyes.

"So you decided to get rid of him. He was sick already so you poisoned him. Nice and slow, just a little at a time."

"What?" Barbara's jaw went slack. "Poisoned Joe?"

"Yes. Did you take him food or a drink when you visited him? Did you slowly poison him and watch him die?"

Barbara's face blanched. "What are you saying? That Joe was murdered?"

"You tell me, Ms. Lowman. Did you kill Joe McCullen?"

MEGAN CLOSED THE door to her office as she waited on the lab to answer. Finally Howard picked up. "Howard, it's Megan."

"I was just getting ready to call you," Howard said.

"Did you finish the tests?"

"Yes. Meet me at the coffee shop across from the hospital."

"I'm on my way." Megan snatched her purse, hurried from her office and locked the door behind her. She caught the elevator from the basement floor where the morgue was housed, then wove through the corridors of the hospital past the gift shop and outside. She had to cross the street to the corner café.

By the time she arrived, Howard was ordering coffee. She ordered a latte and then they claimed a booth in the back corner.

"What did you find?" she asked, unable to stand the wait.

Howard glanced around the coffee shop, then spoke in a hushed tone. "You were right, Megan. There were definitely traces of cyanide in McCullen's system."

Megan's pulse pounded. That meant Joe was murdered.

"What are you going to do with this information?" Howard asked.

Megan blew the steam rolling off her coffee. "I have to go to the police." In fact, she already had.

"Joe was the sheriff's father, right?"

"Yes." And she had no idea how he would react.

"Didn't the sheriff live with his father?" Howard asked.

Megan frowned. "Yes."

"How did someone poison his old man without him knowing it?"

"I have no idea, but I know someone who'll find out." She pulled her phone from her purse and punched Roan's number. His phone rolled to voice mail, and she left a message for him to call her.

"What about Dr. Cumberland?" Howard asked.

"He was close to Joe, but with Joe's illness, I guess he never thought to look for another cause."

"You'll tell him?" Howard asked.

"Of course." She didn't look forward to it, either, not after the way he'd reacted when she'd questioned the tox screen.

They finished their coffee and Howard had to rush back to the lab. She lingered, hoping Roan would return her call, but finally decided to go back to work. When she stepped outside, a chilly wind rippled through the air. The sky was dark with clouds, although it hadn't rained in days.

She shivered, and had an eerie feeling as if someone was watching her. Remembering her encounter with Hummings's brother the night before, she checked around her as she walked to the crosswalk, but she didn't spot the man anywhere.

She stepped up to the street where a group had gathered waiting on the traffic signal. Her phone rang just as the light turned. She pressed Answer and fell into step with the crowd, but suddenly a gunshot blasted the air. The crowd screamed and began to run, and she felt someone shove her from behind, then lost her balance.

She landed on her hands and knees, and her phone went flying across the street.

She looked up and screamed as an oncoming car screeched toward her.

Chapter Four

Roan studied Barbara for a reaction. She seemed shocked at his accusation. "Did you poison Joe McCullen, Barbara?"

Barbara's handcuffs jangled as she waved her hands dramatically in the air. "Of course not. I can't believe you'd ask me such a thing. I loved that man more than life itself."

"You loved him, but we both know you resented the fact that he never married you."

Barbara looked down at the jagged ends of her nails. "Did someone really poison him?"

"There were traces of cyanide in his system."

She jerked her gaze up, eyes flaring with surprise. Or guilt? "Cyanide?"

"Yes. Fertilizer has cyanide in it, Barbara. And you have plenty of that at your house. You use it in your gardening."

Another flicker of unease in her eyes. Then she seemed to pull herself together. "Gardening was a hobby of mine. But a lot of people garden. That's not a crime."

"No, but slipping cyanide into food or a drink that someone ingests is."

"I didn't slip cyanide into anything."

Roan worked his mouth from side to side. "Then maybe your son did."

Anger slashed her tired-looking features. "My son did no such thing."

Roan arched a brow. "Are you sure about that, Barbara? He resented Joe more than you did. He hated all of the McCullens. Maybe he even went to see Joe and Joe told him not to come back, that he didn't want his real sons to know about him." He paused. "Maybe he told Bobby that he'd never be a McCullen. That if he got any of the land, he'd have to work underneath Maddox like he was some kind of servant."

Barbara shot up. "Stop it. Joe wouldn't have talked to Bobby like that. He loved our son."

"But not like he did Maddox or Brett or Ray," Roan pressed.

Rage darkened Barbara's eyes. "Listen to me, Deputy. Bobby and I have suffered enough. We have both been locked up because of that family, but we did not kill Joe. Now leave us alone."

She whirled around and gestured toward the guard. "Take me back to my cell, please."

The guard glanced at Roan, and he shrugged and gestured okay. But before Barbara stepped through the door, he cleared his throat. "Know this, Barbara. If you or Bobby did kill Joe, I'll find out. And any chance of you getting free will disappear."

She shot him a venomous look, then shuffled out the door with the guard.

Roan contemplated her reaction.

Had she been so desperate to protect her son and see him get what was owed to him that she killed the man she loved?

MEGAN'S HEART HAMMERED as tires squealed and the car roared toward her. Terrified for her life, she rolled sideways toward the sidewalk seconds before the car screeched to a stop.

If she hadn't been so fast, the car would have hit her.

Her life flashed in front of her. Playing with her sister when she was little. Losing her. Losing her mother… Her father looking at her like she was nothing.

Being so lonely sometimes she thought she'd die…

Then that night with Roan…his handsome face. Him bending over her, making love to her.

She wanted to live, to be with him again.

Shouts and screams echoed around her, then a man raced to her and helped her up. "Are you all right, miss?"

The driver of the car jumped out, the woman's face ashen as she stumbled toward Megan. "Oh, God, honey, are you okay?"

"Yes," Megan said. She glanced around the street and saw several people watching while others had dispersed in fear. "Someone fired a gun."

"I heard it," the man who'd helped her up said. "But I didn't see where it came from."

"I think it was a car backfiring," a gray-haired man said.

"No, no, it was definitely a gun," another woman said.

Megan didn't know what to think. But…she'd also thought she'd felt someone push her before she fell.

You're just being paranoid.

Although she had expressed suspicions about Joe McCullen's death, the only people who knew that were Howard and Roan. And they were on her side.

Of course Tad Hummings's brother had cornered her in the bar—would he try to kill her because she'd helped send his brother to prison?

"Are you sure you don't need an ambulance?" the driver of the car asked.

"I'm sure." All she wanted to do was call Roan.

Then hide in the morgue where she was safe.

Except she needed to talk to Dr. Cumberland. And he wasn't going to like what she had to say.

ROAN CONSIDERED QUESTIONING Bobby but decided he needed concrete proof before he did. Something that would force Bobby to confess.

He climbed in his SUV to leave the prison and phoned

Megan as he drove onto the highway. Her phone rang three times before she answered. When she did, she sounded breathless.

"Megan, are you all right?"

"No. I mean, yes," she said. "I'm on the way back to the morgue."

"What's wrong?"

"I went to meet Howard to discuss the tox results, but on the way back to the hospital a gunshot sounded. The crowd panicked and started running, and I fell in the street."

Roan went very still. "You fell?"

"Yes, well, I don't know. I thought for a minute I was pushed, but I could have imagined it. Everyone was running to get away."

"Who fired the gun?"

'I have no idea," she said. "The street was crowded and it happened so fast. One man said he thought it was a car backfiring, but I don't think so."

"Did you see anyone suspicious?"

"No. But like I said, it happened really fast and a car was coming so I had to roll out of the way."

He didn't like this one damn bit. First, she'd come to him questioning Joe McCullen's death. Now a gun had gone off in the street and she'd fallen and nearly been hit by a car.

Too coincidental.

Roan clenched the phone with clammy hands. "Who else did you tell about the tox report?"

Tension filled the air. "Just you and Howard, the lab tech and Dr. Cumberland. But I haven't seen him since I met with Howard earlier."

"What were the results?"

"There was definitely cyanide in Joe's system, Roan. Probably administered in small doses over a long period of time so as not to draw suspicion."

Roan veered onto the road leading toward the McCullens' ranch, Horseshoe Creek. He needed to find out who'd visited Joe on a regular basis.

"I know this will upset Dr. Cumberland," Megan said. "He and the McCullens are good friends."

"So how did he miss the fact that his patient was poisoned?"

"Like I said, it was probably administered in slow doses. Since Joe was already ill, Dr. Cumberland must have assumed his weakening condition was due to the disease."

Roan's mind raced. Barbara was his prime suspect, but her shock had seemed real. "But one question is still bothering me—why kill a dying man?"

"Maybe Barbara and Bobby knew about the will, but thought Joe was going to change it and take them out. She could have wanted him dead before he could make the change."

"That's possible. I put a call in to Joe's lawyer to find out."

His phone beeped. Maddox. "Listen, Megan, Maddox is calling. Let me talk to him."

"Are you going to tell him his father was murdered?"

Roan hesitated. That was not a conversation he was eager to have.

"Not yet. I want some proof of a viable suspect before I go to him."

"I don't blame you. The McCullens have been through a lot. But they will want to know."

He was well aware of that. "Don't worry. I'll tell him when the time is right." He hesitated, then remembered her close call on the street. "Be careful, Megan. And don't talk to anyone but Dr. Cumberland about this."

She agreed, and he hit Connect to respond to Maddox. "It's Roan."

"I think I've tracked Romley down. I'm staking out a motel where he was last spotted."

"Do you need backup?"

"Not yet. I'll let you know if I do. Is anything going on there?"

Roan swallowed hard. He hated to lie, but…he wasn't ready to divulge the truth. "No. I'll ride out and check on the ranch soon."

"Thanks. That security detail Brett hired should have it covered. But I'm worried about Mama Mary and Rose staying at the house while I'm gone. I tried to get them to stay with a friend, but they're both as stubborn as they come. Mama Mary said no one would run her off from her home, and Rose insisted on staying with her."

"Don't worry. I'll check on them." In fact, Mama Mary was the one person who'd been by Joe's bedside when he was ill. She'd lived with the family since before the boys' mother passed and was the cook, housekeeper and surrogate mother. According to Maddox, she was as much a part of the family as anyone.

She would know exactly who'd visited Joe. And if he had other enemies, she could provide them with a list of names.

MEGAN COULDN'T SHAKE the uneasy feeling that someone had meant to harm her in the street.

The man from the bar, Tad Hummings's brother?

She should report her altercation with him to the police. To Roan.

But…she had no real proof that he'd pushed her today. And he was already angry with her over the injustice he'd perceived she'd done to his family. If she accused him of pushing her in front of a car or firing a weapon at her, he would be furious.

She didn't want to deal with that kind of rage. Or to falsely accuse anyone of anything.

She finished filing the results on Morty Burns and sent them to the sheriff in Laredo. This was his case, not one for Roan or Sheriff McCullen. But she was curious about the man so she entered his name in her database and ran a background check.

Information filled the screen.

Morty Burns, age fifty-nine, five-ten, a hundred and ninety pounds, no preexisting conditions.

He was married to a woman named Edith Bennett.

Bennett—why did that name sound familiar?

A knock sounded at her office door, but before she could respond, Dr. Cumberland stormed in.

"What the hell are you doing, Megan?" He slashed his hand through the air. "I just found out you ran more labs on Joe McCullen. I thought we settled that issue."

Megan pivoted, forcing a calm to her voice.

She hadn't let her father intimidate her and she wouldn't let this man.

"I'm sorry, Doctor, but the fact that there were two different results bugged me. So I decided to run it one more time."

Dr. Cumberland rammed his hands through his hair, spiking the white strands in disarray. "I can't believe you'd go behind my back—"

"This is not about you," Megan said. "It's about your good friend Joe. If someone did hurt him, wouldn't you want to know?"

"Of course," he stuttered.

"I still don't understand about the false negative."

Dr. Cumberland looked away. "Sometimes our samples get contaminated and it throws off the results."

That had happened before. "I know you cared about him," Megan said softly. "And so did his sons. I just want the truth."

He paused in his pacing and turned to look at her, his expression pained. "What are you saying, Megan? That someone killed my best and oldest friend? That it happened while he was under my care?"

Chapter Five

Dr. Cumberland looked completely distraught.

Megan stepped over to him and squeezed his shoulder. "I'm sorry, Doctor, I know this is upsetting."

The man's face contorted with emotions. "How could I have missed that? I saw him all the time…"

"It happened so slowly, there was no reason for you to look for it, not with Joe already dying."

"This makes no sense," he said. "Why would anyone kill Joe? He didn't have long to live."

"That's the big question," Megan said. "And one I'm sure his sons will want the answer to."

Dr. Cumberland looked stricken, and then he slumped into a chair and dropped his head into his hands. "Good God, Joe…what have I done?"

The guilt in the man's voice tugged at Megan's heart-strings. "You didn't do anything. Joe knew you were his friend. If he'd thought someone was poisoning him, he would have told you."

"But I was his primary physician. I should have realized, should have seen something."

"Like I said, whoever poisoned him did it in small doses over a long period of time." She drummed her fingers on the desk. "Can you think of anyone who had a grudge against Joe?"

"Just Barbara. And maybe Arlis Bennett, but he's in jail." He pushed himself up, but staggered slightly. His pallor was gray, his breathing unsteady.

Megan reached out to steady him. "Are you okay? You aren't having chest pains, are you?"

He shook his head no, then straightened and swiped at the perspiration beading on his forehead. "I have to go."

"Wait." She caught his arm. "Maybe you need to see a doctor."

"I'm fine, I just need some air." He shrugged off her hand and hurried toward the door before she could stop him.

ROAN'S GUT CHURNED with the news of Joe McCullen's murder.

For a fraction of a second, he considered the possibility that this could have been a mercy killing. Mama Mary supposedly loved the McCullens like family—she'd taken care of Joe during his illness.

What if she'd hated seeing him suffer and decided to speed death along?

Although slowly poisoning someone was not merciful. If Mama Mary or someone else, say Dr. Cumberland, had wanted to keep Joe from suffering, he or she would have found a faster way.

As he drove down the long winding drive to the main farmhouse at Horseshoe Creek, he scanned the property. It was an impressive spread. Now it belonged to Joe's three sons.

Horses galloped across the fields while cattle grazed in the pastures. Brett had brought more horses in to train and planned to offer riding lessons and was rebuilding the barns that burned down. He'd taken his wife, Willow, and his son away for a couple of weeks in hopes Maddox would track down the culprit sabotaging the McCullens.

Hopefully Maddox would arrest Romley and the trouble would end.

But the fact that Joe had been murdered changed everything. Was Gates responsible? Or...Barbara or Bobby?

Sunshine slanted across the graveled drive and farm-house as he parked. The ground was dry from lack of rain, although winds stirred dust and scattered leaves and twigs across the yard. Hopefully spring would come soon with warmer weather, new growth and the ranch could get back on track.

But he wouldn't be a part of it. He didn't belong.

Still, he had to get justice for his father.

The sound of cattle echoed above the low whine of the wind, and he spotted a cowboy at the top of the hill herding the cows toward the pasture to the east.

A gray cloud moved across the sky shrouding the sun as he strode up to the front porch.

He knocked, noting that the repairs on the house were complete.

He knocked again, then heard shuffling inside. "Hang on to your britches, I'm coming."

Roan shifted and scanned the perimeter of the property again, searching for anyone lurking around, but nothing suspicious stood out. A second later, Mama Mary lumbered to the door and opened it.

The scent of cinnamon wafted toward Roan, making his mouth water.

The short, chubby lady wiped her hands on her apron as she invited him in. She'd wound a bandana around her chin-length brown curls and flour dusted her blouse and apron. Her brown eyes were so warm and loving that Roan couldn't help but envy the McCullens. Although alarm tinged them at the sight of him. "Deputy Whitefeather, Is something wrong? Did you hear from Maddox?"

"Maddox is fine," Roan assured her. "I spoke to him earlier today. He has a lead on Stan Romley."

Relief softened her face. "Thank goodness. Maybe they'll lock him up, and my boys can get back to work here on the ranch where they belong."

Her boys. She said it with such affection that if he'd ever considered the possibility of her doing something to hurt the family, that thought vanished like dust in the wind.

"May I come in? I'd like to ask you some questions."

Her eyes narrowed. "Something is wrong. Something you don't want to say."

Roan jammed his hands in his pockets. She was damned intuitive. "I'm just trying to help Maddox identify the arsonist."

She nodded, although she scrutinized his face as if she didn't quite believe him. Still, she waved him in. "You want some tea or coffee?"

"Coffee would be good," he said. Maybe it would put them both at ease if he at least acted like this was informal, not a hunting expedition. Although, if she knew her boss and family friend had been murdered, he had a feeling she would want to help.

She gestured toward the den where a fire crackled in the fireplace, and she disappeared into the kitchen while he surveyed the room. A family picture of Joe and his three sons hung on one wall—the boys were teenagers then. A bookshelf held other pictures, a couple of Joe and the woman who must have been his wife, Grace. A third one showed Grace holding a baby in her arms with two toddlers beside her—Ray had to be the baby, Maddox and Brett the toddlers.

How would she have reacted if she'd known that Joe had another son at that time? Roan was probably just a few months older than Maddox.

His hand stroked his wallet where he kept a picture of his mother. There had been no father in the picture because she'd chosen not to tell Joe about him. What would Joe have done if he'd known? Would he have offered to marry Roan's mother?

Would he have grown up a McCullen and lived on a ranch like this?

A wave of disappointment hit him, but he tamped it back. No use wondering. It hadn't happened.

Footsteps sounded, and Mama Mary waddled in carrying a tray with a coffee craft, two mugs and a plate of cinnamon rolls. She set them on the coffee table, handed him a plate with a cinnamon roll on it, then served them both a mug and offered cream and sugar.

"Black is fine," he said as he cradled the warm mug in his hand. Even the coffee cups had an *M* on them for McCullen, another reminder that if his mother had married Joe, that would have been his last name, too.

Mama Mary studied him with a frown. "All right, what's really going on, Deputy? Maddox is after Romley and we know that he worked for Boyle Gates, the man Maddox put away for cattle rustling. I'm aware you all looked into his cousin Bennett. Do you have new information?"

He sipped his coffee, choosing his words carefully. "We're still hoping that Romley will give us a confession regarding the fires."

"So why are you here?"

Roan nodded. "The last few months Joe was sick, Dr. Cumberland came often to check on him?"

She nodded, then stirred sugar into her coffee. "Almost every day. He and Joe went way back. He even delivered Joe's boys."

Except for him. And Bobby. But they obviously didn't count. "Joe and Boyle Gates had trouble?"

Mama Mary sighed. "Well, I guess you could say that. Boyle tried to get Joe to sell some of his land to him. He wasn't happy at all when Joe refused."

"Did Gates visit Joe while he was sick?"

Mama Mary nodded. "A couple of times. I couldn't believe he kept persisting. He must have thought that Joe was weak and would give in, but Joe was adamant that his ranch belonged to the McCullens and didn't intend to let any of it go."

Gates would have had to have administered the poison more than twice for it to show up in the tox screen. Maybe he hired someone to sneak it into Joe's food or drink?

"How about other visitors?"

"Well, a few of the hands dropped by. The foreman and Joe were close. He stopped in at least once a week."

"You said they were close? Did he have any trouble with Joe?"

"No, Joe was always good to him. They were more like brothers than employee-employer." She made a clicking sound with her teeth. "Why are you asking about Mr. Joe's visitors?"

"I'm trying to get the full picture of anyone involved with the ranch or Joe. It's possible Gates paid someone other than Romley to sabotage the ranch."

She chewed on her bottom lip and looked away. "Mr. Brett already checked out the hands. Romley turned out to be dirty, and Maddox found out he was working with another hand named Hardwick. They were both on Gates's payroll."

"What about visitors outside the ranch? Other than Dr. Cumberland, who came to see Joe while he was sick?"

She set her coffee on the tray and rubbed at her knee as if it hurt. "Barbara stopped by a few times, always when Maddox wasn't around. Once I heard her up there crying over him. I tried to stay out of the way when she was here. She didn't much care for me."

"She was bitter," Roan said. "Did she bring Joe any gifts or food when she visited?"

Mama Mary's face crinkled as she scrunched her nose in thought. "Sometimes she brought him cookies. Said they were his favorites, that she made them for him the first time they met."

"Did Joe eat them?"

"One or two here and there. To tell you the truth, he wasn't into sweets that much. He was a meat and potato man."

Still, she could have poisoned the cookies.

"What about Bobby? Did he visit Joe?"

She scoffed. "That boy was like vinegar, sour and bitter as they get. He came some, but I stayed out of his way. He upset Mr. Joe. Sometimes I could hear them shouting all the way in the kitchen." She made a sound of disapproval. "When Joe took sick, you'd have thought Bobby would have softened and been nicer. But one night I heard him asking Joe when he was going to tell the other boys about him. He was always demanding money, too."

Roan's pulse jumped. "What about Joe's will? Did Bobby know he was included?"

"Joe hinted that he'd included him, but more than once he told Bobby if he wanted any part of the McCullen land, he had to get help."

Roan considered their argument. "Did Joe ever talk about changing his will?"

Mama Mary glanced down at her fingers where she was knotting the apron in her lap. "He did. I told him once he should take that boy out. He was ungrateful and a mean drunk, and he didn't deserve what Joe had worked so hard for."

"Did Joe talk to the lawyer about it?"

"I honestly don't know," Mama Mary said with a sigh.

There was one way to find out. Roan had to talk to Joe's lawyer Darren Bush.

MEGAN SPENT THE rest of the afternoon working on the autopsy of a car crash victim.

By late afternoon, she was so concerned about the doctor that she phoned him to make certain he didn't need medical attention, but his voice mail kicked in. Her phone buzzed a second later.

Thinking it was him, she quickly snatched up the phone.

"Dr. Lail, this is Deputy North in Laredo. I got the results for that autopsy on Morty Burns."

"Yes."

"Did you find any forensics?"

"I'm afraid not," Megan answered. "But the bullet that killed him was from a .45."

"Hmm."

"Something bothering you about the report?" she asked.

"Not the report per se. But I talked to Sheriff McCullen from Pistol Whip. Apparently Morty Burns was married to a woman named Edith Bennett."

"Yes, I saw that," Megan said.

Deputy North grunted. "Well, her brother is Arlis Bennett, a man the sheriff suspects is working with Boyle Gates."

There was the name Bennett again. "Has Burns's wife been notified of his death?" Megan asked.

"Not yet," the deputy said. "I phoned and there was no answer at her place. She lives near Pistol Whip, not Laredo."

Megan drummed her fingers on the desk. "I can go out and talk to her."

"We really should have an officer present. This is a murder investigation now."

"All right, I'll get Deputy Whitefeather to accompany me."

"Good. Sheriff McCullen thinks Burns's murder may be related to the trouble at his ranch. That he might have been paid to set the ranch fires and that he might have been killed to cover up what he did." He paused. "Anyway, I was hoping you'd found some DNA to tie his death to Gates or Bennett."

"I'm sorry, I wish I could tell you more."

He thanked her and hung up, and Megan stewed over the information.

It hadn't occurred to her that a murder victim who'd been on her table might be connected to the McCullens.

She texted Roan to relay the deputy's statement and explained that she'd meet him at the woman's home to make the death notification—and question the woman in case she knew who'd taken her husband's life. There was always the possibility that this murder was not related to the McCullens, that it was a domestic dispute gone bad or that Burns had gotten himself in some kind of trouble. Maybe he owed someone money...

Her phone beeped indicating a response to her text, and she read Roan's message. At Horseshoe Creek now. Will meet you at the Burns farm. Wait for me.

She texted back OK, then grabbed her purse and rushed down the hallway.

Outside, the sun was setting, storm clouds rolling in, the wind picking up. The parking lot at the hospital was still full, though; the afternoon-evening shift hadn't arrived, and an ambulance was rolling up.

She hit the key fob to unlock her car, jumped in and headed toward the address for the Burnses' farm.

Traffic was thin as she drove through town, the diner starting to fill up with the early supper crowd. She made the turn to the highway leading out of Pistol Whip, and ten minutes later found the farm, a run-down-looking piece of property that had seen better days.

Overgrown weeds choked what had once been a big garden area, the fences were broken and rotting and the house needed paint badly. Her car rumbled over the ruts in the dirt drive, dust spewing in a smoky cloud behind her.

She scanned the property for life, for workers, but saw no one. Just a deserted tractor and pickup truck in front of the weathered house. She parked and glanced around, suddenly nervous.

She didn't know anything about this woman, except that her husband had been murdered.

Suddenly the door on the side inched open and a cat darted out. Megan's stomach knotted when she noticed blood on the cat's fur and paws.

Fear momentarily immobilized her, but her instinct as a doctor kicked in, and she threw the door open and climbed from her car. She scanned the area for someone suspicious but saw no one. The cat ran into the barn behind the house.

She eased to the porch, one hand on the mace in her purse, her phone at her fingertips in case she needed to call for help. Wind beat at the house, banging a shutter that had come loose against the weathered wood.

She crept up the rickety steps, the squeaking sound of rotting boards adding to her frayed nerves. By the time she reached the front door, perspiration trickled down the back of her neck. Senses honed, she paused to listen for sounds inside.

The wind whistled through the eaves. Water dripped from a faucet or tub somewhere in the house.

The smell of something acrid swirled in the air as she poked her head inside. The living room with its faded and tattered furniture was empty. She took a deep breath and inched inside the door.

A sick feeling swept over her when she spotted the woman lying in the doorway from the kitchen to the den.

She lay in a pool of blood, one arm outstretched as if she was reaching for help, her eyes wide-open and filled with the shock of death.

Chapter Six

Roan polished off the cinnamon roll and thanked Mama Mary. It was the best thing he'd ever tasted. "Mama Mary," Roan said. "Do you know a man named Morty Burns?"

"Can't say as I do," she said with a puzzled look. "Should I?"

Roan shrugged. "How about a woman named Edith Bennett? She was married to Burns."

Mama Mary frowned. "Bennett? Why, yes, Edith used to be good friends with Grace. Although her brother is Arlis Bennett? And she did used to visit Joe from time to time. Why?"

"That text was the ME's office. Edith's husband was found shot to death. I wondered if he worked for Bennett."

She fluttered a pudgy hand to her cheek. "Well…I don't know. I can't imagine Edith and her husband doing something illegal. You think someone killed him because he was sabotaging Horseshoe Creek?"

"At this point, I'm considering all angles." He folded his hands. "Who else visited Joe?"

Mama Mary wiped her hands on her apron again. "Hmm, well there was another rancher named Elmore Clark. He owed Joe 'cause he got in trouble with his mortgage and Joe bought some of his land to help him out."

"So he had no reason to hurt Joe?"

Mama Mary shook her head no. "Not that I'm aware of."

Roan would check out the man. Maybe he hadn't liked the terms of the sale?

"Did Joe tell you how he'd structured things in his will?"

Mama Mary brushed at the specks of flour on her apron. "Not the specifics. He just said everyone in the family would be taken care of." She made a low sound in her throat. "I urged him to talk to the boys about Barbara and Bobby, but he had so much guilt over the affair he'd had. And frankly I think he was too weak to face the hurt he'd see on their faces."

"So you knew about Barbara when he had the affair?"

She blinked and looked away. "I'm not going to gossip about this family. Joe made mistakes, but he was a good man."

"I'm not judging him," Roan said, tempted to confide in her that the man had been murdered. She obviously loved Joe and would want the truth.

Although she was protective of the family and probably wouldn't welcome him into it any more than Maddox or Brett or Ray. "Neither am I, Mama Mary. I'm simply trying to understand the situation so we can catch whoever is sabotaging Horseshoe Creek."

She relaxed a little. "Barbara and Bobby and Boyle Gates are the only three I can think of."

Maybe he should have a chat with Boyle Gates. His phone buzzed and he checked the number. Megan.

"Thanks, Mama Mary. If you think of anyone else who visited or anything else that can help, call me."

She pushed her bulk to her feet with a heaving sound, then caught his arm as he started to stand. "Deputy White-feather, is there something you're not telling me?"

Roan met her gaze. Again he was tempted to confide the truth about the patriarch of the family's death. But Maddox and Brett and Ray deserved to know first. So he shook his head, punched Connect on the phone and headed out the kitchen door.

"Deputy Whitefeather."

"Roan, it's Megan… You should get out here."

His pulse hammered. "What's wrong? Where are you?"

"At the Burns farm…" Her voice cracked. "Edith Burns is dead."

MEGAN TOOK DEEP breaths as she stared at the pool of blood on the floor surrounding the woman's body.

She yanked gloves from her purse and tiptoed inside, listening for sounds that an intruder was still there. The linoleum floor squeaked as she crossed the den to the doorway of the kitchen. She clenched the phone in one hand as she stooped down to check the woman's pulse. Not that she had any doubt that she was dead. The odors and pallor confirmed her suspicions.

But it was routine and she needed to determine time and cause of death.

"Megan, you're sure?"

"Yes." Dried blood soaked the lady's yellow housedress. "It appears that she bled out from a gunshot wound to the chest just like her husband."

"I'm on my way," Roan said. "Wait till I get there to go inside."

"I'm already inside," Megan said. "I saw blood from the doorway and had to see if she was alive."

"Dammit, Megan, what if the killer is still there?"

"He's long gone, Roan. Judging from rigor and body decomp, she's been dead several hours."

"You're alone?"

She twisted to listen for sounds again, but barring the wind battering the wood frame and windowpanes, everything was quiet. "Yes. I'll call a crime team to start processing the house."

"Do you see a bullet casing or weapon anywhere around?"

Megan lifted the woman slightly to search for an exit

wound, but didn't see one. "The bullet must still be lodged inside her. I don't see a weapon anywhere."

She did a quick visual sweep of the kitchen, at least what she could see of it. A bowl of fruit sat on an oak table, fruit flies swarming. A kitchen island held a cutting board where potatoes and carrots lay, a knife on the board as if Edith had been preparing dinner when whoever killed her had struck.

From where she stood, she couldn't tell if the back door had been jimmied or if the killer had broken in.

If so, had Edith heard her attacker?

She checked the woman's fingernails, but didn't see visible signs of DNA or skin cells, but she'd scrape and run tests to make certain. No blood or hair fibers.

What about that knife? Had Edith tried to fight off her attacker with it?

She carefully stepped around her body, searching for footprints or evidence, and spotted blood splatters on the floor near the island, although the knife didn't appear to have blood on it.

She studied the kitchen layout and pieced together a feasible scenario. Perhaps the killer had entered through the back door, which meant Edith was facing away from him. But she'd been shot in the chest.

So…she must have heard a noise and turned to see what or who it was. Maybe she even knew the shooter, so she didn't instantly run.

The killer then fired the weapon. The bullet struck her heart and she grabbed the island in shock. Blood had spurted from the wound immediately, splattering droplets on the floor.

She staggered toward the den and collapsed in the threshold of the door. She was trying to go out the front… maybe to get to her car? Maybe to reach her phone and call for help?

But she'd been bleeding badly, quickly grew weak and

lost consciousness before she could make it to the door or her phone.

A shiver rippled up her spine. Had the same person killed Morty Burns, then came here and shot Edith?

Or…she had to consider the possibility that it was murder-suicide. Morty could have shot Edith then left and killed himself.

Except…the timing didn't seem right. And most suicides were gunshots to the head—Morty's had been to the heart. Also, if he had committed suicide, why wouldn't he have killed himself here beside his wife?

Morty's body had been dumped…

Which brought her back to the intruder theory. What kind of cold-blooded person shot an innocent woman and simply stood there and watched her die?

And why kill either of these people? Were their deaths connected to Joe McCullen's?

QUESTIONS ASSAILED ROAN as he sped toward the Burns farm.

The fact that Edith was related to Arlis Bennett, the cousin of a man who Joe's sons had put in jail for cattle rustling, seemed too coincidental not to raise suspicions.

He had to discuss the situation with Maddox. Finding the couple's killer could be instrumental in determining who'd poisoned Joe.

Storm clouds moved in the sky, painting the run-down farm a depressing gray. The pastures and fields were overgrown, the farm equipment looked rusty and broken down and the barn needed a new roof. He saw no cattle or horses on the land, either.

Had money troubles driven Morty to help Boyle Gates or his brother-in-law sabotage Horseshoe Creek?

His police SUV rumbled and he rolled to a stop beside

Megan's van. On the lookout for trouble, he scanned the perimeter of the property in case someone was lurking nearby.

Dead leaves swirled in the wind across the brittle grass, and the door to the toolshed next to the house banged back and forth. An engine rumbled and he turned to see the crime team's van racing over the hill.

He glanced back at the house and saw Megan step into the doorway. Her hair was pulled back in that tight bun again, her glasses in place. Her expression was stoic, eyes dark with the reality of what she'd discovered in the house.

For a brief second, he wanted to sweep her away from the gruesomeness of her work and his job. Take her someplace cozy and romantic like a cabin in the mountains where they could float down the river on a raft then curl up on a blanket and make love beneath the stars.

Car doors slamming jerked him from the ridiculous thoughts. He was not a man who made love under the stars or…made love at all. Sex was a physical release.

It had been good with Megan. Damn good. But it wouldn't happen again.

She did her job because she liked it and was good at it just as he was good at solving crimes. Dead bodies were their life.

Not cozy mountain retreats.

"Dr. Lail called," Lieutenant Hoberman said as he and two crime techs approached. "She found a body?"

Roan nodded. "Yes, the wife of a murder victim she'd autopsied."

Lieutenant Hoberman's brows rose. "Both murdered?"

"It looks that way. Maybe you can help us pinpoint what happened."

Together they walked up the drive to the porch and climbed the steps. "You okay?" Roan asked Megan.

She gave a short nod, then led the way inside. The stench of decay filled the air, the sight of the woman's body fueling Roan's anger when he spotted her gray hair and gnarled hand reaching out as if begging for help.

Everyone pulled on latex gloves as they entered, and then they gathered around the victim. One of the crime workers began snapping photographs while the other started searching for forensics.

"It looks like she was cutting vegetables when someone entered from the back of the house," Megan said. "I think she heard the noise and turned to see who it was, then he shot her in the chest."

Poor woman was probably in her sixties. Dozens of pictures of her with a slender thirtysomething woman sat on the bookshelves. Then photos of Edith and a dark-haired boy and girl along with a card that read, "Happy Mother's Day, Grandma."

Roan's chest squeezed. She was a grandmother for God's sake.

She hadn't deserved to be gunned down in her home.

Roan's phone buzzed. Darren Bush. He excused himself and stepped on the front porch to take the call.

"Deputy Whitefeather, I got your message."

"Yes, we're still investigating the fires at Horseshoe Creek. When did Joe McCullen make his will?"

"Ten years ago, but he reviewed it each year."

"Did he make any significant changes in the last few months before his death?"

"No. Well, he did purchase a couple more plots of land. He added one of those in the settlement. It went to Bobby Lowman."

Right. "So he didn't plan to change his will and cut Barbara or Bobby out?"

"No, God no. He was adamant about taking care of his family."

That stripped Bobby and Barbara of a possible motive—other than their own bitterness.

Roan thanked him and hung up. Lieutenant Hoberman returned from inside the house carrying a calendar. "Look at this, Deputy Whitefeather. Morty Burns met with his wife's brother Arlis the morning he died."

MEGAN CATALOGED THE details of the crime scene. For some reason the older woman's face had gotten to her. Judging from the pictures on the mantel and bookshelf she was a cookie-baking grandmother who doted on her grandchildren.

It was a senseless death that made Megan determined to find justice for Edith.

"I'm going to notify Arlis Bennett about his sister," Roan said. "If he knows something and is holding back, maybe his sister's murder will be incentive enough for him to talk." He gestured toward Edith as the medics carried her body to the ambulance to transport her to the morgue. "Let me know what you find on the autopsy."

"I will." Megan's phone buzzed as she strode toward her van. "Dr. Lail."

"Dr. Lail, this is Ruth Cumberland. What in the world did you say to my husband to upset him so much? I've never seen him so distraught. I thought he was having a heart attack."

Megan bit her lip. Obviously Dr. Cumberland hadn't revealed her findings. She couldn't disclose the details, either. "I'm sorry he's not feeling well, Mrs. Cumberland. The past few weeks seem to have gotten to him."

A tense moment passed. "There's more to it than that, and I think you're the cause. I realize you're young and think you know everything, but my husband is a good man. So leave him alone."

Megan's pulse hammered at the accusation in the woman's voice.

She opened her mouth to respond, but the phone clicked

into silence. Troubled by Mrs. Cumberland's reaction, Megan started her van and left the farm.

Even if she was upsetting people, Megan had a job to do, and she didn't intend to be intimidated. She'd admired the ME who'd pushed to find the truth about her sister's death, and she would push for the truth for the victims who wound up on her table.

Poor Edith's grandchildren would not have the pleasure of growing up with her or spending holidays in her kitchen baking cookies. Someone had to make that right. Or at least as right as it could be.

Her killer had to pay.

By the time she arrived at the morgue, the medics were bringing Edith's body inside. She struggled to remain professional as she prepared to start the autopsy.

Once she had Edith on the table, she took a few moments to talk to her as she often did her patients. "I'm going to find out who did this to you, Edith. I promise." She stroked the woman's gray hair from her face, the brittle strands breaking off as she did. Dried blood and spittle darkened the corners of her lips, her mouth wide-open in a scream for help.

Forcing her emotions at bay, she donned her gear and began the gruesome task of the autopsy, speaking into her mic and entering the details of stomach contents, scars, injuries and forensics as she worked.

Just as she suspected, Edith had bled out from the gunshot wound. She recovered the bullet. It appeared to be from a .45. Morty had been shot by a .45, as well.

Edith also had a scar from a C-section, suffered from rheumatoid arthritis, had her tonsils removed and had last eaten biscuits and gravy.

Megan put time of death as the night before, being the same day her husband died, only Edith had died hours after her husband. So not a murder-suicide.

The bullet suggested they were murdered by the same

person. But why kill Morty then his wife? Had she known her husband's killer?

If so, why wouldn't she have gone to the police? Instead, she was home preparing dinner.

Because she hadn't known he was dead.

Megan sent the bullet to the ballistics lab to corroborate her suspicions and informed Lieutenant Hoberman about the time of death.

"We'll look at phone records between the couple and others, and their financials. Hopefully some prints will turn up at the house."

She thanked him and hung up, the image of Edith's ashen, shocked face haunting her as she finished documenting the results.

When she finally checked the clock, it was way past dinnertime. The night shift would be on duty now, the hospital quiet as the patients settled in for the night. Of course the morgue was always quiet, especially since it was housed in the left quadrant of the basement.

She hung her lab coat on the peg on the wall and rubbed a hand over the back of her neck with a tired sigh.

But just as she stepped into the hall leading to the cold room and elevators, the hall lights flickered off. She frowned, feeling her way toward the wall for the light switch, but a noise startled her.

Footsteps.

Then suddenly someone slammed her up against the wall and shoved a knee into her back. Megan grunted and tried to fight.

But her attacker stuck the barrel of a gun against her spine.

It was cold. Hard. The click of a bullet in the chamber rent the air.

She screamed and swung her elbow back to fight, but he pinned her against the wall and yanked something thick and heavy over her head, pitching her into darkness.

Chapter Seven

Roan studied the Circle T ranch as he knocked on the door. Thanks to the McCullens, the owner, Boyle Gates, was serving time for cattle rustling.

His cousin Arlis Bennett had moved in to run the business while Gates was incarcerated. The bigger question was if Bennett had known about his cousin's illegal activities and had been an accomplice. So far no charges had been brought against the man.

Judging from the size of the herd on the property, Bennett seemed to be maintaining the ranch. The community and local cattlemen's club were watching, though, just in case he resumed Gates's underhanded methods to add to his stock.

Night had set in, the heavy clouds threatening rain. Megan had texted him with news that Edith was shot with a .45, same as her husband.

Footsteps shuffled inside the house, then the door opened. A tall ruddy-faced man in his fifties stood there, Western shirt neatly pressed, his jeans new and stiff.

Roan doubted Bennett lifted a hand on the ranch himself. He probably had his hands do all the dirty work.

Including the men he'd hired to sabotage Horseshoe Creek.

He just needed some proof, dammit.

"Mr. Bennett?"

"Yes."

"I'm Deputy Whitefeather."

"I know who you are. You work with the McCullens."

"Actually, I work for the people in Pistol Whip."

Bennett held up his hands. "My hands are clean. You can look at my books and see all my stock was bought legitimately."

He was probably smart enough to fake paperwork. "Actually, that's not the reason I'm here. Can I come in?"

Bennett raised a bushy eyebrow. "I guess so."

The burly man stepped aside and gestured for Roan to enter. Roan followed him to a large study with dark wood paneling, a giant cherry desk and credenza complete with a wet bar.

"Drink?" Bennett offered.

Roan shook his head. "I'm on duty. But you can go ahead."

Bennett shot him a dark scowl as if he didn't need anyone's permission. He poured an expensive-looking bourbon into a tumbler, then carried it to a leather chair and took a seat.

Roan claimed the chair opposite him.

"All right, what is this about?"

Roan swallowed hard. He hated this part of the job. "Mr. Bennett, have you talked to your sister lately?"

Bennett's eyes narrowed suspiciously. "Not for a few days. Why?"

Roan folded his hands. "What about her husband, Morty?"

A long sigh. "Two weeks ago. He came begging for money."

"And?"

"Burns was good to my sister, but he didn't know how to manage his land. He also liked to gamble and whittled away their income and savings to the point where they were about to lose their farm."

So he was desperate for money.

"Did you help him out?"

"At first," Bennett admitted. "I talked to Edith. Told her what he'd done. They fought, but she refused to leave him." He shrugged. "I did what I could to help. But finally I had to cut him off."

So Burns might have been desperate enough to take money to do something illegal, like set fire to the barns on Horseshoe Creek.

Bennett sipped his drink. "Now, why are you asking all these questions about Morty and Edith?"

Roan worked his mouth from side to side. "I'm sorry to have to inform you of this, Mr. Bennett, but both Mr. Burns and your sister are dead."

Bennett's eyes widened, then he threw back the rest of his drink. "What happened? How?"

The man's shock seemed genuine. Then again, Roan didn't know him well enough to determine if he was lying.

"They were both murdered. Shot at close range." He cleared his throat. "Mr. Burns's body was found dumped outside Pistol Whip."

Bennett's hand trembled as he clutched the empty glass. "And my sister?"

"She was found in her house."

Bennett pinched the bridge of his nose and blinked as if struggling with his emotions. "When…" his voice cracked "…did it happen?"

"The ME put her death last night." Roan forced a calm to his tone. "Where were you then?"

Anger flared in the man's eyes. "You can't be serious. You think I'd kill my only sister?"

"It's a standard question, Mr. Bennett. Where were you?"

His nostrils flared as he stood. He walked over and poured himself another drink, then turned to face Roan, his eyes seething. "Here on the ranch. My housekeeper can verify that."

"All day and night?"

"Yes."

Roan stood. "One more question, Mr. Bennett. Do you own a .45?"

A muscle ticked in Bennett's jaw. "No."

But a quick flicker of his gaze toward the wall on the opposite side of the room suggested he was lying. Roan scrutinized the area and noticed a painting of a waterfall.

He'd bet his job that a safe was hidden beneath that painting. And that Bennett had a .45 tucked inside.

Dammit. He needed a warrant to look through it.

Bennett gestured toward the door, indicating he was done with the interview. "Instead of hassling me, why don't you look into the men Morty owed money to. Maybe they killed him and Edith because he couldn't pay his debts."

Roan gave a clipped nod. That was a possibility, although how could someone collect money from a dead man who was broke?

No…he had a bad feeling his suspicions were right, that their murders were connected to the McCullens.

That Bennett was offering an alternative person of interest to steer suspicion from himself.

Megan struggled to breathe, but the thick body bag was suffocating. She couldn't see, couldn't think for the fear threatening to choke her.

God…she didn't want to die.

She kicked her foot backward and managed to connect with her attacker's knee. He grunted in pain, but tightened his hold around her neck. Then he pressed his mouth against her ear through the bag.

"Leave Joe McCullen's death alone or you'll end up in this bag for good."

She tried to pry his fingers from her neck and felt latex gloves. Still, she scratched and clawed, desperate to get skin or at least some fibers to help identify him later. If she survived…

He jerked her forward, then something hard slammed against the back of her head. The next second, the world was spinning. She fought to remain conscious, the darkness swallowing her.

Another blow and she collapsed with a groan. Terrified, she blinked, silently willing herself not to black out, but pain shot through her skull, then a numbness crept over her. Blinding colors…black dots…room swirling…

She couldn't move, couldn't lift her hands, make her legs work. She tried to scream, but her voice was lost as he stuffed her in the body bag. The sound of the zipper rasping echoed as if it was far away, and she had the strange sensation of floating…

She looked down at herself in the bag, and then she was lying naked on the autopsy table…

ROAN DROVE FROM Bennett's to the prison where Boyle Gates was incarcerated, hoping to get some answers. A sliver of a moon tried to claw its way through the storm clouds, occasionally adding a tiny flicker of light to the dark sky. Otherwise the land that stretched between Pistol Whip and the jail seemed desolate.

He phoned Megan to see if she'd found anything helpful with Edith Burns's autopsy, but her voice mail kicked in, so he left a message for her to call him.

Then he punched Lieutenant Hoberman's number. "Did you find anything linking the Burns couple to the fires at Horseshoe Creek?"

"Not directly," Hoberman said. "Although there was a can of gasoline in the toolshed. But a lot of farmers have gasoline cans."

"True." Dammit.

"How about his financials?"

"Bank accounts were slim, although there was a deposit of ten thousand dollars made about a week ago."

"Any idea where it came from?"

"No, it was a cash deposit."

Just as he'd expected. No paper trail.

Although it was past visiting hours, he explained to the warden about the Burnses' murders and that he wanted to see Gates's reaction before anyone had a chance to inform him of the news.

Of course, if he'd paid to have the couple killed, he already knew. He and Bennett could have worked together. Or Bennett could have inadvertently told Gates about his sister's troubles and Gates took advantage and offered to help Burns out of his mess if he did him a favor.

Roan settled into the chair in the visiting room, pasting on a professional face as the guard led Gates into the room. He'd seen the rancher around Pistol Whip with his air of superiority and disliked him immediately. He had also given some of Roan's people hell about some land that they insisted belonged to the res. He wanted to buy it and tried to push them off, but thankfully the law had been on the side of the Native Americans.

Even in his prison uniform, Gates still exuded that cocky attitude. "What do you want, Whitefeather?"

The way he said Roan's name sounded condescending, as if he thought Roan wasn't good enough to share the same space with him.

"I thought you might be ready to talk."

Gates rubbed a hand over his smoothly shaven jaw. "I've already said all I have to say."

"Did you hire Stan Romley to set those fires at Horseshoe Creek?"

Gates's eyes flashed with rage. "No. I already told the

sheriff that. And if you think you're going to persuade me to confess to something, you're dead wrong."

"What about Morty Burns? Did you pay him to sabotage the ranch?"

Gates shot up, handcuffs jangling. "This is absurd." He jerked his head toward the guard. "Take me back to my cell."

"Sit down, Gates," Roan said firmly. "I'm not finished."

"Well, I am," Gates said in a tone that brooked no argument.

"No, you're not." Roan jerked his thumb toward the chair, an order to sit down. "Right now I have two bodies in the morgue. Two that I believe you are connected to."

Gates went still, questions flashing across his face. "What bodies?"

Roan thumped his foot for a minute, intentionally making the man wait.

"You came here to talk to me, Whitefeather, so talk. What bodies are you referring to?"

"Morty and Edith Burns."

A brief flicker of Gates's eyes was his only reaction, but it indicated he knew more than he was willing to say. Maybe he'd even known about their deaths.

"What do they have to do with me?"

"The wife, Edith, was Arlis Bennett's sister. I talked to Arlis. He claims that Morty was in financial trouble."

"Again," Gates said, his voice cold. "What does that have to do with me?"

"This is what I think. I think you and your cousin Bennett are working together. You needed someone to do your dirty work, so you hired Romley. Maybe you hired Burns, too. He could have helped with the cattle rustling. Maybe he sabotaged Horseshoe Creek."

"That's ridiculous."

"Is it? The man was desperate to save his farm. Edith

was your cousin just like Arlis is, so you offered to bail out her husband. But things went sour. He wanted more money or tried to blackmail you and you had to get rid of him."

"You're forgetting something. I've been in prison for weeks."

Roan stood, his mouth a thin line. "Yes, you have. But you forget—I know how prisons work. How easy it is to hire someone from the inside."

"You really think I'd kill my own cousin?"

"To protect yourself? Yes."

Gates stared at him for a heartbeat then spit. The guard stepped forward to reprimand him, but Roan gestured for him to wait.

"When I get the proof I need, you'll go back to trial, Gates. And this time you won't be eligible for parole. You'll be on death row."

"Wait just a damn minute," Gates said when Roan headed toward the door.

Roan paused and folded his arms. "What?"

"Instead of trying to pin everything on me, why don't you look at the other people who had a grudge against Joe McCullen?"

Roan maintained a neutral expression, although he was hoping for a lead. "And who would that be?"

"Elmore Clark."

"I know about Clark. But McCullen helped Clark out by buying his land, and he kept it for him in case he got back on his feet and wanted it back."

Gates cursed. "That's a bald-faced lie. Joe refused to give Clark water rights and forced Clark to sell. Then McCullen put Clark out on the street. Clark hated the McCullens for years."

MEGAN'S HEAD THROBBED as she slowly opened her eyes, but an empty, black darkness swallowed her.

She fought for a breath, but the air felt hot, sticky, the air stifling. She reached up to find her way from the empty hollowness, but her hand struck something heavy, thick... vinyl. Then something hard above...

Slowly her memory returned, and fear choked her. The man...he'd attacked her. Covered her head with that body bag.

Panic shot through her and she tried to move, but she was trapped inside the body bag. There was no space, no room. The buzzing sound of the fluorescent lights in the morgue echoed above her.

The truth dawned quickly. Oh, God.

She was locked in one of the drawers in the cold room where they stored the corpses.

Terrified, she started to scream...

Chapter Eight

Roan checked his watch. Too late to talk to Clark tonight. He'd catch up with him first thing in the morning.

Megan still hadn't returned his call, so he punched her number again. The phone rang three, four times, but her voice mail kicked in again. Dammit. Where was she?

Still working on the autopsy?

Knowing her, she wouldn't leave until she'd processed each and every detail of the body and then she'd look for more. He liked the fact that she was meticulous in her job, dedicated and that she took great pains with the bodies that ended up on her table. She had more compassion for the dead than most people did for the living.

But…earlier she'd thought someone had pushed her into the street… What if her questions about this case—or another one she'd worked on—had upset someone enough to want her to stop nosing around?

Anxiety knotted his shoulders as he left the prison and drove back to Pistol Whip. The storm clouds that had threatened earlier opened up and raindrops splattered the windshield. They'd had a dry spell lately, and the farms and ranches needed this rain, but it reminded him too much of the night his mother died.

He'd held her while she'd passed, the rain battering the hogan where they lived in an erratic rhythm that had mirrored his pounding heart. He'd felt so helpless. Had wanted to do something to save her.

But nothing, not his prayers or the chants of the medicine man, not even the modern medicine Dr. Cumberland had brought, had been enough.

He blinked back emotions, but the pain was just as raw as it had been then. Only Megan had stood by him, offering soft soothing words and her comforting arms.

And he'd taken advantage. He'd needed her so damn much that even as he ordered himself to walk away, he hadn't had the strength.

Hell, why was he thinking about her now? Especially in that way…

She was helping him with a case—that's all there could be between them.

Deciding to fill her in on his conversations with Bennett and Gates, he drove by her house, hoping she was home. But her van wasn't in the drive.

She had to be at the morgue.

He spun the car around and headed toward the hospital. Maybe Megan had discovered something concrete that would tie Bennett or Gates to Edith Burns's murder.

MEGAN FOUGHT PANIC. She was trapped in a body bag inside one of the drawers in the cold room.

But she was alive.

At least for now.

She tried to slow her breathing to preserve oxygen. How long could she survive in here? The temperature was meant to keep the bodies from decomposing further before she could complete the autopsy. Even after she finished, the bodies were tagged and preserved before transporting to the funeral home or cremation center.

At this temperature, she might develop hypothermia, but she could recover from that if someone found her in time.

In the morning, Howard would show up for work. Or Dr. Cumberland might stop by.

In spite of her logic and rationale, tears filled her eyes.

What if one of them didn't come in? If they didn't have a new case, Howard might just go straight to the lab. There he would discover the results of her findings on Edith for him to process.

Unless he had questions for her, he'd likely spend the morning analyzing the samples and data she'd collected.

God…she could be here all night, and by morning she'd be too weak to cry out for help.

Cold terror engulfed her, making her tremble. A sob rose in her throat, her pulse clamoring. She was claustrophobic. Always had been.

She didn't like elevators or small spaces. Even as a child, she'd had a panic attack on the submarine ride at the water park.

She struggled to move her hands and arms and managed to feel in her pocket. If she had a scalpel or sharp pen inside, she could rip the bag. But…her pocket was empty. She'd left all her tools on the tray when she'd finished.

In spite of the cold, sweat pooled on her body, soaking her clothes and lab coat. A sob escaped her, and even as she reminded herself to breathe slowly, she struggled for air. Short panting breaths ripped from her lungs and nausea clogged her throat.

She gagged, fighting the urge to throw up. That would only make her situation worse.

Desperate to escape, she used her fingernails to tear at the bag, but her short nails didn't break the surface. Still, she tried to rip the material. When that failed, she pinched together a portion of it and tried to tear it with both hands.

Her hands shook, frustration clawing at her. It was no use. The material was too thick and strong…

Tears mingled with the sweat now, running down her face, into her mouth and down her neck.

She thought she heard a noise from somewhere in the

building. Maybe Howard had come back for some reason. Or maybe Dr. Cumberland.

She held her breath and listened, but the sound was an ambulance…

Frantic, she raised her fists and beat against the top of the drawer, then used her feet to pound the bottom.

ROAN PHONED MEGAN AGAIN, but once again received her voice mail.

Worry kicked in.

Something was wrong. She would have answered or returned his calls by now.

The last time they'd talked, she was headed to the hospital to perform the autopsy on Edith Burns. She might still be there.

Unless something had happened to her.

Vehicles slowed because of the rain, and he veered around them. A truck raced toward him, lights nearly blinding him, and he flashed his lights to warn the driver to watch it.

Rain spewed from the road onto his windshield as the truck flew past. He cursed, flipped his wipers to full speed and turned onto the side street leading to the hospital. He drove through the doctors' parking lot and found Megan's van.

Lights from an ambulance blinked and twirled by the entrance to the ER and a car screeched to a stop behind it. A young couple jumped out just as the medics unloaded an elderly man from the back. They raced in, obviously upset.

He understood the panic. If anything had happened to Megan, he didn't know what he'd do. He should have insisted she give him the results then stay out of the investigation.

He threw his car into Park in one of the visitor spaces, then jogged through the rain to the hospital entrance. He shook off the rainwater as he stepped inside, then hurried to the elevator.

He jumped inside, hoping he was panicking for nothing. That Megan had just gotten caught up in work or silenced her phone.

The doors dinged open. The basement lighting was dim, the halls virtually empty. His footsteps echoed on the floor as he rushed toward the morgue.

The empty dark halls echoed with the dead, the scents of chemicals and antiseptics permeating the walls in an attempt to cover the fact that this place was where the deceased went as a midway stop to their final resting place.

He tried the door but it was locked and the lights were off. Dammit, Megan's car was outside. If she wasn't here, where was she?

Maybe she met up with someone. Maybe she had a date.

The thought irritated him, although he had no idea why. Besides, Megan was in the middle of an autopsy tonight. He couldn't imagine her leaving Edith's body and the questions about her murder to go out for a frivolous evening.

Then again, he could be projecting himself onto her. But…Megan had depth. She was here. He felt it in his gut.

He banged on the door, then peered through the glass partition, but it was hard to see through the blinds, especially with the lights off.

"Megan!" He knocked again, then tapped on the glass. The sound of the glass rattling and his own voice reverberated off the walls. He paused, listening for signs of anyone inside, but heard nothing.

"Megan," he tried again. "If you're here, let me in. We need to talk."

Another hesitation. Seconds ticked by. His heart began to race. His shoulders tightened.

She was in there. He felt it. She needed help.

He sensed it just as he'd sensed when his mother was dying and needed him to come to her side that night.

Fear wrapped his heart in a choke hold. No, this was nothing like that.

Except he couldn't leave until he was certain Megan was safe. What if she was hurt? Injured? Too helpless to call out?

Adrenaline surged through him and he picked the door lock. The door squeaked open and he stepped inside, senses alert for the sound of a voice or breathing. Anything to indicate that someone was there.

The strong scent of formaldehyde assaulted him as he strode through the office and into the autopsy room. The metal trays and pans appeared clean, the gurneys empty, the table and floor hosed down.

Megan had finished the autopsy on Edith Burns and would have then returned her to the cold room. Pulse hammering, he walked through the room and checked the door to the hallway.

The furnace rumbled. Air whistled through the vents, and the fluorescent lights buzzed as he flipped on the light switch. Bright light illuminated the hall, accentuating the walls stained with dirt and the scent of death. No matter how hard they tried, it couldn't be eliminated or erased.

Fear gripped him as he stepped toward the cold room. Edith's body was stored in there, along with whomever else the morgue had received. It was dark. Locked. No sounds from inside.

Again, though, icy fear traipsed up his spine as if the dead had whispered his name, begging for help.

Ridiculous. He did not believe in hocus-pocus, although he had been raised to trust the shaman on the res.

"Megan!" he shouted. "If you're in here, somewhere, show me a damn sign."

He gripped the door handle, heart hammering, breath

trapped in his chest. Silence. The rattling of the building. Rain outside.

Then another sound. Something soft. Muffled. Then a bang.

Was it from inside?

It couldn't be. But…he pressed his ear to the door and listened again. Another muffled sound. Another bang.

Panic shot through him, and he gripped the door and tried to yank it open. It didn't budge. He cursed, quickly picked the lock on that door. He shoved it open with a growl, then flipped on a light and noted the bank of body drawers.

Dear God, was she inside one of those?

MEGAN FOUGHT TEARS and blind panic as she kicked at the drawer and screamed. Her cries came out low and throaty, her voice weak from repeatedly yelling for help. Her lungs ached for air and sweat poured down her face and body, yet she shivered with cold fear.

Had she heard someone outside? A footstep? A voice?

"Help!" she cried. "Please help me." She sucked in a breath, pulled her legs back as far as she could in the small space, then used every ounce of her energy to slam both feet against the bottom of the drawer. At the same time, she pounded the top of the box, but the body bag muffled the sound so much she wasn't sure anyone could hear it from the outside.

Tears trickled down her cheeks as she called out for help again and again. If she escaped, she'd make certain the medical examiner's office installed latches to open the drawers from the inside in case someone were to get trapped again.

Another kick. Another cry. Another pounding of her fist. Her arms were growing weak. Her voice cracking. Low.

Hardly discernible to her own ears. Her feet barely connected with the last kick.

Exhausted, she sagged inside the bag, the heavy plastic clinging to her damp skin, her body weak. She couldn't hold out much longer.

Despair filled her. She was going to die in here and no one would find her until it was too late…

Chapter Nine

Roan stared at the rows of drawers, his stomach knotting. One thing he'd learned on the res was to respect the dead.

But if Megan was in there, he had to look.

He rolled his hands into fists, listening again. Had he heard a noise or was it simply the sound of the rain beating against the building?

A low sound then…barely discernible. A…cry?

Pulse hammering, he crossed the room. Praying he didn't find Megan dead, he jerked open the first drawer, but it was empty. The second one held Edith Burns's body.

"I'm sorry, ma'am," he said in a low voice as he closed her back up.

Suddenly a noise broke through the quiet. Another bang.

He stiffened and hurried to the last drawer where the sound had come from. Hand shaking, he pulled the drawer open. A body bag held someone…there was movement…

"Megan?"

A cry rent the air.

"Megan!" Dear God.

He yanked at the zipper, but it was stuck, so he jerked on it again. Finally the tab gave way and he shoved down the zipper. Megan lay inside, pale and gasping for a breath.

"I'm here, baby." He pulled the drawer the rest of the way open and grabbed her beneath the shoulders. She was fighting, pushing at the body bag, trembling.

"I've got you," he said against her neck as he shoved at the bag and dragged her from the drawer. She struggled to get out of the suffocating vinyl and he yanked it away, then she sagged into his arms. He carried her from the cold room through the autopsy room to her office, his emotions pinging all over the place.

She was crying, her body shaking as she clung to him. He sank onto the small love seat in her office and held her in his lap, pressing her face into his chest and rocking her back and forth.

"You're okay, Megan, I've got you."

He cradled her against him, soothing her and stroking her until she finally calmed and her tears subsided. Slowly her breathing steadied, and he felt her relaxing, felt the panic seep from her.

Dammit, how long had she been in that drawer? And who the hell had put her there?

MEGAN HATED ANY WEAKNESS, but she couldn't stop herself from trembling. It was a natural reaction to the cold and trauma, the scientist in her reminded herself.

But it was more than that and she knew it. She'd been terrified of dying inside one of the very drawers where she stored the corpses she autopsied.

"Megan?"

Roan's husky voice drifted through the fog of fear enveloping her.

"Do you need me to call a medic?"

She shook her head against his chest, still struggling to gather her composure.

He gently brushed her tear-soaked hair from her cheek. "Are you sure? If you need a doctor, just say so."

"I'm…okay," she said, her voice barely a whisper.

His chest rose and fell with his breath, a comforting feeling as she soaked up his strength and the body heat emanating from him. She didn't know if she'd ever get warm again.

He cradled her closer, then lifted her chin with his thumb and forced her to look at him. "You'd tell me if you're hurt?"

Her teeth chattered, but she gave a slight nod. "I'm just s-so cold."

A muscle ticked in his jaw. His eyes were dark with anger. "How long were you in there?"

"I don't know," she said. "It seemed like forever."

His mouth softened slightly. "What happened?"

A shudder coursed through her, and she closed her eyes and buried her head against him. "Someone attacked me."

His body tensed, but he continued soothing her with a gentle stroke of his hand along her arm. "Did you see who it was?"

She shook her head again. "He came up behind me… and he shoved the bag over my face… I tried to fight, but he hit me in the back of my head."

Roan lifted her slightly and angled her head to examine her. "Dammit, you are hurt. You have a knot the size of a golf ball."

"I tried not to pass out," she said in a pained voice. "Then he shoved me in that body bag. I tried to fight him, but… he hit me again, and I blacked out."

"Bastard." He stroked her arms to warm her. "You need to be examined. You might have a concussion."

"I don't want a doctor," Megan said, another chill washing over her. "I just want to go home and take a shower."

"We have to get a team here to see if he left prints."

"He didn't," Megan said. "I tried to scratch him, but he was wearing gloves."

"Still, maybe you snagged a button or something."

"Maybe." She doubted it, but he was right. If there was a chance her attacker had left any piece of evidence behind, it might help catch him.

And she wanted the son of a bitch caught.

Roan captured her face between his hands and looked

into her eyes. Worry furrowed his brows, but he looked so handsome and strong that she lost herself in his dark eyes.

"Hang in there, Megan, I'll call a crime team."

She agreed, although when Roan helped her into the chair and stood to make the call, she missed his warm arms around her.

ROAN PHONED LIEUTENANT HOBERMAN and explained the circumstances. "Thanks. We'll wait here."

When he ended the call, Megan stood on wobbly legs and smoothed her hair back into her bun with her fingers. He wanted to tell her to leave it down, that even shaken and upset she looked beautiful. But he realized she needed to regain control, and part of that was putting herself back together.

"I'm going to the ladies' room."

"Megan, wait. Maybe you shouldn't wash your hands yet, just in case you got some forensics under your nails."

She hesitated, eyes flickering with unease, then acceptance. "You're right." She folded her arms across her chest and straightened her spine. "I wasn't thinking."

Compassion for her filled him, and he stroked her cheek with his thumb. "It's all right. You just went through a terrible ordeal."

Her lower lip quivered, but she clamped her teeth over it as if to calm herself. "I can't believe this." She gestured around her office. "Odd, but I always felt safe here. Now…"

"Your job means you encounter death, Megan. That's not pretty. And you have had three murder victims on your table this week."

"That's true." She paced across the room. "Roan, the man who attacked me told me to leave Joe McCullen's death alone."

Roan's heart jumped. "He said that?"

She nodded, her face paling again. "He said if I didn't leave it alone, I'd end up in that body bag permanently."

Roan cursed. The bastard had threatened Megan's life. He knotted his hands into fists. If he got ahold of him, he'd kill him.

His phone buzzed with a text. Hoberman and his team had arrived.

The next hour the crime team investigators combed the morgue, Megan's office and the cold room searching for anything Megan's assailant might have left behind. They bagged the body bag to take to the lab and scraped beneath Megan's nails.

She resorted to professional mode, answering questions as if the attack had happened to a stranger.

"We found a hair," one of the techs said. "Short, dark."

"It's not mine," Megan said, stating the obvious.

"Could it belong to one of the bodies you have here?" Lieutenant Hoberman asked.

She chewed the inside of her cheek. "I don't think so. But I'll collect a sample from each one for comparison."

Roan admired her strength, and realized taking action was a coping mechanism. He also watched to make sure she hadn't dismissed the blow to her head too quickly, that she hadn't sustained a concussion.

One reason he intended to stay the night with her.

The other…he needed to know that she was alive, and that the man who'd attacked her didn't return to her house to make good on that threat.

MEGAN REPLAYED THE past few hours in her head as the crime team processed the lab. She gathered samples of the hair on the bodies in the morgue, but judging from texture, color and length, none of them were a match.

Maybe her attacker had left a strand of his hair. Hair held DNA.

Whether the person it belonged to would be in the system was the question. If not they'd have to find a suspect to compare it to.

"Who else has been in the morgue and your office?" Roan asked.

Megan massaged her temple with two fingers. "Me. Dr. Cumberland. Howard, my lab analyst. There are a couple of other techs and the chief ME, although he doesn't come in regularly anymore."

"We need all their names and DNA samples," Roan said.

"I'll make a list. Their DNA should be on file."

"Right. Can you think of anyone else? A family member or friend who came in to make an identification?"

Megan searched her memory banks. "The wife of a car accident victim, but she was in her seventies with gray hair."

Roan claimed the seat across from her. "Megan, did you talk to anyone else about Joe McCullen's autopsy?"

She shook her head no. "Just Dr. Cumberland. He was so distraught he left the office. And of course Howard, the tech who ran the tests, knew."

"You trust him to be discreet?"

"Yes. Explicitly. Besides, he didn't even know the Mc-Cullens. Why would he want to hurt any of them?"

"He may not have. But he could have talked to the wrong person without realizing it."

"I know Howard, Roan. I'm telling you he would never discuss a case outside the office. That is, unless it was with me."

Roan seemed to consider her statement. "You said Dr. Cumberland was distraught?"

"Yes. His wife called me, upset. She said she'd never seen her husband so emotional." Megan hesitated, still disturbed by the conversation with the woman. "I think she was afraid I was going to try to ruin Dr. Cumberland's

reputation by exposing that he'd made a mistake. He's supposed to retire this year."

"But you didn't mention doing that?"

"Of course not. I'm sure he didn't realize what was happening to Joe. He loved Joe and his sons. He cried like a
baby at Joe's funeral."

"Have you had trouble with anyone else lately?"

Megan thought back to the man at the bar and relayed
what had happened. "But he has nothing to do with Joe
McCullen."

"True. But he could have shot at you in the street."

Megan shivered. "Or the person who fired that shot
could have been trying to scare me, and it could be the
same man who attacked me."

Roan squeezed her hand. "We will get to the bottom of
this, Megan. Meanwhile don't discuss this case with anyone. I haven't told Maddox or his brothers yet. They deserve to know first."

"I agree. And, Roan, I would never discuss medical findings with anyone not involved or authorized in the case. I
took an oath."

"I'm not questioning you," Roan said in a husky voice
that touched something deep inside her. "I just don't want
to see you get hurt. Obviously our investigation is making
someone nervous."

The crime team finished and Lieutenant Hoberman told
Roan he'd call him with the results of his findings. Megan
stood, anxious to leave.

"Thanks for coming, Roan. I appreciate all you did."

He rubbed her arm, his dark eyes intense. "I'll follow
you home, Megan."

Relief filled her. She didn't want to act like a simper-
ing female, but flashbacks of nearly suffocating taunted
her. "Thanks."

He nodded and she locked up, then they walked to her

car. "I'm right behind you," Roan said. "When you get to your house, don't go inside. I want to search it first."

The idea that someone might be waiting for her at home sent another streak of terror through Megan.

She didn't want to be alone tonight. But how could she ask Roan to stay without making him think that she wanted to be with him again?

You do want to be with him.

Yes, she did. But she'd been raised to be tough and strong. After all, she didn't have her looks to fall back on. She'd have to remember that when Roan was at her house.

Although, as she closed her door and started the engine, she could still feel that man's breath on her neck. His hands nearly choking her.

She could hear the sound of the zipper rasping as he closed her inside that body bag. She could feel darkness choking her when she'd awakened, locked in that drawer…

His menacing warning reverberated in her ears. Had she heard that voice before?

Chapter Ten

Tension thrummed inside Roan as he followed Megan back to her house. He kept his eyes peeled in case someone was following her, but the truck that fell in behind her as she turned through town eventually veered into the parking lot for The Silver Bullet.

He replayed the scene Megan had described in his head a half-dozen times, his anger mounting. If whoever had attacked her saw her with him, would he assume she'd talked? Would he come after her again?

Hell, he was damned if he did and damned if he didn't. Because there was no way he'd leave her alone now.

This son of a bitch wouldn't get away with terrorizing her. And if he'd killed Joe—his father—he had to go to jail.

He had to tell Maddox—soon.

Speaking of Maddox, his phone buzzed and the man's name appeared. Had he heard what had happened?

"Deputy Whitefeather."

"It's Maddox."

"Did you get Romley?"

"No, he escaped. But I'm on his trail now. He hooked up with a woman named Darcy at a bar. She said he told her he's headed west. I'll keep you posted. Anything going on there?"

Roan hated to lie to his boss. But how could he tell Maddox he was his half brother and that their father had been murdered on the phone? That was a conversation to be had in person.

"I'm taking care of things," he said instead.

Maddox thanked him. "Hopefully I'll have Romley in custody by tomorrow and be able to head home."

Twenty-four hours. He needed every second.

Maddox disconnected, and Roan turned into Megan's driveway and parked behind her. The rain had stopped, but the dark clouds still shaded the moon, pitching her yard and house into darkness.

He scanned the perimeter and pulled out his weapon as he climbed from his car. Megan opened her door and slid out. Her face still looked pale, her face gaunt.

"Stay here until I search the house."

She touched his arm. "Be careful, Roan."

He shrugged off her concern. "Just doing my job." Except protecting Megan felt more personal. That one night they'd shared had made it that way.

An animal howled from the woods behind her house, and somewhere nearby a dog barked. She handed him the keys, and he gripped them in his free hand, his other hand tightening around his gun.

The steps creaked as he eased up them. He paused to listen at the door before he opened it. Everything seemed quiet.

Although he doubted Megan's attacker would strike twice in the same night, someone could be lurking inside.

He eased open the door, pausing again, but the entry-way was quiet and so was the rest of the house. He used his pocket flashlight to illuminate the area, then inched into the den, then the attached kitchen. Everything appeared in order.

He eased into the hall and checked the bedrooms. Once again quiet. Nothing out of place.

Relieved, he hurried back through the house to tell Megan. He motioned that it was okay for her to come in, then waited as she climbed the steps.

"The house is clean," Roan said.

"I'm going to take a shower," Megan said. "Thanks for following me home."

He cleared his throat, hating the fear lingering in her voice. "I'm staying here, Megan. Just in case."

Her gaze met his, relief, then some other emotion he couldn't quite define, flickering in her eyes.

He couldn't erase what had happened to her earlier. But he could protect her tonight.

MEGAN BREATHED A sigh of relief that Roan had insisted on staying with her. She detested showing fear or appearing weak, but she also was no martyr. Realistically the man who'd threatened her could be watching her. If he saw Roan, would he assume she'd told him everything? That she wouldn't give up her questions as he'd demanded?

"If you're hungry, there's some homemade soup in the fridge."

Roan raised a brow. "You cook?"

Megan shrugged. "I had to. My mom was too busy with my sister and her beauty pageants to do it."

She realized she sounded bitter and hadn't meant to.

"I'm sorry, that didn't come out right." She'd told Roan about her sister's murder the night his mother died. Another way they'd bonded. "I loved Shelly."

"I know you did," he said in a gruff tone. "But it sounds like you were the caretaker in the family."

Megan shrugged again. "Obviously I didn't do a very good job or my sister would still be alive."

"Don't do that," Roan said, his voice harder. "Your sister's death wasn't your fault."

Emotions welled in her throat, threatening to send her into another sobbing fit. Determined not to fall apart, she turned away and headed toward the bedroom. "I'll heat up the soup after I shower."

She didn't bother to wait for a response. She shut the bedroom door and sagged against it.

But the smell of the morgue and her own fear was wearing on her. She felt vulnerable and weak, like she might throw herself at Roan if she didn't put some distance between them.

Her phone buzzed as she dropped her purse on the chair in the corner. She checked the caller ID—her father.

He probably just wanted to try to convince her to leave the ME's office again like he had the last time they'd spoken. But she'd been adamant that she liked her job, and she didn't intend to follow the career path he'd mapped out for her.

Worse, if he knew her job had endangered her life, he would insist she leave it.

No matter what she did, she couldn't please him.

She let her voice mail pick up and stripped her clothes, anxious to get rid of the sweat-soaked garments. The warm spray of water felt heavenly, but when she closed her eyes to rinse her hair, a chilling fear shot through her.

Thank God Roan had come looking for her tonight, that he hadn't waited until morning.

She soaped and scrubbed her body and hair, desperate to cleanse herself of the stench of her attacker's hands and the smell of the body bag. His voice reverberated in her ears again, and she shook herself, determined to block out the sound.

Finally the water turned cold, and she dried off and pulled on a pair of jeans and a loose long-sleeved T-shirt. She towel-dried her hair, then combed it and left it to dry on its own. She didn't care tonight if it was an unruly mass of curls.

By the time she entered the kitchen, the smell of coffee and the vegetable soup wafted toward her. The warm homey smells helped her relax.

"I hope it was okay that I went ahead and heated up the soup."

"It's great. Thank you, Roan."

Roan gestured to the table and she sank into a chair. His dark gaze met hers, something hot and sensual simmering between them. He looked so big and handsome in her kitchen that for a moment, she imagined waking up to him every day.

"Megan, I know you've been through a lot tonight, but can you tell me anything else about the man who attacked you? Did his voice sound familiar? Did he have a certain smell? Cigarettes maybe?"

The sexual tension she'd felt humming between them had all been in her mind. Roan was here to do a job.

He would protect her, but she couldn't give him her heart. Men didn't want boring plain Janes like her. They wanted beautiful, flirty, fun women, and that was something she would never be.

ROAN FORCED HIMSELF to keep his mind on the case as he and Megan ate dinner.

Her silence concerned him.

Was she reliving the nightmare of what had happened?

Her phone buzzed again, and she glanced at it, then flipped it to silent.

"You aren't going to answer?"

She shook her head. "It's my father."

Roan sipped his coffee. "Why don't you want to talk to him?"

Megan sighed and set her spoon down. "Because he'll want to know what I'm doing and if I tell him, he'll use it as an excuse to lecture me again on why I should leave the ME's office. He thinks it's a waste of my talent to work on dead people when I could be saving lives."

Roan frowned. "He should be proud of you. You're intelligent, you help families find closure by giving them details about how their loved ones died." His throat grew thick. "And you're compassionate to both the dead and the living."

"That's exactly how I feel about the families," Megan said softly. "I wish my father could understand that."

"Maybe one day he will."

She shrugged as if she doubted it, then ran a hand through the damp strands of her hair. They hung loosely around her shoulders, making her look young and impossibly sexy.

Dammit, he wanted to run his hands through the luscious strands.

"So your father is a doctor?"

She nodded. "A neurosurgeon."

If he was unimpressed with Megan's work, he sure as hell would look down on a half-breed deputy sheriff. After all, what did he have to offer a beautiful, smart woman like Megan?

"Let me guess, he wanted you to follow in his footsteps," he said instead.

Megan looked down at her fingers and nodded. "When my sister died, it tore his heart open," she said softly. "Shelly was so pretty and full of life. He used to light up when she walked into the room. She had him wrapped around her little finger just like my mother did."

"I'm sure he loved you, too."

A sardonic laugh escaped her. "Standing beside Shelly was like putting a cactus next to a sunflower."

Roan didn't like the comparison. "He favored your sister?"

"I couldn't blame him," she said with not even a hint of bitterness. "She was so full of life…her outgoing personality drew everyone to her." The sadness in her expression made his gut churn.

"You would have liked her, Roan. Everyone liked Shelly."

"I like you," he said bluntly. "Stop cutting yourself down and comparing yourself to her, Megan."

Megan's lips parted. "I can't help it. My father—"

"Your father should have appreciated you." He couldn't help himself. He reached across the table and captured her hand in his. Her skin felt cold, her fingers tense in his.

"You are not a cactus," he said in a husky tone.

As Megan stared at their joined hands, tears filled her eyes. "Roan, that's nice of you to say—"

"Shut up." He shoved his chair back and stood, then circled the table and pulled her against him. "I'm not the kind of man who doles out compliments just to do so," he said. "When I say something, I mean it." He cupped her face between his hands. "You are not a cactus."

A slow smile curved her mouth. Damn, she was the most beautiful woman he'd ever seen. And the most humble.

Unable to resist the heat simmering between them, he angled his head and slowly lowered his mouth to hers.

It was a mistake.

It was heaven in a kiss.

He told himself to stop. But he didn't listen.

He'd wanted to kiss her again ever since she'd walked back into his life. He'd never forgotten how sweet and erotic she tasted. How her shy touches made him feel strong and virile.

How her silent surrender made him ache for more.

MEGAN SANK INTO the kiss. Roan's lips felt strong and persuasive, offering her pleasure and a reprieve from everything that had happened.

Still shaky from her ordeal, she gripped his arms to keep herself steady, her heart pounding as he rubbed slow circles on her back. His big hard body felt like an anchor against the tirade of emotions overwhelming her, and she savored his calm, tender kiss.

Tender but erotic.

He teased her lips apart with his tongue, and she parted them on a sigh, need and hunger spiraling through her. She slid her hand up his back, urging him closer, desperate to feel the hard planes of his body against her aching one.

He deepened the kiss, his tongue exploring, his chest rising and falling with a labored breath. Desire heated the air between them as he finally ended the kiss, but he didn't pull away. Instead he trailed kisses along her jaw and neck, nibbling at her ear, then lower to the soft swell of her breasts. She arched her head back on a moan and wished she'd dressed in something sexier after her shower, something easy to strip, like her robe.

She wanted him naked and inside her.

He made a low, throaty sound of appreciation, then slipped one hand over her breast and stroked her. Her nipple beaded, begging for more, and he slid his hand beneath her shirt and cupped her through the lacy barrier of her bra.

One stroke, two, he thumbed one nipple then the other, until warmth pooled in her belly. She ran her hands down his back to his butt and cupped his hips, pleasure stealing through her as he thrust his sex against her heat.

A second later, he reached for her shirt to strip it, but his phone trilled, cutting into the moment.

"Ignore it," she whispered.

For a brief second he did. He kissed her again, more urgently this time, the air charged with their breathing. But it continued to trill, and he gave her an apologetic look, then pulled away.

Megan wrapped her arms around herself, trembling with desire as he snatched the phone from the table.

ROAN WANTED TO pound something in frustration. He wanted to kiss Megan. Take her to bed. Make love to her.

Which was a bad idea.

And now the phone. Bad timing or good?

He checked the number. The McCullens' ranch. He quickly punched Connect.

"Deputy Whitefeather."

"Deputy, it's Rose McCullen." Her voice cracked as if she was crying.

"What's wrong, Rose?"

"It's Maddox," she cried. "He caught Stan Romley, but Maddox was shot. The medics just called and they're on the way with him to the hospital."

"Was he in Cheyenne?"

"No, he tracked Romley back near here. They're taking Maddox to the hospital in town."

Roan froze, stomach churning. "How is he?"

"I don't know," she said brokenly. "He's in critical condition."

Roan clenched the phone with a white-knuckled grip. "I'll meet you at the hospital. Unless you need me to drive you."

"No, Mama Mary and I are going together. We'll see you there."

Roan closed his eyes and said a silent prayer that Maddox would survive.

Chapter Eleven

Megan straightened her clothing, disappointed her interlude with Roan was over. But something was wrong.

The worried expression on Roan's face when he faced her confirmed her fear.

"Who was that?"

"Maddox's wife. Maddox was shot apprehending Romley." Roan pocketed his phone, retrieved his gun from the counter where he'd put it and yanked his keys from his pocket.

"Oh, my God, Roan, is he okay?"

"He's in critical condition. They're transporting him to the hospital." He headed toward the door. "I have to go."

"Wait, I'll go with you."

Roan hesitated. "You don't have to do that, Megan. Get some sleep."

She rubbed her arms, a chill going through her. "I don't think I can sleep, not after what happened tonight."

Roan's dark brows drew together. "All right. But I might be there awhile."

Megan grabbed a jacket and her purse. "That's fine. Maybe I can do something to help."

She didn't know why, but Roan seemed upset. At least she could be there for him. He must be closer to Maddox than she'd realized.

She locked the door as they left and followed him to his car. Roan flipped on the siren as he pulled away and sped toward the hospital.

ANXIETY GNAWED AT Roan as he drove. What if Maddox didn't make it?

He hadn't even divulged to him that his father had been murdered. Maddox deserved to know the truth...

And the truth about you?

Did the brothers deserve to know that, or would telling them they were related to Roan rock their world even more?

In spite of the late hour, a few car lights flickered along the highway, and the clouds opened up and dumped more rain on the ground. He flipped his wipers on, the sound of the rain drumming on the car mirroring the racing of his heart.

Megan remained silent. She was probably exhausted, but obviously didn't want to be alone after her earlier attack.

He maneuvered around a truck creeping along, then another car, water spewing from his tires as he turned into the hospital. He threw the car into Park in the ER parking lot and reached for an umbrella for Megan. She accepted it while he tugged on his jacket and pulled on a Stetson.

Together they slogged through the rain and fog to the hospital door. He spotted Rose and Mama Mary as they entered.

"They just took him back." Rose's voice cracked. "They're prepping him for surgery."

Mama Mary wiped at the tears streaming down her face. "He has to be okay, Miss Rose, he has to be."

Rose looked stricken with fear, but she clutched Mama Mary's hands and squeezed them. "He will be. He's strong."

"I'm Megan Lail, Dr. Lail," Megan said. "Where was he shot?"

"The chest," Rose said. "They think the bullet missed his heart, but it may have struck other vital organs."

Megan put her arm around the woman to console her. "Let me get you and Mama Mary some coffee. Surgery will take a while."

A nurse appeared and greeted Rose. "If you want to see him before surgery, you can come back now."

"I'd like to speak to him, too," Roan said.

The nurse narrowed her eyes. "Are you family?"

Roan itched to reply yes. He was Maddox's half brother. But this was not the way he wanted it to come out. "I'm the deputy sheriff. I need to question him about the shooting."

The nurse glanced at Rose for consent, and she gave a quick nod. Then he and Rose followed the nurse through the ER doors to Maddox.

MEGAN RUSHED TO get coffee for everyone. Roan seemed upset—more than she would have thought.

Although, he worked with Maddox and probably considered him a close friend.

When she made it back to the waiting room, Mama Mary was on the phone talking in a hushed voice. "No, Ray, honey, don't cut your honeymoon short. Rose is with Maddox now, and they're taking him to surgery. I'll call you as soon as he gets out."

The older woman sniffed, then dabbed at her eyes with a tissue. "Yes, I already talked to Brett. I assured him I'd call if I thought you two needed to come home."

Megan stood to the side to offer the woman some privacy. The McCullens had the kind of bond that Megan had always wanted in a family.

Mama Mary disconnected and sank into one of the chairs with a pained sigh. Sympathy welled inside Megan. She carried the tray of coffee to her and offered her one.

"Thank you so much, dear," Mama Mary said.

Megan patted the woman's shoulder. "He'll make it through, Maddox seems strong."

Mama Mary gave a little nod, although fear tightened the lines around her big brown eyes. "I thought that about Mr. Joe, thought nothing would ever get him down, but then he took sick." She wiped at her eyes again. "That was hell, watching that big strong man go downhill. Mr. Joe was a proud man. Lordy, how he loved his boys and his land."

"I understand the brothers lost their mother when they were young, and that you raised them."

Affection for the family was obvious in the sad smile that curved her mouth. "That was a rough time when Ms. Grace died. Mr. Joe was all torn up, and those boys…there was a big hole in their lives."

"She died in a car accident?" Megan asked.

Mama Mary nodded. "Ms. Grace, she was a lovely one, but she had her troubles."

"What kind of troubles?"

"That was between her and Mr. Joe."

Megan sensed there was a lot more to the story. "You mean Barbara and Bobby?"

Mama Mary clasped the coffee and took a long slow sip. "I reckon everyone knows about them now. I surely didn't condone what Joe did, having an affair with that woman, but Ms. Grace was so depressed. They were both struggling."

"If you don't mind me asking, what caused her depression?"

Mama Mary's gaze met hers. "I'm not gossiping about that family. I love them and they've been good to me."

"I'm sorry, I didn't mean to pry," Megan said. "And I certainly would never gossip."

Mama Mary searched her face for a moment then seemed to realize she was sincere. "I just told the boys about this a few days ago. Ms. Grace was pregnant with twins but she lost those babies. She and Mr. Joe were both devastated. And Ms. Grace, her hormones were all out of whack."

"I'm sorry, that must have been terrible. Was she being treated for her depression?" Megan asked.

"Of course. Dr. Cumberland did everything he could for her. But some things are just too hard to come back from."

Megan frowned. "I understand how devastating losing a child can be." Her mother had never gotten over losing Shelly.

Mama Mary squeezed her hand, her gaze sympathetic. "You lost someone, too?"

"My sister. My mother committed suicide later. She couldn't stand to go on without her."

"That's tragic," Mama Mary said. "I'm sure you felt alone and abandoned yourself."

Tears clogged Megan's throat. "I'm sorry, I didn't mean to make this about me. We should be saying a prayer for Maddox."

Mama Mary nodded and closed her eyes to pray.

Megan was so moved by the woman's compassion that she did the same. But her mind kept trying to piece together what had happened to the McCullens.

Both Mr. and Mrs. McCullen had ended up dead. The wife from a car accident.

And Joe…

What would Mama Mary say if she knew that Joe hadn't died of natural causes, that he'd been murdered?

ROAN STOOD BACK and gave Rose a few moments alone with Maddox. He was conscious, although he was weak and in pain.

Rose stroked Maddox's face. "You're going to be okay, Maddox. You have to be. I love you and I need you." She pressed his hand to her stomach. "*We* need you."

"Don't worry, darling," Maddox murmured. "I have too much to live for to give up."

A spark of envy ignited inside Roan. Rose was pregnant. The love between the couple was so strong that it made him ache to have a woman feel the same about him.

Megan's face flashed behind his eyes and nearly knocked the breath from his lungs.

Rose kissed Maddox, then turned to him. "Your turn."

Roan put thoughts of Megan on hold as he stepped up beside Maddox's bed. "What happened?"

"I cornered him, and he opened fire," Maddox said. "I fired back and hit him in the shoulder and leg."

"Did he talk?" Roan asked.

Maddox shook his head. "Not yet. They were going to do surgery. A deputy is guarding him 24/7. I want you to interrogate him."

"You got it," Roan assured him.

"Thanks." Maddox gritted his teeth. One of the machines beeped indicating his blood pressure was dropping, and the nurse rushed to Maddox's side.

"The doctor's ready to get this bullet out." She turned to Roan and Rose. "Time for you to leave."

Rose blinked back tears as she kissed Maddox again. Roan hesitated before he left the room. Maddox deserved to know that his father was murdered. He'd probably be furious that Roan had kept the truth from him.

But it would have to wait until he was stable.

MEGAN SPENT THE next two hours trying to comfort Rose and Mama Mary. Persuading Rose to tell her the story of how she and Maddox had met and fallen in love served as the perfect distraction.

Roan seemed agitated, but he'd also retreated into a silent, brooding state that made her feel helpless. She'd tried talking to him, but he didn't seem to want to talk.

He made a couple of phone calls, then stood at the edge of the waiting room as if he didn't belong with Rose and Mama Mary.

Or maybe this situation just reminded him of sitting by his mother's bedside before she died.

"If Maddox hadn't saved me, I don't know where I'd be right now," Rose said softly.

Megan squeezed her hand. "I'm sure he feels like you saved him. That love will help him pull through now."

"I hope so," Rose said.

"It will," Megan said with conviction.

The doctor appeared at the doorway to the waiting room. "Family of Maddox McCullen?"

Rose and Mama Mary jumped up and hurried to talk to him. For a brief second, she thought Roan was going to join them, but then he walked to the window and looked out. Megan wanted to ask him what was on his mind, but decided not to push him. He was probably just anxious about the case and Maddox's injury.

Relief filled Rose's face, and she and Mama Mary hugged, both crying. Roan strode over to the doctor and the women then, and Megan followed.

"He made it through surgery and is in recovery. The next twenty-four hours should tell," the doctor said. "So far he's holding his own."

"Can I see him?" Rose asked.

The doctor removed his surgical cap. "When we move him to a room. That'll probably be a couple of hours. If you want to go home and get some rest or something to eat, we can call you."

"I'm not going anywhere," Rose said.

Mama Mary put her arm around Rose. "Me, neither."

Megan wondered what it would be like to have someone be so fiercely loving and protective of her. If Shelly had lived, would they be close now? Would her father react differently toward Megan?

The day her sister was murdered, a hole had opened up in her, and in him, and they'd never been the same again.

"Call me if you need me," Roan told Rose and the older woman. "I'm going to have a talk with Romley."

"Tonight?" Mama Mary asked. "Son, don't you think it's too late? I'm sure Maddox will understand if you wait till morning."

Roan glanced at the clock, 2 a.m. If the man underwent surgery, he was probably in Recovery. "You're right. I'll go first thing in the morning."

Megan said goodbye to both of the women, her chest squeezing as they hugged her and thanked her for being with them.

It had been a long time since anyone had made her feel so welcome and wanted.

THE THOUGHT OF Maddox dying had done something to Roan. Even though Maddox didn't know it, they were blood kin. Roan had developed a healthy dose of respect and admiration for him both on the job and off.

As he parked in front of Megan's house, he scanned the perimeter again, then kept up his guard as they entered. Their earlier near-lovemaking taunted him. After the tension of the past few hours, he wanted a release. Wanted to take Megan to bed and finish what they'd started earlier.

Dammit, he wanted hot and fast, to pound his body into hers until she cried out his name in pleasure.

He wanted to go slow and easy and slide her clothes off and savor every minute.

He wanted to make love to her.

He silently cursed.

He couldn't do any of those things because as hard as he'd tried not to care about her, he was starting to have feelings for her.

Nearly losing Maddox tonight had served as a reminder to keep his distance from Maddox and Megan.

She looked up at him with that sweet seductive gaze as they walked into her den, and he gruffly ordered her to go to bed and get some sleep.

Hurt flickered in her eyes, but he assured himself it was for the best. She didn't argue. She hurried to her bedroom, making him feel like a heel.

Exhaustion tugged at his limbs, and even though he didn't think he could sleep, he stretched out on Megan's sofa. He laid his gun by his side just in case of trouble, then closed his eyes.

An image of Megan lying in bed wearing a flimsy gown—or nothing at all—teased him. He had imprinted that one night in his memory so deeply that he could almost smell the heavenly scent of her body and feel the luxurious strands of her hair as he ran his fingers through the thick mane.

He could practically hear her whisper his name as if she wanted him to come to her.

Furious with himself, he rolled to his side to face the door, a reminder of the reason he couldn't leave. Megan was in danger, and he wouldn't let anything happen to her.

If anyone tried, they'd have to kill him first.

Chapter Twelve

Megan wrestled with the covers, images of Roan tormenting her. She'd thought they'd connected months ago when his mother died, but obviously she'd been wrong. And tonight, she'd thought she'd seen hunger and desire in his eyes.

Was she simply so desperate for a man to find her attractive that she was imagining it?

She hadn't imagined the heat that had ignited between them earlier or the fact that when they'd made love before that it had been explosive. Sensational.

And that it had stirred emotions inside her that she'd never felt before.

Because you're so inexperienced and naive that you misread sex for affection.

She punched her pillow and rolled over and faced the door. Knowing Roan was on the other side was torture.

Irritated with herself, she turned to the opposite side and faced the wall. It didn't seem to make a difference.

She wanted Roan anyway.

ROAN HADN'T THOUGHT he'd go to sleep, but he must have because the phone jarred him awake. At first he was disoriented, and it took him a minute to realize where he was.

And that, in spite of temptation and his ridiculous obsession to be with Megan, he had managed to stay on her couch.

The phone buzzed again, and he retrieved it from the coffee table where he'd also left his gun.

The number for Horseshoe Creek appeared on the screen. His heart leaped to his throat. What if Maddox... no...he couldn't think the worst. Maddox was strong, stubborn...

"Deputy Whitefeather."

"It's Mama Mary."

He held his breath, his pulse thumping. "Maddox?"

"He's okay, I mean he came through the night and the doc said he's going to make it."

Roan exhaled in relief. "That's good news, then." Except she sounded upset.

"Yes, Miss Rose is still there, but I came home to shower and grab a nap. I told her I'd bring by food later, then she could come home and get some rest. Right now, she won't leave his side."

Once again envy stirred inside Roan. Maddox was a lucky man, in more ways than one.

"But something's wrong?"

"Yes," Mama Mary said, her voice quivering. "Someone broke into the house last night."

"What?"

"It's Mr. Joe's office—I mean Mr. Maddox's. Well, anyway, things are all a mess and torn up like whoever did it was looking for something."

"Are you alone?" Roan asked, concerned about the woman. Where was the security Brett had hired?

"No. The foreman is here. When I noticed that the window had been jimmied, I called him and he came right over. But...I'm worried. Why would someone break in?"

"I don't know but I'll be right there." He grabbed his gun and holstered it on. "Don't touch anything in the office. I'll have a crime team dust for prints."

"All right, thank you, Deputy Whitefeather."

He wanted to tell her it was what family did, but he wasn't part of this close-knit group. All he ever would be was Maddox's deputy. Although hopefully Maddox considered him a friend.

That would have to be enough.

He ended the call, then glanced at the door to Megan's room. He had to at least tell her where he was going. Surely she'd be safe here alone until he returned.

Body taut with tension, he knocked softly on her bedroom door. "Megan?"

She didn't answer, so he knocked again, then heard a noise inside. It sounded…as if she was crying.

Terrified someone had broken in through her window, he shoved open the door. She was thrashing at the covers, kicking and clawing at some invisible force.

His lungs tightened and he raced over to her, sank onto the bed and gently grabbed hold of her arms. "Megan, it's okay, I'm here."

She shoved at his hands and released a sob.

He gently shook her. "Megan, wake up, honey, it's just a nightmare. I'm here and you're safe."

She continued to fight, but he cradled her face between his hands and spoke softly again. "Megan, look at me. It's Roan. You're home safe in your bed."

She went very still then, as if his words sank in, but her body was trembling. She released a cry then sank against him, her breathing choppy.

He pulled her in his arms and rocked her back and forth, soothing her with soft words until her breathing grew steady and her cries quieted.

God…he hated the bastard who'd stuffed her in that body bag.

"Megan, are you okay?"

She nodded against his chest, then lifted her head. Her

tear-soaked eyes and the remnants of fear darkening the depths tore at him.

"I'm sorry," she said in a raw whisper. "I'm not usually a crier."

He chuckled softly. "Somehow I knew that." He raked her hair from her cheek. "But you're allowed. Someone did attack you last night."

"I know." She shivered again. "I'll be okay, though. I will."

The pride and determination in her voice made him smile again. "I don't doubt that." He stroked her back, once again vowing to find the bastard who'd hurt her. "Listen, I hate to leave, but Mama Mary called."

She instantly straightened, her concern for everyone else taking precedence over her own fears. "Is Maddox okay?"

He nodded. "He's stable. Rose is with him. She won't leave his side."

"It's obvious how much they love each other," she said in an almost wistful tone.

"Yeah. But someone broke into the ranch house."

Megan gasped. "Is everyone okay? Was Mama Mary there?"

"Not at the time, and she's fine. Just shaken. It sounds like they were looking for something in the study. I'm meeting a crime team there."

Megan reached for the covers to get up. "I'll go with you."

He caught her hand. "You don't have to do that. Get some more sleep or take a shower."

"There's no way I can go back to sleep, Roan." She pushed her legs over the side of the bed. "But I can use some coffee and I probably need to get to work."

"Do you really want to go back to the morgue today?"

Her face looked stricken for a moment. "No, but I refuse to let anyone drive me away from my job. I have to face it sometime."

He admired her courage. "Then let me drive you. We'll pick up coffee on the way to the hospital."

She agreed, and he reluctantly stepped back into the living room while she dressed. If he didn't, he'd forget the case, take her back to bed and chase her nightmares away with the hot pleasure of sex.

But Megan deserved better than that, so he fortified his resolve to keep his hands off her, then phoned Lieutenant Hoberman to request the crime team.

MEGAN WAS SURPRISED to find the chief ME, Dr. Mantle, waiting in her office when she arrived. He didn't look happy.

His round face was red with anger, his eyes bulging behind his bifocals. "Megan, what in the hell is going on?"

Megan folded her arms in a defensive gesture. She'd never seen him so furious. "What are you talking about?"

He motioned for her to shut her office door, and she did, her nerves on edge. What had she done wrong?

"Dr. Cumberland's wife called me upset. She thinks you're trying to ruin her husband's reputation before he retires."

Megan shifted, choosing her words carefully. "She also called me, Dr. Mantle, but I assure you I'm not out to hurt Dr. Cumberland. I admire his work and know how much he cares about his patients."

"But you questioned the autopsy results and went behind his back and had samples retested."

Megan sucked in a sharp breath. "First of all, I was just doing my job. When I first read the report, I noticed something odd about the tox screen. I mentioned it to Dr. Cumberland and he acted like I'd made a mistake, then he showed me a contradictory report that had been sent to his office."

Dr. Mantle ran a hand over his balding head. "So there was a mix-up in the reports?"

"That's what he said," Megan replied. "But with contradictory tox screens, I had to run another test to make sure."

"And you did?"

"Yes, with another sample I preserved." She paused. "Isn't that what you would have done?"

He removed his glasses, rubbed at his eyes, then put them back on his face and adjusted them.

"Wouldn't you?" Megan pressed.

He coughed, obviously stalling. "Yes, I guess I would. But Dr. Cumberland says you implied that he was incompetent."

"Oh, my God," Megan said. "That's not true. I respect him. I'm not sure exactly what happened with those two reports, but I couldn't be satisfied without verification."

"Why was it so important to you?"

"Because the tox report indicated that Joe McCullen was poisoned."

His eyes widened beneath his glasses. "You're saying he was murdered?"

"That's what the report indicates. And," she said, her voice raw with memories of her attack, "last night someone knocked me unconscious, put me in one of the body drawers and warned me that if I didn't stop asking questions about McCullen's death, that he'd kill me."

Dr. Mantle staggered backward against the desk. "You're serious?"

"I wouldn't joke about this. I've already talked to the deputy sheriff. He's investigating Mr. McCullen's murder. But this is strictly confidential. He hasn't told the McCullen sons yet."

"Oh, Megan. No wonder the Cumberlands are upset."

He wheezed a breath. "You're good, I admit that. And I appreciate your initiative. But you are not to disparage Dr. Cumberland in any way. I don't want this office liable, and I certainly don't want you to ruin that nice man's reputation just as he's close to retirement."

Megan bit her tongue to stifle a sharp retort. Wasn't the truth more important than the man's reputation?

"Besides, Dr. Cumberland was Joe McCullen's friend. I'm sure if anyone wants the truth it's him."

Megan nodded, although if that was true, why not thank her instead of sending her boss to ream her out?

MADDOX WONDERED HOW Megan was handling going back into the morgue after her close call the night before. She was strong and tough, but that experience would have shaken anyone.

He pulled down the drive to the ranch house, morning sunlight dotting the green pastures and hills with golden light. The rain the night before left droplets on the leaves and grass that fell as the wind shook the limbs.

Although even with the beauty of their land, the McCullens had trouble.

He parked and jogged up the steps to the porch. Mama Mary met him, wringing her hands together. "Thanks for coming, Deputy Whitefeather. I didn't want to bother the boys with this, not when they're all worried about Maddox."

"I understand. But you will have to tell them." Just like he had to tell them about their father. And soon.

"Is anything missing?" Roan asked.

Mama Mary led him inside. "Not that I can tell, but Maddox will have to look in the office and safe to make sure."

They crossed the entryway into the office. He scanned the room, noting the papers scattered around, the open desk drawers, the wall of family photos...

"I didn't touch anything," Mama Mary said.

Roan yanked on a pair of latex gloves. "Do you mind if I look around?"

"Of course not. I just don't understand who's doing this. Who set those fires. It has to stop."

"Don't worry," Roan assured her. "I'll get to the bottom of it."

"Thank goodness you're here." She yawned and rubbed her head with her fingers. "I think I may have to lie down a bit."

The poor woman had been up all night. "Get some rest. I'll let the crime team in and we'll lock up when we leave."

She thanked him, then shuffled from the room.

Roan began to comb through the office. The files on the desk included records of cattle sales, horses that had been bought, expense reports and a business plan the brothers must have put together for further expansion.

He searched the desk drawers and found other information related to the ranch's operation. But wedged between the wooden bottom of the drawer and a corner, he felt the edge of something stuck.

Curious, he yanked at it and realized it was a business card. He pulled it free and skimmed the card.

Barry Buchanan, Private Investigator.

He frowned, wondering if the man worked for the McCullen brothers—or if he'd worked for Joe.

He entered the PI's number in his phone. There was one way to find out.

His thoughts took a dark turn. What if Joe had suspected that someone wanted him dead?

Chapter Thirteen

Roan punched the number for the private investigator, Barry Buchanan. The phone trilled three times before a woman answered.

"Hello."

He'd expected a business greeting. Did he have the right number? "This is Deputy Roan Whitefeather from Pistol Whip. I'm calling for Mr. Buchanan. Who am I speaking with?"

"His wife, Carrie."

"I see. Is the number for his private investigating firm?"

"Yes, but his business is closed," the woman said tersely. "I can refer you to another agency."

"No, I don't need a reference. I wanted to speak to him personally. Is there another number where I can reach him?"

A long awkward pause followed. "I'm afraid not. My husband died two weeks ago."

Roan tensed. "I'm sorry to hear that. Do you mind telling me what happened?"

"A car accident, or at least that's what the sheriff said."

Suspicion laced her voice, making him more curious. "I'm sorry, ma'am. You don't believe it was an accident?"

Another pause. "No. The sheriff said Barry's brakes failed, but my husband was a stickler for keeping his car in tip-top shape. His father owned an auto shop and he worked for him for years."

"What do you think happened?"

"I think someone tampered with his brakes."

Roan tensed. "Did Mr. Buchanan have any enemies?"

"My husband was a private investigator, Deputy White-feather. Of course he ticked off some deadbeat cheating husbands and wives. And that's only a few of the cases he worked on."

"You think one of the cases he investigated got him killed?"

"That's exactly what I think. Although the sheriff here doesn't agree."

Under the circumstances, Roan had to take her seriously.

"Why are you interested in my husband's business?" she asked.

The CSI van rolled down the driveway, and Roan acknowledged them with a flick of his hand. "I thought your husband might have worked for a murder victim I'm investigating."

"Well, I don't know details about Barry's cases. And he never told me his clients' names."

"Would you mind if I stop by his office and look at his files?"

Her breath hitched. "I guess not. That is, if you'll do me a favor."

"What kind of favor?"

"If you find something suspicious, someone who held a grudge against Barry enough to kill him, you'll let me know."

"I promise I will, ma'am."

She agreed to meet him after lunch, and he hung up and went to greet the CSI team.

WITH NO AUTOPSIES to perform, the morgue was eerily quiet. A fact that only reminded Megan of the night before and that someone had nearly killed her.

She made a phone call to follow up on Tad Hummings's

brother and spoke to the prosecutor who'd tried the man's case. His name was Gerard, and she admired and respected his opinion.

"There were witnesses, the evidence was clear. You didn't make a mistake, Megan."

"Has his brother been a problem?" Megan asked.

"His brother is a mean drunk, but he's also a coward. He doesn't have the guts to follow through on anything. He's just a bully who likes to throw his weight around."

He had plenty of that—he must have weighed 275.

"Do you want to file a complaint against him?"

"No," Megan said. "I just…wanted to make sure he wasn't dangerous."

His breath echoed over the line. "You're not telling me something, Megan. What's wrong?"

There was a lot she wasn't telling him, but she didn't feel like spilling her guts now. Especially with no proof. "It's nothing, Gerard. It's just that…well, the day after I ran into him, I was in a crowd and I thought someone pushed me into the street. But I probably just stumbled."

"What the hell, Megan? Why didn't you call me?"

"I told the deputy sheriff in Pistol Whip," she said. "So no need to call in the cavalry."

"Just to be on the safe side, let me check up on the brother. What day did this incident in the street happen?"

Megan gave him the date and time. A second later, Gerard cleared his throat.

"Megan, Hummings didn't push you. He couldn't have."

"Why do you say that?"

"He was arrested on a DUI the night before and spent the next two days in jail before he made bail."

Megan went still. If Hummings hadn't pushed her, then someone else may have. An eerie chill swept over her. Maybe the same person who'd attacked her last night…

MADDOX MET LIEUTENANT HOBERMAN back inside the ranch house's office. "Did you find anything?"

"A few prints, but considering the fact that the sheriff and his brothers probably all use this office, I'll have to run a comparison."

Roan showed him the private investigator's business card. "Mama Mary had no idea what the intruder was looking for, but I found this PI's card. I called the number to see if he was working for Joe, but his wife answered and said he's dead."

"You think they're connected?"

"It's possible. I think it's time to talk to Maddox." His keys jangled in his hand. "I'm going to the hospital to question Romley, then I'll drop in on Maddox."

Hoberman agreed to let him know as soon as he found anything, and then Roan drove to the hospital. A guard stood at the man's hospital room door, so Roan identified himself.

"You can take a break and grab some coffee or a bite to eat if you want."

The guard nodded, then walked down the hall, and Roan let himself inside Romley's room. The man was hooked up to an IV and a heart monitor. Bandages wound around his thigh and shoulder. His face was pale, dirty-blond hair disheveled, eyes closed.

Roan didn't bother to try to be quiet. His boots pounded the floor as he crossed the room. Romley opened one eye, anger glinting. "I'm not in the mood to talk, just in case you're wondering."

"You shot the sheriff," Roan said. "If you want leniency on that charge, you'd better get in the mood."

Romley groaned as he tried to sit up in the bed. "I need a lawyer."

"Yeah, you do," Roan said. "And I need some answers."

"I got rights," Romley said in a low growl. "That means I don't have to talk to you."

"No, you don't," Roan said. "But as I mentioned, if you want leniency you should cooperate." He crossed his arms and glared down at the man. "Did you set those fires at Horseshoe Creek?"

Romley rubbed at his leg. "I talk, you gonna cut me a deal?"

"That depends on what you have to say."

Romley twisted his mouth into a grimace. "I shot the sheriff in self-defense."

Roan laughed. "Nice try, but that's not gonna fly. You had a warrant out for you. You ran, then resisted arrest." He made a clicking sound with his mouth. "You're racking up the charges."

Romley rubbed at the bandage again. "Gates hired me and Hardwick to keep an eye on Horseshoe Creek's operation and report back what the McCullen men were doing."

"So you reported that Brett was building his equine operation. Adding barns and stock."

Romley nodded.

"Then what?"

"Then...hell, he told me to do something about it."

"Gates paid you to set the fires?"

Romley shrugged, then winced as if the movement caused him pain. "He said there'd be a big bonus if I slowed down their progress."

"So it was your idea to set the fires?"

Romley looked away. "I needed the money."

"You needed money bad enough to commit arson? What if someone had been inside those barns or the house? You could have killed one of the McCullens or their housekeeper."

"No one was supposed to be home that night," Romley said.

"But they were," Roan said. "And what about those horses? How inhumane are you?"

"I only set fire to the empty one." Romley's tone grew defensive. "I figured the McCullens would put it out before it spread and no one would be hurt. The financial damage would have set them back, that's all."

"What about Arlis Bennett? Was he working with Gates?"

Romley clammed up. "I don't know. Gates wasn't exactly my buddy, you know. He paid me. I did what he said."

"Did he pay you to kill Morty Burns and his wife?"

Romley cut his gaze back to Roan. "What the hell are you talking about?"

"Arlis's cousin Morty was in a lot of debt. We think he worked for Gates, too. That he and his wife were murdered because they had information that could expose all of you and send her brother Arlis to jail."

"Listen here," Romley said. "I don't know anything about that. Like I said, I was a hired hand."

"You were a hired killer," Roan said. "You shot Morty and Edith Burns. And you killed Joe McCullen for Gates."

Romley nearly came off the bed. "You're crazy. I didn't kill anyone."

"You expect me to believe that? You shot Sheriff McCullen."

"That's different," Romley said. "He was after me. But I didn't kill anyone. And you're not going to railroad me into prison on a murder rap."

Roan studied him, searching for the truth. He would ask the ballistics lab if the gun that shot Maddox was the same type that had killed the Burnses.

But if Romley hadn't killed the Burnses or Joe McCullen, who had?

MEGAN RECEIVED A text from Roan saying he intended to tell Maddox about his father. He wanted her to join him.

She dreaded the conversation, but Maddox deserved to know the truth. He might even be able to help. After all, Maddox had lived with his father, so he'd probably know who else had visited him.

Still nervous about the attack, she kept her eyes peeled for trouble as she hurried to the floor where Maddox was. She found Rose at the coffee machine. She looked exhausted, but she still offered Megan a smile.

"How is he?" Megan asked.

"Sore, but stable," Rose said. "At least he's out of the woods."

"You should go home and rest, Rose."

"I will." She stirred sugar into her decaf coffee. "I just couldn't bear to leave him yet." She shrugged, a blush staining her cheeks. "I'll go home tonight."

"He's lucky to have you," Megan said.

"We're both lucky."

Megan sighed, wishing Roan felt that way about her.

"What are you doing here?" Rose asked as if she suddenly realized that there was no reason for the ME to visit.

"Roan is on his way. He talked to Romley about the shooting. And there's more information he had to discuss with Maddox."

"I hope they finally figure out who's trying to hurt the family," Rose said. "Maddox and his brothers lost a lot. First their mother, then their father, then there was the trouble with Barbara and Bobby. And now the sabotage with the ranch."

Guilt tugged at Megan. There was still the bomb Roan had to drop about his father's murder.

Roan appeared then, his big body filling the space.

"You have news?" Rose said.

"I just talked to Romley. He admitted that he set the fires. Gates was behind it."

"What about the Burnses?" Megan asked.

Roan shook his head no.

"Who are they?" Rose asked.

"If you come in with Maddox, I'll fill you in."

"Dr. Cumberland is with Maddox now," Rose said.

Megan's pulse jumped. Roan frowned, then turned and strode down the hall. She and Rose followed.

As soon as Roan opened the door, Maddox's angry voice boomed into the hall.

"What do you think you're doing, Whitefeather?" Maddox shouted. "You find out my father was murdered, and you don't tell me?"

Chapter Fourteen

Roan silently cursed.

His gaze met Dr. Cumberland's. Dammit, the doctor had already broken the news to Maddox.

"I'm sorry, Deputy Whitefeather, but I felt it was my duty to tell Maddox what I knew about his father. He had a right to know."

Anger shot through Roan, but he tamped down a reaction. After all, the doctor was a friend of the McCullens. Maybe he had felt compelled to inform Maddox.

"Why the hell didn't *you* tell me?" Maddox asked, his voice gruff.

"I was coming here today to do just that," Roan said, although judging from Maddox's look of disbelief he realized that argument sounded weak. "But I wanted to verify my information before we talked. And then you were shot and I couldn't tell you last night."

Maddox planted his fists on his sides, pressing them into the bed to sit up. "So it's true?"

Roan gave a clipped nod, then glanced at Megan. She offered him a sympathetic look, then spoke. "Actually, I brought my suspicions to the deputy."

"You did?" Maddox said in a gruff tone.

"Yes. I detected something suspicious in your father's autopsy, but—" She glanced at the doctor, and Roan wondered if she'd confess that Dr. Cumberland had implied that she'd made a mistake.

"But what?" Maddox asked.

"But there were two contradictory reports, so I ran a third test to verify the information. You were out of town so I contacted your deputy and relayed my findings."

Rose moved over to stand by Maddox and laid her hand on his shoulder in a comforting gesture.

Maddox inhaled sharply. "What exactly were those findings?"

Roan forced a neutral tone to his voice. Maddox couldn't know how personal this case was to him. "Dr. Lail found poison, specifically cyanide, in your father's tox screen."

Maddox stared at him, stunned. "Cyanide?"

"That's correct," Megan said.

"I'm so sorry," Dr. Cumberland said, his voice cracking. "Your father was so sick that I didn't notice the signs. That is, if there were any." He wiped a handkerchief over his sweating head. "When your father complained of nausea, I assumed it was his illness coupled with a reaction to the pain medication."

Which made sense, Roan had to admit.

"I feel terrible." Tears leaked from the doctor's eyes. "Maybe if I'd known, I could have bought him a little more time."

"Don't blame yourself," Maddox said to the doctor. "But I don't understand. Why would someone kill my father when he was already dying?"

"That's the reason I wanted to investigate before I came to you," Roan said.

"Do my brothers know about this?" Maddox asked.

"No, of course not. I was going to talk to you as soon as I had something concrete."

"And do you?" Maddox asked.

Roan sighed. "Not exactly."

"What does that mean?"

Roan jammed his hands in his pockets and glanced at the doctor. "Maybe we should discuss this in private."

Maddox studied him for a moment then agreed and asked Cumberland and Rose to step outside.

Roan waited until they'd left before he spoke again.

"I questioned Barbara about the poison, but she seemed shocked when I implied that someone hurt Joe. I haven't spoken with Bobby, although of course Barbara defended him."

"You suspected them because?"

"I thought your father might have planned to change his will to cut them out. If they found that out, it would have been motive."

"True."

"But your father's lawyer claims Joe had no intention of changing his will. He insisted that Barbara and Bobby be taken care of."

He drew a breath. "Arlis Bennett and Gates are top on the list, but so far I have no proof that they poisoned your father. Stan Romley confessed that he set the fires at Horseshoe Creek. He said Gates paid him to keep tabs on the farm and instructed him to do whatever was necessary to slow down your progress."

"Son of a bitch," Maddox muttered.

"There's more," Roan said.

Maddox released a tired sigh and dropped his head back against the stack of pillows. "What else?"

"Gates pointed the finger at another man named Clark. He said that your father refused to give Clark water rights and that eventually caused him financial trouble. That your father forced him to sell."

"So he had reason to hate my father. Or at least in his mind he did."

"It appears that way. I'm going to investigate him, too."

Maddox pinched the bridge of his nose.

"There are a couple of other developments," Roan continued. "Arlis Bennett's sister Edith and her husband were murdered. I'm not sure their deaths are related to your father's death or the fires, but both were shot with a .45, so it's definitely a possibility that they're connected."

"Edith?" Maddox asked.

Roan nodded.

"She used to visit my father a lot," Maddox said. "She and my mother were friends way back in the day."

Mama Mary had said something similar. If Edith had been friends with Maddox's mother, surely she wouldn't have hurt Joe. Would she?

"I talked to Mama Mary about your father's regular visitors," Roan said. "Of course Dr. Cumberland, Bobby and Barbara. Edith came, too. And your foreman."

"He would never hurt Dad," Maddox said. "He's the most loyal man I've ever known."

"But Barbara and Bobby might have," Roan said. "I found fertilizer at Barbara's. It contains cyanide."

"But if the same person killed my father and the Burnses," Maddox said, "it couldn't be Barbara or Bobby. They're both locked up."

"True. There's something else," Roan said, knowing he had to make full disclosure.

"Go on."

"Someone knows we're looking in to your father's murder and that Megan had a part in it. She was attacked and almost murdered last night."

The protective instincts of the McCullens darkened Maddox's face as he looked at Megan. "Are you all right, Dr. Lail?"

"Yes, but call me Megan. Please."

Maddox studied her for a second then nodded.

Roan folded his arms. "This morning Mama Mary called. Someone broke into your house, into your father's office."

Maddox made a move to get out of bed, but Roan

shook his head. "She's all right, Maddox. I talked to her. She's safe."

"Then why did they break in? More sabotage?"

"I don't think so," Roan said. "I think they were looking for something."

"Looking for what?"

"I was hoping you might know. Were there any deeds in question? Any bank accounts or transactions that looked suspicious? Did your father keep cash in his safe?"

"No, none of that."

Roan removed the private investigator's business card from his pocket and offered it to Maddox. "I had a crime team dust for prints. In the desk, I found this card. Do you know who this PI is?"

"No. I didn't hire him." Maddox frowned as he skimmed the card. "And I don't recognize his name."

"Do you know why your father might have hired him?"

Maddox wrestled with the sheet as if to get out of bed again, but Roan firmly held his arm. "I know you're upset, but you have to rest, Maddox. I can handle this."

"My father was murdered and this man might know the reason. I have to talk to him."

Roan cleared his throat. "I'm sorry, but that's not going to happen."

"Why the hell not?"

"Because he's dead," Roan replied.

A tense silence fell.

"How?" Maddox asked, frustration in his voice.

"Brakes failed on his car. His wife said it was ruled an accident, but—"

"She thinks he was murdered?" Maddox filled in.

Roan nodded. "When I leave here, I'm meeting her at her husband's office. She agreed to let me look through his files."

Maddox rubbed his eyes again. "Dammit, I want to help."

Sympathy for his half brother settled in Roan's chest. "I understand. But I swear that I'll find the truth, Maddox. I owe you for giving me a chance to prove myself in this town." He owed his father, too, although Joe McCullen had never done a thing for him.

Still, he was his biological father and Roan didn't intend to let his killer go free.

MEGAN FELT FOR MADDOX. But the questions kept adding up. There were too many to dismiss anything as coincidental. Too many that seemed to be connected for them not to be.

She was a woman of science. Concrete evidence.

Proof.

Rose came back in, and Maddox quickly filled her in.

"Trust me, Sheriff," Roan implored Maddox. "I'll find the answers for you."

"Let him handle the investigation," Rose said softly. "You have to rest, honey."

Maddox winced at her endearment, but his hand was shaky as if his injury was wearing on him. He had lost a lot of blood.

"Only if you keep me abreast of what you find every step of the way," Maddox said. "I may have been shot, but I'm not dead. And this is *my* father we're talking about."

Megan bit her lip at the spark of anger in Roan's eyes. She didn't quite understand it, except that sometimes prejudice still existed, and maybe he'd had to struggle to get where he was.

"I'll call my brothers," Maddox said. "Ray is a PI. Maybe he's heard of this guy."

"Let me know what he says." Roan's phone buzzed, and he checked the number, then answered. "Deputy White-feather." A pause. "Yes. All right, thanks."

When he hung up, he sighed. "Romley's gun, the bullet that he shot you with—it's not the same as the one that killed Morty and Edith Burns."

"So someone else killed them," Maddox said as if thinking out loud. "Maybe Arlis?"

"You think he'd kill his own sister?" Megan asked.

Roan and Maddox exchanged questioning looks. "Hard to say. I don't know Arlis that well."

"Could be Edith discovered that your father was murdered, and she was killed because of it."

ROAN HATED THE seed of resentment sprouting in his gut. He couldn't resent Maddox for what he'd said about *his* father when Maddox didn't know the truth. Still…sometimes he had wondered what his life would have been like if Joe had known about him.

If he'd acknowledged him as his son.

But if Maddox found out now…he'd probably not only fire Roan, but by withholding the truth, Maddox would consider him a liar and be suspicious of his motives.

"I can drop you at home or at a friend's," Roan offered. "With that maniac who attacked you still out there, I don't want to leave you alone."

Megan offered him a brave smile. "I'll go with you. Maybe I can help."

He studied her for a moment, but agreed without an argument, and they hurried to his SUV.

"Are you okay?" Megan asked as he drove from the hospital parking lot.

"Why wouldn't I be?" he said, his voice tight.

Megan frowned. "You seemed upset when you were talking to Maddox. Has there been tension between you two before?"

He shook his head. The last thing he wanted was for Megan to figure out the truth. To see that he cared, for God's sake.

Anyone he cared about ended up dead.

"Don't read so much into things, Megan. I'm just working a case and trying to keep you alive."

Megan lapsed into silence, and he studied the road, unwilling to pretend that he wanted to talk when the last thing he wanted was for someone to get inside his head.

Twenty minutes later, the tension was still thick as he parked at a small office building in a business park. Several other businesses occupied offices in the complex, and the lot was filled with cars.

He opened the car door, then adjusted his Stetson as he and Megan walked up the sidewalk to the PI's office. When he knocked, a woman with white-blond hair greeted him and introduced herself as Carrie Buchanan.

Roan made the introductions, and he and Megan both expressed regrets for the loss of her husband.

"You believe he died because of a case he was working on?" Roan said.

The fortyish woman toyed with her gold wedding ring. "Yes. Like I told you, Barry was meticulous about keeping his car in good shape."

"Did he mention any specific problem or person?" Roan asked.

"No, but he was agitated lately. He kept getting odd phone calls that upset him, but when I asked about it, he refused to discuss it."

Maybe Roan could look at those phone records, find out more about the calls.

Megan ran her hands through her hair, pushing the wind-tousled strands back behind her ears. For some reason, she'd forgotten the bun today.

It was damn near distracting, too.

That bun had kept him from touching her the first few times he'd seen her. He needed her to wear it again.

"Did your husband ever mention a man named Joe Mc-Cullen?" Maddox asked.

"No, like I said, he never revealed his clients' names." She led them inside the office. The front held a receptionist's area divided by a door that must lead to the back and Buchanan's private office.

Roan watched as Megan studied the pictures on the walls. Photographs of the man's credentials, then pictures of several families, smiling and hugging, all nostalgic scenes.

"Mrs. Buchanan," Megan said softly. "Did your husband specialize in any particular type of investigations?"

Mrs. Buchanan adjusted a stack of folders, which didn't need adjusting. They were already neatly stacked. "Yes. He worked with people trying to reconnect with lost family members. Missing kids. Adoptions. Runaways."

Roan scraped a hand over his beard stubble, wondering how that fit with Joe McCullen. He had knowledge of Bobby, his illegitimate son, so he hadn't been searching for him.

But…what if he suspected he had another son? That Joe was looking for *him*?

No…that was impossible. His mother had kept her secret to the end.

"Do you mind if I examine his files?" he asked. "I need to know the reason Joe McCullen hired him."

She gestured toward the door that led to the back, and he and Megan followed her through the hall to an office with metal furniture and hard vinyl chairs. Mrs. Buchanan flipped on the light, then gasped.

Someone had been inside the office and tossed it. Files were strewn all over the office, the file cabinet drawers opened, the files dumped helter-skelter across the floor and desk.

Roan cursed, frustration knotting his belly. He had a bad feeling the file he was looking for was missing.

"My God, it wasn't like this last week," she said in a pained whisper.

Last week he and Megan hadn't been asking questions about Joe McCullen's death.

*McCord, are you there? Are you okay?" Rising to a
point of whisper.*

Last week he said he was finishing the puzzle.

Oh, she hadn't come in calls.

Chapter Fifteen

Roan scanned the mess of papers strewn across the office
with skeptical eyes. An intruder had ransacked the place,
obviously looking for something.

Mrs. Buchanan spun the ring around her finger in a nervous gesture. "Who would do such a thing?"

"Someone who didn't want us to see what was in one of
your husband's files." Roan surveyed the room and desk.
"Your husband had a computer?"

"A laptop."

"Where is it?"

Her gaze swept the room. "I don't know. I thought it
was in here."

The laptop was gone.

Megan encouraged the woman to sit down, and Mrs.
Buchanan sank into a chair in the corner.

"So he really was murdered?" she said in a haunted
whisper.

"I can't say for certain," Roan said.

"Was there an autopsy?" Megan asked.

The woman lifted a shaky hand to push at her hair. "Yes.
He was killed on impact when his car struck a boulder."

"Would you mind if I reviewed that autopsy report?"
Megan asked.

Mrs. Buchanan inhaled sharply. "No, that would be fine.
I want the truth about my husband's death."

Megan rushed to get the woman a glass of water while
Roan yanked on gloves and began to comb through the pa-

pers, searching for anything that might have Joe's name on it. Of course, if the killer had stolen the file, he wouldn't find anything.

The PI had organized the files by case number, so he sorted the miscellaneous pages by matching numbers. His wife had been right, most of the cases involved reconnecting birth parents and biological children. Three cases revolved around a kidnapping—all led back to a parent kidnapping a child from the other parent.

So why had Joe been using the PI?

Determined to unearth the answer to that question, he checked the filing cabinet. Most of the files had been dumped on the desk and floor, but a few remained inside, although their contents had been rifled through.

He examined them, but didn't find Joe's. Dammit.

He checked the drawer labeled *M-P*. Empty.

Frustrated, he searched the desk drawers. Sticky notes, pens, stapler, paper clips.

He fumbled through the mess, then noticed a sticky note with the word "Grace" written on it—a question mark was behind the name.

Grace…

"Do you know anyone named Grace?"

The man's wife shook her head no. "What is her last name?"

"It doesn't say."

"Grace," Megan said in a low voice. "Wasn't that Maddox's mother's name?"

Roan's gaze jerked to Megan's. She was right.

He stared at the slip of paper again, his heart pounding. Joe McCullen's wife had died years ago when the boys were small. Hadn't she died in a car accident?

So had the PI…

Questions ticked through his head, but he had no answers. But the fact that the PI had a question mark by

Grace's name made him wonder if whatever Buchanan was looking into for Joe had something to do with his wife.

As soon as they stepped outside Buchanan's office, Megan phoned to request a copy of his autopsy.

"I wish I knew what this means," Roan said.

"Maybe Maddox will have some insight."

"I hate to bother him again. He needs rest to recover."

Megan gently rubbed Roan's arm. "Maddox would want to know, Roan. You heard him earlier. This is about his father, and now…maybe his mother. You can't not tell him."

A muscle ticked in his jaw. "You're right."

The sky had darkened with the threat of another storm, and the wind had picked up, swirling leaves and dust across the parking lot. Shadows played across the sky as the clouds rolled and shrouded the remaining sliver of sunlight.

Megan's phone buzzed that she had an email as they climbed in the car. She checked it and found the autopsy report.

She clicked to open the attachment.

The medical examiner who'd performed the autopsy was a doctor named Lindeman. She skimmed the results of the cause of death—head trauma. His brain had swollen with blood from the impact of the collision. Other lacerations, bruises and a broken femur, ribs and collarbone. Glass fragments pierced his skin, one had embedded in his leg causing more blood loss.

So far the injuries were consistent with the accident.

She skimmed further, though, and frowned at the tox report. "It says here that the doctor found a high level of alcohol in his blood."

"Mrs. Buchanan didn't mention that he'd been drinking."

"No, she didn't." Megan massaged her temple with two fingers. "Maybe the ME decided to spare her the detail."

"Could be. But with her suspicions, we have to ask."

"I'll call her."

"And I'll phone the sheriff who covered the accident and see if he investigated."

Megan punched the woman's number. "Mrs. Buchanan, I'm looking at your husband's autopsy. Did the medical examiner mention that your husband had a dangerous amount of alcohol in his system?"

"No. That can't be. Barry hadn't had a drink in twenty years."

Megan sucked in a breath. "So he was an alcoholic?"

"Yes, a recovering one. He attended AA meetings regularly."

"Perhaps he fell off the wagon."

"No," she said vehemently. "Barry *never* touched alcohol. He messed up when he was young because of drinking and caused an accident that seriously injured a friend. He never forgave himself. He made it his mission to visit schools where he spoke to teenagers about the dangers."

ROAN GRIPPED THE phone and explained to the sheriff in Laramie about his talk with Buchanan's wife. "Did you see the autopsy report?"

"Of course I did," the sheriff said. "The fact that the man had alcohol in his system suggested he lost control. That explained his accident."

"What about the brakes failing?"

"According to the mechanic, there was a slow leak in the brake lines."

"Did you consider the possibility that the brake lines had been tampered with?"

"Why would I? The man was drunk or he wouldn't have been going so fast. If he'd been going slower, he might have been able to stop in spite of the leak."

"The wife seems to think that this wasn't an accident."

"She was in denial," the sheriff said. "Didn't want to

believe that her husband was drunk and caused his own accident. She even claimed he didn't drink, but he was an alcoholic. Husbands don't tell their wives everything, you know."

True. But Roan wasn't satisfied.

But the sheriff cut him off and hung up. Roan filled Megan in as he drove from the parking lot. "The sheriff knew about the alcohol, but didn't find it suspicious."

"I know people fall off the wagon all the time, but Barry's wife insisted that her husband never drank. He felt guilty over an accident he caused when he was younger, so he spoke to teen groups about the dangers of drinking and driving."

Roan arched a brow. "If he didn't willingly take a drink, someone could have forced it in him."

"It's possible," Megan said.

Roan mentally contemplated the random pieces they'd learned so far. Gates and his plan to sabotage the McCullens, Morty and Edith Burns's murders and now Barry Buchanan's murder.

Joe had hired the PI. His wife's name had been scribbled on a sticky note suggesting she had something to do with why Joe had hired him.

The clouds opened up, once again dumping rain on the dry land and slowing him down. Just as he reached the turn-off for the hospital, though, a dark van raced up on his tail. Tires screeched. The car sped up and started to pass him.

Roan scowled and gripped the steering wheel, ready to flip on the siren and chase the bastard. But suddenly the van raced up beside him, and a gunshot blasted the air.

Megan screamed, and he swerved sideways. The bullet missed the glass window by a fraction of an inch.

Another shot rang out, and Roan swerved again. "Get down and hang on, Megan."

She ducked, and he jerked the car to the left to slam into

the van. The van swung sideways, tires squealing as it careened forward.

Roan pressed the accelerator, determined not to let him escape, but the van disappeared around a curve.

Roan sped up, but another car pulled out just as he soared over the hill, and he had to brake and swerve to the shoulder of the road to avoid hitting it.

MEGAN TRIED TO compose herself as Roan pulled over and climbed from the car to examine it. He retrieved something from the trunk.

Five minutes later, he climbed back in the front seat and dropped a baggie on the console. "I managed to dig one of the bullets out of the side. I'll have the lab analyze it and see if it came from the same gun that killed the Burnses."

He covered her hand with his. "Are you all right?"

She nodded. "You know, I thought Barbara and Bobby had the most to gain if Joe McCullen was dead, but they can't be doing this."

"You're right. I'm beginning to think Joe's murder didn't have anything to do with them. That whatever this PI was working on for him got them both killed."

Megan considered his suggestion as the storm raged around them and they parked in the Pistol Whip Hospital parking lot.

The rain had slackened, but still water dripped from the trees. She pulled her jacket hood up to shield her from the rain, and Roan settled his Stetson on his head. Then they hurried inside.

Rose and Mama Mary were huddled together in the room with Maddox.

"I tried to get Rose to go home," Mama Mary said as she greeted them, "but she refused to leave."

Maddox laid a hand on his wife's belly. "She's going home tonight if I have to get up and drive her."

Rose laughed softly. "Now I know you're going to be okay. You're getting bossy."

Her casual joke seemed to ease the tension.

Maddox laid his spoon on the tray. "Thanks for the soup, Mama Mary."

She flattened her palms on her big hips. "Well, I couldn't have my boy eating that nasty hospital stuff they call food. If a man wants to get well he needs nourishment."

Maddox chuckled and tolerated her fawning over him. But as soon as she took the tray, he sobered and looked up at Roan. "What did you find out?"

"Actually, I have more questions." Roan explained about his visit to the PI's office and his conversation with the man's wife.

Megan slid into a seat beside Rose and Mama Mary.

"When I spoke to the sheriff who investigated Buchanan's death," Roan continued, "he didn't seem suspicious. But Mrs. Buchanan was adamant that her husband didn't drink. And that he was meticulous about keeping his car in tip-top shape."

Maddox pulled at his chin. "You still don't know why my father hired him?"

Roan glanced at Megan, and she understood his hesitation. Joe McCullen had one illegitimate son with another woman. Could he possibly have had another?

"At this point, we don't know, but Buchanan specializes in connecting families with lost members."

"You mean like adoptions?"

"Yes. He's handled a couple of kidnapping cases, but mostly works with adopted children or birth parents trying to find one another."

Maddox wheezed a labored breath. "But that makes no sense. Dad knew about Bobby."

The air grew hot with tension. Finally Maddox looked

at Mama Mary. "You knew about Bobby. Did Dad have any other indiscretions?"

Roan fisted his hands by his sides. That was how Maddox would look at him—as an indiscretion. A mistake.

"No, Joe didn't have another affair, if that's what you're asking. I told you, your folks were going through a rough patch when that happened." She puffed up her chest. "Your daddy loved Ms. Grace. But she was extremely depressed over losing the twins."

"I knew about them," Maddox said, "but not that Mama was that depressed."

"Speaking of your mother," Roan said, his pulse hammering at the defensive look in Maddox's eyes. "I found a sticky note with her name on it in Buchanan's desk drawer."

"My mother's name," Maddox said beneath his breath. "I don't understand."

"Someone broke in and ransacked Buchanan's office. If he had a file on your father, it was gone."

"So we're back to nothing," Maddox said, his voice gravelly with frustration.

A dozen questions settled in the air. Mama Mary made a low sound in her throat.

"You said Mr. Joe hired this man. And that he had Ms. Grace's name on a sticky note."

Roan swung his head her way. "That's right."

Mama Mary wrung her hands together. "Oh, my word… it can't be."

Roan's chest thumped. Maddox pushed himself straighter in the bed, although the movement cost him and he clutched at his bandaged torso.

"What is it, Mama Mary?" Maddox asked.

The sweet woman's eyes looked troubled. "I…don't know. I can't be sure…"

Rose patted her hand. "It's okay, Mama Mary. Did you remember something?"

The older woman nodded, worrying her bottom lip with her teeth. "It's just that Ms. Grace, she was so upset about losing the babies. They were both boys you know."

Pain wrenched Maddox's face. "Go on."

"Like I said, she was depressed and she wasn't sleeping at night. She kept saying her babies couldn't be dead, that she heard them crying for her."

A chill went through the room. Judging from the strained expression on everyone's face, they felt it, too.

"I thought she was just in denial." Mama Mary dabbed at her eyes as she looked at Maddox. "She loved you boys so much. You all and your daddy were her life. And she wanted those two other little babies so bad."

"What happened, Mama Mary?" Maddox asked in a gruff voice.

"Dr. Cumberland said Grace was suffering from depression. Postpartum and grief, it was eating her up, so he gave her some medication."

"She was drinking on top of that?" Maddox asked.

"That's what he said the night she died." She wiped at the perspiration trickling down the side of her face. "But the night before…I heard your mama and daddy arguing."

"What were they arguing about?" Roan asked.

Mama Mary sniffled. "Ms. Grace said she didn't think her babies were dead. That she remembered holding them when they were born and hearing them cry. Then suddenly they were gone. Doc said they died at birth, and Ms. Grace was so traumatized she just dreamed she heard them crying. When he told her they didn't make it, she was so hysterical he had to sedate her."

Anguish flared in Maddox's eyes. Confusion also blended with the shock. "My mother thought her babies were alive?"

Mama Mary nodded, her lip quivering. "That's what they argued about. Your daddy was so worried about her that he called the doc that night. He thought she might be going over the edge."

"But she died the next day in that accident," Maddox said.

Mama Mary nodded. "Mr. Joe never forgave himself."

"So your parents argued about whether the twins survived," Roan said, piecing together the facts. "And before Joe died, he hired Buchanan, a man whose specialty was finding missing children and connecting adopted children with their birth parents."

Mama Mary whimpered. "Do you think he discovered something about those babies? That maybe Ms. Grace was right? That someone stole them from her arms and made her think they were dead?"

Chapter Sixteen

Roan considered the possibilities. If someone had stolen Grace McCullen's babies, and Grace kept probing, insisting they were alive, the kidnapper might have panicked and tried to silence her.

And she *had* ended up dead. With her, the questions had died, as well.

Until recently when Joe had hired Buchanan.

Now Joe and the PI were both dead, too.

Mama Mary sniffed and wiped at more tears. "I can't believe this…all these years, I thought those babies were dead, too. Thought Ms. Grace just couldn't accept that she lost them…"

"We're just speculating right now." Maddox turned to Roan. "But if there's a possibility that the infants were kidnapped, that means I…Brett and Ray and I have two brothers we never knew about."

Roan's throat thickened with the need to confess that he was their half brother, but now wasn't the time. Maybe there never would be a time.

He would have to live with that.

He wasn't doing this to gain favor with the McCullen brothers. He was a lawman who believed in justice.

"Poor Ms. Grace," Mama Mary said. "No wonder she was so depressed. If she had reason to think her babies were kidnapped and no one believed her, she must have felt so alone."

Pain lined Maddox's face. "Did she say anything specific about why she thought they were alive?"

Mama Mary rubbed her forehead in thought. "Just that she heard them cry when they were born, then she passed out and when she came to, Doc told her they hadn't made it."

Maddox rubbed at his chest. "I remember Mama being sad for a while, and Dad said she lost the babies, but I was so young I didn't really understand. I do remember them talking about a nursery."

"She had just started it when she lost them," Mama Mary said. "Your daddy painted over it in a hurry, thinking it would help. But it only made Ms. Grace mad."

Maddox seemed to absorb that information. "Because she thought the babies were alive."

Mama Mary nodded. "Losing those boys tore him up, too," Mama Mary continued as though reliving those days. "Then he and Ms. Grace started fighting, and she slipped away."

"That's when he met Barbara," Maddox said.

Mama Mary nodded gravely. "I think he just needed some comfort, but it didn't last long. He loved your mama more than words, and wanted to help her get better."

"Except she couldn't because she believed her babies had been kidnapped." Roan chewed the inside of his cheek. "Where are the babies buried?"

Mama Mary's eyes widened. "Well…they…they didn't bury them. Dr. Cumberland had the babies cremated. He said it would be easier on the family that way."

"What?" Anger hardened Maddox's tone. "Did my parents ask him to do that?"

Mama Mary fumbled with the tissue in her hands. "I don't really know. Mr. Joe and the doc talked behind closed doors. I…assumed that was what your daddy wanted."

"I have to talk to Cumberland." Maddox reached for the phone. "He has some explaining to do."

HE CERTAINLY DID, Megan thought.

And without bodies, she couldn't perform an autopsy to determine cause of death or use DNA to verify that the McCullen infants had actually died.

"Good Lord," Mama Mary muttered. "Here, all this time I thought Ms. Grace took those pills and had a drink and drove into that wall to kill herself."

Maddox scrubbed a hand over his face as he punched the doctor's number.

"So if those twins lived," Megan cut in, "who took them?" She paused, mind spinning with more questions. "And if Grace suspected foul play and was asking too many questions, maybe her death wasn't an accident or suicide."

Hushed murmurs of worry echoed through the hospital room.

Megan waited until Maddox left a message for Dr. Cumberland to call him, that he had questions about his mother and the babies she'd lost. He put the phone down, his face strained.

"Was an autopsy performed on Grace?" Megan asked.

"I don't believe so," Mama Mary said. "Mr. Joe and the doc talked and said they didn't want it coming out that she was drinking and taking pills. That Ms. Grace had suffered enough. He wanted her to rest in peace." Mama Mary gave Maddox a sympathetic look. "Mr. Joe was worried about you boys, too. Pistol Whip's a small town, and he didn't want people gossiping."

"That sounds like Dad." Maddox squeezed Rose's hand, and she rubbed his shoulders.

"So we're looking at the possibility that someone kidnapped the twins, then drugged your mother, causing the accident that killed her," Roan said, summarizing what they were all thinking.

"But who would take those babies?" Rose asked.

A thick silence fell while everyone contemplated that question.

"Someone who either wanted them for themselves," Megan suggested.

"Or someone who wanted to hurt Grace, and possibly Joe," Roan finished. "What about the doctor?"

Mama Mary frowned. "He loved this family. He was distraught over losing the babies, too."

"But if they're still alive, he must know something," Roan pointed out.

"I think he had a young doctor working with him at the time," Mama Mary said. "Maybe he had something to do with it and Dr. Cumberland didn't know."

"I'll find out." Maddox rubbed at the bandage on his chest again. "What if Barbara knew my father before my mother lost the twins? Maybe she thought if she could drive my parents apart by kidnapping the babies, she'd have a chance with Dad?"

Maddox angled his head toward Mama Mary. "Did they know each other before?"

Mama Mary ripped the tissue in her hands into shreds. "Ms. Grace met Barbara at the garden club. Later, I remember hearing your father tell Barbara to stay away from your mother, that it was over between them, that Grace had already been hurt enough."

Compassion for the family engulfed Megan.

Barbara was a gardener. She had access to cyanide—Roan had found it at her house.

Had Barbara pretended to be Grace's friend, then killed her in an attempt to keep Joe for herself?

ROAN SHIFTED, FOLDING his arms. "Barbara is the most viable suspect, but there are a couple of problems. She had the opportunity and means to kill your parents. But someone attacked Megan and threatened to kill her if she didn't leave your father's murder alone. Barbara and Bobby are both locked up, so it's impossible that they threatened her."

"They could have hired someone." Maddox reached for his IV to remove it. "I need to get up and do something."

"You are not going anywhere." Rose put a hand on Maddox's to stop him, and Mama Mary moved to her side for reinforcement.

"Listen to your wife." Mama Mary gestured toward Rose's baby bump. "You need to take care of yourself. You got folks who need you now."

Maddox grunted in frustration, but sank back against the bed. "I hate this. I should be working leads."

"Roan will take care of things," Rose said. "Won't you?"

"Of course." Roan had more reason to find the truth than anyone thought, but he kept that to himself.

"I'll have the IT team dig through Barbara and Bobby's financials to see if they made any large payments to anyone," Roan said. "And I want to talk to Dr. Cumberland."

"He was upset when he left," Maddox said. "He still can't understand how someone poisoned my dad while he was under his care."

Roan gritted his teeth, but said nothing. He had no personal attachment to the physician like Maddox and his family did, so he was more skeptical.

"What about Clark?" Roan asked. "He was bitter about losing his land."

"But that happened long after my mother died," Maddox said.

Still, if Grace McCullen's death hadn't been murder, Clark could have killed Joe. But it was looking more and more like Grace was murdered first, and then Joe discovered something that made him suspicious, hired the PI and then he and the PI were killed because of it.

"Didn't you say Edith Burns visited your father when he was ill?" Roan asked.

Maddox nodded. "A few times. She said she promised my mother that if anything ever happened to her, she'd always look in on us kids."

Close friends did that, but considering the fact that Edith and her husband had been shot to death, it made Roan wonder if there was a connection. Maybe a cover-up that had gone back years.

A cover-up that was about to be exposed when Joe McCullen hired Buchanan.

FEELING ANXIOUS, MEGAN swept her hair back into its bun and pinned it in place as Roan drove toward the doctor's office. She didn't like the train of thought her mind had taken. "If those babies didn't die and were kidnapped, that means Dr. Cumberland had to know something about it."

A muscle jumped in Roan's cheek. "That's what I was thinking. Maddox has to be thinking it, too."

Dr. Cumberland had a private practice in Pistol Whip in the square. Two cars sat in the parking lot. A gray Lexus and a black SUV.

"You've known the doctor through the ME's office. Do you think he's capable of such deception?"

Uncertainty crept through Megan. "I don't know. From what I've seen, he's truly caring and kind to his patients. He listens to elderly people, is patient with children and everyone in town knows him and has been to his office for one reason or another. He's delivered most of the babies in town and he's never had a lawsuit filed against him." She paused. "In this litigious society, that's a miracle."

"Maybe we're jumping to conclusions," Roan said. "Joe could have hired this PI to look into Clark or Gates."

Megan nodded. "But it still doesn't explain why Grace's name was on that sticky note in the PI's office."

"It's possible that there was another Grace."

Megan nodded again, although he didn't sound con-

vinced and neither was she. They knew for a fact that Joe
had been poisoned. Maybe Joe had hired the PI because
he'd received some kind of threat or suspected someone
was trying to hurt him?

Together, she and Roan walked up to the doctor's office
and went inside. The receptionist, a gray-haired woman
with a kind smile, greeted them. "What can we do for you?"

Roan identified himself and introduced Megan. "We
need to speak to Dr. Cumberland."

"I'll let him know you're here. He's with the new doctor
now." She pressed an intercom button and announced their
arrival. Dr. Cumberland told her he'd be right with them.

"A new doctor?" Megan asked. "Is Dr. Cumberland ex-
panding his practice?"

The woman's smile faded slightly. "No. Dr. Cumberland decided to retire so he's bringing in a replacement."

Roan studied the pictures on the waiting room walls—
photographs of babies Dr. Cumberland delivered along with
families and individuals he'd treated.

"I thought he wasn't retiring until next year," Megan
commented.

"The doc's wife is pushing him to travel more."

Interesting, Megan thought. The timing could be coincidental, although it also could indicate that he wanted
to get out of town to escape scrutiny over Joe McCullen's
autopsy report.

Perhaps the reason he'd been so upset with her when
she'd run the test a third time was because he didn't want
anyone to know that he'd doctored the report to hide the
fact that his friend was murdered.

THE PHOTOGRAPHS ON Dr. Cumberland's wall chronicled the
story of a well-loved, small-hometown doctor who'd served
his community since he was a young man.

Roan had to tread carefully or he might wreck an innocent man's life.

Or...expose the truth and tear the town apart with lies and secrets that dated back decades.

The door leading to the offices in back opened, and the older man appeared wearing a worn shirt and dress pants. He looked tired, the age lines around his eyes carving deep grooves into his skin.

A younger man, probably early thirties, with thick dark hair and dressed in Western attire including a bolo tie, appeared beside him.

Dr. Cumberland raised a brow when he saw them, then introduced the doctor as Seth Griffin.

They shook hands and made introductions, and Roan gestured toward the back office. "Can we talk in private, Dr. Cumberland?"

He adjusted his glasses, his face sagging with fatigue, but nodded, and Dr. Griffin left.

Roan and Megan followed Cumberland to his office. He offered coffee or water, but they both declined. Cumberland poured himself a cup of coffee, though, and claimed a seat behind his desk, but his hand shook as he set the mug down.

"Dr. Cumberland, we need to ask you some more questions," Roan began.

"I don't know what's going on with you two, but I've apologized to Maddox and explained that I don't know how I missed what was happening with Joe."

Roan cut his gaze toward Megan, then back to the doctor. "There's more," Roan said. "We discovered that Joe McCullen hired a private investigator named Barry Buchanan."

Dr. Cumberland's face paled. "What would Joe need a PI for?"

"We were hoping you could explain," Roan said.

"I have no idea."

"I think you do," Roan said, cutting to the chase. "Joe was murdered. So was the private investigator."

The doctor's breath whooshed out. "Good God."

"Buchanan's office was also ransacked, some of his files stolen. The file on Joe McCullen was gone."

"You think the man was murdered because of what he was working on for Joe?"

"Yes," Roan said.

"It probably had to do with that cattle rustling ring," Dr. Cumberland suggested. "Joe suspected someone in the community was stealing from others and was determined to find out who it was."

"That's possible, but I found a sticky note with the word 'Grace' written on it. I think Joe hired the PI because of her death."

"But Grace died in a car accident years ago," the doctor said.

"You didn't request an autopsy on Grace, did you?" Megan asked.

He swung a startled look at Megan. "No, didn't need to. I smelled the alcohol on her, and knew she'd been taking antidepressants. I didn't want to put Joe through any more suffering."

"But autopsies are standard in that kind of situation," Megan pointed out.

Dr. Cumberland's voice took on an edge. "Maybe in big cities where there's lots of crime, but not here in a small town. Not when everyone knew the family. Joe loved Grace, but she was severely depressed. There was no need to drag her name through the mud."

Roan arched a brow. "Grace was depressed over losing her babies, correct?"

Dr. Cumberland drummed his fingernails on his coffee cup. "Yes. But that was understandable. She had two stillborn infants."

Roan and Megan exchanged a look. "Were they still-born?" Roan asked.

The glare Roan received indicated he'd hit a nerve.

"Yes," Dr. Cumberland said through gritted teeth.

"Tell us about the night they were born," Megan said. "Were the babies premature?"

"Yes, about four weeks, but that's not uncommon for twins. Joe was out of town, had gone to buy more cattle. I called him when Grace went into labor, but he was hours away. He never got over the fact that he didn't make it back in time."

"She delivered at the hospital?" Megan asked.

The doctor shook his head. "No, there was no time. Edith came over and took the other three boys to her house for the night. I wanted to get Grace to the hospital, but her contractions were one on top of the other. I tried to make her comfortable and help her through it, but when I delivered the babies, they weren't breathing. And one of them, well, he was also deformed." Emotions twisted the doctor's mouth. "I tried to resuscitate them, but failed."

"Did you request an autopsy to determine cause of death?" Megan asked.

"Look, it was thirty years ago. Rules and regulations weren't so tight." He shrugged. "Besides, Grace was so distraught. She didn't want anyone desecrating their little bodies, and I respected her wishes."

"Did she hold the babies?" Megan asked.

He shook his head again. "No, like I said she was distraught. I had to give her a sedative to calm her."

"And you had the babies cremated instead of letting the family bury them?" Roan pressed.

The doctor's mouth tightened. "It was what the McCullens wanted. Grace said she didn't think she could bear to look at those tiny graves."

"What happened to the ashes?" Megan asked.

"Joe and Grace scattered them in the pond on Horseshoe Creek."

So there was no chance of testing the ashes.

Roan folded his arms, his voice hard. "Are you certain that's the way it happened?"

"Of course. It was a terrible time. I loved that family and afterward did everything I could to help Grace and Joe mourn their loss."

"I don't believe you," Roan said. "I have reason to think that Grace suspected her babies hadn't died, that someone kidnapped them."

Dr. Cumberland gasped. "That's ridiculous. For God's sake, I was there."

Roan leaned across the desk, hands planted firmly on top, eyes boring into the doctor's. "Exactly."

The man's eyes narrowed to slits. "Just what the hell are you implying?"

"That for some reason you took those babies and gave them to someone else. Maybe for money. Maybe it was someone you knew. Either way, later Grace questioned it, and she was killed because she refused to stop looking for them."

Chapter Seventeen

Dr. Cumberland stood, his nostrils flaring. "I don't like the implications, Deputy Whitefeather. Does Maddox know that you're here making these kinds of accusations?"

Roan met his gaze with a cold stare. "Yes."

That sucked the bravado out of the man. "This is unreal. I've devoted myself to this town and the McCullens were my personal friends. I'd take my own life before I'd hurt one of them."

"Then how do you explain all the inconsistencies and the deaths," Megan interjected.

"We know for a fact that Joe was murdered. We suspect Grace might have been, as well. The private investigator Joe hired was also killed in a suspicious car accident, an accident similar to Grace's." Roan hesitated. "Also, Morty and Edith Burns were shot to death. You knew them, didn't you?"

"Yes, but…" Dr. Cumberland shook his head in denial. "When did that happen?"

"A couple of days ago," Roan answered. "Did you say that Edith took care of Maddox and his brothers the night Grace gave birth?"

The doctor nodded, although he suddenly looked ill. "Edith and Grace were good friends."

"Then Grace probably confided her fears to Edith."

More questions ticked in Roan's head. What if Edith was killed because she found out that Dr. Cumberland had kidnapped the McCullen twins? Or what if she actually aided in the kidnapping?

"If you want to know who would kill Joe, look at Barbara," Dr. Cumberland said. "She was bitter toward both Grace and Joe."

"We've already questioned her," Roan said. "She claims she would have never hurt Joe."

"But she might have killed Grace." Dr. Cumberland stood, eyes fixed with anger. "Now, I've answered your questions, it's time for you to leave."

Roan planted his hands on the desk again. "There's one more thing, Doctor. The day Megan ran that third test on Joe McCullen's blood, someone pushed her into the street. And shortly after she got the results, someone attacked her in the morgue and threatened her."

Nerves fluttered in the doctor's eyes.

"Other than the lab tech who ran the sample, you were the only person who knew about that test and the results."

A coldness seeped into the doctor's eyes that struck Roan as guilt. A second later, the doctor swung his hand toward the door.

"Get out, Deputy. I'm done with your accusations."

Roan refused to be intimidated. "Know this, Dr. Cumberland, if you were involved in either of the McCullens' death or the Burnses', or if you're lying about what happened to the twins, I will find out." He leaned closer, eyes pinning the man to the spot. "And nothing had better happen to Dr. Lail. Do you understand?"

Another tense second passed, and then the doctor gave a clipped nod.

But Roan didn't trust him. As soon as he and Megan left the office, he phoned the lab and asked them to examine the doctor's phone and bank records going back three decades.

If someone had paid Cumberland to fake the twins' death, that would be a place to start.

MEGAN WORRIED HER lip with her teeth. "If Barbara had something to do with Joe's death, maybe we should talk to her again."

"She's not going to confess," Roan said. "She's just as defensive as Dr. Cumberland."

"Then talk to Bobby. If his mother killed Joe and he didn't know about it, he might turn on her."

"Good point. Let's pay him a visit."

She struggled to make sense of the situation as he drove to the prison where Bobby was locked up. He was being held in a minimum-security facility that provided mental health.

"I still find it hard to believe that Dr. Cumberland would deceive the McCullens like that," she said, thinking out loud. "He seemed to genuinely care for them. And no one has ever filed a complaint against him."

Roan scrubbed a hand through his thick, long hair. "You never know what people will do if they're pushed into it."

"What do you mean?"

"It was a long time ago," Roan said. "We don't know what was going on in the doctor's life back then. Hell, what if he and Barbara had had a thing?"

"That doesn't seem likely," Megan said. "But I guess you're right. I just hate to think that he betrayed that family's trust."

They parked at the prison, then cleared security, and Roan explained to the warden that he needed to visit Bobby. "How is he doing?"

"He has his good days and bad days. The therapist is working with him on anger management issues. He's been sober now for weeks, so that helps."

One of the guards led them to a visitor's room, and a few minutes later another guard escorted Bobby into the room. He wore prison garb and was handcuffed, but lacked the shackles. The gray pallor of his skin indicated he hadn't seen much sunshine, and the glint of anger in his eyes indicated he still harbored bitterness toward the world.

"You can remove the handcuffs," Roan said.

Bobby seemed wary, but muttered a thanks when the guard unlocked the cuffs. For a moment, he rubbed at his wrists as if the cuffs had hurt. Or maybe he just hated confinement.

She remembered being confined in that body bag and understood the suffocating feeling of having your freedom stripped away.

"Hello, Bobby, I'm Deputy Whitefeather, and this is Dr. Megan Lail, the medical examiner in Pistol Whip."

Bobby cut his steel-hard eyes toward Megan, and a spark of male appreciation replaced his resentment. "To what do I owe the pleasure?"

Megan forced a neutral expression, determined not to let him bait her. "We need to talk to you about your father."

"My father is dead," Bobby said matter-of-factly.

"Yes, he is," Roan said. "But we know the truth about how he died now."

Bobby's eyes flickered with emotions that Roan couldn't quite define. "What is that supposed to mean?"

"I performed an autopsy on Joe," Megan said. "He didn't die of natural causes. Someone poisoned him."

Bobby gaped at them in shock. "My father was murdered?"

Megan nodded slowly.

"That's impossible," Bobby said. "He was sick. He had emphysema…"

"Yes, he did," Megan said. "But his illness didn't take his life. I found traces of cyanide in his tox report. Someone slowly poisoned him to death."

"Cyanide?" Bobby's voice grew shrill. "But that's crazy." He spread his hands in front of him and stared at his bruised knuckles.

"You had the most to gain from your father's death," Roan said bluntly.

Bobby's head jerked up, rage darkening his face. "You think I killed my own father?"

Megan swallowed hard at the pain in Bobby's voice. Was he lying or was he really shocked by his father's murder?

ROAN NARROWED HIS EYES, scrutinizing Bobby. "Maybe you already knew what your father put in that will and you weren't happy about it."

"But I didn't know," Bobby stuttered.

"Then you thought he was going to change his will and cut you out completely, and that wasn't fair." Roan lowered his voice. "Hell, man, I get it. You were just as much a son to Joe McCullen as Maddox or Brett or Ray, but he never treated you the same. You got bits of his time and attention when he could fit you in."

Pain wrenched Bobby's face.

"I don't blame you for being angry, for hating the Mc-Cullens. Joe should have made you a part of his family. He should have given you the riding lessons and the land and his name—"

"Yes, he should have," Bobby growled.

"You visited him when he was sick?"

Bobby nodded. "He apologized, said he knew he'd let me down, but that I had to shape up. Hell, I bet he never talked to his other sons that way. They didn't have to prove they were worthy of being a McCullen like I did."

How could Roan not understand the man's animosity? "Even when he was dying, he didn't acknowledge you to your half brothers?"

Bobby shook his head. "He was ashamed of me."

Roan's heart pitched. Would he have been ashamed of him if he'd known he was his son?

"So you decided to get back at him, didn't you?" Roan

asked. "You slipped some poison in his drink and slowly watched him die."

Bobby shot up from this seat, outrage flashing in his eyes. "That's a lie."

The guard stepped forward, stance aggressive, handcuffs in one hand, his other on the gun at his waist. He motioned for Bobby to take a seat.

"Damn this." Bobby glared at the guard, but sank back in the metal chair. He rolled his hands into fists on the table, then took several deep breaths.

"That's total crap. Yes, I was furious at my father, and I never made any bones about the fact that I resent my half brothers. They've never done anything for me. I'm sure they're pissed that Dad included me in the will." His eyes darkened. "Have you considered the fact that maybe one of them wanted to get back at him for his affair with my mother?"

"That makes no sense," Roan replied. "First of all they had no knowledge of you. And secondly, if they did, they would have tried to convince Joe not to include you in the will. Killing him only meant you got your share sooner."

Bobby's face fell. Apparently he hadn't thought his theory through.

"Listen to me." Bobby lowered his voice. "I was mad at my father, but I didn't kill him. Like a fool, I…kept hoping he'd make things right before he died."

Roan chewed the inside of his cheek. The pain and raw hope in Bobby's voice sounded sincere.

"What about your mother?" Megan asked. "Barbara had just as much reason to be angry at Joe as you did."

Bobby twisted his head toward her. "She loved Joe until the end. She would have never hurt him."

"Really?" Roan said. "She was obsessed with Joe for years. She wanted him, but even after his wife died, he refused to marry her."

Bobby's lips thinned into a straight line.

"In fact, we now believe that Grace McCullen might also have been murdered."

"What?" Bobby stuttered.

"Did you know that Grace McCullen was pregnant with twins a few months before she died? That she lost those babies?"

Bobby looked from Roan to Megan, then shook his head. "I have no idea what you're talking about."

"Then I've got a story to tell you," Roan said. "Joe married Grace and had three sons. Later she got pregnant with twins. Somehow Barbara had met Joe and had a thing for him, but she knew he wouldn't leave his wife. So she hires someone to help her kidnap those babies when they're born. Grace and Joe think the babies died, but Grace can't get over it. That was Barbara's plan—she wanted to drive Grace and Joe apart."

"You're crazy," Bobby muttered.

"It worked for a while. Joe hooked up with your mother, and they had you. But Joe still loved his wife and refused to leave her. A few months later when Barbara realized her plan hadn't worked, she decided the only way to have Joe was to get rid of Grace. She discovered Grace was on antidepressants, so somehow she found a way to get some alcohol into Grace. Mixed with the pills, Grace passes out and is killed in what appears to be a car accident."

Roan paused. "But that doesn't do the trick. Joe still won't marry her. He still keeps you and your mother on the side. Barbara puts up with it for years but her resentment grows. Then eventually Joe gets sick. She finds out about the will and is irate at how he left things and poisons him."

Bobby shook his head in denial, but said nothing.

"She took your father from you before his time was up,"

Roan said, pressing harder. "Maybe if she hadn't, he would have found a way to introduce you to your half brothers."

Bobby's face blanched. "My mother wouldn't have done that."

"Can you be sure, Bobby? Just look at what she did a few months ago. She pulled a gun on Scarlet Lovett and threatened the McCullens."

Bobby looked down at his hands, his face anguished. His breathing was choppy as he stood. A cold resignation framed his eyes as he met Roan's gaze. "I want to see my mother."

Roan's pulse jumped. He was hoping he'd say that. "I can arrange that." He paused. "But only if you let me listen to your conversation."

A vein throbbed in Bobby's neck. "You want me to try to trap my mother into confessing to murder?"

"I want the truth," Roan said. "I think you do, too."

Bobby squared his shoulders, his body ramrod straight. "Fine, set it up. But I'll prove you wrong."

Roan gave a small nod, although Bobby's voice lacked conviction, as if he didn't think that would happen at all.

As if he thought his mother was guilty.

Chapter Eighteen

Sympathy for Bobby welled in Megan's chest. If his mother had murdered Joe and Grace and kidnapped the twins, she would spend the rest of her life in prison.

Bobby would also lose the only parent he'd ever really known.

But at least if Bobby confronted her, they'd learn the truth.

Although it was early evening, Roan didn't want to put off the interview with Barbara until the next day. If he did, Bobby might change his mind. He might also find a way to contact his mother, which could work against getting that confession.

She and Roan stopped and had dinner at the local diner while he arranged the transport and meeting. Two hours later, they sat in a room with a two-way mirror that allowed them to view the conversation between mother and son.

Bobby looked even more agitated than he had when they left him. Barbara looked…excited, happy about seeing Bobby again.

"Son, I'm so glad to see you." Barbara swiped at tears and folded Bobby in her arms. Roan had instructed the guards to remove the handcuffs so the two could talk openly. If the situation spiraled out of control, the guard would step in.

Roan was prepared to back him up.

"Mother, you look…good," Bobby said.

Barbara blushed and shook her head. "Orange has never

been my color. And they won't let me have my makeup. It's a travesty."

Megan almost laughed. The woman was harping on her looks when she was locked up for months. If they made this kidnapping or murder stick, she would be inside for the rest of her life.

"I've missed you so much, Bobby. You look good. Although you're a little thin." Barbara fluttered a hand down her cheek, then sank into the metal chair, but kept one hand clasped in her son's.

"The food sucks," Bobby said.

"Well, one day we'll be out and I'll fix you all your favorites again." Barbara pressed Bobby's hand to her cheek. "I dream about that all the time. Making that pulled pork you like and that coconut cake with the three layers."

Bobby looked torn. "Yeah, that'd be great."

"How did you arrange this get-together?" Barbara asked. "Are you getting an early release?"

Bobby had plastered on a smile, but it faded. "No early release, but I'm working through rehab."

"That's good, son. I want you to do well, to get out and prove to those McCullens that you deserved to be one of them."

"I don't care about being a McCullen anymore," Bobby said.

"But you're inheriting your own piece of land, Bobby. You'll have your own spread one day just like I always dreamed about for you."

Bobby gritted his teeth. "I know, Mom. I need to ask you something."

Anxiety knotted Megan's shoulders as she watched Bobby. She couldn't imagine confronting one of her parents in this kind of situation.

"What is it, honey? You want to talk about your therapy?"

"No, Mother, I want to talk about my father."

Barbara thumbed a strand of hair from her cheek. "All right."

"The police said Dad was poisoned. Did you kill him?"

Barbara gasped. "How can you ask me that, Bobby? You know how much I loved Joe."

"Yes. But I also know how much you hated his wife. The police say she was murdered, too."

"Yes, I hated that woman," Barbara admitted. "And I wanted her to die so I could have Joe, but I didn't kill her."

"Joe was poisoned with cyanide." Bobby leaned closer to her, his voice a conspiratorial whisper. "You kept cyanide, Mother. You used it in your gardening. And you visited Joe multiple times, and you were always making him cookies."

Rage slashed Barbara's face as she pushed herself to stand. "I can't believe you of all people would accuse me of such a thing." She glanced at the guard, then around the room.

"Did you do it?" Bobby asked. "Did you kidnap those twins, then kill Grace so Joe would be with you?"

Barbara went stone-cold still. She turned slowly and looked at the mirror on the wall, then spoke as if she knew they were watching. "How dare you force my son into trying to trap me to confess. I did not kill that damned woman, and I certainly didn't kill Joe." Her eyes turned menacing. "You will pay for turning my son against me. You'll pay."

She flicked her wrist and motioned to the guard. "Now get me out of here. I'd rather be in my cell than visiting with a son who would stab me in the back."

"THAT DIDN'T GO as I expected," Roan said.

"I know you were hoping for a confession." Megan fastened her seat belt as they drove toward Pistol Whip. "But maybe we have it wrong. Maybe Barbara wasn't the killer."

Roan grunted in frustration. "Could be. Everything leads back to Dr. Cumberland and that night the twins died…or disappeared. He could have covered up Grace's and Joe's murders, too."

"But he spent his whole life helping people in this town," Megan continued.

Roan phoned the doctor, but his voice mail picked up, so he left a message.

He hung up, but couldn't get the doctor off his mind. A second later, his phone buzzed. The lab. "Deputy White-feather."

"Roan, it's Lieutenant Hoberman. We researched Barbara Lowman's accounts as well as Dr. Cumberland's. There were a few deposits made in Barbara's account that could have raised red flags, except we cross-checked with Joe McCullen's and they match."

"Joe was supporting her and Bobby?"

"Yes, for years."

No surprise there. Would he have helped Roan's mother if he'd known she'd given birth to his son? Or would he have denied having a Native American child? "How about the doctor?"

"His are a little more interesting. His income has been stable, but we dug deep into when he first started practicing."

"He owed a lot of money?"

"That's not it. The year before the twins died, he made a mistake that cost a patient her baby," Hoberman said. "The couple claimed he took some uppers to keep him awake during a delivery. The delivery went south and the baby died. The couple was going to sue, but something changed their mind and the case was dropped."

Roan's chest constricted. "They were paid off."

"Probably. I'm trying to get the couple's names, but it's difficult to access medical files."

Yes, it was. But the incident suggested a motive for Dr. Cumberland to take the McCullen babies. Maybe he was trying to pay the couple off by giving them another child.

MEGAN'S CHEST ACHED as she listened to Roan explain the CSI's findings. "Oh, my God. A mistake like that would have cost him his license, his entire career."

"But it was swept under the rug," Roan said. "Probably for money, or maybe Dr. Cumberland came up with another solution."

"What do you mean?"

"He could have replaced the child with another baby. Or two."

Megan's heart pounded as she considered his theory. Unfortunately, it made sense. If Dr. Cumberland had caused that infant's death, guilt could have forced him to kidnap the McCullen babies.

But to steal a child—no, two children—from his own friends? And why would he have chosen the McCullens?

Because they already had three children...?

Megan stared into the dark woods they passed as night set in. Farm and ranch land spread for miles and miles, the hint of wild in the rugged ground and boulders interspersed between lush pastures.

Birds sailed above treetops, diving for food, and a bobcat darted through the woods.

Roan pulled down a narrow street just outside of Pistol Whip. It wasn't a street, but a long driveway that led through the woods to a private estate.

"Dr. Cumberland lives down here?"

"Yeah, apparently he's done well for himself."

Dr. Cumberland's house was a rustic two-story with a wraparound porch complete with planters and a porch swing. It looked so homey and inviting that Megan couldn't imagine anything sinister inside—especially a small town doctor with deadly secrets.

Roan parked beneath a giant tree with limbs that resembled arms stretching toward the sky. The door swung open before they could make it to the front porch, and Mrs. Cumberland barreled down the steps toward them.

She folded her arms under her ample bosoms, her eyes flaring with accusations. "Where is my husband?"

Megan came to a halt beside Roan.

"Actually, we came to talk to him," Roan said evenly.

The woman huffed. "Well, he's not home. I talked to him earlier and he was upset, said the two of you are treating him like he's a suspect in Joe McCullen's murder." She shook her finger at them. "You should be ashamed of yourselves. After all my husband's done for this town and those McCullens. Those boys can't possibly think he'd hurt their father."

"Mrs. Cumberland," Megan said, "we're just asking questions to figure out what happened."

"Because someone did murder Joe McCullen," Roan finished. "We also know that your husband had a case that went bad a few years ago. A baby died. A couple threatened to sue him."

The color drained from the woman's face. "That happened years ago," she said with a confused look.

"What about the night the McCullen twins died?" Roan asked.

One hand fluttered to her heart. "They were stillborn, for God's sake. That wasn't my husband's fault."

Roan cleared his throat. "Actually, we have reason to believe that your husband faked the babies' deaths and gave the twins to someone else."

"What?" The doctor's wife threw up her hands. "That's ridiculous."

Compassion for the woman filled Megan. But if their suspicions were true, her husband had destroyed lives.

"You're going to be sorry you did this," Mrs. Cumberland said. "I'm going to talk to Sheriff McCullen. Maddox would never put up with you treating us like this."

Roan's jaw tightened. "I'm just doing my job."

"A job you never should have been given," she said. "Why don't you go back to the reservation with your own people?"

Megan's breath caught. She started to say something, but Roan stopped her with a hard shake of his head.

"If you hear from your husband, tell him he can either come in on his own, or I'll pick him up," Roan said in a dark tone. "Either way, as long as I am the deputy sheriff, he will answer my questions."

"Get off my property!" Mrs. Cumberland shouted.

Emotions welled in Megan's throat. She knew some folks still harbored prejudices, but she hadn't expected it from Mrs. Cumberland.

Then again, the woman was shaken up over the accusations they'd made and was probably lashing out any way she could.

It still didn't make it right, though.

Was she so defensive because her husband was innocent, or because she was trying to cover up for what he'd done?

ROAN'S PHONE DINGED with a text as he drove away from the Cumberlands' house. He handed it to Megan. "Read that."

Megan took his cell phone and skimmed it. "It's from Dr. Cumberland. He wants to meet us at the morgue. He's ready to talk."

Roan's heart hammered. "Good. Maybe we'll finally learn the truth."

He pressed the accelerator, veered onto the road leading through town and flipped on his siren. It might not be an emergency, but Megan's life had already been endangered, and finding whoever had threatened her and shot at them was imperative.

Already too many people had died.

Ten minutes later, he swerved into the parking lot and threw the vehicle into Park. Megan was getting out before he could make it around to open the door for her.

He hurried to walk with her, his gaze scanning the hospital parking lot. Bushes lined the exterior, adding greenery and color, but also provided places for a predator to hide.

Footsteps sounded behind them, and he jerked his head to the left to search for trouble, but a man and child were walking toward the entrance, carrying a bouquet of pink roses and a white teddy bear, along with a "Congratulations, it's a girl!" balloon.

Such a happy occasion in the midst of so much death in the town.

The man and child were oblivious, though, hugging and laughing as they hurried inside to welcome the newest member of their loving family.

A pang of longing tugged at Roan, something he'd never felt before. The need for a family.

For a wife and a child of his own.

He glanced at Megan, and an image of her holding his baby son taunted him.

Megan caught his arm as they followed the man and child in, and he wondered if she might be thinking the same.

She gestured toward the elevator, a reminder they weren't headed to the nursery where new life was being celebrated, but to the morgue where loved ones met with death, murder and grief.

They rode the elevator in silence, then walked down the hall toward the morgue. The dreary paint on the walls needed a new coat, preferably something with color. The lights seemed dimmer down here, and the smell was suffocating—a blend of strong antiseptics and cleaner meant to disguise the more acrid odors of what happened between the cement walls inside, but failed.

This was Megan's world. She was unlike any woman he'd ever known. Tenderhearted yet strong, determined to find the answers for the families grieving for their lost loved ones.

A diamond in the rough.

She swiped her ID card to get inside, then glanced through the window to the autopsy room, but it was empty. The lab was empty as well, indicating the employees had left for the day.

"He must be in my office."

"Dr. Cumberland has a key to your office?"

She shook her head no. "But if he arrived before Howard left the lab, he would have let him in."

Roan nodded, but he didn't like it. This place was creepy. Set away from the main hospital in the far corner of the basement, Megan and her workers were virtually isolated.

Which meant they could be walking into a trap.

Honed for trouble, he pulled his gun and followed her down the short hallway.

When they reached the door to her office, he caught her arm. The door was closed.

Fear clouded her eyes as she looked up at him, and he gently coaxed her behind him and turned the knob. The door squeaked open. Roan held his gun at the ready as he stepped into the doorway.

Darkness bathed the room, but the faint light from the hall illuminated the inside, enough for him to tell that the chair behind Megan's desk was occupied. All he could make out was a man's head, though. No movement.

"Dr. Cumberland?" Megan said softly as she inched into the doorway.

Silence echoed back.

Roan detected the metallic scent of blood.

Dammit.

Roan held out his hand to stop Megan from entering as he flipped on the light. He knew what he was going to find, but the sight of blood and brain matter splattering the walls still made bile rise to his throat.

"Oh, God." Megan's legs buckled.

He caught her and pulled her up against him to shield her from the grisly sight.

Chapter Nineteen

Megan struggled to breathe through the shock. Dr. Cumberland was…dead. In her office.

"Don't touch anything," Roan said.

Megan dug her nails into his arm. "I know the drill, Roan. What…do you think happened? Do you think…he killed himself?"

"I don't know." He handed her his phone. "Call the crime team and stay in the hall."

She found the number in his contacts, keeping her feet rooted to the floor. He didn't have to tell her twice not to go inside.

She'd seen a lot of dead bodies, but she knew this man, had spoken with him, had conferred with him.

Worse, she and Roan had been asking questions. Had they gotten him killed?

The phone rang three times then a man answered. "Lieutenant Hoberman."

"It's Dr. Lail. Deputy Whitefeather asked me to call. I'm with him now."

"What's going on?"

"We're at the morgue, my office. It's Dr. Cumberland… he's dead."

"Good God." The lieutenant released a loud sigh. "I'll get a team and be right over."

She thought she thanked him, but she couldn't be sure. Her eyes were glued to Roan, who'd pulled on latex gloves and was walking around the front of the desk to examine the doctor.

Megan held her breath, her head spinning from the scent of fresh blood.

"He was shot?" Megan asked.

"Yes." Roan scrutinized the scene. "Shot in the temple, close range, right side."

"He was right-handed," Megan said.

"He's holding a .38. I'll have to follow up and see if he owned the gun." He stooped and examined the man's hands, then looked up at her. "Powder burns on his hands indicate he fired the weapon."

Megan's mind spun. "Why would he text you to meet, then kill himself before you arrived?"

"Good question." Roan retrieved his phone, then snapped pictures of the office and the doctor's body position.

"Do you think someone else was here?"

Roan shrugged. "It's a possibility."

That would explain why he died before they arrived. Someone knew he was going to finally talk and wanted to shut him up.

Megan scanned the office. The files she'd stacked on her desk seemed undisturbed, her favorite coffee mug in the same place she'd left it. Her books were in order on the bookshelf, desk lamp in place.

There were no signs of a struggle.

Roan made a low sound in his throat as he peered at Megan's desk, his brows furrowed. "Damn."

Perspiration beaded on Megan's neck. "What?"

"He left a suicide letter on your computer."

Roan read the note aloud.

"Dear Dr. Lail,
I know you and the deputy have been asking questions and you're close to uncovering the truth. My

conscience has bothered me for a long time, and it's time I tell the real story about what happened years ago.

I made a terrible mistake earlier in my career and should have performed a C-section on a woman. Complications arose because of it and the woman lost the baby. She and her husband blamed me. I tried to settle with them out of court, but the woman couldn't have more children. Her husband threatened to ruin my career if I didn't help find them another child.

I panicked. I didn't want my career to end. I loved the people in Pistol Whip, and couldn't live with myself and my mistake. So the night Grace McCullen went into labor, I decided to take her babies and give them to this couple.

I realize it wasn't right, but Joe and Grace had three boys already. They had a family, and I thought Grace would eventually get pregnant again.

But she never recovered from that night. She started asking questions. She said she wouldn't stop looking until she found her missing boys.

I honestly thought she'd mixed the antidepressants with alcohol and had an accident, though. But once you raised questions, I started having doubts myself.

I made some calls, and I think the man I gave the twins to had Grace killed. I also think he poisoned Joe because one day Joe was on a buying trip and came back and told me he'd seen a young man who looked a lot like Maddox. Joe started probing then, wondering if his wife was right. He hired a PI to find the truth.

The man I gave the twins to was Bart Dunn. He won't give up the truth easily, but it's time the McCullen boys knew the real story.

I can't live with these secrets and lies any longer.

I left my wife a letter explaining everything. She had no idea what happened. Please tell her that I love her, and I'm sorry for keeping secrets. Most of all I'm sorry I betrayed my friends. If I could go back and change things, I would.

But some mistakes can't be taken back.

Also, let Maddox and Brett and Ray know that I really loved their father and them. I never meant to hurt anyone."

"My God, he really did it." Megan's pained voice echoed across the room. "His poor wife, she's going to be devastated."

"I'm sorry, Megan," Roan said quietly. "I understand that you considered the doctor a friend."

Megan shrugged. "He did have a good side," she said. "He did a lot for the people here in Pistol Whip."

"But he also betrayed one of his best friends, and he hurt Grace McCullen terribly."

"I know. I can't imagine giving birth and losing my child. No wonder Grace slipped into a deep depression." Megan sighed. "If she suspected foul play, and that the twins were still alive and no one believed her, she must have felt so scared and alone."

THE NEXT TWO hours passed in a blurry haze for Megan.

The crime team took photographs, processed her office, made copious notes on the scene and their findings and searched for forensics. They dusted her computer for prints to verify that Dr. Cumberland had typed the note and that it hadn't been written by another party.

Under the circumstances, she phoned the chief ME to perform the autopsy.

Megan's stomach roiled as they finally moved the

doctor's body from her office and carried him to the morgue.

"We have to notify Mrs. Cumberland," Roan said.

"I can take care of that if you want," Lieutenant Hoberman offered.

"That might be best," Roan agreed. "She wasn't too happy with us the last time we spoke."

Megan felt weary. "She's going to blame me for her husband's death."

"It's not your fault," Roan said matter-of-factly. "Her husband started this a long time ago."

"I realize that, but her life will be shattered by the news."

"A lot of lives will be," Roan agreed. "Just look at what his actions did to the McCullens."

"They'll want to find their brothers," Megan said.

"Yes, they will." Roan angled his head toward the lieutenant. "I'm going to track down Bart Dunn. If he or one of his people killed Grace and Joe McCullen, it's time they paid."

Megan followed Roan as they stepped away from her office. She would never be able to work in there again without seeing an image of Dr. Cumberland slumped in her chair with her head blown to pieces.

"Let me call our tech team and see if I can get a current address for Dunn," Hoberman said.

Roan thanked him, then phoned Maddox to relay the news of the doctor's death.

Megan stepped inside the autopsy room where Dr. Mantle stood studying the doctor before he began the autopsy.

"You were friends, weren't you?" Megan asked.

The chief ME shrugged, his expression torn. "Yes. He delivered my two girls."

"I'm so sorry," Megan said.

He stared at her for so long that Megan's pulse clamored. Did he blame her for the doctor's death?

"You were right, Megan. Damn, I didn't want to think that he'd do anything underhanded."

Megan offered him a tentative smile. "For the record, I didn't want to believe it, either."

He adjusted his glasses. "Your questions got him killed, though."

"That wasn't my intention."

He grimaced. "No, but it was theirs." His voice dropped a decibel. "Be careful, Megan. I'd hate to have you lying here next."

Megan's heart pounded at his dark tone. Was he concerned about her safety, or was that a threat?

ROAN ENDED THE call with Maddox, his chest tight as Megan reappeared in the hallway. "Maddox is going to call Brett and Ray and fill them in." A text dinged through, and he checked it.

"I've got the address for Bart Dunn. Let's go."

Megan was pale and quiet, but he didn't push her. God knows she'd been through enough the past couple of days, then to find a coworker with his head blown off in her own office? It was enough to shake anyone.

"Where does he live?"

"A ranch about fifty miles from here."

"Are you going to call ahead and see if he's there?"

"No, I want the element of surprise on my side. If he kept those babies, well, they'd be adults now. I don't want to spook them."

Night had definitely set in, the wind howling as they left Pistol Whip. The rain had slackened, but dark clouds still shrouded the moonlight, making it seem later than it was.

His tires churned over the road leading toward the Dunns' ranch, the wilderness becoming more vast and reminded Roan of his life on the res. Megan laid her head back against the seat and closed her eyes.

For a second, he thought she might fall asleep, but she kept twitching, obviously agitated. Traffic was minimal, the area growing more desolate as he approached the ranch.

The sign for the ranch hung askew and was so faded that Roan couldn't read it. He turned down the long drive, noting overgrown pastures and fields, and a barn that looked as if it was rotting. No animals were in sight, and the white clapboard house was dingy, shutters in need of repair.

"It looks like Dunn hasn't kept up his land," Megan said.

A rusty truck sat in front of the house, a beagle lying on the porch. Roan parked and they walked up to the house together. He kept one hand on his gun, alert and ready in case they were walking into an ambush.

He rapped the door knocker, slanting a look at the dog who groaned and lifted his head, then dropped it back down as if he was too tired or old to do anything else. Footsteps shuffled inside, and the door squeaked open.

A pudgy woman with short curly brown hair answered, leaning on a cane.

"Mrs. Dunn?" Roan asked.

"Yeah, that's me."

Roan identified himself and Megan. "We'd like to talk to you and your husband."

She made a sarcastic sound. "My husband doesn't live here. He hasn't in a long time."

Roan frowned. "What about your sons?"

The woman pinned him with angry eyes. "I don't know who you think you are, but I don't have any sons."

Chapter Twenty

Megan studied the woman's reaction as she gripped the door edge. Why was she denying she had children? They could easily find that out.

"I beg your pardon," Roan said, "but I was told you had twin boys."

The woman's face turned ghostly white. "Where did you hear that?"

"From Dr. Cumberland," Megan said, the doctor's eyes haunting her.

Mrs. Dunn shook her head in denial. "You have the wrong information. I…can't help you."

She started to slam the door in their faces, but Roan caught it and shouldered his way inside.

"Stop it, you can't come in here!" Mrs. Dunn shrieked.

"I can and I'm going to," Roan said bluntly.

Sympathy for the woman tugged at Megan, but if she'd kidnapped the McCullen babies and knew about the murders, she wasn't an innocent.

"But…I haven't done anything wrong," she protested.

"Nobody said you did," Roan said, his tone indicating he didn't believe her.

Ignoring her, he strode through the foyer then into the hall and den. Mrs. Dunn chased him, and Megan followed, her gaze sweeping the walls for pictures of the family.

Of the McCullen boys—men.

But only a couple of oil landscapes and a saddle adorned

the walls. No family pictures or chronicling of children as they grew up.

Roan paused in front of the stone fireplace. The furniture looked worn and old, the house was cold and seemed almost…empty.

Mrs. Dunn clung to her cane, panic tightening her face. "Please, I don't know why he told you that, but I lost my baby a long time ago. I…couldn't have children after that."

"Listen, Mrs. Dunn, cut the act," Roan said. "We know that your husband blackmailed Dr. Cumberland into stealing Grace and Joe McCullen's twin babies to give them to you."

She gasped, then staggered sideways. A moment later her face crumpled, and she sank onto the threadbare sofa with a sob. "I told Bart it was wrong…not to take them…"

Megan sucked in a sharp breath. "So you did know he kidnapped them?"

She made a strangled sound. "We were having a rough time, I was depressed. He was…drinking too much. He wanted to make me happy."

Megan and Roan exchanged looks. "Go on," Roan said.

"Losing our baby ripped us apart," she said in a muffled whisper. "I guess he thought giving me another child would fix things, make us closer." She dabbed at her eyes. "But when I heard him talking to his foreman about what he planned, I told him no. I didn't want to tear out some other woman's heart the way mine was."

"You told him to call it off?" Megan asked.

She nodded miserably. "But he said it was too late. We argued and I told him I didn't want someone else's children, that if he would do that, he wasn't the man I married. We…said awful things, and he left."

Roan let the silence stand for a heartbeat. "But he came back with the babies?" She looked up with such a desolate expression on her face that Megan did feel sorry for her.

"No. He said he'd risked everything for me, but I didn't appreciate it." She sighed. "Then he drove off and never came back."

Megan sat down beside the woman and rubbed her shoulders. "What about the twins?"

"I have no idea what he did with those babies." She wiped at her eyes. "Frankly, I told him I didn't want to know, that he should give them back to their family. I...prayed he did." She wiped at tears. "I even searched the news for mention of a kidnapping, but nothing ever came out, so I thought they must have been back with the family."

"Nothing came out because Dr. Cumberland lied to the parents and told them their babies died," Megan said.

The woman gasped, anguish streaking her face.

"When was the last time you talked to Bart?" Roan asked.

She grabbed a tissue and scrubbed her face. "He sends me a Christmas and birthday card every year. But he never says much in it."

"He never mentioned the babies or sent pictures of them?" Megan asked.

She shook her head. "No, like I said, I thought he gave them back." She turned a terrified look at Roan. "Why are you asking about all this now?"

ROAN STUDIED MRS. DUNN. The woman seemed sincere, and he certainly didn't see any signs that a man or any children had been around for a long time. "Because the father of those babies was recently murdered. We believe it was because he hired a PI to find his sons."

She blanched again, fingers frantically working at the tissue in her hand.

"Did you keep any of those cards and the envelopes with the postage on them?"

She bit down on her lip. "I kept them all. I...loved Bart,

and I kept hoping he'd come back and we'd work things out. But losing the baby, then the whole thing with him talking crazy…it completely destroyed our marriage."

"Would you mind getting the cards and envelopes," Roan said gently. "It might help us track him down."

Panic flashed across her face. "If you find him, what are you going to do to him?"

Roan ground his teeth. "We just want to talk to him, Mrs. Dunn. If he took those babies, the family has a right to know where they are. Don't you agree?"

"Yes," she said in a choked whisper. "But…he meant well, and I still love him. I don't want to see him hurt."

Roan reached out and patted her hand. "I promise that if we find him, I'll do everything I can to make sure he's not hurt. Right now we just want to talk, that's all."

She hesitated, her expression anguished, but finally she inhaled a deep breath, stood and lumbered down the hall.

A minute later, the woman returned with a box filled with cards and envelopes. "The most recent ones are on top," she said, her tone worried.

"Thank you." Roan lifted the top one and studied the envelope. The address and postal stamp indicated it had come from Cheyenne.

Not too far away.

Roan gestured toward the box. "Do you mind if I take these with me?"

Mrs. Dunn looked hesitant, but finally nodded. "I would like them back. Please."

"Of course." He patted her hand again. "I'll take good care of them."

The woman escorted them to the door. As soon as they stepped outside, the wind picked up, swirling leaves around their feet as they hurried to his SUV.

"The last address was Cheyenne."

"For her sake, I hope we can keep that promise," Megan said as they drove away.

So did he. But if Dunn was behind these murders, and behind the threat against Megan, he'd do whatever necessary to bring him in.

THIRTY MILES DOWN the road, though, Roan sensed they weren't alone. Someone was following them. The bright lights of a van nearly blinded him as the vehicle closed in. A van with tinted windows.

"Hang on," he told Megan. "We've got company."

Megan darted a glance over her shoulder and winced. "He's speeding up."

Roan pressed the accelerator and rounded a curve, tires squealing, but the van raced closer.

"Dammit." Roan pressed the gas again, an oncoming car's lights flashing as the driver swerved to avoid him. The van let the other car pass, then sped up beside Roan.

Suddenly a gunshot pierced the air. Just like before.

He cursed again, then jerked the wheel to the left to slam into the van, but it swerved toward him at the same time and knocked him into a spin.

"Hang on and get down, Megan!" He tried to maintain control, but a bullet shattered the windshield on his side, and when he ducked to avoid being hit, the van slammed into them again and his vehicle sped out of control.

They skidded, his SUV hit a boulder, bounced back, then flipped and rolled.

Megan screamed. He tried to put a hand out to keep her from hitting the dash, but the air bags exploded, pinning them against the seat. The car skidded a few more feet then careened into a ditch.

"Roan!" Megan shouted.

"I'm here."

Seconds later, the scent of gas assaulted him.

"We have to get out!" He fumbled, pushing at the air bag as he reached inside his pocket for a knife. He jerked it out and frantically ripped away the bag and his seat belt, then did the same for Megan.

The scent of gas grew stronger, then a spark ignited. God, the car was on fire. It would explode any minute.

"We have to hurry, Megan. The car's about to blow."

She frantically jerked at her door, but the impact had crushed the side in, and she couldn't open it. His was the same.

Flames darted up, visible through the back window. "Cover your head!" he shouted.

Megan dropped her head to her knees and covered it with her arms, and he shifted, then kicked at the front windshield. It took several attempts, but finally the glass cracked and shattered. He removed his jacket, wrapped it around his fist and used it to knock the remaining glass free.

He crawled through the opening first, kicking away broken shards on the hood, then reached for Megan. The flames bounced higher, smoke starting to fill the air. Heat seared his hands and face as he dragged Megan from the car.

Her ragged breathing punctuated the air as she gripped his arms. By the time they cleared the car, flames shot up along the doors and the sizzle of an impending explosion rent the air.

"Come on!" They ran for cover and collapsed against a tree just as the SUV burst into a fireball.

MEGAN CLUNG TO Roan as the flames lit the sky. The scent of burning metal and rubber filled the air, the sound of hissing flames echoing shrilly around her.

A second later and they would have died in that explosion.

"You didn't see him?" she whispered.

"No, but it was a van with tinted windows just like before. I couldn't get the license, though."

Megan fought a sob. She was not going to fall apart here. Even if they had come within a hairbreadth from burning to death, they were alive.

Roan rubbed her arms, his own breathing labored. Sweat beaded his face and droplets of blood dotted his arms. In spite of the jacket he'd wrapped around his fist, the glass shards had punctured his skin.

"You're hurt, Roan."

"No, I'm fine." He shrugged off her concern, retrieved his phone and called for help.

Megan tried to compose herself as an ambulance and fire truck arrived along with a deputy sheriff from Cheyenne.

The paramedics cleaned his arm and examined them both while the deputy snapped photos of the scene and listened while Roan explained about his investigation and what had happened.

"He shot at you?" the deputy asked.

"Yeah. I think it was the same man who shot at us before."

It was nearing midnight as the crime team arrived to process the car.

"I'll have one of my men carry you home. I'm going to try to locate Bart Dunn," the deputy said. "If he's at the address you gave me, I'll bring him in."

"We'd rather go with you tonight," Roan said. "I don't want this man to get word that we're on to him and disappear."

"Ma'am, are you sure you're all right with that?" the deputy asked.

Megan nodded. "Whoever did this has nearly killed me three times now. If Mr. Dunn knows who did it, I want him locked up."

The deputy and Roan spoke to the crime team, then

she and Roan climbed in the deputy's SUV. The deputy plugged the address into his GPS and eased onto the highway. Megan rode in back while Roan sat up front with the deputy who asked question after question about the investigation.

The gloomy weather intensified her anxiety as they neared the trailer park where they hoped Bart Dunn still lived.

The trailer park was run-down, weeds choked the tiny yards and battered kids' toys were scattered around.

"Dunn lives in the end one," Roan said.

The deputy cut his blue lights and coasted to the last trailer. An old rusted Impala sat on three wheels, obviously in need of repair and bodywork. There were no other cars in the drive.

"Doesn't look like anyone's home," the deputy said.

Still, he and Roan pulled their weapons as they crept from the deputy's SUV and inched up the graveled drive.

Megan held her breath, half hoping the man was there with answers, and praying he wasn't armed and dangerous.

ROAN CLENCHED HIS Glock in a white-knuckled grip as he climbed the rickety stairs to the trailer door. The deputy veered right and inched around the back of the trailer, scanning the property beyond and searching for a back door in case the man was inside and tried to run.

Roan pressed his ear to the door and listened, but heard no movement inside. He leaned to the left to peek through the window, but the lights were off and he didn't see movement.

Shoulders tight, he raised his fist and knocked, his gun at the ready. The wind howled, rustling trees and sending a tin can rolling across the yard. He knocked again, but no one answered.

Braced for trouble, Roan turned the doorknob and eased

open the door. The stench of rotting food, stale beer and cigarettes sucked the breath from him. He covered his mouth with his handkerchief, visually sweeping the den and kitchen, but no one was inside.

The couch was not only threadbare, but birds must have gotten inside, pecked the stuffing from the cushions and nested. The floor creaked as he crept to the hall and glanced in the one bedroom and bath. Mold grew along the wall and floor, trash was overflowing and the bed had fared like the couch.

He quickly surveyed the walls and furniture for photos, for some clue that Dunn had lived here with one or both of the twins, but the place was empty.

He checked the dresser drawers, desk, then returned to scour the kitchen for mail, bills or a paper trail that would clue him in to Bart Dunn's location.

Frustration knotted his gut. Dammit, they had to find the man. He was the key to locating the McCullen twins.

Chapter Twenty-One

Megan was still shaken as the deputy dropped them at Roan's cabin. The deputy had driven them first to her place, but Roan insisted she come home with him. He was ever the gentleman, the bodyguard, and refused to let her stay alone, so they took her car to his cabin. "You can use the shower first," he said as he combed the rooms to make sure no one was waiting inside.

Grateful they'd run by her house for an overnight bag, she ducked into the bathroom, stripped and stepped into the shower. Bruises colored her torso, arms and chest, and her ribs ached from the impact of the air bag.

The warm water felt heavenly, easing the tension from her limbs, and she washed the sweat and scent of smoke from her hair, although she couldn't erase the image of the burning vehicle from her mind.

As an ME, she'd seen the results of fire and smoke, and how it ravaged the human body. It was a painful way to go.

She rinsed off, desperately trying to obliterate the thoughts. Too exhausted to care about dressing again, she pulled on a pair of pajamas, combed her hair and left it damp around her shoulders.

When she left the bathroom, she felt warm and cozy, yet she still shivered at the memory of the explosion.

Roan handed her a glass of wine as she entered the kitchen. He was halfway through a beer. She thanked him, well aware that he looked fierce and rugged with that leather tie holding back his hair. His eyes were dark with emotions—anger, worry…hunger.

"My turn."

She wanted to tell him she didn't care if he showered, that she wanted him to hold her and comfort her and…love her. But the scent of smoke lingered on him, a reminder of their close call with death.

Besides, if he stayed in the room she might throw herself at him, and if he rejected her, she wouldn't be able to stand it.

Tonight of all nights, she didn't want to be alone.

He disappeared, and she walked to the window and looked out. A few stars struggled to fight their way through the clouds, but the woods looked eerie, dark and filled with places predators could hide.

Shivering, she jerked the curtains closed, heard the shower water kick on, imagined Roan standing naked beneath it and her body heated with desire. Trembling with the urge to go to him and wait in his bedroom, she phoned Dr. Mantle and explained about the ambush, then left a message telling him she was staying at Roan's and for him to call her if he had any information on Dr. Cumberland's autopsy to share.

Too antsy to sit still, she headed to the den to pace, but as she passed the kitchen table where his computer was, her hip brushed a stack of papers and they fell onto the floor, scattering across the wood.

She stooped to pick them up, shoving the stack together, but one of the pages caught her eye.

A birth certificate. Roan's.

Curious, she couldn't help herself. She'd met his mother, but when she'd asked about his father, he'd clammed up and refused to discuss him.

She glanced down at the line where the father's name was listed and stared in shock.

Joe McCullen.

Her breath stalled in her chest. God… Roan was Joe's son. Which meant he was Maddox, Brett and Ray's half brother…

ROAN TOWEL-DRIED HIS hair as he stepped into the kitchen. He'd yanked on jeans and a shirt, although he hadn't buttoned it yet, but he was so damn hot he had to wait until he cooled down from the steam.

A startled gasp echoed from the kitchen, and he spotted Megan stooped down holding some papers. Others were scattered across the floor.

Her stunned gaze drifted up to his, and his gut knotted when he realized she was holding his birth certificate.

Anger hardened his voice. "What are you doing? Snooping through my papers?"

"No." Her voice faltered. "Of course not. I accidentally knocked the file off and was picking it up."

He tossed the towel onto the kitchen chair and grabbed the papers from her. She made another surprised sound, then slowly stood.

"I'm sorry, Roan. I didn't mean to pry."

His jaw tightened. Suddenly his heart was beating ninety miles a minute. "But you did."

She reached for his arm, but he stepped back. "That was private."

Megan clamped her teeth over her lip, her expression full of regret. "I really didn't mean to," she said in a whisper. "Why didn't you tell me?"

He blinked, forcing emotions from his throat with a hard swallow. "Because it's none of your business."

"Did you tell Maddox?"

His eyes turned steely. "No, none of the McCullens know, and you'd better not tell them."

Hurt and bewilderment crossed Megan's face. "Why haven't you told them, Roan? They deserve to know."

"You're living in a fantasy world if you think anything good could come of that." He shoved the papers in the file and jammed it inside the desk, then slammed it shut with a bang.

"But they're your half brothers. You've been working this case because…it's personal to you." She hesitated, her breath rasping out. "That's why you've been so driven. Why it bothered you when Maddox made comments about his father and family."

"Maddox and Brett and Ray are not going to find out." He rammed his hand through his wet hair. "For God's sake, Megan, after what they went through with Bobby, they might think I had something to do with Joe's death."

"But that's ludicrous," Megan stammered. "You've been leading this investigation."

"And they could say that I steered it into one direction to deter suspicion from myself."

Megan shook her head in denial, her eyes filled with emotion. Anger…at him? Remorse?

"Maddox knows you, Roan. He knows you're an honorable man." She took a step toward him, her voice softening. "You lost your mother, you deserve to connect with the family you have left."

"Do you really think that the McCullens are going to accept me into their tight-knit family?" Roan's voice rose in pitch. "They didn't want to accept Bobby. They sure as hell aren't going to accept a half-breed. Especially when Joe didn't even know about me."

"Roan…don't put yourself down—"

"I'm not. I live in reality, Megan." He paced across the room, picked up his beer and chugged it, then set the bottle down with a thud. "You think prejudices don't exist anymore? You heard Mrs. Cumberland. She's not the only one who feels like that, either."

Megan shook her head again. "You don't know that the McCullens will feel that way, Roan. You have to at least give them a chance."

He strode back to her and gripped her arms, angry and hurting and wanting her so bad his damn teeth ached. "Let it go, Megan. The McCullens are not going to find out. I am going to track down the person who killed Joe and his wife. But I want nothing in return." He shook her gently. "Do you understand?"

Her eyes glittered as she stared at him, a tear sparkling on her eyelash. "Yes, Roan, I promise, your secret is safe with me."

Dammit, he released her so swiftly she stumbled backward, then he looked down at his hands. Had he been too harsh and hurt her?

He'd never forgive himself if he had.

MEGAN SENSED ROAN'S withdrawal and couldn't allow him to believe that he didn't deserve to be a McCullen.

She gingerly touched his arm. "Roan, look at me."

He stepped away in an attempt to escape her touch. But Megan moved faster than he'd anticipated and cradled his face between her hands. "Look at me," she whispered. "Don't sell yourself short. You may not have been raised a McCullen, but you're a self-made man. That's even more admirable."

He dropped his head forward, his jaw clenched. "Stop it, Megan. I don't want anything from the McCullens."

"I understand," Megan said softly. "But that still doesn't mean that you aren't as good as they are." She stood on tiptoe and brushed a kiss across his cheek. "You are strong and honest and you protect others. You sacrifice yourself to keep the people in this town safe, including the half brothers who are clueless as to how much you're sacrificing by keeping your silence."

"You can't give up something you never had," Roan said gruffly.

She brushed another kiss along his other cheek. "Yes, you can. You can miss family. You can miss having the love and support of people who are like you. And whether you realize it or not, even without Joe McCullen or his other sons knowing about you, you became an honorable decent man. A selfless man who has been fighting for justice for Joe even though you expect nothing in return."

Roan's breathing sounded choppy in the dark silence that followed. Megan's heart pounded with the need to comfort him and convince him he was worthy of love. Of the McCullen family.

At the same time her blood heated with the need to be closer to him, to feel his lips against hers. His mouth on her mouth. His hands on her body.

Her breath hitched, and his tortured gaze found hers. Something hot and passionate burst to life between them.

"Megan…"

"Don't think about it," she said in a raw whisper. "I know there are no promises, and I don't care. I just want to be with you tonight."

Roan's expression softened, although the intensity still remained, but instead of pain, hunger flared in his eyes. Emboldened by that sign, her own hunger spiraled out of control, and she pressed her lips to his.

Roan grunted, then suddenly gave in to his need and the chemistry between them, and swept her in his arms. Megan's heart raced as he carried her to his bedroom.

The room was just as masculine as Roan. Evidence of his Native American roots shone in the arrowheads and art on the walls. His bed was covered in a quilt designed with

Indian symbols and a painting of a wild herd of mustangs hung above his bed.

He was like those mustangs in his raw primal energy and connection to the earth, but even with his fierce hunger for her, he possessed a tenderness that made her desire grow with every touch.

He stripped her pajamas and she pushed at his clothes. The sight of his bare chest bronzed with water droplets from the shower still clinging to his skin made her pulse pound.

He plunged his tongue inside her mouth, tasting and exploring, and she met him thrust for thrust, each sweet kiss growing hotter until her body burned with need.

She trailed her hands across his bare torso, her breath hitching again as his muscles bunched beneath her touch.

She lowered her head and planted her lips where her hands had been, teasing him with kisses and flicks of her tongue, sweeping her lips across his nipples. Heat pooled in her belly at his guttural moan of pleasure.

She had a feeling Roan rarely took pleasure for himself, and she wanted this night to be one he would remember.

She pushed him back on the bed, raking her hands across his chest and down his body, looking her fill, then teasing his belly and trailing her fingers south until she reached his sex.

He groaned, then suddenly flipped her over and crawled on top of her. She cried out in pleasure as his mouth made a path down her neck to her breasts. Seconds later, his lips teased and tormented her nipples until they were hard and begging for more.

He drew one into his mouth and suckled her until she whimpered his name. Then he did the same to the other, his fingers traveling along her hips to her stomach and lower to tease her lips apart and taunt her with his fingers.

She wanted him inside her.

"Roan," she murmured. "I need you."

He hesitated, then lifted his head to look into her face. The flare of emotions that darkened his eyes hit her with such force that she felt the first strains of an orgasm coming.

Desperate to have him join her, she lowered her hand and closed it around his thick length.

His chest heaved as he inhaled. Once more he gave in to primal needs as he covered her hand with his. For a moment, he guided them both closer to the brink, closer to planting himself inside her.

Then he muttered a protest and pulled away.

She reached for him. "Roan, please…"

"Condom," he said in a gruff whisper.

She nodded, grateful he'd thought of it, yet hating to wait a second longer until he could be inside her.

ROAN FOUGHT THE intense need to make Megan his, but her fingers and mouth had robbed him of any rational sense. All he knew was that he couldn't walk away from her tonight.

She didn't expect more. She'd said that.

But dammit, he wanted to give her more.

Don't think, she'd told him.

With the hunger burning through his blood, how could he think?

He grabbed the condom from his nightstand, ripped the foil packet open with his teeth, rolled it on and pressed the tip of his erection against her wet center.

Megan undulated her hips, at the same time clawing at his back and pressing him closer. Skin against skin. Heat against heat.

Passion, need and a hungry desperation drove him inside her. She arched her back, raised her hips and met him thrust for thrust, her throaty cry mimicking his own male sound of pleasure as they rode the waves together.

Her body convulsed, her nails dug into his back and he closed his eyes and lost himself in the woman beneath him.

He'd never lost himself in anyone before.

The words *I love you* teetered on the edge of his tongue, but he caught himself and whispered her name again instead.

As his release claimed him, he memorized the moment to keep him company when she was gone.

MEGAN STARTLED THE next morning when her cell phone rang. She felt sore and sated and…content. In spite of the fact that they'd almost died last night, making love to Roan had made her feel more alive than she'd ever felt before.

She snuggled next to him, raking her fingers along his smooth chest, smiling as he groaned in his sleep. They had made love over and over during the night, sometimes slow and tender, at other times fast and furious as if they knew they only had one night to experience the passion.

The phone buzzed again. Damn.

Remembering they had unanswered questions and that Bart Dunn was still missing, she grabbed her phone from the nightstand and checked the number.

Dr. Mantle.

Instantly her nerves jumped to alert.

She rolled sideways and punched Connect. "Hello."

"Megan, I finished Dr. Cumberland's autopsy last night. I need you to meet me at the morgue to discuss the results."

Megan's heart thudded. "What did you find?"

"I can't talk about it over the phone. Just come to the morgue asap."

Megan glanced over her shoulder at Roan, who was now wide-awake and watching her like a hawk.

"All right, I'll be right there."

She disconnected, then grabbed her robe and slipped it on. She had to shower before she met her boss. But Roan caught her arm.

"What was that about and where are you going?"

His possessive tone both disturbed her and awakened a tender feeling toward him. Maybe they had the possibility of more than one night.

"That was the chief ME calling about Dr. Cumberland's autopsy. He said I needed to meet him. He must have found something."

"It wasn't a suicide?"

"He wouldn't say. But, Roan, I have to go."

"You're not going anywhere without me." He slipped from bed and strode naked to the bathroom, leaving her to admire his muscular backside and wanting him all over again.

DAMMIT, ROAN WANTED Megan again. And again. And again.

Maybe he wanted her all the time.

Not a good idea.

Remembering his vehicle had died a fiery death the night before, he quickly showered so he could ride with Megan to the hospital.

No way in hell he'd allow her to go anywhere alone today. Not after last night.

Not with a killer still on the loose.

By the time he made it to the kitchen, she was dressed and ready, her hair pulled into that tight bun again. The ME back in control.

A smile curved his mouth. He could rip out that bun and ram inside her and make her lose control again.

Make her want him the way he wanted her.

He had a serious problem.

"Do you want me to drop you somewhere?" Megan asked. "Maybe to get another police car?"

"I'm going with you first, then I'll get another vehicle," he said in a tone that brooked no argument.

She retrieved her keys from her purse and they hurried to her van together.

She drove through the drive-in at the local hamburger joint and picked up coffee while he phoned to arrange another car for himself and to fill Maddox in. Maddox was sleeping, so he told Rose to have Maddox call him.

The rest of the ride to the hospital, he silently argued with himself over how and when to end this thing with Megan.

Because it had to end.

They'd had wild, crazy, erotic sex because they'd almost died last night. They were high on adrenaline and fear. Nothing more.

Except maybe…he wanted it to be more.

He wanted what his brothers had.

Not the land or money or name. The love.

But all his life that had seemed as elusive as a father whose name he hadn't known.

How could he think of Maddox, Brett and Ray as brothers when he'd lived all his life as a loner? When they wouldn't ever consider him a real brother.

Megan parked, and they walked up to the building in silence. Was she having regrets about sleeping with him?

Dawn cracked the sky as they entered. The elevator ride was short, and the halls seemed empty and dark. The hair on the back of his neck stood on end as she used her key card to enter the morgue. Déjà vu struck him. The last time they'd come here they'd found Dr. Cumberland dead. Blood everywhere.

The doors swished open, and he hesitated to search the hall before they went into the autopsy area, but Megan suddenly made a strangled sound.

He jerked his head toward her, at the same time reaching for his weapon. It was too late.

Dr. Mantle was nowhere to be seen. Instead, a white-haired, craggy-faced man grabbed Megan around the neck and pointed a gun at her head.

Chapter Twenty-Two

Roan barely controlled his rage at seeing the man's arm tighten around Megan's throat. She coughed, gasping for air, but he dragged her in front of him, shielding himself with her body.

Coward.

Roan pulled his Glock and aimed it at the man. "Let me guess, you must be Bart Dunn."

"You should have left things alone like I told you to." He cocked the gun at Megan's temple, and her eyes widened in terror. "Now drop it or I shoot her in the head."

"Just like you did Dr. Cumberland," Roan said through clenched teeth.

"I didn't shoot him. He was so driven by guilt he took care of that for me." His gun hand trembled, making Roan's lungs squeeze for air.

"Listen, Dunn," Roan said in a quiet tone—a struggle when he wanted to rip the man apart limb by limb. "We know what happened, all about you and Dr. Cumberland. How you killed Grace McCullen and stole her twin babies, then the doctor covered it up."

His beady gray eyes bore into Roan's. "All that, and my wife wouldn't even take those babies," he growled. "I loved her so much. All I wanted to do was make up for losing our son."

Roan lowered his voice to a sympathetic pitch, hoping to connect with the man. "That must have been awful. I lost my mother and it damn near ripped my heart out. I can't imagine losing a child."

"We were going to name him after me," Dunn said in a voice that warbled with grief. "Little Bart. We had his crib all ready, the room painted blue, my wife decorated it with trains…but then everything went wrong."

"And you blamed Dr. Cumberland," Roan said.

Rage flared on the man's face, contorting the grief-stricken man to a bitter one. "It was his fault. My little Bart died before we even had a chance to hold him." He had a faraway look in his eyes as if he was reliving the nightmare.

"I'm sorry," Megan said in a rough whisper. "Really sorry, Mr. Dunn."

He seemed to loosen his hold on her for a second. "You can't know what it was like, seeing that tiny infant lying there. So cold. Not moving. We kept waiting on him to cry, hoping and praying, but he never did." Tears leaked from his eyes. "My wife was so devastated I thought I was going to lose her, too. She was bleeding a lot and almost died. But Dr. Cumberland managed to save her." The gun wobbled in his hand. "It still didn't make up for little Bart being gone."

"Nothing could," Megan said softly.

"So you told the doctor to get you another baby," Roan said, filling in the blanks. "Did Morty Burns and his wife, Edith, help you? Were they in on it?"

"No, but later Morty had heard me and my wife aruging and figured it out. He wanted money to keep quiet," Dunn spit out. "I paid them at first, but it got to be too much."

"So you killed them," Megan whispered. "And you pushed me into the street and later attacked me in the morgue."

"But you kept asking questions."

Roan gritted his teeth. "All those people dead—Grace,

Joe, the PI? You murdered them all to keep them from finding those twins."

Dunn wiped sweat from his neck. "I couldn't go to jail, not when I'd already lost so much."

"How did you poison Joe?" Megan asked.

The man huffed. "It wasn't that hard. Even when he was sick, Joe insisted on his nightly scotch. I had a bottle sent to him as a gift from the Cattlemen's club. He never tasted a thing."

"Dr. Cumberland kidnapped the McCullen babies and told Grace they died?" Roan asked.

"He didn't want to, but he messed up that day with us and I told him I'd ruin his reputation. After all, he destroyed my life."

Roan inched toward him. "Now the truth has come out, Dunn. We talked to your wife."

Pain wrenched his face. "She told me to take those babies back, but how could I? The deed was done. After all I sacrificed for her, she didn't want them."

"Because they belonged to another mother," Megan said. "She didn't want that woman to feel the same kind of pain she felt."

He pressed the gun at her temple again. Roan froze, terrified the man would shoot.

He couldn't lose Megan.

"You did what you could for your wife," Roan said, hoping to assuage the man's pride. "But killing Dr. Lail is not right and you know it. Nobody can bring your son back, but she had nothing to do with your loss. Don't let anyone else die. If your son had lived, he wouldn't want that."

An anguished sob escaped the man, but instead of releasing Megan, he dragged her backward. "I'm not going to jail," he said bitterly. "I'll release her once I get away."

Megan gave Roan a brave look, but Roan had a bad feeling that if he didn't save Megan now, the man would shoot her before he disappeared.

One more step and Dunn was near the rear door. Roan gave Megan a signal to drop, and she elbowed Dunn and ducked as Roan charged the man with his weapon.

"Drop it!" Roan shouted to Dunn.

Dunn fired. Megan screamed and rolled out of the way. Roan vaulted toward Dunn, but he fired again. This time the bullet pierced Roan's chest.

Roan fired a round from his own gun, and Dunn's body bounced against the wall, blood spurting from his chest. Dunn dropped his gun to the floor, his look startled as he fell to his knees, then collapsed.

Roan struggled to remain on his feet, but blood oozed from his wound and he staggered sideways. He managed to kick Dunn's gun out of the bastard's reach before he went down on his knees.

"Roan!" Megan scrambled to help him, and he slumped against her.

Roan still kept his gun trained on Dunn. "Where are the McCullen twins?"

Dunn looked up at him with dazed eyes, then coughed blood. "I…couldn't get caught…"

Roan jammed the gun at the man's forehead, praying he hadn't hurt those babies. "What did you do with them?"

"I left them at a church," he rasped.

"Where are they now?"

He coughed, spitting blood. "Don't…know."

"What was the name of the church?"

Dunn gagged for a breath.

Roan shook him. "Tell me the name of the church."

But Dunn's eyes rolled back in his head, and his chest jerked with his last breath.

Dammit. Roan reached for Megan to keep from passing out, but lost the battle.

MEGAN SWIPED AT tears as she eased Roan to the floor. The gunshot looked…bad.

She called the ER for help while she grabbed some cloths, folded them up and pressed them against Roan's wound to stem the blood flow. Terrified Roan would die, she sank to the floor and cradled his head in her lap while she waited on the medics.

"Please don't die on me," she whispered. "I love you, Roan. You're the only man I've ever felt this way about."

Tears blurred her vision, but she blinked them away. She had to be strong. Should call someone.

Maddox. Brett. Ray. Roan's half brothers.

A helpless feeling overcame her. She would let Maddox know Roan had been shot, but she couldn't tell them the truth about his paternity. She'd promised Roan.

"Dr. Lail?" A voice shouted to her from the cold room, and she frowned.

"I'll be right back, Roan. Help is on its way."

She gently laid Roan's head back on a pad, then hurried to the cold room.

"Megan! Get me out of here!"

"Dr. Mantle!"

"Some bastard made me call you and locked me in here," he yelled.

"So there was nothing odd about Cumberland's autopsy?" Megan asked.

"Just that he shot himself."

She hurried to retrieve her keys, then unlocked the door. Dr. Mantle appeared to be unharmed, but he was steaming mad. "Is that crazy man still here?"

"He's dead," Megan said as she led him back to Roan. "He shot the deputy sheriff, too."

His shocked gaze flew to hers. "What the hell?"

She stooped to check Roan's pulse while she explained to her boss what they'd learned about Dr. Cumberland.

Seconds later, footsteps pounded, and the ER team raced in. They checked Roan's vitals, then hoisted him onto a gurney and rushed toward the elevator.

Megan followed, her heart in her throat. Roan couldn't die and leave her. She needed him.

THREE HOURS LATER and Megan thought she was going to go insane. Roan's prognosis wasn't good, but he was in surgery.

What in the world was taking so long?

She'd paid Maddox a quick visit to inform him about what had happened. He was supposed to be released, but insisted on joining her in the waiting room. Rose and Mama Mary both showed up to hold vigil, as well. So had Brett and Ray.

"Dunn didn't say what happened to the twins?" Maddox asked.

Megan shook her head. "I'm sorry. He said his wife told him to take them back. He was afraid of being caught so he dropped them at a church."

Brett cleared his throat. "What church?"

Megan knotted her hands together. "He died before he could tell us."

Ray cursed, and Megan's heart went out to the three men. They wanted to find their missing brothers.

Yet they had no idea that the man who'd found their parents' killer and discovered they had twin brothers was also their blood kin.

It wasn't fair to Roan.

She paced to the nurses' station again. "Have you heard anything from the doctor about Deputy Whitefeather's surgery?"

The nurse's brow furrowed. "He's coming out to talk to you in a minute."

Megan thanked her and strode over to the door of the waiting room to keep watch.

Seconds dragged into excruciating minutes. When the surgeon finally appeared, his grave expression made her stomach revolt.

"What's wrong?"

"I'm afraid he's not doing too well. We got the bullet out, but it punctured his heart, and he was bleeding internally. He needs a transfusion, but we're short on his blood type. He also has a rare genetic marker."

The doctor ran a hand over his surgical cap. "Does he have family? Someone who could possibly donate blood for a transfusion. Even then, it may be touch and go for a while."

Fear clawed at Megan. She'd vowed to keep quiet about Roan's paternity, but how could she keep that promise if his life depended on his half brothers?

There really was no other choice.

"Let me talk to the McCullens and I'll get back to you."

He nodded. "We're asking around other hospitals to try to locate a blood match."

Megan thanked him, took a deep breath and hurried to talk to Maddox and his brothers.

"How is he?" Maddox asked.

"He lost a lot of blood and needs a transfusion." She explained about his blood type and that a family member would be the best bet.

"Does he have family?" Brett asked.

"He never mentioned any to me," Maddox said. "He lost his mother a few months ago."

Megan wet her parched lips with her tongue. "Actually, he does have some family."

"Who?" Ray asked.

Brett gestured toward his phone. "I'll call them."

"That's just it," Megan said. "It's not that simple."

Mama Mary gave Megan a sympathetic look. "What is it, honey?"

Megan sighed, prayed the McCullens wouldn't balk at what she had to say, then began to explain.

Maddox sat with his head down, shaking it back and forth in denial. Brett looked shell-shocked while Ray's dark look reeked of suspicion.

"Why didn't he tell us?" Ray asked.

"He didn't know until his mother died and he found his birth certificate. She met your father long before he married your mother. Apparently when she got pregnant, she never told Joe. I guess with the cultural differences, she didn't want to cause trouble."

"But Roan has known for months and works for me," Maddox said. "How could he keep this from us?"

Megan crossed her arms. "He didn't know how you would react. He was afraid you'd accuse him of wanting something from you like Bobby did."

Brett winced. "What *does* he want?"

"Nothing," Megan said, a trace of anger in her voice. "That's the point. He didn't want anything from you, but when he discovered your father—his father—was murdered, he did everything possible to find his killer."

A tense silence ensued. Mama Mary clapped her hands. "He's a good man, boys. He figured out Ms. Grace was murdered and that her babies might still be alive."

"That's right," Megan said. "And he was shot and almost died searching for the answers for you."

Another silence, then Maddox gripped the edge of his wheelchair. "I'm going to get tested to see if my blood will work."

Brett nodded. "I'm right behind you."

Ray followed. "Me, too."

Mama Mary hugged each of them as they filed out to see if they could help save Roan.

Chapter Twenty-Three

Megan waited with Mama Mary and Rose while Maddox, Brett and Ray had blood drawn. Brett and Ray must have called their wives because Willow and Scarlet both showed up. Mama Mary introduced them to Megan, then took Brett's little boy to the cafeteria for ice cream.

The older woman was far more than a cook and housekeeper—she was a mother to them all and the glue that held the McCullens together.

Maddox and Brett returned a few minutes later without Ray. Their faces looked strained, the night's revelations still sinking in.

"Ray is a match," Maddox said.

"Thank God." Megan couldn't hide her relief. Both Maddox and Brett looked at her with narrowed eyes, but their wives squeezed her arm as if they completely understood.

The next few hours dragged by excruciatingly slowly. Ray did the transfusion, but still they waited to see how Roan would respond.

Meanwhile, Ray made some calls and learned that Elmore Clark had nothing to do with the trouble at Horseshoe Creek. Apparently he'd left town a couple of years ago and settled in with his daughter and her children.

Since only family was allowed, each of the men had taken a turn visiting Roan.

But Megan wanted to be with him. She needed to touch him, to feel that he was still alive, to see his chest rising with each breath and the color returning to his complexion.

It *would* return. He *would* be all right. She couldn't allow herself to think otherwise.

Mama Mary drove Brett's little boy home, and the Mc-Cullen men insisted their wives go with her. They were possessive, protective and three cowboys who adored the women they'd married.

Megan wanted that with Roan.

But what would he want when he woke up?

ROAN REACHED FOR his mother's outstretched hand. "I've missed you, son."

Washed out sunlight cast shadows around her angelic form, but he recognized her face. Her sweet smile. Her long, dark braid.

Chants in his Native American language echoed from somewhere in the distance, maybe behind the moon. The shaman stood over him, his feathers swaying as he waved his arms and hands above Roan, performing one of the sacred songs that their people sang when someone passed.

He was dead.

His mother...the light...the music...

Darkness swallowed him, and he was spinning and falling, clawing the emptiness for his mother's hand, for the light, but his hand connected with air and the light faded.

Was he headed into Hell?

The sound of another voice cut into his confusion, soothing his fears. "Roan, you're going to be all right."

He struggled to open his eyes, but his lids felt heavy and he hurt all over. Pain burned through his veins and his skin felt like it was on fire.

He was in Hell.

"Come back to me, Roan, please, I need you."

That sweet voice...if he was dead and in Hell, so was she. But that wasn't right. Megan was too kind and honorable, too good to land in the fiery depths below the ground.

"I'm right here, and so are Maddox and Brett and Ray. They're outside in the waiting room."

Waiting room?

He wasn't in Hell, after all. It just felt like it.

An image of Megan crawling on top of him, naked and so beautiful he could hardly breathe for wanting her, floated to him, wrapping him in the seductiveness of her voice.

Her gentle hands brushed his cheek, and then her lips touched his, and he floated off, dreaming he was in Heaven.

Some time later, hours or days, he had no idea, pain wrenched him from his peaceful sleep. He stirred with a moan and reached for the image of Megan naked and loving him. It was the only comfort he'd known.

But when he opened his eyes, Maddox stood beside his bed, looking serious and worried and…angry.

Roan blinked, squinting through the fog of drugs and the haze of his muddled mind, then saw Brett and Ray beside him. Arms crossed. Frowning faces. Suspicious eyes.

They didn't have to say a word. Somehow they knew the truth about who he was.

A sense of betrayal cut through him like a knife. The only person who could have told them was Megan.

And she'd promised to keep his secret.

But she had lied.

MEGAN THANKED THE nurse for updating her on Roan's condition. She'd also been kind enough to sneak Megan in for a visit during the long, dark hours of the night. Only after she'd seen that Roan was indeed breathing did Megan allow herself to doze in the waiting room.

Morning coffee in hand, she stepped to the edge of the room and saw the three McCullen men standing by his bed.

"You should have told me," Maddox said. "I would have understood."

Roan wheezed a breath. He still looked pale, and wires

and tubes were strung from him to machines that beeped and got on her nerves, but at least he was alive. "You had enough trouble on your plate," he said gruffly. "Besides, I don't want or expect anything from you. You owe me nothing."

He said it with such conviction that Megan's heart ached for him. Roan had gotten the raw end of the deal, but unlike Bobby, who'd allowed his bitterness and self-pity to turn him into a vindictive person, Roan had thrived and made a man of himself.

"You found the man who killed our father," Brett said, his voice thick with emotions.

"And our mother." Ray pinched the bridge of his nose. "You don't know what that means to us."

Maddox cleared his throat. "We would have never known the truth," he said. "Or that we have two more brothers."

"That is, if they're still alive," Brett muttered.

"Dunn said he left them at a church," Roan said. "That's a place to start."

The three McCullens nodded, then one by one shook Roan's hand. Megan blinked back tears at the scene.

Maybe Roan had been wrong about them accepting him. For his sake, she hoped so.

"We should let you get some rest," Maddox said.

The other two agreed, and they assured Roan they'd be back.

"Thanks for the transfusion," Roan said to Ray. "You saved my life."

Ray gripped Roan's hand. "That's what brothers do." He angled his head toward the door. "You can thank Megan, too. I think she wants to see you."

The three men left together, and Megan crossed the room, but the smile faded from Roan's face. Instead a bitter scowl darkened his eyes.

"You made a promise and you broke it."

The coldness in his tone cut Megan to the bone. "I'm sorry, but you were dying, Roan. I had to do something."

"It doesn't matter. I trusted you and you betrayed me." His Adam's apple bobbed as he swallowed. "Leave me alone."

Megan reached for his hand to tell him how much she loved him, but he closed his eyes and turned away from her, shutting her out as if he was cutting her out of his life.

ROAN DIDN'T KNOW what to say to the McCullens. He'd been alone so long that he was far more comfortable by himself than having other people in his life.

And Megan…

She'd only been gone a few hours now and he missed her. His dreams after she'd left had been mixed with visions of them making love and with her walking down the aisle with another man.

Then there were horrible nightmares about Megan being murdered, of finding her in one of the drawers at the morgue.

Of losing her forever.

He'd woken in a cold sweat with tears streaming down his face.

He couldn't survive loving Megan and having something bad happen to her.

Besides, he had nothing to offer her.

It was better to break it off before anyone got hurt.

HURT SWELLED INSIDE MEGAN.

It had been three days since Roan's surgery. He was improving, and the doctors expected him to make a full recovery. The McCullen men and Mama Mary had visited him daily. Mama Mary seemed to have had already adopted him as another son and had snuck him homemade soup and some of her huckleberry pie.

Megan's heart twisted. She was glad the family had accepted him.

But Roan refused to see her.

Was he simply angry that she'd told the McCullens about his relationship to them? Or…did he really not care about her?

Had he only taken her to bed because they'd been thrown together and in danger and she was…available?

Self-doubts assailed her as she finished an autopsy on a man who'd had a seizure while driving and ended up wrapping his car around a tree.

Determined to reach Roan, she washed her hands, removed her lab coat and headed to the second floor where he was recovering. When she reached his room, he was trying to get out of bed and arguing with one of the nurses.

"Tell the doctor I'm ready to go home. I'm not a damn invalid."

Megan laughed at his obstinate tone. He was definitely feeling better.

Still, he winced as the nurse helped him back to bed, a sign he had a long way to go before he was back to normal.

Her stomach fluttered with nerves as she stepped aside to allow the nurse to exit the room. When she walked in, she was so anxious to see him that his scowl didn't faze her.

"Hi, Roan."

A muscle ticked in his jaw. "What are you doing here? The case is over."

His look indicated they were also over.

She inhaled a deep breath and stepped closer to his bed. "I know that. But I miss you."

Some emotion she didn't understand flickered in his eyes. "Megan, don't."

"Don't what? Don't be honest?" she said softly. "Don't care about you?"

"Don't make something out of what happened between us. It was just one night of sex. Nothing more."

She'd been afraid he felt that way, but hearing the words felt as if he'd stabbed her in her heart.

"But—"

"There is no but." He jerked the sheet up over himself, but the movement only caused her to notice his bare legs poking out from that hospital gown.

God, she wanted to crawl in bed beside him, run her foot up his calf, her hands over his chest. She wanted to love him and for him to love her back.

All the things her father said to her growing up rose to the surface. She had her brains, her job. Hell, she was married to her job.

No man would ever marry her because she wasn't the pretty girl they wanted on their arm.

"I understand," she said, grateful her voice didn't break. "I won't bother you again." Terrified, she might break down in front of him, she turned and ran from the room.

She made it all the way to the elevator before she burst into tears.

She swiped angrily at them as the elevator doors opened and out stepped Mama Mary.

Embarrassed, she forced a smile, but her tears must have given her away.

"What's wrong, dear? Is it Mr. Roan? Did something happen?"

She shook her head. "He's all right. It's just…he doesn't want me."

Mama Mary gaped at her, then folded her in her arms. "Come on, honey, and tell me all about it."

Megan had stood alone for so long that she welcomed the woman's motherly embrace and allowed her to usher her to the cafeteria for coffee and a good cry.

ROAN WAS TIRED of the hospital, tired of the nurses hovering, tired of feeling weak and damn near helpless.

He wanted to go home and sulk by himself in his own place.

Except Megan had been there with him, leaving her sweet feminine scent on his sheets, and images of her climbing on top of him and tormenting him with her body in his mind.

How could he sleep in his own bed now without remembering that night?

You told her it meant nothing.

This time he'd lied.

It had meant everything.

He squeezed his eyes closed, desperately trying to blot the memory, but he could see her head thrown back, her breasts swaying above him, her lips parted and closing around his sex.

Dammit…

Mama Mary knocked, then lumbered in. "Mr. Roan, I hear you've been giving everyone here fits."

In just a few short days, he'd come to love the older woman. He especially loved her pies.

Did she have one with her today?

No…her hands were empty. And for the first time since she'd taken it upon herself to cheer him up daily, she wasn't smiling.

"I'm ready to go home."

"Yeah. You also made Ms. Megan cry." She huffed and planted her hands on her ample hips. "And that girl seems like a tough one. Not like a crier."

She *was* tough. "She was crying?"

Mama Mary marched over to him. "If you don't love her, I get that, but that girl was plumb devastated with worry the

night she brought you in. She waited here all night praying and frettin'. She's crazy in love with you, Mr. Roan."

Roan clenched the sheets in a white-knuckled grip. He
didn't know how to respond. Megan had never said she
loved him.

Because you didn't give her the chance.

"Worst thing is, she thinks you don't want her 'cause
she's not one of those beauty queen types."

That took him by surprise. "What?"

In spite of the fact that he was bandaged, she actually
poked him in the chest. "You heard me. Seems her daddy
did a number on her. Told her she wasn't pretty like her sister, that girls like her had to use their brains to get by." She
made an indignant sound. "Now, I sure as heck agree with
that. But Ms. Megan is strong and brave, and she cares about
folks with all her heart, and that makes her ten times more
beautiful than any of those plastic model types with their
fancy clothes and three-inch heels and gobs of makeup."

Roan remembered the way she'd looked with her hair
tumbling around her shoulders, with her eyes dark with
passion. Then her comment about being a cactus. "I agree."

Mama Mary narrowed her eyes. "You do?"

"Yes, of course. She's the most beautiful woman I've
ever met."

She stared at him with a confused look. "But you don't
have feelings for her?"

Roan looked away. Mama Mary was way too perceptive.
"I didn't say that. I just don't have anything to offer her."

"What kind of foolishness are you talking about?" She
tsked at him. "All a woman really wants is a man to love
her." She poked him again. "*Do* you love her?"

Roan chewed the inside of his cheek. "It's not that
simple."

"It is if you want it to be. If you love her, get up out of
that bed and tell her."

Roan looked at the door, then at Mama Mary, and an image of Megan crying taunted him. She thought he didn't love her because she wasn't beautiful enough.

He wasn't accustomed to being part of a family, to having brothers, or a mother figure, to…having someone love him.

But hadn't he envied Maddox and Rose?

He had wanted what they had. Maybe he had it with Megan.

But he'd been too stubborn and cowardly to admit his feelings. Too afraid of losing her and being hurt.

In protecting himself, he'd hurt her. The one person who loved him for himself.

He shoved at the covers. "Push that wheelchair over here. I'm going to see her now."

"Hot damn." Mama Mary gave him a big hug that nearly tore out his stitches, but he chuckled as she pulled away and pushed him into the chair. He wheeled himself to the elevator and started toward the morgue, but decided to stop at the flower shop instead.

Fear pressed against his heart as he made his purchase and rode the elevator to the morgue. What if he'd hurt her so badly that she couldn't forgive him?

Chapter Twenty-Four

Megan splashed cold water on her face and patted her tear-swollen eyes dry.

Good grief, she couldn't believe she'd poured out her heart and soul to Mama Mary. But that woman had a way of wrapping her arms around you that made you feel like you'd come home.

Maddox, Brett and Ray had missed growing up with their birth mother, but they'd been blessed by having a wonderful woman like Mama Mary in their lives.

Roan would be blessed with that now, too. She could already hear the affection in the woman's voice when she said his name. One of the nurses had told her that Mama Mary had been doting on him and spoiling him rotten.

Roan deserved it.

She blew her nose, then gave herself a pep talk before returning to work. She was fine. She might be alone, but she had her job.

Yep, all those dead people waiting on her. But dead people didn't talk to you or hold you at night and keep you warm when your nightmares crept up on you.

Maybe she'd get a dog. Or a cat. She could become one of those cat collectors who had half a dozen...

She tossed the paper towel in the trash, dabbed a little powder on her cheeks, then stepped from the bathroom and headed back to the morgue. When she arrived, she was surprised to see Roan in a wheelchair.

"What are you doing here?" She skimmed her gaze over

his torso. His bandage was still in place, but his coloring was better.

"I came to see you." His jaw tightened as if he might have come under duress. "You've been crying."

Compassion softened the accusation, and a blush heated her neck. She didn't intend to tell him about her meltdown. "What do you want, Roan?"

Her voice sounded harsher than she'd intended, but he had dismissed her earlier as if she was nothing. Better he think she was angry than hurt.

"I'm sorry for hurting you," he said, his voice hoarse.

So much for hiding her feelings.

"You were just being honest, Roan. I'm a big girl. I'm fine."

"Well, I'm not fine."

Worry knifed through her. "What's wrong? Are you in pain? Are your stitches coming loose?"

He pushed himself to stand and pulled a bouquet of sunflowers from behind his back. "This is not about my gunshot wound." He took a step closer to her, and Megan's chest squeezed.

"Roan, you shouldn't be down here. You need to go back to your room and rest."

"I can't rest until I make things right."

Her heart fluttered, but she ordered herself not to latch on to hope.

"What do you mean?"

"I mean you're not a cactus, you're a sunflower." He thrust them in her hand. "And I was a coward," he said bluntly. "I lied to you before."

She smiled at the sunflowers in her hand. Was he saying what she thought he was saying? "Lied about what?"

"About that night meaning nothing. It was…" He cradled her hand in his and pressed it over his heart. "It was everything to me. *You* are everything to me."

Megan's heart pounded. "I am?"

"Yes." A smile curved his sensual mouth. "It hurt so much when I lost my mother that I vowed never to love anyone ever again. I…didn't think I could stand that kind of pain."

Megan's heart fluttered.

"Then I found you and my brothers and I didn't think I deserved any of you."

"Oh, Roan, that's not true. You are the most honorable man I've ever met."

He lifted her hand and kissed her fingers. "And you are the most beautiful woman I've ever met."

"Roan, you don't have to stay that. It's not true—"

"It is true." He stroked her arms with his hands. "Your father was wrong to make you think that you aren't beautiful."

Her breath caught. "My God, Mama Mary told you."

He nodded, but his eyes didn't hold pity. They held a tenderness that made her heart fill with warmth.

"I love you, Megan. I…don't want to lose you." He leaned closer and brushed a kiss across her lips. "I have three brothers now. I'm just getting used to that. But I still need you." He kissed her again. "I still want you."

"I want you, too," she said breathlessly.

"I love you," he whispered.

"I love you, too."

His kiss came hard and fierce this time, a give-and-take, a dance of love and promises.

When he finally pulled apart, they were both panting. "You really do need to get back to bed," she whispered.

"Not until you promise me something."

The fact that she'd broken her other promise echoed in her mind. "What? Anything…"

A teasing smile flickered in his eyes. "Promise me that you'll marry me."

Megan's heart soared with love and happiness. She threw her arms around him and they both fell into the wheelchair, the sunflowers fluttering to the floor as she kissed him and told him yes.

Epilogue

Three weeks later

Megan smiled as Mama Mary adjusted her veil. She was marrying Roan today. The McCullen wives had welcomed her like a sister into their family and helped her put together the wedding, which was taking place at Horseshoe Creek.

Rose had found a wedding gown through her antiques shop, Vintage Treasures, that reminded Megan of the dress her mother had worn. In the dress, she felt…beautiful.

Willow and Scarlet had helped decorate the gazebo by the pond on the property that the McCullens had given Roan as a thank-you gift and a wedding present. But it meant more than a piece of land—it meant they accepted Roan as part of the McCullens.

A knock sounded at the door of the cabin where she and Roan were living temporarily until their house was built. Mama Mary answered, then returned a moment later.

"Megan, there's someone here to see you."

Megan finished applying lip gloss. "Who is it?"

"It's me, your father."

The deep baritone voice made Megan swirl around. She stared at her father, speechless for a moment. He looked older, his hair was graying and he wore a dark suit, but he still stood tall and imposing.

Mama Mary and the McCullen women slipped quietly out the door.

Her heart fluttered with dread. "Hello, Dad. What are

you doing here?" Had he come to try to talk her out of marrying Roan?

"I heard you were getting married."

She nodded, braced for an argument. "I am. To Deputy Roan Whitefeather. He's a wonderful man."

Her father studied her for a second, his face twisting with emotions. "I tried to reach you several times lately, but you didn't return my calls."

"I was busy. Working."

"I know. I read about you and this deputy and what you did." His voice thickened. "I came to say I'm proud of you, Megan. I...know it's late in coming, but I'm so proud."

Tears clogged Megan's throat.

"I was...not always the most understanding father, or at least it didn't come out that way. I didn't handle losing your sister and your mother well at all, and I guess I retreated into some kind of shell."

"We were both grieving, Dad," Megan said softly.

"Yes, but I pushed you away, I let you down."

"I understood. I wasn't pretty like Shelly or Mom, not the girly girl—"

"That's just it, you are so beautiful, Megan, but in a dif-ferent way. You're strong and smart and kindhearted and... you always seemed so independent. I suppose I doted on Shelly because she was easy, and she didn't have the brains and drive you did. I thought she needed me more."

"Oh, Dad, I needed you, too." Megan swallowed, bat-tling more tears.

"I realize that now." Her father rubbed a hand across his forehead. "Anyway, I've thought a lot about it and I want us to see each other again, to be...to build a relationship."

Megan bit down on her lip. "I'm not leaving the ME's office, Dad."

"I know that." A smile graced his mouth. "And I'm not

asking you to. All I'm asking is that you give me a chance to be your father again. To have a place in your life."

How could she say no to that?

He removed a velvet box from his pocket and held it out to her. "Here, sweetheart, please open this."

Her hand trembled as she accepted the box and lifted the top. Her breath caught at the diamond earrings sparkling back. They were stunning.

"Those were your mother's. She wore them at our wedding." His tone grew gruffer. "I thought you might want to wear them today."

Tears filled Megan's eyes and she stood and rushed to her father. "Thank you, Dad. I don't know what to say."

"Just know that she loved you, honey. I wish she was here to see you now."

"I wish she was, too," Megan said through her tears.

He closed his arms around her. "I love you, Megan. I really do. I'm sorry for wasting so much time."

"I love you, too." She kissed his cheek, then took his hand and squeezed it. "Will you walk me down the aisle?"

His gaze met hers, the pain and turmoil of their past fading away. "I would be honored."

ROAN ADJUSTED HIS bolo tie, smiling at his half brothers who'd joked about how uncomfortable they all felt in a suit. They'd been grateful he'd asked them to wear jeans and a Western duster instead.

He'd been moved when Maddox, Brett and Ray had given him the land their father had bought from Clark. They assured him he'd earned it, and they wanted him to be part of Horseshoe Creek.

His half brothers filed out from the cabin and they took their places at the gazebo the womenfolk had decorated in front of the pond on what was now his land.

Tears clouded his eyes as Megan walked across the field

on her father's arm. Mama Mary had told him that the senior Dr. Lail had shown up, and he'd been nervous that Megan would be upset.

But her radiant smile as she looked up at him and then her father told him they'd made peace.

His wife-to-be looked stunning in an antique ivory lace dress. A shoulder-length veil was held in place by pearl combs, and today she'd worn her hair down, long and flowing and blowing in the wind.

He stepped up to take her hand, and she kissed him before the ceremony even started.

Laughter erupted from the McCullens and Mama Mary, and Brett's little boy clapped. Dr. Lail gave him a serious look, then shook his hand.

"Take care of my girl, she's special," he said in a gruff voice.

Roan nodded. "Yes she is, sir."

Megan kissed him again, and Roan laughed and drew her in his arms. The kiss was just a prelude of the life they were starting together.

And one day they would have a family of their own.

But today Megan was all he needed. Although he was grateful for the McCullens and the land he and Megan could now call home.

* * * * *

*Find out what really happened to
the missing McCullen twins when*
THE HEROES OF HORSESHOE CREEK
*continues later this year! Look for them
wherever Intrigue books are sold!*

The thought that he could have lost her today—had come so close to losing her— had him crushing her to him.

He wrapped one arm around her hips and threaded his other hand through her hair, bringing her lips to his.

The heat was instant, as always. It chased all traces of cold away.

"I thought I'd lost you tonight," he murmured against her mouth.

"I had the same fear when I couldn't get you to wake up in the car," she responded, her lips never moving away from his.

There was no more talking. Neither of them wanted to think about death. Not right now. Liam didn't want to even think about whether this was a good idea or not.

All he wanted to think about was her body pressed up against his.

ARMORED
ATTRACTION

BY
JANIE CROUCH

First Published in Great Britain 2016
By Mills & Boon, an imprint of HarperCollins*Publishers*
1 London Bridge Street, London, SE1 9GF

© 2016 Janie Crouch

ISBN: 978-0-263-91907-3

46-0616

Our policy is to use papers that are natural, renewable and recyclable products and made from wood grown in sustainable forests. The logging and manufacturing processes conform to the legal environmental regulations of the country of origin.

Printed and bound in Spain
by CPI, Barcelona

Janie Crouch has loved to read romance her whole life. She cut her teeth on Mills & Boon Cherish novels as a preteen, then moved on to a passion for romantic suspense as an adult. Janie lives with her husband and four children overseas. Janie enjoys traveling, long-distance running, movie-watching, knitting and adventure/ obstacle racing. You can find out more about her at www.janiecrouch.com.

To my parents, for being a constant example of God's goodness, faith and love. Thank you for being a blessing not only to me but so many others.

Chapter One

A leisurely walk along the beach in the evening was a chance for many people to ponder the meaning of life. Not for Vanessa Epperson. She rarely had time to walk along the beach at all anymore, much less waste that valuable time *pondering*.

She was way too busy to ponder. But, ahh, how she loved the feel of the sand on her toes.

She should have as much time as anyone to walk along the beach: her career as a social worker for a private organization—The Bridgespan Team—was technically nine to five, Monday through Friday. But in reality it rarely worked out that way. A call from a woman needing housing immediately because she'd finally gotten the courage to leave her abusive husband didn't always come during normal business hours. Nor did a call from someone who had his first critical job interview in weeks and needed a ride at 7:00 a.m. because his car had broken down.

Both of those scenarios had happened to Vanessa in the past forty-eight hours.

Her coworkers told her she got too involved, that she needed to keep more of a professional distance between herself and her clients. Vanessa just shrugged her colleagues off. Sometimes people needed help beyond what was required from the job. When she could help, she did. Because there were far too many times when there was just nothing she could do.

If they knew about it, she guessed most people would say she could dip into the five million dollars her parents had made readily available to her. But Vanessa couldn't do that. *Wouldn't* do that. She didn't plan to ever touch that money.

She pushed all thoughts of her family away as she walked along the sands of the Roanoke Sound of the Outer Banks of North Carolina. She wouldn't let them intrude on her rare moments of solitude and quiet.

But this sand—this particular sand—in her toes renewed her. Helped her to remember that everything would be okay. Helped her to clear her mind and leave the problems she couldn't solve somewhere else for a little while.

It was the beginning of October. The sun had set a few minutes ago, casting the beach in a purple hue. It was empty. With summer gone, most of the tourists had long since left the Outer Banks; they would've been on the ocean side anyway, rather than the more boring sound side. Most locals weren't out, either, having made their way to their homes or wherever they spent their evenings. Everyone was settling in.

Vanessa would need to do the same soon, too. Tomorrow's alarm at five thirty in the morning would come all too soon. She needed her sleep to fortify her for whatever the day would bring.

But since the beach was so quiet, the sand so nice and cool in her toes, the breeze so gentle in the ever-darkening sky, she decided to keep walking. She would just walk up to the beached log she could barely make out a couple hundred feet ahead, then turn around and go back to her car.

As with her family, she would categorically *not* think about other times she had walked along this very beach and whom she had walked along with. Thinking about it never led to anything but sadness anyway. Vanessa refused to be sad all the time. Life was too short.

Before she knew it she had made it to the log and was about to turn to walk back—until the log groaned and began to move.

Vanessa shrieked before she could help herself and jumped back. It was a *person*.

She looked around for any other people—aware after the past few years at her job that danger could be found in the most innocent-looking places—and grabbed her pepper spray from her bag. A gun would've been better—she was licensed to carry a concealed weapon in North Carolina—but hers was back at her car.

The log moaned again.

Vanessa worked her way closer, cautiously, running scenarios in her head. It could be a drunk person who had passed out on the beach. Didn't usually happen here, but it was possible. It could be someone who had fallen asleep.

It could be someone waiting to ambush her, although a mugging on the beach in October at this time of night was not very likely. Still, Vanessa kept her pepper spray close.

"Excuse me, are you okay?" When there was no answer she took a step closer. "Hello?"

Maybe it was someone hurt. She didn't let her guard down, but walked a few steps closer. Now she could see more of the person's shape.

If this person meant Vanessa harm, he or she must have a weapon. Now that Vanessa could see more clearly, she realized how small the person really was. Couldn't be much taller than Vanessa's own five feet two inches.

"Are you okay? Hello?"

Vanessa walked the rest of the way to the form. It was a female. She was lying unconscious on her stomach, long brown hair strung down her back, wet and full of sand and seaweed.

Vanessa reached down and pressed gently on the woman's shoulder. Her skin was icy to the touch.

Whoever this was needed help.

"Hello? Can you wake up?"

She could possibly have a head or spinal injury. Vanessa didn't want to move her. She cursed the fact that her cell phone was back in her car, although even if it was here, she probably wouldn't get a signal.

Vanessa rubbed up and down on the woman's arm. "Hello? Can you hear me?"

Vanessa jumped back when the woman suddenly scurried away from Vanessa's touch, chest heaving, breaths sawing in and out. She put an arm out in front of her in a defensive posture.

Not a woman. A girl. A teenager. Maybe fourteen or fifteen years old.

Vanessa's heart broke. She knew what that arm held out meant: abuse.

At least there didn't seem to be any spinal injury to worry about.

"Hi, I'm Vanessa." She spoke very slowly, softly. "Are you okay? How can I help you?"

Vanessa made no move to get any closer to the girl, not wanting to scare her further.

The girl shook her head, not saying anything.

Vanessa realized the girl was wearing a dark T-shirt that was ripped and falling off her body. She didn't seem to have anything on under it. Vanessa began to unbutton the lightweight jacket she was wearing.

"I'm just going to take off my jacket. You might feel a little better if you have on more clothes."

Vanessa worked it the rest of the way off then stretched out her arm and dropped it. It landed close enough for the girl to grab, but not so close that it would touch her if she didn't want it.

"Is there anyone I can call for you? Parents? Friend? Boyfriend?"

Vanessa was relieved when the girl reached for the jacket, but she didn't answer any of her questions.

"Can you at least tell me your name?"

The girl looked up at her, big brown eyes seeming to swallow her entire face.

"Ka-Karine," she finally whispered. "My name is Karine."

Her English was broken at best, heavily accented—sounding Eastern European. That was probably why she hadn't answered Vanessa's other questions. She didn't know enough English to understand what Vanessa was saying.

And unless she had family visiting here, she was also a long way from home.

"Hi, Karine," Vanessa said gently, slowing her speech significantly to see if it would help the girl understand any better. "Can you tell me how you got here?"

"Boat," Karine whispered.

"You were traveling on a boat? With your family? Was there an accident?"

Karine began to cry. "No. Men took us. Put us on boat for many days."

"Someone kidnapped you? From here in the Outer Banks?"

Vanessa could tell she had lost Karine again.

"Where are you from?" Slowly again. "Where is your home?"

"Estonia."

Vanessa wasn't sure where that was. The United States? An entirely different country?

"Is Estonia here in the United States?" Vanessa asked.

"No, it is near Russia."

Vanessa's breath whistled through her teeth. Was she understanding correctly?

"Some men came and took you from Estonia and put you on a boat?"

Karine nodded. "First one boat and then the smaller boat with the men who spoke only English."

Vanessa could see the girl begin to visibly shudder at the thought.

"And there were other girls with you?"

Karine nodded again. "Yes. There are seven more."

Vanessa felt nausea roll through her stomach. Karine and the other girls were obviously part of a human-trafficking ring right here in the Outer Banks.

"How did you get here, Karine?" Vanessa asked. "How did you get away from the men?"

She held up a hand covered in bruises around her wrist, obviously from handcuffs or other restraints.

"Man tie us when no one is on boat with us. But I got out. And then I jump in water. I rather die from sharks than let them touch me again." Karine closed her eyes and lowered her hand.

There weren't any sharks in the Roanoke Sound, Vanessa knew, although there could be painful jellyfish at this time of year. Either way, it had been an amazing feat for the small teenager to undertake. The Sound was more than five miles wide at some parts. There was no way Karine could've known how far she would have to swim when she'd jumped in.

Whatever had been waiting for her on that boat had to have been bad enough that Karine was willing to risk her life to get away from it.

Vanessa needed to get the girl to a hospital. Report this to the authorities. Get the cops or National Guard or Marines or all three to start looking for those other girls.

"Karine, you were so brave," she whispered. "I know it is hard, but do you think you could come with me? I can take you to the hospital. Get you the help you need."

"I promised other girls I would help them if I lived," Karine whispered.

"Yes." Vanessa nodded. "Absolutely. We will go to the police so they can help find the other girls."

Vanessa thought for a moment that Karine might refuse her help, but she finally nodded and got up off the ground, wrapped in Vanessa's jacket.

"Okay, I go with you."

Karine didn't seem to have many significant injuries. She was able to walk unassisted from the beach to Vanessa's car. Dehydration was obviously an issue—she gulped down the contents of the water bottle Vanessa offered in seconds—as was hunger. She made short work of a package of crackers. Vanessa wished she had more to offer. She gave Karine a pair of yoga pants to put on, which were too big for the girl but at least were better than nothing.

Vanessa took a direct route to the Nags Head Regional Hospital. She'd brought in enough clients over the years that she was pretty well known there. She walked Karine in through the emergency entrance, relieved to see her friend Judy working the desk.

"Hey, Judy." Vanessa spoke only loud enough that the other woman could hear her. The last thing Karine needed was the media circus that would come along with anyone finding out she had been part of a probable human-trafficking ring in the area. "I have an assault victim here. Doesn't speak much English. Probably also suffering from dehydration. She swam a long way to get away from the person or persons who were holding her against her will."

Judy shook her head and smiled softly at Karine. "I'm so sorry, honey. We'll help you." She turned to Vanessa. "It's crazy busy in here tonight. Can we put her in temp room one? Just until something else opens up. We won't do any exams there."

Temporary room one was at the front of the trauma unit.

They rarely put assault victims there because it was so busy nearby and was only separated by curtains. Judy wouldn't put them there if she had another choice.

"Okay, sure. I'll take Karine in myself."

She led the girl into the room and helped her to sit. She seemed to stare blankly out the crack in the curtain.

Should Vanessa get her some food? She didn't want to leave Karine alone, but who knew when she'd last had a decent meal? Maybe Judy could get something for them.

A moment later Karine bounded out of the chair and backed away to the farthest point in the room. Her face was devoid of all color and her eyes were huge.

"Leave. Leave." The young woman was shuddering so hard that was all she could get out.

Vanessa had no idea what was going on. Why was Karine freaking out now when she had been so docile since they'd arrived? Vanessa looked out through the crack in the curtain to where Karine had been looking.

A uniformed member of the sheriff's department was talking to Judy at the main desk.

Had Vanessa misunderstood the whole situation? Was Karine running from the law?

She turned back to the young woman and found her slipping under the curtains of the room. Vanessa rushed over, stopping her gently.

"Karine. The policeman out there… Is he looking for you?"

Karine clutched at Vanessa. "Man. Man on boat."

"That man was on the boat?" A sheriff's deputy?

"No." Karine shook her head. "That clothes."

Not that particular guy, but someone wearing the same uniform. Dear God. Was Karine telling her that someone from the sheriff's office was part of a trafficking ring?

Vanessa stared at her for a few more moments. She had no idea exactly what was going on, but she was willing to give Karine the benefit of the doubt. If Vanessa was wrong, she'd deal with the consequences later.

"Okay, let's get you out of here."

They slipped under the curtain and were out of the hospital in a matter of minutes. Karine was still shuddering, glancing from side to side frantically, obviously searching for anyone who might be following. Vanessa put an arm around her, tentatively, to guide her through the parking lot to her car. Karine stiffened briefly before leaning into her.

Vanessa started the car and pulled to the edge of the parking lot. She didn't know which way to turn. If someone from the sheriff's office really was in on this, it wouldn't take long for them to figure out Karine was with her. She couldn't take Karine to her house. She needed to get her out of the area.

"Karine." Vanessa turned to the girl, who was sitting low in her seat so no one could see her. "I'm going to drive you to Norfolk, okay? It's a city about an hour and a half from here. There are police, FBI, who can help us."

"No!" Karine sat straighter in the seat. "I cannot leave. I must stay here to help the other girls. Must find them."

"Yes, we'll get help and then come back here."

"No!" Karine repeated, grabbing for the door handle. "I stay here."

"No, wait. Don't get out," Vanessa said.

Karine was exhausted, traumatized and injured. Vanessa prayed she had been mistaken about the police uniform. Many of the men in the sheriff's department Vanessa had known most of her life. She couldn't imagine they would be involved with the victimization of girls.

But she wasn't about to put Karine out on her own, no matter how unlikely the scenario may be.

"Okay, we'll stay here in Nags Head," Vanessa told her, watching her visually relax. "We'll go to a hotel."

Karine nodded and eased lower into her seat.

If Karine was going to refuse to leave the area, Vanessa was going to need to see about someone coming here to help them. Contacting the local police was out of the question. She needed someone outside that circle, someone in federal law enforcement.

Liam Goetz.

He was DEA, which maybe didn't deal with trafficking directly, but at least she knew he wasn't local. He'd know how to help or tell her who to contact.

Of course, she hadn't talked to Liam in eight years. Didn't even know if he would be willing to talk to her now. But he was her best chance in this situation. She had to try.

Vanessa sped to her apartment to get his phone number, which was written on the back of a picture of the two of them. She should've thrown it away years ago but hadn't been able to make herself do it. Now she was glad she hadn't.

She grabbed a couple changes of clothes from her room, but nothing to make it look as though she wasn't there, then ran back out to the car. She had no doubt one of the first places the police would start looking for Karine was at Vanessa's apartment.

As she pulled away, she Bluetoothed the number on the back of the picture. She forced herself not to look at the much younger, more innocent version of herself in the photo. That girl was gone forever.

The phone rang twice before someone answered.

"DEA call center."

"Um, yes, I'm trying to reach an agent. At least he used to be an agent." Vanessa wasn't sure exactly what she should say. Maybe Liam didn't even work for the DEA anymore. "He gave me this number."

"Please provide the name of the person you are trying to reach and I'll direct your call." The operator was briskly efficient.

"Liam Goetz." Vanessa had no idea what department he worked for or even what city.

"Please hold."

Vanessa drove toward some older hotels closer to Nags Head. They weren't very expensive, which was pretty much all Vanessa could offer Karine right now. Plus, the police were probably less likely to look for her there.

The longer Vanessa was on hold, the more convinced she became that this whole call to Liam was probably useless.

"Hello? You're trying to reach Liam Goetz?" A briskly efficient female voice this time.

"Yes. But I don't know which division he's in—"

"I'm going to connect you to his voice mailbox. Please leave a detailed message. We will make sure he gets it."

Okay, so evidently he did still work for the DEA. That was good.

"Okay."

"Please hold. Leave a message when you hear the beep."

Vanessa was startled, caught off guard, a moment later when she heard the beep. There had been no outgoing message.

"Um, Liam, it's Vanessa. Vanessa Epperson."

How much should she tell him?

"I'm still living on the Outer Banks, but I'm actually staying at a hotel at the moment." She gave him the name and address of the hotel they'd just pulled up to. "I need your help. I have a situation here and believe local police might be involved, so I need federal law enforcement. If you could just point me in the right direction, I would really appreciate it. I wasn't sure who else I could trust. Just call if you can."

She was rambling, so she left him her number and then disconnected the call. She'd done all she could do there. She knew she needed to have a backup plan in case Liam didn't call her back. After all, the last thing she'd heard him say about her eight years ago was that she was a selfish, spoiled brat who didn't have it in her to care about another person.

Yeah, she definitely better have a backup plan in place.

Chapter Two

Liam listened to the voice-mail message for the umpteenth time.

Vanessa Epperson.

He could honestly say he'd never expected to hear her voice ever again. After all, she hadn't even cared enough to leave him a voice mail eight years ago when she'd decided he wasn't good enough to marry.

Or a letter. Or an email. Or a face-to-face explanation.

But evidently she'd gotten over her phone aversion. Good for her.

Liam played the message again.

She needed help and was contacting him because she thought he was still DEA. He hadn't been DEA for more than five years, since Omega Sector's Critical Response Division had recruited him to lead their hostage rescue team.

Fortunately for Vanessa, since Omega Sector was made up of agents from multiple different law-enforcement agencies—FBI, Interpol, DEA… Hell, Liam had worked a mission with a damn Texas Ranger last month—her message had been recorded and immediately forwarded to him.

She didn't mention what sort of trouble she was in, just wanted Liam to drop everything and help her. Like how she'd always wanted everyone to drop everything to do what she wanted. Some things didn't change.

He listened to the message one more time.

Liam should call one of his many friends from the head DEA office in Atlanta and have them send someone to Nags Head. Or he might even know someone at the FBI field office in Norfolk he could call.

It was the logical thing to do; probably the most professional answer to this situation. He could have someone there handling Vanessa's problem in three or four hours.

But who was Liam kidding? He wasn't going to make those calls. He was already walking down the hall of the Critical Response Division's headquarters to his boss's office.

He wasn't sure what he was going to tell Steve Drackett. Just that he needed some time off to help an old friend. God knew Liam had enough time off saved up.

He knocked on Steve's office door, his back office door that led directly to Steve himself, rather than pass through the main office entrance guarded by Steve's four assistants.

Four young, attractive, quite competent and intelligent female assistants.

Liam knew them all, flirted shamelessly with them all. He'd spent so much time in the office with those women that Steve had threatened to fire him several times.

Not that Liam dated any of them—he knew better than to date anyone who might have his life in her hands—but at any given moment he'd be leaning on their desks chatting, and keeping them from their work.

Liam smiled. Steve's main office was one of his favorite places in the world to be.

But not today. Not right now. He could not go in there and flirt with those beautiful women with Vanessa's voice still filling his head.

Steve's door opened.

"Hey, Liam. Come on in." Steve said, still reading from a file in his hand as he returned to his desk. "I didn't even think you knew this door existed. Hell, I wasn't really sure you knew any offices existed outside those belonging to my assistants."

Derek Waterman and Joe Matarazzo—both Liam's colleagues and good friends—were sitting in chairs across from Steve's desk. They held similar files.

"Hey, Goetz," Derek murmured. Joe muttered something unintelligible without looking up from the file in his hand.

"I don't mean to interrupt, Steve," Liam said.

"It's no problem. What's on your mind?"

"I'm going to need a few personal days."

Now the guys looked up from their files. Liam was pretty sure he'd never taken personal days except to go on actual vacations planned well ahead of time.

"Everything okay?" Steve's concern was also evident.

"Yeah." Liam shrugged. "Everything's fine. I just have a friend who called needing some help back in the Outer Banks. My friend said this might be a little sticky with the locals so wanted some outside help."

"You grew up there, right? You haven't been home in a long time."

"Yeah, not since my grandmother died. Not much there for me."

Steve nodded. "Is your friend's trouble serious? Do we need to send in a team?"

"Nah. I'm sure I can handle it."

"What sort of trouble?"

Liam sighed. "To be honest, I'm not exactly sure. My friend called my old DEA contact number. They forwarded it to me."

"Has anybody else noticed Goetz's complete lack of pronoun usage?" Joe said, leaning back in his chair.

Damn it. This was about to become a thing.

"As a matter of fact, I did," Derek responded, grinning. "So are we to assume this *friend* is of the female variety?"

Liam realized he should've just mentioned that from the beginning. "Yes, she is."

"Um, Joe, do you ever recall Liam being shy about mentioning a female friend to us before?" Derek quipped.

Liam knew his reputation. He'd worked pretty hard at making sure everyone knew he was a ladies' man. Girl in every port. Shameless flirt.

At times he almost believed his own press. Because it was a hell of a lot easier to believe that he was some sort of modern-day Casanova than that he still pined over a woman who'd left him cold eight years ago.

"A female from his hometown, no less," Joe responded. "I've never heard him mention any such creature before."

"Very curious, indeed." Derek waggled his eyebrows.

"All right, enough, you two," Steve cut in. He turned to Liam. "Like I said, is there anything we need to know about your friend or her situation?"

"Not as far as I know," Liam said. "She didn't provide much detail. If it looks like something I can't handle, I'll let you know."

"You're not going to call her first? Get more details?"

"No, I'm just going to go."

Thankfully none of the three men in the room pointed out what Liam already knew: dropping everything and traveling from Omega headquarters in Colorado Springs to the Outer Banks of North Carolina because of a vague phone call from someone he hadn't talked to in nearly a decade was overkill.

But from the first moment he had heard Vanessa's voice, figured out she was asking for help, Liam knew he would be doing just that.

"Okay, I think one of the Omega jets is heading out to DC in the next few hours if you want to catch a ride there," Steve responded. "Be safe and keep me posted as to when you'll be back."

Joe and Derek didn't say anything, although they were both staring at Liam with mouths slightly agape. Liam ignored them.

"Okay. Thanks, Steve."

Liam just left. He didn't want to explain himself to his friends, especially when he could hardly understand what he was doing himself. All he knew was that he had to see Vanessa.

He wasn't really surprised that she was still living in the Outer Banks. The two-hundred-mile stretch of land, a string of barrier islands running along the northeast coast of North Carolina, held a great deal of prime property and the Eppersons owned a good chunk of it.

And Vanessa was princess of it all. She had been her whole life.

Liam had found out the hard way that her love for her pampered way of life outweighed any promises she might make to any poor sap fool enough to fall in love with her. Fool enough to believe her when she said she loved him, too.

Did she think of him when she felt the sand of the Roanoke Sound on her feet? On her back? Think of all the many hours they'd spent there together?

Did she ever think about him asking her to run away and marry him right there in that sand? About saying yes?

About not showing up where they were supposed to meet? About refusing to talk to him at all when he'd come by to see why she had changed her mind?

Probably not.

The address she had given him in the message was not her family mansion in Duck, which was slightly north of Nags Head and the preferred location for million-dollar mansions. It was some hotel he didn't recognize at Mile Marker 13, pretty much in the middle of nowhere.

Liam drove to his apartment and packed his things. He'd try to catch a ride with the team going to DC as Steve suggested. If not, he'd drive to Fort Carson, the army base in Colorado Springs. Omega worked pretty closely with the military when needed, and Liam had lots of contacts there from his days in Special Forces.

The commanding officers might lock their daughters away when Liam was in sight, but they would gladly welcome him on board an aircraft to give him a lift wherever he was going.

The thought brought a quick smile to Liam's face. His playboy reputation was well deserved. He'd certainly earned it since he'd been in Colorado.

Except for the past couple of years when he seemed to have lost his taste for fun, fast hookups. Yeah, he still flirted with all the gals—young or old—and kissed just about every woman he came across. But he wasn't particularly interested in more than that.

The thought of pseudo intimacy with another woman whose face he'd fondly remember but name he'd probably forget? Not as interesting anymore.

Maybe it had something to do with watching two of his best friends—and fellow Omega agents—fall in love with strong, beautiful women over the past few months. Jon Hatton and Derek Waterman's love for the women in their lives was downright palpable. Liam wanted something authentic like that for himself.

Then it struck him. *That* was why he was going to Nags Head. Because until he could put what had happened there behind him, he was never going to be able to have something real with any woman.

It was time. He was going to lay the ghost of Vanessa Epperson to rest once and for all. Her call was finally the excuse he needed.

LIAM WASN'T GOING to call.

Vanessa had accepted that reality when she woke up this

morning, sleeping in a pretty dingy hotel, a traumatized teenager curled into the tightest of balls in the bed next to her. He'd had all evening, all night and some of this morning to respond, but hadn't.

Maybe he hadn't gotten the message. Maybe he was off on some important mission with the DEA or something.

Maybe he still hated her.

The reasons why he wasn't contacting her didn't really matter. All that mattered was that Vanessa was on her own in helping Karine.

That was okay. Vanessa had learned in the hardest way possible that she was capable of handling *on her own* almost anything that came her way. This situation was no different.

But Liam's lack of contact still stung a little bit.

She dragged herself out of bed, careful not to wake Karine. She knew from the girl's whimpers and cries throughout the night that she couldn't have gotten very good rest.

Karine needed help. Probably medical and definitely psychological—both more than Vanessa could provide. If the hospital and police weren't safe around here, then Vanessa was going to have to talk her into leaving the Outer Banks, at least for the day.

Vanessa poured water into the cheap four-cup coffeemaker on the bathroom vanity. Once she had coffee, no matter how bad it was, she'd be able to figure out a plan.

While she waited she turned on the local morning news. Although she doubted it, she was curious to see if there was any mention of Karine.

At first nothing, just weather and tides—an important part of life on a string of islands. But then the breaking news...

The sheriff's office had set up roadblocks at the bridges on both sides of Nags Head. They were looking for a federal fugitive—considered armed and very dangerous—and were stopping all cars leaving the island to search them.

Since there was only one road leading off Nags Head at the north and south bridges, she knew the police could, in essence, search every car attempting to leave the island.

The rest of the news report was about the traffic havoc the car-by-car search was creating. No one from the sheriff's office seemed willing to comment.

Vanessa turned the television to mute and just stared at the screen.

Dangerous federal fugitive, her ass. Vanessa was one hundred percent certain the "dangerous federal fugitive" was curled up on the bed whimpering in her sleep every few minutes. But it meant that it would be impossible to get Karine off the island, at least today.

Not to mention that it confirmed that someone, at least one person pretty high up in the sheriff's department, was definitely a part of what had happened to Karine and the other girls.

The thought made Vanessa downright sick.

She grabbed her coffee, looking around. They weren't going to be able to stay here all day. They would need food—God only knew when Karine had last had a decent meal—and some other supplies. She'd given the girl a pair of shorts and a T-shirt she'd grabbed from her house, but they were too big.

She couldn't leave Karine alone while she went to get food, so she'd have to wait until she woke.

Vanessa needed to come up with a plan pretty darn quickly. But right now her options were limited.

A soft tap at the door startled her. She rushed to it but didn't say anything. She put her ear against the door. Maybe whoever it was—housekeeping?—would go away. She'd put the do-not-disturb placard on the doorknob.

"Vanessa, it's Liam. Open the door."

Chapter Three

Liam tapped on the door softly again. He was almost positive he had the wrong place. This was the address of the
hotel Vanessa had mentioned on the voice mail, but this
could not possibly be right.

Was it some sort of trap? Liam pulled his weapon from
the belt holster attached to his jeans, but kept it low to his
side. Had one of his enemies—and he had made plenty of
them over the years—found out about his past with Vanessa
and planned to use her against him in some way?

Because if that was someone's intent, it had succeeded
brilliantly. Here Liam was, completely out in the open, at
every possible tactical disadvantage, all because Vanessa
had called.

But his history with Vanessa was long ago and buried
pretty deeply. He hadn't even told his best friends about
what had gone down between them. So he didn't really
think there was any devious master plan, such as someone
forcing her to make a phone call against her will.

But he still didn't put his weapon away. There was no
way in hell Vanessa Epperson would be staying at a hotel
like this if she had any other choice.

You really couldn't call it a hotel. It was more of a run-
down motel, with all room doors leading directly outside
to a parking lot that desperately needed repaving. There
was no room service, spa or concierge.

Ergo—and obviously he'd been hanging around too many overthinking profilers at Omega if he was using words like *ergo*—no Vanessa.

He must be at the wrong place. He eased his weapon back into the holster and was turning to leave, not wanting to disturb whatever non-Vanessa person was sleeping in the room, when the door cracked open just the slightest bit.

"Liam?"

It was her. He couldn't see her through the crack, but he would know her voice anywhere, even if he hadn't heard it in her message recently.

"Yes. Are you okay? Let me in?" He took his weapon out again.

For a minute he didn't think she was going to do it, but then she stepped back and opened the door far enough for him to enter.

"What are you doing here?" she whispered. The room was dark because of the pulled shades and he could hardly see her.

Liam looked around but didn't see anyone else that could be threatening Vanessa in the darkened room. He reholstered his weapon. "What do you mean, what am I doing here? You called me, needing help. That's what I'm doing here."

"Oh," she whispered again. "I thought you'd just call me back and leave me the contact info of someone in the DEA or something similar. Were you in the area?"

"Something like that." Absolutely nothing like that. "Why are we whispering?"

Vanessa turned and pointed over her shoulder. "Her."

There was a very small person balled up on the bed.

Okay. *This* was definitely not what he'd expected. The dumpy hotel. The hiding. The kid sleeping in the bed. "Vanessa, what the hell is going on?"

She shushed him with her finger then grabbed his arm,

pulling him into the bathroom and closing the door behind her.

Now he could see her.

He refused to let his breath be stolen just because he was seeing her again for the first time in eight years. But damn if he could stop himself from staring at her.

Her hair was shorter now. Stopping just past her shoulders rather than flowing down to nearly her waist as it once had. But it was still that same deep auburn color that reminded him of fall leaves or russet chrysanthemums. Her eyes were the same soft brown—although she had often worn colored contacts when she was a teenager, always wanting to be more *dramatic*. That had never made sense to Liam. Her eyes were stunning just the way they were.

She was still tiny. God, he'd forgotten how little she was. Her personality was so big, people tended to forget that she was barely five foot two and couldn't weigh more than a hundred pounds. Standing beside her now, Liam towered over her. As always, it didn't intimidate Vanessa.

Something was different about her now. He couldn't quite put his finger on it exactly, but something about her had changed.

Of course she was more mature, in her looks, even in her movements. But it was more than just that. Something in her eyes was different—a depth that hadn't been there before.

A depth that was only caused by living through pain. *Real* pain.

He knew that look, had seen it often enough when he served in Afghanistan with other men who had known heavy loss. A pain that would never be fully erased.

Liam couldn't even reconcile seeing a look like that on Vanessa. It just wasn't possible. He had known her since she was fifteen years old. Knew firsthand how selfish and self-centered she was.

So he had to be wrong about whatever he thought he saw in her eyes now.

"That girl out there is what the hell is going on," she said.

Liam had been so deep in his own thoughts he had forgotten he'd even asked the question.

"Who is she?"

"Her name is Karine. That's all she's told me so far. I found her when I was walking the Sound yesterday evening." Her eyes shot away from his as she said the words. "She was unconscious on the ground, in only a T-shirt. A teenager."

"Runaway?"

Vanessa cracked open the door so she could check on the girl and then closed it again. "No. I think she was part of a human-trafficking ring, Liam. She's from Eastern Europe somewhere—Estonia, I think she said—and was being held on a boat. Says there are other girls. Seven of them."

Liam muttered a curse under his breath. Human trafficking had been a huge issue up and down the entire east coast for years. He wasn't surprised to hear something had popped up in the Outer Banks. The string of islands was an ideal place to bring in a boat unnoticed. Easy access and tourists year-round, so locals wouldn't pay particular attention to a boat they didn't recognize.

What Liam didn't understand was why Vanessa felt local law enforcement might already be aware or even a part of the situation.

"Explain more why you don't want to go to the local police. They would be best equipped to handle this, or at least begin the investigation. Have the most knowledge of the area."

Vanessa shrugged. "I'll admit I may be wrong about this. But I took Karine to the hospital yesterday evening so she could get checked out. She seemed to be keeping it together pretty well until she saw a sheriff's deputy at the nurses' station. She freaked out, Liam. Completely panicked." She touched his arm as she said it, then immediately dropped her hand again as if burned. "Sorry."

Liam had no idea what to say about her touch, so he just ignored it. "Did you press her about it?"

"Yes. It wasn't that particular officer she recognized, but she was convinced it was someone wearing that uniform."

The sheriff's uniform hadn't changed in the years that Liam was gone from the Outer Banks. It was still brown; still ugly. But it wasn't the only ugly brown uniform in the area—Liam hated to think they were suspicious of law enforcement when it could actually be a package delivery guy who was the perpetrator. A traumatized girl could easily be forgiven confusing two brown uniforms.

"There are a lot of brown uniforms out there," Liam said.

"I know. And I'm trying to keep that in mind. But she was *convinced.* And I thought it was better to be wrong and have to apologize than her be right and back in her captors' clutches." She shrugged. "So we snuck out of the hospital without anyone seeing us."

He couldn't disagree with that line of reasoning. Under similar circumstances he probably would have done the same.

"The clincher for me was when I woke up this morning and there was a 'fugitive alert' and the police were checking cars trying to leave Nags Head." She shook her head. "I tried to take Karine to Norfolk last night, but she refused to go. Says she has to stay and help the other girls."

"She sounds like quite a kid," Liam said. "Strong."

"Yeah, but she needs help. I can't keep her cooped up in this hotel room. She needs a doctor and a counselor."

"I was wondering about this place. Why are you here? If you were trying to pick a place no one would ever search for Princess Vanessa, you certainly found it."

Her eyes narrowed. *Princess Vanessa* obviously still struck a nerve.

Her voice was tight. "I couldn't take her back to my place. And, yeah, I didn't want anyone to find me."

Liam had never been afraid to poke the tiger. "Your dad would probably not be interested in a teenage misfit staying in the Epperson mansion."

She turned all the way from him then, in the guise of cracking the door to check on Karine again, but he could tell the topic didn't sit well with her.

"I don't live in my parents' house on Duck any longer, so I wouldn't take her there anyway. But, yes, I'm sure my dad wouldn't like it."

Duck, despite its corny name, consisted of mostly million-dollar mansions rather than the much less expensive vacation rentals, restaurants, and putt-putt golf places of the other islands in the Outer Banks.

Elitist in a word.

He shouldn't be surprised that she didn't live at home any longer. She was twenty-eight, for heaven's sake. No one would still live with their parents at that age if they had other options. Especially if Daddy paid for those other options, of which Liam had no doubt.

"So, where's your place?"

"In Kitty Hawk."

He raised an eyebrow. "On the beach?"

"No."

"On the Sound, then?" She had to live on the water. Vanessa Epperson had always lived on the water.

"Look, where I live is not important, okay? I just couldn't chance taking her to my place. Not if the police are after her and someone at the hospital reports she's with me."

He could agree that Vanessa's suspicions of the police were grounded, given Karine's fear of the uniform and the car-search tactics this morning. Until they knew for sure, they would keep all actions under wraps.

"Why don't I go in to the sheriff's office today and feel things out? I could tell them I'm here on vacation or something."

Her eyebrow rose. "You really think they're going to talk to you at all? You have a history with the Outer Banks police. They probably haven't forgotten that."

It was true. Liam had been a hell-raiser back in his juvie days. His grandmother had done the best she could with the wild child she'd been forced to raise after both his parents had died suddenly when he was ten. But even her loving yet strict hand hadn't been enough to keep him out of pretty regular trouble with the law when he was a teenager. Nothing too serious: some fights, occasional vandalism, a few nights of disturbing the peace after he'd been able to talk some poor tourist into buying him alcohol.

He was actually thankful for a lot of his misspent youth. During one of the times the sheriff's office had handcuffed him to a chair, he'd met Quint Davis, the DEA agent who had taken the time to look past Liam's rather gruff exterior and talk to the half boy, half man underneath.

Quint had gotten Liam to join the army and then picked him up as a DEA agent immediately after Liam's discharge, which had eventually led to his job at Omega. Liam owed the man his life.

But, yeah, anybody who had worked at the Outer Banks sheriff's office for more than ten years was going to remember him. He doubted they would even know he was law enforcement now, unless they ran a background check on him.

"Well, this time I'm not some kid they've arrested for stumbling drunk down the beach."

Their eyes locked. He had met Vanessa on just such an

occasion. She had stuck her snooty little nose up at him and told him to go find a bench and sleep it off.

He hadn't been able to help falling in love with her right then and there.

"I'll just be checking in as a professional courtesy, as a fellow law-enforcement officer," Liam continued, ignoring the shared memory between them. "When I heard about the escaped fugitive, I wanted to see if there was anything I could do to help."

Vanessa was nodding, about to respond, when they heard a cry from the bedroom.

"Miss Vanessa?" The voice was lost. Sorrowful. Frightened.

Vanessa ran to the young girl, but Liam kept his distance. He had no doubt she would not want to be near a man right now.

"I'm here, Karine. I was just in the bathroom."

Karine all but jumped into Vanessa's arms.

Vanessa sat on the bed and smoothed the girl's hair, holding her loosely so she wouldn't feel trapped.

"Who is that man?" Karine asked.

"He's my friend. His name is Liam. He's going to help us get you and the other girls to safety."

Karine reached over and turned on the lamp next to the bed. Liam just stood there as she watched him with eyes that had seen too much. Even if they got this girl to safety today, away from the horror she had lived through, she would never have a child's innocence again.

Her childhood had been finished from the moment someone had kidnapped her and thrown her on a boat.

Finally she nodded. "Okay," she said to Vanessa.

Liam guessed he'd passed the test.

They needed a plan. But first Liam knew that everyone needed food.

"I'll go grab some breakfast from—"

His words were interrupted by a pounding on the door. "This is the Outer Banks Sheriff's Department. Open the door."

Chapter Four

Vanessa stood. The sheriff's department had found her? How? She hadn't used a credit card.

This was the problem with living in a relatively small town. There were no secrets. One call from the police to the front desk in a systematic search and the clerk would undoubtedly have remembered her and told them. It was pretty odd for Vanessa to be at a hotel of this caliber, since most people knew her face and reputation—the Outer Banks princess—but didn't really know anything about her. They assumed she still lived off her parents' money, just as Liam had assumed in the bathroom.

She didn't. She hadn't for more than eight years.

It really didn't matter how the officer had found her. She had to figure out what to do.

They couldn't get out the one window of the room; it was right next to the door. There was no window in the bathroom, either.

The pounding on the door came again. Not obnoxiously loud, but firm enough to know whoever was on the other side meant business. "I need to speak with Vanessa Epperson."

Tears were running down Karine's face but she made no sound. Vanessa glanced frantically around the room before her gaze settled on Liam.

Who was taking his shirt off?

"Get her into the bathroom, then come back out here." He looked at Karine. "Stay very quiet in there. We'll take care of this."

The young girl nodded and ran to the bathroom. As soon as she turned away, Liam kicked off his shoes and socks and started unbuttoning his jeans, before pulling them, and his underwear, all the way off.

Liam was naked.

Vanessa pulled the bathroom door closed behind her and tried not to stare but could not help herself.

Liam was *naked*.

He ruffled his own hair so it stood on end, then turned and walked to the door, opening it a few inches.

"Man, what is going on? Do you know what time it is?" Liam looked down at an arm that didn't have a watch on it. "Neither do I. But it's like the butt crack of dawn."

"Um, excuse me, sir."

Vanessa couldn't see the officer but could hear the discomfiture in his voice.

"We were told that Vanessa Epperson was staying in this room."

"Well, she is, man." Liam yawned and ran a hand through his hair. "But she's a little worn out right now if you know what I mean."

Liam opened the door a little farther, his nakedness causing the man to step back rather than step closer to look inside.

"Um, could you put some clothes on, sir? I'd like to talk to Miss Epperson, please."

The officer wasn't going to be deterred, although Liam was doing his best. Vanessa wasn't sure if the officer could enter the room without a warrant, since it was a hotel, not a home, but she didn't want to find out.

She pulled off her pajamas—T-shirt and shorts—so she was also naked, grabbed the sheet off the bed and wrapped it around herself. She wasn't as bold as Liam and willing to answer the door buck-naked.

"Hey, baby." She walked up behind Liam and slid her arms around his chest, running them over his pecs and abs, feeling them tighten under her fingers. "What's going on?"

This is all just an act. This is all just an act. This is all just an act.

Liam put an arm around her and pulled her in front of him so the sheet was covering them both from the officer outside.

But her very naked back was pressed to his very naked front. *All* of his naked front. Vanessa couldn't stop the shiver that ran through her entire body when he reached down and kissed the tender skin joining her neck and shoulder.

This is all just an act.

"This officer of the law was looking for you," Liam said in that friendly mocking voice only he seemed to be able to pull off without offending people. "Have you been a naughty girl?"

Vanessa could tell the more intimate she and Liam pretended to be, the more uncomfortable the young officer became. She turned partway in Liam's arms so she was half facing him. "What if I have?"

He leaned down and kissed her, biting her lip with his teeth and pulling on it before letting it go. "Well, I'd have to do something about that, wouldn't I?" He nipped at her lip again. "First I'd have to—"

The officer cleared his throat in an embarrassingly loud manner, stopping whatever scene Liam was about to describe.

This is all just an act. This is all—

"Excuse me, sir…ma'am. I'm Officer Atwood. I just have a few questions. Then I'll let you get back to your… business."

Vanessa kept the sheet clutched at her chest, making sure

it didn't fall too low. But she could feel Liam's hands on her waist, rubbing tiny little circles with his fingers. Moving down to her hips and back up again. The feeling was delicious. She wanted to push his hands away but couldn't if she didn't want to give the officer of the law a peep show.

Liam pulled her back, flush against his body. Vanessa barely kept in the moan that wanted to escape her.

This was all just an act.

"Yes, Officer Atwood. What's your question?"

Evidently the act was working, because the poor officer standing in front of her didn't know where to look and barely seemed to know how to pose his question.

"Um, last night, did you have a teenage girl with you?"

Liam's fingers stopped their rubbing and gripped her hips tightly in warning. She knew she couldn't totally deny being with Karine. Obviously the sheriff's department already knew that, had probably been told that by Judy at the hospital. There wouldn't be any reason for her not to tell them.

"Yeah, that runaway kid? Bless her heart. She was not looking so good. I picked her up off Highway 158. We went by 7-Eleven to get some food—I don't trust runaways with cash, it's often used to immediately buy drugs—and then I took her to the hospital, since it looked like she might have some injuries or something."

Liam's fingers resumed their circles.

"Did she tell you her name, where she was from?"

Vanessa shook her head. "Katy or something, I think? She didn't really talk much at all. I think she might have been on something. Why? Did she do something bad after I left her at the hospital?"

"You just left a minor at the hospital? Don't you work in social services, Miss Epperson?"

Uh-oh. The officer was right. Vanessa would never have

left a teenager alone at the hospital. She felt Liam's fingers tighten again.

"Yeah, but I'm not a social worker around the clock." She smiled at the officer. "It was after eight. I had other plans that very definitely did not involve a teenage girl." Vanessa allowed herself to melt back into Liam. He pulled his hand up from her waist to tilt her head back against his shoulder so he could kiss her.

She was instantly thrown back into old times. The heat between them had always been almost palpable. They might have yelled at each other, fought and wanted to kill each other at times, but whenever they had been this close, an undeniable passion had flared between them.

Vanessa couldn't help herself; she twisted, trying to get closer to him.

Until she heard the officer clear his throat once more.

Damn it. *This is all just an act.* Remember that.

Liam brought his lips up from hers. "*I* was her other plans," he said to the officer, winking, deliberately downplaying his intelligence. Anything to keep the other man's guard down.

It worked. Atwood rolled his eyes. "Yeah, I got that. Thanks." He looked at Vanessa. "So you left the girl at the hospital?"

"I checked her in with one of the nurses, asked her to call social services—you know, someone who was actually on the clock—and pretty much left. Because, like I said…other plans."

"And you didn't have her with you for the rest of the night?"

One of Liam's arms came to rest across her chest, hooking around the top of her opposite shoulder, pulling her farther back against him. "Officer, if we had a kid in the room with us while doing some of the stuff we did last night, you would have to arrest us right now." He winked again.

"Hey!" Vanessa feigned outrage and elbowed him in the stomach. Or rock-hard abs.

"Sorry, baby," he whispered, "but you know it's true."

"Is the girl in some sort of trouble?" she asked Atwood.

"She's a suspect in some burglaries of homes in the area, so we're trying to find her."

"Darn it. I was hoping she was just a runaway who could be reunited with her parents. Some kids get away from home and when faced with the reality of the streets realize that home wasn't such a bad place, after all."

Officer Atwood shook his head. "She's definitely wanted by the police."

"Okay, well, if for some reason I see her again, I'll be sure to let you know."

Liam was starting to play with her bare shoulder with his fingers as though he was getting impatient for the officer to be gone.

"Okay. Thank you for your time. Sorry to have interrupted your…rest."

"No problem, man. I think we might go back inside and play out our own version of good cop, bad cop."

Vanessa giggled as Liam dragged her inside and shut the door.

"Do you think he bought—"

Her words were cut off by his mouth swooping down and devouring hers.

This time it was not just an act.

Vanessa gave herself over to the kiss, to the heat. As always, she didn't have any choice. It consumed her. The thin bed sheet was the only thing between them as he lifted her and pressed her against the door they'd just closed.

She couldn't hold back the moan. She didn't even try. She wrapped her fingers in his brown hair, still as silky and thick as she'd remembered it, and pulled him closer.

It was as if all the years they'd been apart melted away; all the pain they'd caused each other never happened.

Except it had. Both seemed to remember that at the same time.

And that they had a very scared teenager in the bathroom.

Liam eased back and Vanessa slid down the door until her feet were on the floor. She unwound her hand from his hair and grabbed the sheet that covered her again, since it was in danger of falling now that they were no longer pressed together.

"You okay?" he asked.

Was she okay? No, not by any stretch of the imagination was she okay. "Yeah, I'm fine."

He nodded then turned away to start dressing. She kept her back to him and did the same, in her clothes this time rather than her pajamas.

"I'm going to check on Karine," she said without looking at him. Vanessa wasn't sure she was ever going to be able to look at Liam again.

That was too bad, considering he was still just as ridiculously gorgeous as he had been eight years ago. Brown hair and green eyes. She had always been so damn jealous of those clear green eyes of his.

She tapped on the bathroom door and opened it a crack.

"Karine? It's safe now, honey."

She didn't hear anything so she opened the door farther. "Karine?"

She wasn't in the bathtub or behind the door. There was no window in the room for her to have climbed out.

"Miss Vanessa?" The sound came from the cabinet that ran under the length of the sink vanity.

Vanessa crouched and opened the cabinet. Oh, God, the girl had crammed herself in there to hide. It couldn't have been comfortable.

"Come on out, honey. It's safe now." She helped Karine unfold herself from her small hiding space.

"I want to make sure nobody find me."

"You did great, Karine." Vanessa wrapped her arms around her and pulled the girl close. Even though she was so young, she was almost the same height as Vanessa. "It was the perfect hiding spot, but you're safe now."

"I was scared."

"I don't blame you."

Liam turned from where he stood at the window. "Ladies, we can't stay here."

"Do you think that officer will come back?" Vanessa asked.

"Not him. I think we traumatized him enough. But once he reports that he found you, Vanessa, but did not actually search the room, somebody else—higher up who won't be scared by a couple of naked people—will be coming back here. We need to get out now."

Vanessa took her arm from around Karine. "I'll go get your clothes so you can change, okay?"

She grabbed the same clothes from yesterday—yoga pants that were too large and another T-shirt—and walked them to Karine. She left the bathroom and closed the door behind her.

Liam was standing a few feet away directly in front of her. He folded his arms over his chest and she couldn't help noticing the bulge of his biceps. Liam had always been in good shape, even when they'd known each other before.

Now he was rock solid. Everywhere. This morning's theatrical performance had proved that.

It was totally unfair that he looked just as good in clothes as he did without them. And that she was still so *affected* by him.

"I think you owe me an explanation." The intensity of his voice caused parts of her deep inside to flutter.

"About what? I told you pretty much everything I know about Karine."

"Not about Karine. About you. What the hell is going on with *you*?"

Vanessa shrugged, confused. "I don't know what you mean."

"Well, let's start with the two words I never thought I'd hear used to describe you. *Social worker*."

Chapter Five

Liam felt as if he were having an out-of-body experience.

To get rid of that young Deputy Atwood, he'd had to think fast. Sordid affair was the first thing that had come to his mind when he looked at this place, so he'd decided to play that angle.

He definitely hadn't expected Vanessa to jump in and help with the ruse when the officer wasn't buying it despite Liam's best efforts to make him so uncomfortable that he just went away. And her actions had made the difference.

Of course, the officer couldn't just barge in without a warrant—a hotel was considered a temporary home in the eyes of the law and most of the same rules applied—but if they refused him entry with no grounds whatsoever, Atwood would've been suspicious. He would've called it in and then the sheriff's department would've just waited them out. Sooner or later they'd have to leave and the hotel room only had one entrance and exit.

Sitting ducks.

So Vanessa's help in fooling the officer had just bought them some desperately needed time. Not much, but enough.

Vanessa's naked body pressed up against his naked body? That searing kiss that threatened to turn his bones to ash?

Yeah, out-of-body experience.

All of that was nothing compared to hearing the words

social worker used to describe Vanessa Epperson's profession. There was no way the spoiled, selfish, but full-of-life woman he'd known eight years ago had become a social worker. Someone who took care of other people.

But he couldn't deny the tenderness she'd showed as she'd cared for Karine since he'd arrived. It was hard to reconcile the Vanessa gently holding a traumatized teenager with the Vanessa he'd known before.

There were pieces of the puzzle—many of them, it seemed—that he was missing. Some were obvious now that he was looking for them.

For example, what were these clothes she was wearing? A pair of non-designer, off-the-rack jeans and a simple green cotton T-shirt. Liam could very clearly remember her teaching him about silk, cashmere and Pashmina—by wrapping her naked body in each and making him guess—scoffing that cotton shirts for women were only as a last resort.

Evidently, this situation was a last resort, then.

Her tennis shoes were no-name brand, also. He was pretty sure you could pick them up at the local supercenter.

Vanessa Epperson at the local supercenter?

Out-of-body experience.

She was looking at him now as if she didn't know quite where to start. And it didn't matter anyway, because they had to get out of there.

"You know what?" He cut her off as she began to speak just as Karine opened the bathroom door. "Save it. We've got to move."

He took a step closer. "But I will be told exactly what is going on."

Vanessa nodded.

Liam winked and smiled at Karine, not wanting her to think any tension between him and Vanessa should worry her. She smiled back at him, albeit timidly.

"I'm going to go drive around for about five minutes, see if we have anybody watching the room."

He pulled his cell phone out of his pocket and texted Vanessa so she would have his number.

"That's me." He nodded in the direction of her phone when it chirped. "You two be ready to go in case I have to come get you in a hurry."

He hoped it wouldn't come to that. Nags Head—really none of the Outer Banks islands—wasn't big enough for them to escape in a high-speed chase with the police. Their best bet was to get out now while they could.

"Is your car hidden somewhere?" he asked Vanessa.

"No." She shook her head. "I didn't think I needed to. I didn't think they would be looking for me so fast."

"That car right out front is yours?" Liam couldn't keep the shock from his voice.

She nodded, eyebrow raised, as if daring him to say something further.

At sixteen she'd had a BMW. And now she was driving an early 2000s–model Camry? Not that there was anything wrong with a Camry: safe, dependable, known to last. If she'd had the latest model, he would've considered it a wise, mature choice.

But a model that was at least a dozen years old?

The out-of-body experiences just kept on coming.

"Okay, well, just be ready in case you need to drive it. Don't open the door or peek through the window until you hear from me in case someone is watching the room."

"Be careful," Vanessa said. Karine had come to stand right beside her and she slipped an arm around the girl.

"I will. Be ready."

Liam walked out the door, whistling and tossing his keys. If anyone was watching the room, he wanted it to look as if he was in no hurry, that he was just a happy, sated guy going to grab some coffee.

As he got to his car, which he'd parked toward the front of the lot away from Vanessa's, he missed the keys he was tossing on purpose so they fell to the ground. As he crouched to get them, he stayed down to fake tying his shoe, taking survey of the parking lot as he did so.

There were two other cars in the lot and both had been there before Liam arrived. One was near the front desk, probably the clerk's. The other was a few spots down from Vanessa's Camry, not an optimal place for surveillance, but not terrible.

Liam honestly didn't think they were watching the hotel yet. No doubt they would be soon after the officer made his report. Liam was willing to bet the young officer probably didn't know the importance of what he had been tasked to do. He thought he was looking for someone who had last been seen with a teenage, petty burglar. He probably felt he'd drawn the short straw this morning and wouldn't be in any hurry to report questioning a naked guy that hadn't resulted in anything useful.

They needed to use that situation to their advantage.

Liam drove slowly out of the parking lot. There were no cars around the streets with anyone sitting in them in stakeout fashion. Nor any vans that could be used for surveillance.

The hotel was clean.

He'd drive around for a few minutes just to make sure. See if anyone followed him. He also needed to figure out a larger game plan now that he was also convinced someone at the sheriff's office was in on the trafficking ring. Too much time was being placed on finding Karine for him to think otherwise.

He needed to find a safe place to stash both Karine and Vanessa. Nothing that was connected to Vanessa in any way. He knew just the place but he didn't know if Vanessa would like it.

Too bad.

After driving around the block twice, and turning around and driving a different block in another direction, Liam was sure no one was following him. He stopped at a doughnut shop for coffee and doughnuts, as one last precaution, and because they needed food anyway.

And Vanessa could not survive without coffee.

The thought popped into his head unbidden. But to be honest, Liam wasn't sure if that was true anymore. He had no idea what was true about Vanessa. He got her coffee anyway.

Right before he left the shop, he texted her to let him know he was coming. ETA five minutes. Watch for me through the peephole and get out fast. Keep K's head covered.

This was it. Either the hotel was under surveillance or it wasn't. Regardless, now was when they were going to make their move.

Liam drove back to the hotel as if he wasn't in any particular hurry. Still no sign of any tail. The moment he pulled up to the hotel, the door to the room opened and Vanessa flew out, her arm around Karine, her jacket draped over the girl's head. She opened the back door to his SUV and they both piled into the backseat.

Liam was pulling out of the parking spot before Vanessa's door even closed.

This time he did not drive leisurely. He didn't drive fast enough to attract attention to them, but he got out of there with purpose.

The problem when trying to lose a tail in the Outer Banks was the lack of main roads. Highway 158 was the main four-lane drag, and that was about it. There was also Highway 12 that ran parallel to 158, but it was a two-lane and much slower. All Liam could do was take the back roads and cut-throughs that he remembered from his youth.

This wasn't his first time trying to get away from the Outer Banks police without calling attention to himself.

Vanessa and Karine kept crouched in the backseat so it would look as if Liam was driving alone. If they did happen to pass anyone studying the drivers of vehicles, they wouldn't be looking for him.

"Do you think anyone is following us?" Vanessa asked after a few minutes.

"No, I think we got out in time." If someone was following them, he'd know it by now. The winding route he'd taken over the past mile would've made it obvious.

"What about my car?"

"I think it's better to leave it there. Maybe it will buy us a few hours' time if they think we're still in the room. This car wasn't parked near you, so hopefully Officer Atwood didn't notice."

"Okay. What are we going to do? I'm sure they're still searching cars, right? We can't make it off the islands."

"No leave, Miss Vanessa," Karine said. "Must help other girls. *Must.*"

The girl didn't know a lot of English, but she knew what she wanted.

"It's okay, Karine." He glanced back at them in the rear-view mirror. "We're not leaving. We want to help them, too."

"Can you call your DEA contacts in, Liam?" Vanessa asked. "Or the FBI or whoever handles cases like this? Obviously we don't know who we can trust with the local police."

"I'm not actually with the DEA anymore. Haven't been for the past five years."

"But I left a message for you with the DEA. How did you get it if you don't work there?"

He glanced at her again. Confusion was evident on her face.

"I now work for an interagency task force called Omega Sector, in their Critical Response Division. I'm head of the hostage rescue team."

He watched as her eyes widened and her mouth fell open before turning his gaze back to the road.

"Sounds like you're pretty qualified to handle what's going on here, then. You have people you can call in? People with big guns who can shoot the bastards responsible for this?"

Liam rolled his eyes. "Generally we arrest the bad guys unless they shoot at us first, but, yes, I can get a whole team here."

"Then why haven't you done that yet? Those girls are somewhere out there, trapped. Hurt and desperate."

He glanced in the mirror again and saw Karine's face growing paler. He caught Vanessa's eye and gestured with his head toward Karine. Vanessa looked down at the girl and immediately slipped an arm around her.

"I'm sorry, sweetie. I shouldn't have said that."

"It's okay," Karine whispered. "They need help."

"And we will help them. We'll get Liam's friends here—people who help others all the time—and we'll get the other girls out."

Liam caught Vanessa's eye in the rearview mirror again. "We'll talk specifics later."

She nodded, tugging Karine closer.

"Where are we going right now?" Vanessa asked.

"We've got to get off the streets. Once they figure out we're not in the hotel, they'll start searching again. I'm going to take you somewhere not related to you at all."

"Another hotel?"

"No, that will always leave witnesses. A house."

She shook her head. "A friend's? Are you positive you can trust the person?"

"No. My grandmother's house. I still own it."

That silenced her.

He had a cleaning service come in once a month to clean, keep it in shape and take care of any repairs. He even paid for power and water each month, which wasn't much because it was so small.

After his grandmother died, he hadn't been able to sell it. He had said it was because she'd been his last living relative—the only roots he'd ever had—and he didn't want to part with it if he didn't have to. But he couldn't deny the other part of that truth now.

He'd kept the house because it was the first place he and Vanessa had made love.

Chapter Six

An hour later they were safely tucked away in Liam's grandmother's house. His house now.

They had stopped briefly at a grocery store, Vanessa and Karine tucked low in the backseat as Liam ran in. They had agreed it was better to go to the store now to get what they needed so they were prepared for as long as possible.

In the house of a million memories.

But Vanessa would accept living with the memories, as painful as some were, if it meant they were safe. If it meant Karine could get some real food and the real rest that she needed. If it meant they could figure out where the other girls were being held and do something about it.

She still didn't understand why Liam hadn't just called in the SWAT cavalry or whatever. But he had been right; they didn't need to talk about those details in front of Karine.

Liam had come back to the SUV in less than fifteen minutes. He hadn't said anything as he opened the hatchback and put the grocery bags inside. Hadn't hurried around to the driver's side. Hadn't done anything that would call attention to himself.

He was good, Vanessa could definitely see that.

He hadn't talked until he was pulling out of the parking lot.

"You girls okay?" he asked.

"Yes. Any problems?"

"Nope. Got food and even a couple T-shirts and sweatpants. I had to get four different sizes, so I explained it was for my family while we're visiting."

"Because you buying a size extra-small pants and shirt might have been memorable."

"Exactly. All the cloak-and-dagger was probably unnecessary, but always better to be safe."

He *was* good. He'd thought of details Vanessa probably would've missed.

The drive to his grandmother's house—*his* house—took about twenty minutes. They had gone to a grocery store on the opposite side of Nags Head just in case someone remembered seeing him or his car.

But now they were inside, car pulled behind the back, Karine well fed and sleeping in one of the bedrooms.

"She still needs medical and psychological help. Professional help," Vanessa said. It was probably too late for any sort of assault kit to yield any results, but everything should still be documented.

"Yeah, those bruises on her wrists are pretty bad. And I hate to say this, but I'm sure she was assaulted, right?"

Vanessa rubbed a hand over her eyes. "She won't talk about any specifics, but, yes, I would say most definitely."

Liam reached out and pulled her down next to him on the seat at the table.

"She's a survivor," he said. "She's strong."

"I know. I just can't bear to think about what she's been through."

"We'll get her a counselor and a doctor. We just have to figure out who we can trust."

She nodded. "Why haven't you called in some sort of attack team yet?"

"Because if we send in a blitz attack on the sheriff's office, not knowing who exactly is involved and to what degree, the first thing the kidnappers will do is kill the remaining girls. They're liabilities."

Nausea pooled in Vanessa's stomach. "I hadn't thought of that. But you're right."

She rested her face in her hands.

"That doesn't mean we're not going to stop them, Nessa. It just means we're not going to roll in guns blazing."

He'd called her Nessa. He was the only one who ever had, ever dared. She hadn't heard that name in eight years.

"Not to mention," he continued, "it's the word of one small foreign girl, supposedly wanted by the law, against the word of people who may have lived in this area their whole lives."

"But I know she's telling the truth," Vanessa said. She had no doubt about it at all.

Liam nodded. "I believe her, too, but it's about what we can prove when it comes down to a court of law."

"I just can't stand the thought of more girls trapped and scared." Karine had told them that the youngest of the girls was only eight years old. Fortunately she was being "kept" for someone special—some sick buyer, no doubt—so she hadn't been assaulted. The older girls hadn't been so lucky.

Liam reached over and grasped her hand. "I know. I feel the same. But it's important that we keep whoever is behind this in the dark as long as possible. That is our best chance at saving those girls. By convincing law enforcement that you don't really know anything about Karine and that you certainly don't know where she is now."

Vanessa nodded. He was right.

"Okay, then I need to call my office, let them know I won't be coming in. If I just don't show up, everyone there will be worried."

Vanessa stood and called her supervisor at Bridgespan. It wasn't a long conversation. Vanessa told her she was sick but that she would hopefully be in tomorrow. Her boss understood and told her to take care of herself.

"That seemed pretty painless," Liam said after she finished. He was sitting back in his chair, long legs stretched out in front of him, arms crossed over his chest.

He looked relaxed, lazy even, in that way Liam could pull off so well. But Vanessa had no delusions. He intended to have answers from her about the changes in her lifestyle.

She didn't want to fight with him. Didn't want to go back to eight years ago in some epic battle of "who was right and who was wrong when we were young and stupid." But she could at least give him the basics.

"You want answers."

"I would just like to know what is going on. I find I do better in any tactical situation when I know all the information."

Was that what she was? What they were? A *tactical situation*?

"There's not a whole lot to the story. I grew up. Decided I couldn't live on my parents' money forever."

"And became a social worker. Like with a degree and everything?"

She could tell he tried very hard to keep any trace of incredulity out of his voice, and almost succeeded.

It stung a little. But it was the most common sentiment among people who had known her then and knew her now. Why would Liam be different?

Vanessa ten years ago would never have been a social worker. An interior decorator? Maybe. Buyer for some fashion line or upscale boutique? Perhaps. Professional country club attendee and beach bunny? Absolutely.

Helping other people for barely over minimum wage? No.

But she wasn't that person anymore. Thank God, she

wasn't that person anymore. Although the change had come at a high price.

"After you left…after…" She trailed off. She didn't want to talk about that. About him leaving or what had happened afterward. "I decided to go to college. I didn't want to just sit around here anymore. I really enjoyed my basic psychology and sociology classes, and so followed that route. Ended up with a degree in social services." In less than three years, she might add.

"Wow." He shook his head. "I just never would've figured—"

"That I would ever be anything but a selfish, spoiled brat who didn't have it in her to care about another person?"

Silence fell between them. That was the quote, almost word for word, that he'd told his friends about her when he left. After he'd asked her to come away with him and get married and she'd said yes but then hadn't.

For reasons he didn't understand. And, once she'd found out what he'd really thought about her, for reasons she'd had no plans to ever tell him.

"You made a promise and then broke it." Liam rubbed a hand over his face. "I was angry. Hurt. Plus, it was the truth." He sat straighter in his chair. "How did you find out I said that?"

"I went looking for you. Your friends were happy to relay the message." They'd never liked her. Had always thought she was a snob.

"When did you come looking for me?"

"Maybe a week after you left?"

"Why then?"

Because it was the first time she had been able to. But again, not telling him that. "I wanted to see if there was any chance you were still around."

That mocking smile, so fake and handsome—the one that had always gotten under her skin—covered his face now. "Why? Didn't think I'd actually leave? Even though you didn't even have enough guts to explain to me yourself that you were no longer interested in marrying me? I had to find out by knocking on your door and your father telling me?" He stood from the table and walked over to the sink, farther from her. "Nope. I left and never looked back."

This was the fight she'd been trying to avoid. It was a situation too many years past, water having long since washed under the bridge. Pride and stubbornness and tragedy conspiring together to keep them apart.

Vanessa turned and walked over to the window. This place was so bittersweet for her. Every time Liam's grandmother had gone off to the grocery store or her bridge club or, heaven forbid, a weekend trip up to Norfolk to see her cousin, Vanessa and Liam immediately jumped into his big bed. They'd never been able to get enough of each other. She was surprised they hadn't burned down the whole house with the passion between them.

Yeah, she'd been selfish and spoiled, but she'd loved Liam Goetz with every fiber of her being. Hearing that he'd said how selfish and undesirable she was—combined with everything else she'd gone through at that time—had cut her to the quick. Him walking away and never looking back? That had just proved to her that he hadn't loved her in the same way she had loved him.

It had caused her to do something she hadn't done in the entirety of her selfish, spoiled life.

Give up.

She should've fought for him. For them. But hadn't had the strength at the time.

So after she'd healed, she'd gone to college, waiting tables to pay for classes. She hadn't wanted a dime of her parents' money. She'd gotten a degree in helping other people. It didn't take much of a psychologist to figure out that Liam's words had influenced her career choice.

She'd survived. Found an inner strength she hadn't known existed. Left selfish and spoiled behind her.

Liam had walked away and never looked back.

"I hope you've been happy, Liam," she whispered from the window. "I never wished you ill."

She wasn't sure the same was true in what he wished for her.

Chapter Seven

She'd come after him?

A week later. But still... If he had known she had come looking for him, would it have made a difference? It was too late to ever know the answer to that now. Nearly a decade stood between them.

Vanessa looked so tiny standing over there by the window. He wanted to go and wrap his arms around her.

Not for the young woman he'd known then, but the woman she'd turned into now. Caring, passionate, using her strength for things that mattered.

No, he hadn't wished her any ill over the years. He'd been mad. Had sometimes thought about the few choice words he'd say to her if they ever happened to run into each other. But he'd never wished anything bad would happen to her.

He still felt as though he was missing part of the story. Something had happened between her and her parents, but evidently she didn't want to talk about it.

And maybe he should just leave it alone. He'd come here to lay the ghost of his past to rest. The hows and whys and should'ves and could'ves couldn't be changed and didn't matter.

But that kiss earlier. *That* he couldn't get out of his mind. His body started to respond just thinking about it. It was time to change the subject, move it away from the past and back to solving the case and saving those girls.

"I never wished you ill, either, Vanessa. Not ever."

She turned a little from the window and smiled slightly, nodding.

"How about if I don't ask any more questions and we concentrate on finding the other girls?"

She walked toward him. "Yes, I think that's a good idea."

"I need to contact Omega," he told her. "Unless you have someone else in mind, someone you know can be trusted, we should probably bring an outside doctor in to talk to Karine."

She nodded. "That's probably better. I do have lots of contacts at the hospital. I'm there quite a bit with my work. But all of them would probably believe the police over something a teenager says."

"Okay. I'll get rolling on that. Omega has contacts all over the country, not just in Colorado Springs where headquarters is located. They should have someone here in a few hours."

"Good."

"Also, tell me where you found Karine. I can look at tide patterns, which will give us at least a general direction and possible distance she came from. We need to ask her how long she thinks she was swimming."

He walked over to a long drawer attached to a buffet in the dining room and pulled out large tidal maps of the area. Almost everyone who lived here year-round had a set. They were needed for just about any fishing or water-sport activity.

He rolled out the one for their area. "Where did you find Karine?"

Vanessa stared at the map for longer than Liam expected. Was she confused? She'd always been so good with maps.

"We're here," he said, pointing to a spot on the map

where his grandmother's house would be, not far from the Sound.

Then he noticed the blush that had stolen over her entire face.

"What?" he asked.

"Nothing." But her face was burning. "I was here when I found Karine." She pointed to a place on the map.

Oh.

Liam knew exactly where that was. Undoubtedly, by her flush, Vanessa knew exactly where that was, too.

A very secluded section of the Roanoke Sound where rarely anyone went. Its difficulty to access and mediocre views and beach made it not worth the effort by most. Sand dunes blocked it from the rest of the Sound.

It was their special place. The place where they'd gone when they'd wanted to get away from everything and everyone else.

They had made love there dozens of times. He could still remember the feel of the sun, of the sand, of the sweetness of Vanessa's body as if it had happened five minutes ago.

It was where Liam had asked her to marry him.

He didn't question why she'd been walking there yesterday and she didn't offer the information. Whatever reason she had been, he was glad; otherwise Karine might've been in a lot more trouble right now.

"Okay." He nodded. "You found her here at about 6:30 p.m., right?" He looked over at her for confirmation.

"Yes. Maybe a little closer to seven, but not much."

"We need to ask Karine how long she was swimming."

A soft voice answered from the doorway, "It felt like very long time."

Vanessa rushed over to the girl. "Hey, honey, how are you doing? Done sleeping?"

Karine looked down, embarrassed. "I am hungry again."

"That's fine. Let's get you some more food." She put

her arm around the girl and led her to the kitchen. Liam followed them.

"How long do you think you swam, Karine? Do you have any idea how much time?" he asked as Vanessa began to make them all a sandwich.

"I do not know exact time," Karine said softly. "I swam until I could not move my arms anymore. Then I just used my legs. I was very cold."

Hours, then. But then again, Karine was not very big and hadn't had decent calorie intake in days or maybe weeks. So she might have become exhausted after just a few minutes.

Karine sat at the table and pulled her legs up to her chest, wrapping her arms around them. She was wearing the Outer Banks sweatshirt and sweatpants he'd bought at the grocery store. She rested her head on her knees and looked out across the room.

"We all were in same room that was in bottom of ship. Every morning and every evening, one of the three mans come. They bring food and water. Let us use bathroom and walk around. Sometimes choose a girl and drag her out." She wrapped her arms more tightly around her knees. "He said they would enjoy us for the week we were there."

Liam caught sight of Vanessa behind Karine. She had stopped what she was doing, listening, tears rolling down her cheeks. He didn't blame her. Anger burned like acid in his gut for what Karine had gone through, what the others were still going through.

"Karine, how many days had you been on the boat? Do you know?"

"That boat? *Divi*." She held up two fingers. "Two days. Before that, we were on other big ship for many, many days."

Karine's only having been on the little boat here in the Roanoke Sound for two days was good news. If the men planned to keep them for a week before selling the girls to whatever buyers they had lined up, that meant they still had five more days before the girls were forever out of their reach.

Unless the men decided to cut their losses and just kill the girls outright since Karine escaped. Liam prayed they would be too greedy to do that. Especially until they knew for sure someone was on to them.

"When man left yesterday morning, he did not close my…" She put her finger and thumb around her wrists in demonstration. "How you say?"

"Handcuff," Vanessa and Liam said in unison.

"Yes. He did not close my handcuff. I waited until he was gone, then showed the other girls. They agreed I should try to get help. They gave me all the day's food to eat." Now Karine began to cry. "I broke the door and got out."

"Could you see the land from the boat?" Since the boat was in the Sound, she could've been anywhere from half a mile—Liam didn't think the perps would dare keep a boat with kidnapped girls closer than half a mile in—to about four miles at the widest part of the Sound if the boat was being kept in the very center.

Honestly, Liam didn't think Karine would've made it that far. She would've drowned.

"Yes." Karine nodded. "I could see some land far away and some land closer. I swam toward the close one."

"Of course you did." Vanessa put a sandwich on the table in front of her. "Smart."

"Where was the sun when you got in the water? Straight overhead? Were you swimming toward it?"

Karine took a bite of her sandwich and thought as she chewed. "At first sun was straight, but then behind me." She shrugged.

"Good, that's good," Liam said. That meant she had been swimming east in the mid to late afternoon.

"Once I was on land I was too tired to walk. I slept for

long time before I got up. Walked little more then lay down again. Miss Vanessa find me."

She would've been swimming with the tide, thank God. That undoubtedly was a factor in Karine's making it to shore. Based on his knowledge of the area and the map, Liam could make an educated guess that the boat was in a certain two-mile radius on the Roanoke Sound. He took a pencil, wrote an X where Vanessa had found Karine and a circle where he thought it most likely the boat had been moored.

Unfortunately, there would probably be hundreds of boats in that same two-mile radius. Not to mention, the perps had probably already moved the boat. That was the main reason boats were so often used for human trafficking. Because they could be easily moved.

Vanessa put a plate with a sandwich next to him on the table. She looked over his shoulder at the map nodding.

"Now what do we do?" she asked.

"Now I make that call I was talking about earlier, getting the professional help needed."

"Good." Vanessa nodded, touching Karine gently on the shoulder. "That shouldn't wait."

"Then, if you think it's okay—" he turned to Karine to include her in the conversation, too "—and if it's all right with you, Karine, I think we should take a boat out to this area on the map—" he pointed with his finger "—to see if we can find anything."

"Do you think it's likely?" Vanessa asked.

"Honestly, no. But I do know that the longer we wait, the more endangered those girls become. They are bound to move the boat soon if they haven't already."

"Yes." Karine was already standing. "Yes, Miss Vanessa. Please, let's look. We must try."

Liam could see Vanessa was torn. It was dangerous, he

knew. Any number of people would be looking for both her and Karine.

"Is it worth the risk?" Vanessa asked softly. "I just can't stand the thought of anything happening to Karine."

Honestly, it probably wasn't worth the risk. The chances of them finding the girls were slim. But they were better than their chances of finding them from here in the house.

"I'm not going to let anything happen to you two. You can bet on that."

Chapter Eight

The search for the girls all that afternoon and the next day proved fruitless. Liam had rented a boat and taken them all around the area they'd determined on the map as the most likely place Karine had been held. But they hadn't found anything useful. Most likely the boat had already been moved. Vanessa's frustration mounted.

Liam was infinitely patient when working with Karine. He showed her different boat sizes so she could have a reference to better describe the one she'd been held in. He pointed out landmarks she might have seen in the distance while swimming that might have been familiar. He never got frustrated with her no matter what she could or couldn't remember.

Even though his focus had been torn—looking for boats that could be holding the kidnapped girls and also for anyone who might be trying to find Vanessa and Karine—he was never short with Karine when she asked any questions or had any sort of language barrier that needed clarification. It was easy to see that Karine was becoming more comfortable with Liam.

Liam would make a great father.

Maybe he was already a father. The thought cut something deep inside Vanessa. Eight years was a long time. He could've been married before. Have a whole gaggle of kids.

"What? Are you okay?" Liam was looking at her. Reaching out one arm from where he was steering the boat. "Are you sick?"

"Have you ever been married? Do you have any kids?" The questions were out of her mouth before she could stop them.

He tilted his head to the side. "How do you know I'm not married now?"

"You never would've kissed me at the hotel if you were." Vanessa had never even questioned that. Liam would be true to the woman he married.

"No, never married. No kids." He grinned in that way that was so uniquely Liam and winked at her. "Although many of my colleagues would argue that *I* am a kid."

She couldn't help smiling back. "I don't doubt it."

He nodded and then turned his face back to watch the water in front of them, answering a question Karine had.

Although the search hadn't led to any positive results, the doctor Omega Sector had sent, Dr. Jennifer Giandomenico, both a medical doctor and psychiatrist, had been wonderful. She had been waiting when they'd returned from searching the Sound yesterday afternoon. She had examined Karine and documented all possible physical evidence in case it was needed later. Then she had talked with the girl for hours.

Vanessa wasn't sure exactly what the doctor had said to the girl, or what Karine had said to the doctor, but Karine had looked better, calmer, after their conversation.

Omega Sector had also sent profiler Andrea Gordon to help out in any way she was needed: profiling, surveillance, hanging out with Karine.

Vanessa had wanted to dislike the agent—the young, gorgeous, leggy blonde agent—on sight. Was this the type of colleague Liam worked with all the time at Omega?

But the woman had been nothing short of immaculately professional with both her and Liam. No flirting, no touches with him or anything that could be considered unprofessional. As a matter of fact, Vanessa would have thought Andrea was downright cold if it wasn't for how she treated Karine. Andrea might be all business with her and Liam, but with Karine she was friendly and kind. Something in Andrea identified with Karine, Vanessa could see.

Vanessa had to go back to work today. She had called in sick the past two days, but any more than that would really be suspicious. She'd be wearing the same jeans and blouse she'd worn three days ago—she'd washed them yesterday—since she didn't dare stop by her house to get new clothes. Fortunately the organization she worked for—a privately funded aid organization that helped families, women and children in need—encouraged casual dress. Many of the people Vanessa went out to see and help on a daily basis would not respond well to a suit.

"Remember, be as vague as possible when answering any questions your colleagues ask," Liam told her. "Cough a lot and tell them you're still not feeling one hundred percent. That will usually keep people away."

Liam was going to drop her about three blocks from the hotel where they'd left her car. She was going to drive to work from there.

"The police are still looking for their 'fugitive,' so don't freak out if you're pulled over," Liam told her. "Just let them search your car then move on. Don't ask questions."

"How long do you think they'll keep doing that?"

Liam shrugged. "It's a smart move on the perp's part, actually. Having a fugitive on the loose provides them with an opportunity to search cars—in the name of citizen safety—they'd otherwise need a warrant to search."

"I know a few cops. Why don't I use my contacts at work to see if I can find out who provided the information about said fugitive? That would give us our bad guy, right?"

Liam shrugged. "Maybe. Or maybe it would just be

someone who was following someone else's orders." He helped her slip on her button-down sweater. "Don't do anything that will draw attention to yourself or the trafficking ring. Our greatest asset right now is making them think that Karine made it to shore, you helped her and she ran without telling anyone anything. If they think we know about them, it might make them move up their timetable or do something drastic."

"Okay." Vanessa nodded. *Drastic* meant kill the girls. That was the last thing she wanted.

"Andrea is going to rent a house on the other side of the island in her name. If somebody recognizes me, this place won't be usable as a safe house any longer. Our past history is too well known."

She looked over to where Andrea and Karine were eating cereal and watching old sitcom reruns on television.

"Yeah, Karine seems pretty comfortable with her. I think that will be good." She watched as the two females looked at each other then laughed at something on the television. "How old is Andrea, anyway?"

Liam cocked his head to the side. "I'm not sure. I never thought about it. She pretty much keeps to herself all the time at work. I guess I assumed she was in her late twenties."

Vanessa doubted the woman was over twenty-two or twenty-three, although she didn't voice her opinion. Andrea tried hard—maybe a little too hard in Vanessa's opinion—to be professional. But underneath, Andrea seemed to be much more relaxed and carefree. Maybe she just felt she needed to keep up a front around her coworkers. Vanessa didn't care, because the woman seemed as drawn to Karine as Karine was to her. Kindred spirits.

"Okay, I'm ready," she said to Liam. "'Bye, girls," she called out to Andrea and Karine. They both waved but barely even looked at her. Vanessa rolled her eyes. At least she didn't have to worry about Karine being upset she was leaving.

Liam opened the door for her at his SUV. "After work, drive straight back to your house. Try to act as normal as possible. Text me and we'll work out a plan. Andrea is going to get Karine a phone today, too, so she can talk to you or text if she needs something."

That was good. Vanessa knew both Liam and Andrea were competent and cared about what happened to Karine. But Vanessa felt responsible for her. She wanted the girl to be able to easily get in touch with her if she needed something.

"Great. Thank you." Vanessa was nervous. Jittery.

When they were almost to where Liam was going to drop her off, he reached over and grabbed her hand. It was lying on the leg she couldn't quite keep from bouncing with nervous energy.

He looked over at her. "You're going to do fine. It's just another day at the office."

"I'm not a great liar. I've always just voiced my opinions about everything, usually not caring what other people thought." She shrugged and looked away. She was certain that was part of why he thought her so selfish and self-centered.

He squeezed her hand. "Honesty is a trait to be admired, so don't beat yourself up over it. Just don't volunteer information and try to sidestep any questions."

Easier said than done.

He stopped at the parking lot of a diner a few blocks from the hotel where her car was parked. He turned off the SUV and looked at her. "The key to a good lie is to keep it as close to the truth as you can. If anyone seems suspicious about how you're behaving, take them into your confidence."

She shot him a blank look, frowning.

He turned toward her and leaned a little closer. "Tell them, in truth, you weren't really sick but called in because your old flame showed up in town and the two of you were naked in a hotel room before you even knew what happened."

VANESSA WAS STILL thinking about Liam's outrageous statement two hours later when she sat at her desk pretending she was catching up on paperwork. Not only the statement but the kiss that had come afterward.

She was sure he'd probably meant it as a playful, go-get-'em, tiger-type kiss. Instead, within seconds they'd been all but crawling over each other. Continued proof there were some things time didn't change. The heat between the two of them was one of those things.

When they had finally broken apart, Vanessa had been halfway over the center console into his lap and both of them were breathing heavily. The windows were completely steamed up and Vanessa's blouse was half unbuttoned.

It had taken them five minutes before they could pull it together enough to even get out a coherent sentence. By then Vanessa had no idea what she would say to him, so she had straightened her shirt and bailed out the door, walking to her car without looking back at Liam.

But she'd felt his eyes on her. And known what his look meant. And everything in her body had tightened at the thought as she walked.

So yeah, making up something about how her old flame was in town and had gotten her completely discombobulated would not be any stretch of the truth at all.

Fortunately, nobody seemed to care. Everyone was busy with their own set of issues—there was always more than enough work to go around—and didn't even notice if Vanessa looked a little flush. Or if they did they just attributed it to whatever supposed sickness she'd had for the past two days.

Vanessa had multiple voice-mail messages on her phone. Some were from families she worked with, which she listened to and took notes on. Two were from Judy in the hospital.

"Hey, Vanessa, it's Judy. I just checked you and that teenage girl in a few minutes ago. Then the police showed up looking for her and you guys were gone. I just want to make sure you're okay. She didn't look like much of a threat, but you just never know with some of these kids today. Call me."

Another one from her the next day.

"Hi, Vanessa, it's Judy again. I talked to your boss and she said you'd called in sick. I just wanted to make sure you were really okay. The police came by here again this afternoon looking for you or that girl. Just want to talk to you for myself to make sure you're okay. Call me."

She'd better call her friend before Judy did something crazy such as go to the police herself with concerns about Vanessa's behavior. Vanessa liked Judy a lot, but the older woman did tend to be a bit paranoid.

Vanessa was just picking up her phone when it buzzed on her desk. She pressed the intercom button to talk to her boss.

"What's up, Maureen?"

"Vanessa, can you come out to the lobby? There are two officers here and they said you need to go with them to the sheriff's office for questioning."

Chapter Nine

Vanessa hung up with Maureen and immediately called Liam. He picked up on the first ring.

"What's wrong?"

"The police are here." She tried to keep the panic out of her voice but couldn't quite manage. "What do I do?"

"Damn it," Liam muttered. "They must have been watching your office. We knew this was a possibility. Just stick with the story of me and you as lovers. That will also be corroborated by Officer Atwood's statement from what he saw on Tuesday."

"Okay," she whispered, staying hidden behind her door so no one could see her from the clear windows opening out to the lobby. "But I thought we were trying not to let them know who you are."

"I'm sure it will be suspicious that an Omega agent just happened to show up the day after one of the victims escaped."

She could hear the tension in Liam's voice.

"But the perp might buy that you and I are just rekindling our relationship."

She gripped the cell tighter. "But he might not. Which would put the girls in danger."

The phone on her desk buzzed again.

"I've got to go," she whispered.

"See if you can keep my name out of it, but if you need to tell them it's me, that's okay, Nessa. All right?"

There was a loud knock on her office door. Evidently the officers were tired of waiting.

"I'll do my best. Bye."

She disconnected the call and slipped the phone into her purse. She didn't know if she'd be allowed to use it again or not once they took her to the station.

She opened the door. "Can I help you, gentlemen?"

"Vanessa Epperson, we need you to come with us to the sheriff's office."

"Guys, I've been out sick for two days." She glanced over their shoulders and saw that everyone in her entire office was watching the spectacle. "I've got a ton of paperwork and cases that need my attention. Does this need to be done right this second? Could you come back tomorrow?"

"No, ma'am," one of the officers, the shorter, chunkier one, said. "We've been instructed to bring you in right now."

"Am I under arrest? Are you going to put me in handcuffs?" Vanessa laughed lightly, but neither man even cracked a smile.

"Only if you refuse to come with us, ma'am."

"Fine." Vanessa walked over and made a show of straightening papers and organizing her desk. She knew she was stalling but didn't know why. There was no help coming.

She didn't want to be arrested. Didn't want to answer their questions. Didn't want to take a chance on letting Liam and Karine down by saying something wrong.

When the officers stepped closer to her, she gave up. She just put everything down and went with them. She didn't want to be arrested in front of her colleagues, but they were all staring at her as if she were already in handcuffs anyway, so she guessed it didn't matter.

"I'll be back later, Maureen," she said as she passed her boss, both officers flanking her. "Sorry for the ruckus."

As the men put her in the back of their police car, Vanessa vaguely wondered if anyone else would think it was overkill that the department had sent two large officers to bring her—half their size and weight—in. Probably not.

The drive was short to the sheriff's office. Vanessa expected to be fingerprinted or have her mug shot taken or something. She realized she really didn't have a good idea of what happened on this side of law enforcement.

Liam would. He'd been here often enough when he was younger, and he worked in law enforcement now. But Vanessa was determined not to bring up his name no matter what.

They brought her into an interrogation room—she'd seen enough television shows and movies to recognize the two-way mirror for what it was—sat her at a table that had four uncomfortable chairs, read her the Miranda rights and left.

Nobody came in and yelled at her. Nobody came in and threatened her with jail time. Nobody took her belongings or searched her person. As a matter of fact, they were nice enough to leave a bottle of water out on the table. So Vanessa waited.

And waited.

She had a signal on her cell phone, but she didn't want to make any calls or send any texts. She was sure this room was being watched, to see what she did, who she contacted.

Finally, more than an hour after she'd been placed in the room, someone came in. Handsome, young, maybe not even as old as Vanessa's twenty-eight years. But it was plain to see he was all-business, looking to make a name for himself.

She disliked him on sight.

"I'm Assistant Sheriff Tommy Webb," he said, sitting

across from her at the table. "You've been read your rights, correct, Miss Epperson?"

"Do I need a lawyer?" she asked.

The man cocked his head sideways and gave her a smile she was sure was meant to put her at ease.

Liam would've done it much better.

"I've found that criminals are the only ones who need lawyers, Miss Epperson. But, certainly, it is your right, if you'd like to call one."

It was probably better to try to get out of this without a lawyer. Not that she knew one to call, anyway. Her parents had one on retainer, but Vanessa wouldn't call him even if she knew the contact info.

"I don't need a lawyer."

"Good." Webb looked pleased with himself. "Let's just start with an easy question, like, where have you been for the past couple of days?"

That wasn't an easy question at all. It was probably one of the most difficult questions he could ask. Vanessa thought fast. Should she try to pretend she'd been sick? Or should she do as Liam had suggested and bring him into the equation?

Of course, she also wanted to keep his identity a secret so they didn't know an Omega Sector agent was sniffing around their backyard.

"You called in sick to work, Miss Epperson," Assistant Sheriff Webb said, probably trying to make her think they knew quite a bit about it. But she knew they didn't know the truth. "Why don't you start there?"

She would follow Liam's advice and go with the "hot lovers" story. That was pretty darn close to the truth anyway.

"Look, Officer Webb…"

"Assistant Sheriff Webb," he corrected.

Vanessa barely refrained from rolling her eyes. "Assistant Sheriff Webb." She leaned a little closer in her chair. "Is what we say here going to be reported back to my boss?"

"We're under no obligation to report what you say here to your boss."

Vanessa noticed he didn't actually say they *wouldn't* tell her boss, but she left it alone. "Okay, yeah, I called in sick, but I wasn't actually sick."

"You were with someone," Webb continued for her.

"I'm sure you don't want all the dirty little details, but it was a guy that I met last year and he came back into town. Things got pretty hot and heavy between us."

"Can you provide us with his name?"

Damn it. "Um, no."

Assistant Sheriff Webb's eyebrow rose. "Why not?"

"Let's just say he, um, wasn't supposed to be with me. And that he has a definite aversion to anything having to do with the police."

Webb wrote down a bunch of notes. Probably that Liam was a criminal or married or something. Good. The more shady they thought him, the better.

"We'll come back to that," he said. "You were with him for the whole two days?"

"Yep." Vanessa smiled dreamily, which wasn't too difficult when she thought about her kiss with Liam this morning. "That Officer Atwood guy who came to the hotel Tuesday morning saw us."

"Yes, but that was early Tuesday. Did you stay at that hotel until this morning?" Webb didn't look up from his notes as he asked the question.

Because they knew she hadn't been there. Webb was hoping to catch her in a lie.

"No." Vanessa shook her head. "We went to another place. I think the cop kind of freaked my friend out."

"And where was that place?"

Vanessa realized she was digging herself in deeper. "I

don't mean to be rude, but what is this all about? I haven't done anything wrong… Well, at least not illegal, and neither has my *friend*. Why do you have so many questions about what I've been doing the past couple of days?"

Webb didn't respond, obviously trying to decide whether to push it or not.

It was time to take a page out of the Liam Goetz playbook: stand naked in the doorway.

"Look, I'll be glad to give you a blow-by-blow," she snickered a little at that, "of the entire past forty-eight hours. What we did at a friend of a friend's house. On the bed. And on the kitchen table. And even right outside on the back deck. Come to think of it, maybe we did do something illegal. But I don't think that's what you want to write down in your little notebook."

She leaned back in her seat and crossed her arms over her chest, feigning a smug confidence she didn't have.

Liam would be proud if he could see her right now. She knew it without a doubt.

And it worked. Webb grimaced and took some papers out of another file on the table. "Fine, if your actions for the past couple days are not fit to be written, then let's talk about the girl you picked up on Monday evening."

Vanessa rolled her eyes as if she was bored. "Seriously? I told that officer guy all I knew about her."

"And what was that?"

It was important for her to remember the details she'd told Officer Atwood. "She was walking on the side of the road. I'm in social work, like you know, so I was concerned about her. I took her to 7-Eleven for some food and Gatorade."

"Did you talk to her? Ask her about her situation?"

"She didn't say much. Honestly, I think she was probably on something. She didn't really seem to understand much of what I said."

Hopefully, if Webb was the one in on the trafficking ring, he would think Vanessa just thought Karine had been on drugs, not that she'd noticed the girl was from a different country.

"So what did you do after getting her something to eat and drink?"

"I took her to the hospital. She still seemed dehydrated and possibly on drugs. More help than I could give her. Plus, I had other plans for the night."

"So you didn't really talk to her and you didn't really care what happened to her. You just dumped her at the hospital. Odd behavior for a social worker."

"It wasn't like that. Look, most of the time I get up early and work late to help people. Any of the families I partner with can attest to that. But I had plans, so I couldn't take this kid on."

"It sort of looks like you took the kid on." He took a picture and slid it over to Vanessa. It was of security footage of her and Karine at the hospital, Vanessa hovering close and protectively over the girl.

Vanessa shrugged. "I'm not a monster. Just because I couldn't stay there with her doesn't mean I didn't care about what happened to her."

"We need to find this girl, Miss Epperson." Webb's voice took on a very grim tone.

Vanessa watched as his face seemed to get harder, eyes flintier.

Yeah, this guy was pretty desperate to get his hands on Karine.

Too desperate.

Webb took out some other pictures and placed them in front of Vanessa. "These are from Tuesday night, the night after you dropped the teenager at the hospital."

The pictures weren't very clear, no real visual of a face, but it was definitely someone with long brown hair, about

Karine's height and build. The person was obviously robbing a house, grabbing valuables and stuffing them in a bag.

"Is that her?" Vanessa asked. She knew very well it wasn't Karine, but played along. "Officer Atwood mentioned something about her being wanted for burglary."

Webb slid the pictures back and then took out another stack. "Unfortunately, your teenage runaway is now wanted for more than burglary. When the woman whose house she broke into came home, she hit her in the head with a metal fire poker. The woman died."

Vanessa gasped as the next set of pictures Webb set out showed the girl hitting a woman and the woman falling to the ground.

"Evidently the suspect didn't realize there was a security camera at the house." He pulled out another picture. "Moreover, the person she was with didn't realize there was a camera, either."

He pushed another picture in front of her. A woman, also dressed in black, like the one who had brandished the fire poker, stood by the shadow in the doors.

Again, you couldn't make out many details about the person. But her height, her build, the hair coming out from under the dark ball cap she wore?

Looked quite similar to Vanessa.

"This was Tuesday night?" she finally blurted. The pictures were jarring. The knowledge that someone seemed to be setting her up even more so.

"That person." He pointed to the woman in the shadow. "Looks pretty similar to you."

"That's n-not me," Vanessa stuttered.

Assistant Sheriff Webb's eyes were hard. "I'm getting a lot of pressure to get this case solved, Miss Epperson. More than that, I'm *determined* to catch the person who did this—whether it's your teenager friend or not—and the woman she was with."

Vanessa swallowed. "That's not me. And I don't know the location of the girl you're looking for. I can't help you. I'm sorry."

"Well, you are our best link in this case. Our only link right now. So you have two choices—you either provide me with the name of the man you were supposedly with for the past forty-eight hours for an alibi, or we arrest you and continue this questioning later."

Chapter Ten

As soon as Vanessa had disconnected the call with Liam, he sprang into action.

"Ladies." He didn't want to frighten Karine, so he kept his tone as light as possible. "I don't mean to interrupt your television viewing, but we need to vacate a little sooner than planned."

Andrea was on her feet in an instant.

"Trouble?" she said softly.

"Locals picked up Vanessa."

Andrea grimaced. "I'll get dressed."

"What means *vacate*?" Karine asked as she brought the cereal bowls over and began washing them in the sink.

"It means leave. We knew we needed to go to another house, remember? We're just having to do it a little earlier than we'd planned." He touched her shoulder gently, slowly. It was the first time he'd initiated any sort of physical contact, and was glad when the girl didn't flinch or pull away.

"Miss Vanessa?" Karine asked.

"She'll be fine. Promise." He'd see to it personally. "She'll meet us there soon, okay?"

"Okay." She reached up and squeezed his hand.

They were completely packed and ready to leave less than twenty minutes later. He and Karine followed Andrea as she went to a local rental property office and secured a house for the next two weeks. Then they drove to the house.

Andrea had chosen well. It was a great location, directly on the Roanoke Sound, but far enough away from the action that no one would accidentally stumble onto them. It had a boat dock and a small fishing boat, which could allow for a second means of escape if needed.

Most of all, the rental agreement was solely in Andrea's name. There was no tie whatsoever to Vanessa or Liam. So if something happened to them—although Liam planned to make sure that didn't happen—Karine would still be safe. Andrea would get her out. Hell, the only reason they didn't get her out right now was to help the other girls. But if they had to, Omega could have a helicopter in here and out again in under an hour. The sheriff's department would be none the wiser.

But that was a last resort and only if there was no hope for getting the other girls out alive. Karine would not leave them behind willingly.

Once Andrea and Karine were safely in the house, Liam left. He had to get to the sheriff's office to see about Vanessa. Hopefully she was holding up under the questioning. They wouldn't have any grounds to hold her, he was sure—you couldn't be arrested for helping a runaway teenager—but knew that questioning could be uncomfortable at best. Downright wearying at worst.

Everything in him said to get her out of there right now. Liam was a man of action. But he knew in this case, rushing in there, pulling rank—and he could do it—wouldn't help their cause. Wouldn't help those girls.

Vanessa was strong. She could handle it.

He put a call in to his boss at Omega on his way to the sheriff's office. If things went sour, he was going to need backup. More than just Andrea could provide.

"Liam. How's it going?" Steve Drackett asked as soon as the call was connected.

"Locals have taken Vanessa in for questioning." Steve

already knew about the trafficking ring from when Liam had called and Andrea had been sent.

"Okay, let me put someone on that to get info. Hang on."

Steve was back on the line in just a few moments. "What's your plan?"

"I'm on my way to the station now. So far my presence on the island, and the fact that I'm law enforcement, is unknown. Vanessa is trying to keep me unknown to them, but I'm not sure if she'll hold up."

"That's a lot for someone with no training to keep hidden during questioning. You. Karine. The trafficking ring."

"Exactly." Liam took a turn. He was almost there. That was the good thing about the Outer Banks islands being so small—nothing was too far away. "Andrea has already gotten Karine to a new safe house, so even if Vanessa crumbles, they won't find her anywhere having to do with me."

"Good. What do you need?"

"If we can keep whoever is behind this thinking we don't know anything about the trafficking ring, I think we have four more days until the sale goes down. Bastards wanted to use the girls themselves for a little while."

Liam heard Steve's curse and agreed with the word he'd said. "I'm going to go ahead and send Derek and Joe. You'll need them."

When they found out exactly where the girls were being held and it came down to actually getting them out, there was no one Liam would want more at his back than Derek Waterman and Joe Matarazzo. They'd saved his ass more than once.

"It will probably be a couple days at the most." Liam pulled into a parking spot at the sheriff's office.

Steve cursed again.

"What?"

"It looks like someone is trying to run a warrant through to arrest your girl."

"*What?* For what?" Liam's teeth ground.

"Aiding and abetting a criminal."

"Damn it. It looks like I might need to blow my cover here, Steve. I'm not going to let them arrest her if I can be her alibi."

"I agree. But be careful."

"I'll call with an update later." Liam disconnected the call and was jogging across the parking lot in moments. As he got to the stairs he was stopped by someone sitting on a bench under a tree right outside the door.

"Liam Goetz. I should've known if Vanessa was about to be arrested, you would be somewhere in close vicinity."

George Epperson. Vanessa's father.

Liam stopped. "What are you doing here? Did Vanessa call you?" Liam shouldn't be surprised at that. Vanessa had always been able to call her parents whenever she wanted something—a trip to Paris, a diamond bracelet—and they'd made it happen. This situation wouldn't be any different.

The man's soft bark of laughter held no humor whatsoever. "No, my daughter very definitely did not call me. Fortunately, I have friends here at the station. Or rather, I should say, people who want to stay in my good graces. One of them let me know she was here."

"Oh." The man looked older, much older, than he had when Liam had last seen him. Eight years ago when Liam had gone to his house, asking to see Vanessa, wanting to know why she hadn't showed up at their planned location to meet and go get married.

George Epperson had made it very clear that his daughter was no longer interested in marrying a "hoodlum—reformed or not" and that Liam was not ever welcome on their property again.

Obviously, Epperson's attitude toward Liam hadn't changed very much. But he couldn't get over how much more haggard the man looked. Maybe he had health problems or something.

"My lawyer is inside with her right now, taking care of whatever charges the department is threatening to bring together."

Relief flowed through Liam. He might not be a personal fan of George Epperson's, but if his money and lawyer got Vanessa out of the sheriff's office unscathed, Liam would be the first to applaud. Not to mention that Epperson had just saved Liam from going in there and pulling out his badge—putting those kidnapped girls in extreme danger. So if Epperson wanted to blame him for Vanessa being in this mess, it was a small price to pay.

"Did you do something to her? With her?" Epperson asked. "I understand the possible charge against her is aiding and abetting a criminal. That sounds about up your alley."

Either Epperson didn't remember that Liam had been entering the DEA when they'd last met or he just didn't care. The man had never been able to get much past Liam's run-ins with the law when he'd been a teenager. As far as George had been concerned, Liam had never been good enough for his daughter.

Liam didn't know what the man had to be so bitter about now. In the unspoken war between them—Liam had never thought of it that way, but figured Epperson had—the older man had definitely won.

For years when he was younger, Liam had held his tongue around Mr. Epperson. Vanessa loved her family and Liam hadn't wanted to force a wedge between them. But he and Vanessa had both known her parents were never going to give them their blessing for a wedding, so they had agreed to get married and then just tell them. At least that was what Liam had thought they'd agreed. Until Vanessa hadn't showed up.

Liam took a step closer to the man so he wouldn't have to speak louder. "You know I'm law enforcement. Knew it when I left. I'm here to help Vanessa, not get her in any trouble."

Epperson shrugged, not willing to admit it. The look he gave Liam made him feel as if he were still twenty years old and bringing her home from a date. He'd always respected the Eppersons' rules and had always had her home on time, but it had never been enough. Epperson had always looked at Liam just as he was looking at Liam now: like an annoyance and a peasant.

Liam shook his head. Some things never changed. "I don't know why you still hate me. You never thought I was good enough for Vanessa. I get that. And, honestly, Mr. Epperson, I even understand it. But why in God's name would you still dislike me so much now?"

Liam knew he should stop, that he should just walk away, but couldn't bring himself to do it. "She didn't marry me. Obviously she agreed with you about me not being good enough. She chose you guys. You've still got her."

The look on Epperson's face changed. All the years came crushing down on his countenance and he looked so old to Liam, although he couldn't have been more than his mid-fifties.

"You're an idiot, Goetz." There was no sting to the words. "We're both idiots."

Liam cocked his head to the side. That second comment he hadn't expected. "Not that I disagree, but what are you talking about?"

For the first time George looked at Liam like a person, an equal. "Liam, I'm pretty sure you don't know all the facts about—"

"What are you doing here?"

Liam's words were cut off by Vanessa's hiss behind him. At first he thought she meant him, coming here and possibly ruining his cover. But when he turned he found all her anger focused on her father.

Epperson shrugged. "I got word that you were being detained. So I called Michaels and had him meet me here."

The emotional distance between Vanessa and her father was palpable. When Liam had known Vanessa before, she hadn't always agreed with her parents, had thought they were old-fashioned and overprotective, but they had always been close. She'd always been the apple of her father's eye.

Now it looked as though she wasn't interested in being her father's anything. She wasn't even interested in being in his presence.

"You shouldn't have come here at all, Dad. Shouldn't have sent Michaels."

"It's good your father sent his lawyer, Vanessa," Liam told her. "I didn't have to break my cover. I was on my way to do just that."

She took a deep breath. "Yes, you're right," she said to Liam. Then she turned to her father. "I do appreciate your help. There's a situation—I'm not at liberty to talk about it—but your assistance really helped. So, thank you. But, Dad, I still want you to stay out of my life."

"Vanessa…" Mr. Epperson said, reaching his hand toward her.

She stepped away from him. "Save it, Dad. As always, too little, too late."

Liam didn't really understand what was happening between Vanessa and George. Obviously this chasm between them wasn't anything new; both knew where they stood in this battle and were accustomed to the war.

Liam would've thought seeing an emotional distance between Vanessa and her family would make him happy. Would make him feel justified.

Instead it just left him with a lingering sadness.

It was another piece of the puzzle, an important piece,

to understanding exactly what had happened between him and Vanessa, but Liam had no idea where the piece went.

Why would Vanessa tell her father to *continue* to stay out of her life? Something must have drastically changed in the past eight years. Was it long ago? More recent?

Whichever, Liam found himself wanting to help the two of them bridge whatever gap lay between them. While Epperson looked as if he would give anything to sit and talk with his daughter—hell, Liam even felt sorry for the man—Vanessa was obviously not interested.

She turned to Liam. "Are you ready? You sticking around out here is probably not the best idea."

She was right. He nodded.

Epperson sighed. "At least call your mother. She is worried about you. She's always worried about you—in your line of work—but now she's even more distraught."

Vanessa rolled her eyes. "Social work isn't dangerous, Dad."

It was obviously not a new conversation.

"I know. But your mother…worries."

"Fine. I'll call her in a few days." She turned to Liam. "Let's go." She didn't wait for him, just began walking.

Epperson looked at Vanessa as she stalked off. Then he turned to Liam. "Like I said, we're both idiots."

He turned and walked off without another word, joining his lawyer at the doorway to the station. Liam jogged in the direction of Vanessa in the parking lot.

"Whoa," he said when he reached her. "Are you okay?"

He saw her quickly reach up and wipe her eyes with the back of her hand.

"Vanessa—"

"No, I don't want to talk about it. I just want to get out of here."

He took her arm and led her in the direction of the SUV.

"You don't want to talk about your father or you don't want to talk about the questioning?"

"My father."

"Okay." He helped her inside the vehicle then went around to the driver's side. When he got in, she had her head laid back against the seat rest, eyes closed. Her stomach growled loudly in the silence.

It was already midafternoon. She had to be starving. "Food first. Then we'll talk."

She nodded. "But don't go far. We'll need to come back here."

"Is that such a good idea?"

"I want us to follow someone."

"Who?"

"Assistant Sheriff Tommy Webb, the guy who was questioning me. I think he's the one who's behind the trafficking ring."

Chapter Eleven

They got fast-food burgers and immediately headed back to the sheriff's office parking lot. Vanessa explained everything that had happened in questioning.

"Obviously those pictures can't be Karine," Vanessa said between bites. "She was with us the entire time."

"Someone is setting up a case against her. A preemptive strike," Liam said. "So if she does come forward with her story, they'll be able to discredit her."

"Killing someone?" Vanessa shook her head. "I can't believe they'd go to that length."

Liam's real concern now was for those other girls. Someone willing to kill a complete stranger to possibly discredit Karine would not hesitate to kill the other girls to keep themselves from getting caught.

They were running out of time.

"It sounds like you did good in there," he said.

"I don't know. I tried." She shrugged. "That guy Webb is determined to catch Karine. Like 'nothing will get in my way' sort of determined."

Liam chuckled at her imitation of Webb. "Who is he? I don't recognize him from when I lived here."

"No, he's young to be assistant sheriff. Midtwenties maybe? He's all about the power."

Liam had already called Omega for any info about Webb. That should be coming in soon.

It was a long shot, but a long shot was better than doing nothing.

Vanessa had been texting Karine pretty constantly since he'd given her the girl's new phone number. Karine was happy with Andrea. They were watching television again and about to eat dinner. Liam could tell that knowing Karine was safe took a lot of stress off Vanessa.

Now they were waiting for Webb to leave so they could follow him. It might be a while. They were sitting in a section of the parking lot where they had a good line of sight of the back door and the parking area the officers used. When Webb came out, they would see him.

Liam rolled down the windows a little bit to let some breeze through the SUV and then asked the question that had been on his mind for the past hour.

"What's going on between you and your parents, Vanessa?"

Her sigh was audible. "I don't want to talk about it."

"He saved our asses, you know, by bringing in his lawyer to get you out." Liam was a little irritated that he hadn't thought of the plan. It was perfect. Who would Vanessa call if she was in trouble?

Daddy.

No one would've suspected a thing. It would've kept him, and especially the fact that he was law enforcement, out of the equation.

"We should've made that the plan from the beginning," Liam continued. "You calling your father for help."

"I wouldn't have agreed to it."

She would've. To save those girls, Liam was convinced, Vanessa would do just about anything. But that wasn't the point he wanted to argue with her. What he wanted to know was why there was such a rift between her and her dad.

"Why?"

"We don't talk anymore."

"At all?" Liam could hardly believe that. She was the Eppersons' only child. They doted on her. Spoiled her. Gave her all their love and attention.

"No, not really. Although my mom calls, so I let her know I'm okay."

"Did you guys get in a fight? George said your mom worries about you doing social work—is that it?" Liam could understand Mrs. Epperson's concern. But for it to cause a rift of this size between them?

"No, that's not really it."

"Then what?"

She stared at him in the gathering darkness from the sun's descent. For a long time he didn't think she was going to answer him.

"We fought. It was a long time ago. I don't really want to talk about it."

Liam couldn't seem to let it go. Even if he'd never been accepted by them, he knew how much Vanessa loved her parents. "You can't find a way to work it out? I know how close you all are...were."

"Some things just can't be fixed. The shattered pieces are too many to be glued back together."

That same look he recognized from the hotel Tuesday morning was back in her eyes: pain, loss, emptiness.

Liam found the resentment he'd held toward her for the past few years begin to melt away. Yeah, she'd hurt him, broken his heart when she'd changed her mind about marrying him. He'd nursed that wound for a lot of years.

But whatever had happened to her since he'd left— whatever had put that look in her eyes—Liam was willing to let go of all his past anger and hurt if it meant he'd never have to see that look on her face again. That heaviness, as if she carried the weight of the world on her small shoulders.

"Nessa—"

"I can't talk about it, Liam." She buried her face in her hands. "I'm sorry."

He reached over and smoothed his hand down her hair. "You don't have to talk about it, okay? I'm here. I just want you to know I'm here and you don't have to carry whatever this is alone anymore if you don't want to."

He could tell she was wiping tears from her eyes. Then she leaned her face into his hand, which had moved to cup her cheek.

The heat was there between them. It always had been and probably always would be. But there was something more between them now.

A warmth.

"I'm sorry you were so hurt eight years ago," she whispered.

"You were twenty. I was twenty-two. God forbid we be judged for the rest of our lives solely by the decisions we made at that age."

She nodded and started to say something else but then their attention was caught when the back door of the station opened. It was Webb.

"Showtime," Liam murmured.

The man didn't seem suspicious, not looking around for anyone tailing him, but that didn't necessarily mean anything. They followed him to a nearby diner, where he went inside and fortunately sat by a window booth. They could see that two other men joined him.

Three men. Just as Karine had mentioned.

What Liam wouldn't give for audio surveillance on them right now.

"Do you think that's them?" Vanessa whispered.

"I don't know, but it sure seems possible."

They watched for verbal cues as the men talked, but

without knowing the topic, understanding their expressions and gestures was impossible.

Liam's phone buzzed and he looked down at it. It was the report about Tommy Webb. He read through it.

"What?" Vanessa asked when Liam grimaced.

"It's the background info Omega Sector sent me about Tommy Webb."

"Something bad?"

Liam shook his head. "The opposite, actually. The guy was literally a Boy Scout. Grew up in Raleigh but vacationed here. After he went to college—with a 4.0 GPA, by the way—he moved to the Outer Banks. Was a deputy and then worked his way up to assistant sheriff. Pretty impressive for someone twenty-six years old. He's driven."

"So he's not our guy?"

"Not necessarily. He could still be behind the trafficking ring. But if so, he's very good at making himself look like what he's not."

"Well, whoever made the video of 'Karine' hitting someone with a fire iron is also good at making stuff look like something it's not," Vanessa shot back, leaning forward to look closer at the men in the diner.

She was right. It looked as though Webb was a perfectionist. That could translate very well to running a successful human-trafficking ring.

Except for one small girl who'd bravely escaped. The cog in Webb's wheel.

They needed to know who those other guys were. Liam cursed again at their lack of surveillance equipment.

"I'm going to go in and try to get pictures of the two other men with my phone," he told Vanessa.

"What if someone recognizes you?"

"I'll have to take the chance. We have to know who those guys are and get someone following them." Liam was thankful Derek and Joe were on their way. They were needed.

Stress was clear on Vanessa's face. "Be careful."

He reached over and gave her a quick, forceful kiss.

"Hey." He winked at her. "It's me."

She was still rolling her eyes when Liam grabbed a ball cap from the backseat and hopped out the door. He pulled the cap low over his head and prayed no one would recognize him as he went inside.

He sat at the bar and immediately ordered coffee. The waitress smiled as she brought it, but Liam didn't engage in any casual conversation with her. That might just call the men's attention toward them.

Liam tried to make it so his phone would take a picture of the men from the back lens. That way it would appear that Liam was looking at his screen—as almost everyone in the diner was—but, really, he could take a picture.

He muttered a curse when he couldn't get the right angle. He'd have to hold the phone up too high, which would bring attention to his actions.

He'd have to walk by the men's table and try to get the picture. It would be tricky, and if he didn't get the photos on the first attempt, he wouldn't be able to do it at all. Walking by their table more than once was another sure way to attract their attention.

Liam asked the waitress where the bathroom was located and then made his move. As he passed by the table, he kept his phone on video-record mode. They would be able to pick up a still photo from the video. When he got to the bathroom he checked the footage. He'd gotten what he needed of one of the guys. As he walked back he'd get footage of the other one.

He waited a few moments before going out, but when he opened the door he realized the men were getting up to leave. He'd missed his chance for the second guy, damn it.

Keeping his head averted as they were paying, Liam threw a five-dollar bill down by his coffee cup and walked out the door. He needed to be back at his SUV before Webb left so they could continue to follow him.

It was beginning to rain in the darkness, which gave Liam an excuse to jog toward his car. His heart skipped a beat when he opened the door and realized Vanessa was no longer in the vehicle.

Adrenaline coursed through him. Where the hell had she gone? Had someone grabbed her? He was getting back out to look for her when the passenger door opened and she climbed in.

"Where were you?" Liam demanded.

"I could tell you only got pictures of one of the guys from the angle you were walking to the bathroom."

"So?" His heart was still beating a little too fast from thinking she had been taken.

"So, when I saw they were getting up to leave, I snuck to the window and took a picture of the other guy myself."

She was grinning like an idiot. Liam couldn't help smiling himself.

"I hope they didn't see you," he said, shaking his head.

"I don't think so," she said. "I kept to the shadows. If they did notice, they didn't act any differently."

"Here comes Webb." Liam started the SUV just as the assistant sheriff started his. "I think we should keep following him until we figure out who the other guys are."

He followed Webb at a safe distance. Enough people were leaving the diner that it wasn't too obvious they were following, but surveillance with only one car, at night, in a small place like the Outer Banks, was difficult. It wouldn't take long before Webb would become suspicious. Unless Webb was going out to the boat, following him wouldn't give them any sort of tactical advantage. If he was just going to his house, it wasn't worth the suspicions it would raise in Webb's mind.

Right now they were on the four-lane Highway 158. Everybody used that road, so it wouldn't grab Webb's attention.

"Getting out to take pictures of those guys could've been dangerous, you know," he said to Vanessa, who was straining to keep her eyes on Webb's car. "There's no doubt they're willing to kill to cover their tracks."

She shrugged. "No more dangerous than you going in there."

Liam gave a short laugh. "I'm a trained agent, not to mention I have nearly a foot and probably close to a hundred pounds on you."

She shrugged again. "It was worth the risk."

Liam had emailed the photos of both men to Omega as they'd waited at a stop light before moving on to the highway. Hopefully they would have positive IDs by morning, though Liam knew they couldn't be arrested or brought in for questioning. They would never give up the location of the girls; it would be too incriminating against them. The girls would die alone on that boat.

Not an option.

But they could at least follow the men and put full-time surveillance on them.

Webb pulled off Highway 158 onto a smaller, darkened road. Things were about to get tricky.

Liam tossed Vanessa his phone. "Check the file with his info. Is his house on this road? If so, we don't want to follow. That will just make him suspicious."

She found the file quickly and her face jerked up to his. "No, his house is on the north side of the islands, near Kitty Hawk. Isn't this the road that leads out to the bridge to Riker's Island?"

She was right. An old wooden bridge that led out to a small island in the Sound the locals had nicknamed Riker's. The island was popular with young people during warm weather for lying out, sneaking a few illegal substances and just generally being young and stupid. Liam had spent time there himself as a teenager. A place to get away from endless tourists during the summer.

Right now, during the off season, it would be the perfect place to keep a small motor boat to get out to the bigger one where they were keeping the girls.

Liam switched off his headlights just before he turned onto the road leading out to the bridge. There was no way Webb wouldn't notice them behind him.

"If he gets in a boat, we don't have one," Vanessa reminded him.

"I know. We'll have to follow him as best we can with binoculars. It's better than nothing. Maybe they aren't far. Then we can come back out later tonight."

They kept a pretty good distance behind Webb. The island wasn't the only place these back roads led to, but it was a good bet. When Webb began slowing down, Liam stopped and backed up around a curb.

"I don't know if he sees us or what, but we need to stay out of sight for a minute. The last thing we want to do is spook him."

Of course, they didn't want to lose him, either. But if he was going to Riker's Island, that was a dead end.

Liam waited a full two minutes before easing the SUV around the bend again. He couldn't see Webb's taillights any longer.

They drove at a steady pace toward the bridge, slowing as they were about to ease onto it. Seeing the road without headlights was difficult.

"All right, let's see if the bastard went—"

He caught Vanessa's terrified look past him out the window as she threw out her arm toward him. He felt the jarring impact of another, much larger vehicle slamming into theirs.

Then everything went black.

Chapter Twelve

Why did she have her feet in cold water? Vanessa blinked, trying to wake all the way up.

Were they on a boat? They were rocking as though they were out on a boat.

She brought a hand to her head. Everything hurt. Was that blood on her hand? She couldn't see. And she couldn't really breathe because her seat belt was too tight.

As she blinked again and wiped her hair out of her face, her eyes adjusted.

Oh, God, she was in the car with Liam and they were *in the water*. The cold, salty water was already beginning to fill the vehicle. The windows were already below the water line.

How deep was the water here? Vanessa didn't know. But as the SUV continued to sink she realized it was deep enough to kill them.

She couldn't get a deep breath because so much of her weight was being forced against her seat belt from the angle the vehicle was sinking.

And Liam was sitting there, still. Arms floating eerily from his angle in his seat.

He was too still. And whatever vehicle had hit them had connected on his side.

"Liam!" Vanessa yelled. She could now feel water inching up over her ankles.

He didn't move at all. She couldn't see any blood on him, but it was dark.

It was even darker in the water outside the windows.

She tried to reach over to touch him, but couldn't with the awkward angle her body was stuck in. She pushed at the release mechanism on her seat belt, panicking for just a second when it wouldn't give. Then it did and she fell forward.

The car shifted slightly with her movement. It was still filling with water.

"Liam," she yelled again, bracing herself against the dashboard so she could get closer to him. "Liam, wake up."

She shook his shoulder, then reached over and cupped both his cheeks with her hands.

"Liam, baby, I need you to wake up." She kissed him then patted his cheeks sharply.

The water was rising in the car. They were running out of time.

Liam moaned and she released a breath she hadn't even realized she'd been holding.

"That's right, you big old hunk of handsome. Wake up."

He groaned. "I prefer hunk of burning love."

Vanessa snickered and kissed him on the forehead. "I'll call you hunk of anything you want if we can get out of this vehicle alive."

It only took a moment for the cobwebs to clear in Liam's mind.

"We're already submerged. The water is rising inside the car." She could feel the cold creeping up toward her knees. The car was still sinking at an angle.

Liam reached for the controller to ease the window down, but it wouldn't work. "Electrical is already out."

Vanessa shrieked a little when the car hit the bottom and evened out. Her weight was thrown down into her seat.

Water was entering the car much faster now, pouring in through the floorboards.

"Okay, good, we're at the bottom," Liam said.

"That's good?"

He unhooked himself from his seat belt then took his gun out of his holster.

"Going to shoot some fish?" she asked. Maybe he could just shoot her. That would be a less painful way to go than drowning.

"No, I'm going to shoot your window out. Once the water fills the vehicle, we'll be able to swim out."

"Okay." It was a good plan in theory. "I don't know how far down we are. We were already sinking when I regained consciousness."

"Kick off your shoes," he said. "We're both good swimmers. We can make it."

She nodded but really wasn't sure.

"It might be disorienting when you first get through the window. You can't tell which way the surface is in the dark." He grabbed her hand. "If that happens, stop swimming and let yourself float for a second. You'll automatically start rising toward the surface. Then swim that way."

"Have you done this before?"

He reached over and kissed her. "Nah. But I was Houdini in another life."

She smiled. He'd always been able to make her smile, even in the craziest of circumstances or when she'd been so angry at him she was ready to hire a hit man.

He cupped her cheek. "The water coming in will be the hardest part. Don't panic, baby. We can't do anything until the car is full of water. The pressure of it coming in through the window will be too strong to swim against."

His eyes were serious.

Liam serious was frightening. She grasped his hand and squeezed.

"Cover your ears," he said as he pointed his gun at the window.

She did so, turning to the side. The sound of the gun—shooting three times in rapid succession—was so loud. But just as frightening was the sound of the water now pouring in through the window. The force of it tore through the holes the bullets had made and ripped the window open like a gaping wound.

Panic poured over Vanessa like the cold water. Her breathing became shallow and tears pooled in her eyes. Water was up to her waist in seconds.

"Nessa, look at me." He grabbed her hand in the water. "Concentrate on your breathing. You're going to need a deep breath before we swim up."

He breathed right in front of her. She tried to follow his pattern, but the water was up to her shoulders now.

"You can do this, baby. You're the strongest person I know. The strongest person I've ever known."

Vanessa focused. He was right, she *could* do this. She had to do this or she would die. The water now was just a few inches from the ceiling of the car.

"One deep breath and then we swim, okay?"

"Okay," she said. They both had their heads tilted straight up so they could get the last bit of air. She heard him suck in a breath, then did the same, her hand clutching his.

This was it.

Swimming, knowing you couldn't just pop up for air if you needed it, was much different than a regular swim. Vanessa had to force herself to remain calm. The pressing darkness all around her didn't help.

Liam swam through the window first. He had to let go of her to do so and she fought the panic once again. She couldn't see him at all.

Part of her shirt got caught on something as she took her turn through the window, so she just pulled on it with all her strength, causing it to rip. But at least it hurled her through the opening.

Where was Liam? Had he already gone toward the surface?

Which way was the surface?

She was running out of air and she hadn't even started swimming yet.

She remembered what he'd said about disorientation in the dark water. She tried to stop moving but couldn't tell which way her body was floating.

Now Vanessa really began to panic. She was at the last of her air. The overwhelming urge to gulp was almost unbearable, but she knew all she would get was water. And then she would drown.

She began to swim, because that was better than doing nothing, but she had no idea if she was heading toward the surface.

She felt a yank on her hair. Liam.

He kept a hand on her hair and reached out with the other one until he had hold of her hand. She was glad. She didn't want him to let go of her even for a second in this darkness. Together they swam.

Vanessa kept her breath as long as she could; the pressure became unbearable.

She held on another couple of seconds—fighting—but then couldn't any longer.

She opened her mouth and inhaled.

But instead of air, all she got was the painful sting of the brackish Sound water.

She couldn't fight the darkness anymore. Her last hope was that she didn't take Liam down with her as she drowned.

LIAM FELT VANESSA stop kicking a few feet from the surface. His own lungs burned with an agonizing intensity. He forced himself to give one more giant kick and their heads burst past the surface and into the life-giving air.

It only took him a moment to realize that Vanessa wasn't conscious. Wasn't breathing.

The vehicle had sunk father than he'd thought; probably nearly twenty feet. That was a long way to travel on one breath. Especially in Vanessa's panicked state.

He swam with her motionless form to the bank and pulled her up. Ignoring the cold that was making his movements sluggish, he tried to check her pulse. It was weak and thready, but it was still there. Pulse but no breath.

He had to get the water out of her system and air in or she wouldn't have a pulse soon. He turned her onto her side and thumped. Hard. She would have bruises on her small frame, no doubt.

"Come on, Nessa," he said, voice hoarse. "Stay with me."

He pulled her limp frame up, holding her with one arm across her chest, clasping her upper arm. He thumped again, leaning her forward as if burping a baby.

"Come on, sweetheart."

The sound of her retching was the most beautiful thing he'd ever heard.

He held her as she coughed and threw up the rest of the water in her system, replacing it with oxygen. Then he fell back onto the ground, taking her with him. They both lay exhausted.

"That wasn't fun," she finally whispered, obviously unable to make her voice any louder.

"Which part, the drowning or the epic vomiting?"

She chuckled weakly. "Both were equally gross."

Liam knew he had to get them up and going. The water had felt a lot colder than it actually was—it was only the first of October, so it wasn't dangerously cold—but they were both still freezing. They needed to warm up. Vanessa especially. She didn't have the same muscle mass he had to keep himself warm.

Whatever vehicle had pushed them into the water was gone. Could it have been Webb? Could he have seen them, doubled back and been waiting for them to make their way onto the bridge?

They'd have to figure that out later. Right now? Warmth. Of course, they had no vehicle, no working phones and no shoes. At least Liam still had his wallet.

He helped Vanessa up and they began walking. They'd head for the nearest hotel—thank God, the Outer Banks was fairly littered with them—get warm and call this in.

He kept Vanessa pinned to his side as they walked, slowly and pretty painfully, down the side road.

They were both alive. That was what mattered.

Chapter Thirteen

Vanessa's teeth were chattering and she was miserable.

If Liam reminded her one more time that shivering was a good sign, that it meant she hadn't gone into any later stages of hypothermia, she might pop him in the mouth. She didn't want to hear that the castanets playing in her head were a good sign. She just wanted to get warm.

They hadn't had to walk far for a hotel, thank goodness. He had kept her pinned to his side the entire time except when he'd reluctantly let her go so he could check in. Vanessa sat outside on a bench waiting, since they both looked like something out of *The Creature from the Black Lagoon*. Plus, he didn't want the clerk to possibly recognize her in case the cops started searching again.

Even in her physical misery, Vanessa couldn't ignore the overwhelming joy that permeated her body.

They were alive.

Both of them were walking, no broken bones, no obvious head injuries, no floating facedown in the Roanoke Sound. They had some cuts and definitely some bruises, but they were *alive*.

Liam walked back outside. "Okay, I've got us a room and extra bottles of shampoo and conditioner."

This hotel was pretty nice. Not luxury, like something her family would stay at, but certainly not as scary as the other place she'd been with Karine. Liam led her inside, into the elevator and up to their room. He immediately went to the heating unit and cranked it to high.

Vanessa wanted to fall face-first on the giant king-size bed, but definitely needed a shower first.

She wondered if she could talk Liam into joining her. That would warm both of them up. She looked over at him, but he was already grabbing the phone and stretching it over to the table by the window.

"I'm going to make a call to Omega Sector," he said. "Make sure we have backup on the way and that they are bringing everything we need."

She knew she should be happy that he was in super-agent mode. He was getting things done. Making sure those girls were going to make it out of this situation alive. Calling in the guard.

Was it bad that she wished—just a little bit—he would be in let's-celebrate-we're-alive mode and join her in the shower?

Probably.

"Do you think that was Webb who rammed us into the water tonight?" she asked him.

He nodded. "Maybe. Him or one of his friends. They could've noticed we were following him."

"It's a good thing we sent those pictures already. My phone didn't make it out of the Sound."

"Mine did, but it's completely useless. We'll need to get replacements tomorrow. And figure out a plan about everything. I'm thinking the best bet is for you to go to work as if nothing happened. That would completely throw Webb, or whoever tried to kill us, off."

"Won't he just bring me in again?"

"Not with your dad's lawyer there to get you out. I know you don't like your dad's interference, but nobody is going to bring me in for questioning unless they are absolutely sure they can charge you with something. The Epperson lawyer made sure of that, I have no doubt." He turned back to the phone.

Yeah, Liam was definitely in super-agent mode. That was good, she reminded herself. Good.

She spun and made her way to the shower, by herself. Good.

LIAM CATEGORICALLY REFUSED to think about Vanessa in the shower as he made his calls. First one was to Andrea to check on Karine and to make sure she knew to be even more diligent. Andrea assured him everything was okay there.

He knew Vanessa—who was not being thought of naked in the shower—would be glad to know everything was fine on the home front.

His next call was to Omega, reporting to Steve Drackett about the attack. It didn't change much. Derek and Joe would be in the Outer Banks tomorrow morning. They hadn't had any luck identifying the men Liam and Vanessa had sent pictures of, but the facial recognition software was still running them.

Of course, facial recognition programming was limited. Unless the men had a record or were public figures, the software might not come up with any helpful results.

By the time Liam got off the phone with Steve, the shower had stopped. At least now he could stop not thinking about Vanessa naked in the shower.

And while he was not thinking about things, he definitely should not think about that explosive kiss between them this morning before she'd gone to work. How he'd dragged her across his lap and every window in the vehicle had fogged in under ten seconds.

The bathroom door opened and she stepped out, wrapped only in a towel.

Add that to the don't-think-about list, also.

"It's all yours. I rinsed out my clothes because they were so gross with the Sound water. They're on the sink."

Liam looked everywhere but at her. "Okay. I don't blame you."

"Everything okay with Karine and Andrea?"

"Yes, no problems whatsoever." He glanced over at her, drawn by the expanse of her shoulders not covered by the towel, then quickly away. "Andrea is on high alert, but I don't think they can tie anything having to do with you and me to her, even if they know who I am, which is doubtful. So they're safe."

He glanced at her to gauge her reaction, but was instead transfixed by a drop of water that found its way from the damp hair at her temple down her cheek and neck. It moved on to her chest, only to disappear in the track between her breasts.

All Liam could think about was backing Vanessa up against that wall and following with his lips the same path that droplet had taken.

Of untying that towel wrapped around her and letting it drop to the floor. And following the routes a few more droplets of water had taken down her body, or just make up his own.

Damn, he was not supposed to be thinking of any of this.

"I'm going to shower." He didn't look Vanessa in the face; just went into the bathroom.

That was what he needed: a little distance, a nice hot shower to wipe out the lingering cold and salt clinging to his skin; time to just let everything that had happened today go.

Five minutes into his shower, he realized it wasn't going to help at all.

The more he tried not thinking about Vanessa—naked, fully clothed or otherwise—the more he couldn't get her out of his mind. He was going to have to get another room. That was the only way he'd be able to leave her alone.

He didn't rinse out his clothes, but put them back on grudgingly, wincing at their stiffness and smell. He needed to go down to the lobby to ask for a second room. He stepped out of the bathroom still drying his hair with a towel.

"Hey, Nessa, I was thinking. It would probably be prudent for me to get my own—"

He looked up from under his towel and halted his words. Vanessa was lying on the bed, under the covers, curled up in a ball. She was fast asleep.

"Room," Liam finished in a much softer voice.

It would probably still be prudent. But Liam had never been particularly good at prudent.

Besides, he trusted himself not to molest a sleeping woman. Even if she was the most gorgeous, feminine, sexy woman he'd ever known.

Liam went back into the bathroom and rinsed out his clothes. He laid them next to Vanessa's to dry then turned out the lights. He got into the bed, moving carefully so he wouldn't wake her.

So he was quite surprised when, a few seconds later, a very naked Vanessa pressed up to his side.

"I tricked you," she said, giggling, then covered her mouth as if she was surprised at the sound.

That sweet laugh. Lord, how he had missed it. He hadn't realized until right now that Vanessa's infectious laughter was probably what he had missed most about her over the past eight years.

He hadn't heard it once since he was back, until now. Sure, circumstances were dire, he knew that, but it was almost as if that sweet laugh wasn't part of Vanessa's regular makeup anymore. More than ever, he was determined to understand what had changed for her. What had made her stop laughing?

But he'd have to worry about that later. Right now it looked as though the laughing Vanessa had other plans.

The time for prudence had come and gone. Liam could hardly fight his own desires. There was no way in hell he could fight his *and* hers.

He turned onto his side so they were face to face and wrapped an arm around her, pulling her closer. "You certainly had me fooled, Miss Epperson."

"I had to get you out of super-agent mode. This seemed like the easiest way."

Liam cocked an eyebrow. "Super-agent mode?"

She rubbed a hand over his chest. "Yeah. I didn't need an agent. I need Liam."

"Well, he's here now."

He pulled Vanessa so she lay all the way on top of him. The thought that he could have lost her today—had come so close to losing her—had him crushing her to him. He wrapped one arm around her hips and threaded his other hand through her hair, bringing her lips down to his.

The heat was instantaneous, as always. It chased all traces of cold away.

"I thought I'd lost you tonight," he murmured against her lips.

"I had the same fear when I couldn't get you to wake up in the car," she responded, her lips never moving away from his.

There was no more talking. Neither of them wanted to think about death. Not right now. Liam didn't want to even think about whether this was a good idea or not.

All he wanted to think about was her body pressed up against his.

He rolled them over so she was tucked underneath him, catching his weight on his elbow and using his other hand to run down the length of her body. He heard her breath catch as he became reunited with the body he had once known so well.

She reached up and threaded her hands in his hair, pulling his lips down to hers. He got one last glimpse of the endless brown in her eyes before he closed his and gave himself over to the passion between them.

As if they'd never been apart.

Chapter Fourteen

Liam was hard-pressed to remember a time he'd been as relieved to see anyone as he was to see his fellow Omega agents Derek Waterman and Joe Matarazzo the next day. Without them Liam's focus had been too torn: trying to make sure Vanessa was safe at work, getting some sense of where Tommy Webb was and what he was doing, plus keeping an eye out for either of the two men he'd been with, since the facial-recognition software still hadn't netted any results.

It was too much for any one person.

Now Liam had the backup he needed. He trusted these men in a way he didn't trust anyone else. He'd learned how to put his life in other people's hands when he'd entered the army and then qualified for Special Forces. His multiple direct-action missions in Afghanistan had taught him the very essence of teamwork. He'd thought the camaraderie would be gone forever after he'd left Special Forces, but he'd found the same brotherhood at Omega Sector.

Of course, right now they were giving him a hard time and he wished he wasn't stuck with them.

"Are we certain it wasn't one of Goetz's ex-girlfriends who rammed him off the bridge?" Joe asked, stretched out in the backseat of Liam's new rental car.

Derek, sitting next to Liam in the front, shook his head. "Joe, you need to be serious."

Liam nodded. "Thanks, Derek."

"We all know there is not enough law-enforcement man-power in the world to track down all the women who would like to run Liam off a bridge," Derek continued, causing Joe to chuckle. "We'll have to just hope it's some criminal. Then we have a chance."

"Very funny," Liam muttered. Although Liam guessed he deserved it after how much he had teased Derek about his wife, Molly, the forensic lab director at Omega.

They had already inspected Webb's vehicle, at least the one he'd been driving last night, which he had parked at the station today. There was no damage to the front of his car. It could not have been the vehicle that had pushed them off the bridge.

That didn't mean it hadn't been one of his buddies, though.

"I'm going to leave you two comedians here to watch Webb. Particularly to see if he meets up with our unknown suspects again." Both Joe and Derek had the pictures he and Vanessa had taken at the diner and they each had a car in case they needed to split up.

Liam had also gotten new phones for him and Vanessa. Being out of touch was not an option.

"I should probably check in with Andrea, make sure everything is okay there. I don't want to take Vanessa to that house in case someone is following us. Webb might have surveillance on her that we don't know about."

Joe looked at him, all joking now aside. "You need to be careful out there, man. Whoever is behind this is hard-core."

Liam nodded. "I'm just hoping those girls are still alive and the perps haven't moved up their timetable. We need to watch them, but nothing that will arouse unwanted suspicion."

"Let's just hope they're more greedy than they are

smart," Derek said. "They won't want to lose the money those girls will provide unless they absolutely have to."

"I'm going to stick with Vanessa. They couldn't get her out of the way through legal channels, so now it looks like they're trying to get rid of her altogether."

There was no way Liam would be leaving her side once she was out of her office, in case whoever had tried to kill them yesterday decided to come back and finish the job while Vanessa was alone.

That decision, of course, had nothing to do with the lovemaking that had occurred last night. And this morning. Twice.

It was Friday afternoon and Vanessa would be done with work soon. He wouldn't have to let her out of his sight all weekend. He wished he could keep her naked that whole time, but knew they had work to do.

Plus, what the hell was he doing? He had come here to the Outer Banks to put Vanessa's ghost to rest. To finally be able to move on without the thought of her hanging over every action he made.

That definitely was a mission fail.

As he waited outside her office—still not completely able to wrap his head around the fact that Vanessa was a social worker—Liam knew he had to face some hard facts.

He had never really gotten over Vanessa.

The situation had just become a great deal more complicated based on last night's—and this morning's—actions.

Vanessa was not the same person he'd known eight years ago. Of course, he wasn't the same person, either. They'd both grown up. But something had changed her. She didn't want to share it, but before he left this place, Liam was going to know what it was.

And how was he going to leave her again? He'd barely survived leaving her once. And that was because he'd been forced to. But even if they could work out their differences, her life was here and his was in Colorado.

There was one thing he had better remember and consider more than anything else: he had been in this exact place before. Eight years ago. Sitting there making future plans for him and Vanessa. Sure that all the love and heat and passion between them was two-sided.

Then she had just up and changed her mind.

How stupid would he be to allow the exact same thing to happen? Yeah, they'd had sex, but she'd given him no indication that there was anything permanent between them.

Hell, even when she *had* promised him things were permanent between them, she hadn't meant it. How much less so now when she wasn't making any promises at all?

He would be best served by keeping that forefront in his mind.

He was here to exorcise her ghost. Maybe a few rolls in the hay were necessary to accomplish that mission. But his heart needed to stay *way* out of it.

Liam saw Vanessa coming out the office door and shut down his thoughts. He usually wasn't one to sit around overthinking things. Liam preferred action.

Unfortunately this time he wasn't sure what action to take.

IT HAD BEEN a pretty damn stressful day at work.

First, she'd had to wear the same clothes—again—except this time they were even worse because they'd been in salty water and even rinsing them thoroughly at the hotel hadn't gotten them completely clean.

Not to mention Vanessa had arrived utterly exhausted this morning. Sure, a lot of that had been from the absolutely fabulous bouts of lovemaking between her and Liam. But the exhaustion had also stemmed from almost being killed and spending half the day being questioned by the police.

Her body had had enough.

Her boss, Maureen, had wanted answers as soon as Vanessa walked through the door. Why had she been taken by the police? Why was she being questioned? Did any of this have to do with any of her cases? Did she really think it was a good example if any of the families she worked with had seen her being marched down to the sheriff's office?

Vanessa hadn't been able to easily defend herself, since telling the truth wasn't an option. So in the end Maureen had thought it better if Vanessa take a leave of absence until things were more settled. She would review and make a final decision about Vanessa's continued employment at Bridgespan once all the facts were available.

Vanessa had spent the rest of the day phoning some families she worked closely with to let them know she wouldn't be around for a while. She used the excuse of a family emergency. Seemed fitting.

She also spent a few hours going over her cases with other counselors in her office. Vanessa wasn't sure how long this nonsense with the sheriff's office was going to drag out and she wanted to make sure her families were taken care of in the meantime.

All her colleagues were wary of her. They didn't say anything outright, but Vanessa could tell. After all, it wasn't every day not one but two uniformed officers came and escorted someone out of the office. Especially not an Epperson.

And then, as the long day finally finished, she went out to the car ready to see a friendly face—*Liam's* friendly face—but instead he'd been cool and reserved. Maybe he'd just been in super-agent mode again, but it still had stung. They had decided she should drive her car home and he would follow her in the new rental. She was no longer trying to stay away from her apartment now that Karine was with Andrea at a different location.

So now here they were, parked and walking up the stairs to her second-floor unit. He was only a couple feet behind her, but the chasm between them seemed huge to Vanessa.

Sadly, she didn't know Liam well enough anymore to know what was causing the distance. Was this just how he did his job? She could understand if he didn't want to be focused on her if he was trying to see if they were being watched or whatever.

Did he regret last night? Resent that she'd tricked him into getting into bed? She'd meant it in a lighthearted fashion, and he seemed to have taken it that way, but now she didn't know. He'd seemed fine this morning but hadn't touched her since she'd gotten off work.

He did finally touch her as she took the key out to open her apartment door. He touched her hand to take it from her.

"I'm going to go in and check it out first, just in case."

She stepped back as he drew his gun out of the holster under his jacket. She knew he carried a weapon, but still wasn't used to seeing it up close and personal. She hadn't even thought about checking her apartment before going in.

"Stay here," he said.

He was inside the door, weapon raised, before she could even respond. She watched from the entrance as he looked around corners and in closets. It didn't take him long to search her apartment—the two-bedroom, one-bath place wasn't very big—and he came back out, gun out of sight.

"Okay, all clear." He stood to the side so she could come through the door.

Still very much not touching her.

She stepped through, closed the door behind her and walked into the kitchen.

Maybe something had happened today that she didn't know about. His colleagues had arrived, she knew from the text he'd sent her. She now had their numbers in her phone as well as Andrea's and Karine's—although Karine's was just listed in her contacts under "Kay."

Maybe he had bad news and didn't want to tell her. Some info about the men they'd seen with Webb. Or, God forbid, the girls.

She turned to him, reaching out to touch his arm on the biceps. She stroked softly. "Is everything okay? Anything bad happen today?"

For just a second he leaned into her touch. She slid that hand up to his shoulder and reached her other arm up to the other shoulder, too, pulling him to her, even as she stepped toward him.

She thought for a moment he would meet her in the embrace, but instead he stiffened and pulled away.

"Everything's fine." He took another small step back. "I just want to get those girls out, that's all."

Vanessa didn't want to nag, didn't want to pressure him into talking if he didn't want to. But this tension around them was hard. She didn't like it and wanted to ease it if she could. She took another step toward him.

"Are you sure that's it? You seem…" She searched for the right word. Mad. Cold. "Distant. After last night, I just want to make sure everything is okay with us."

She smiled and reached for him.

His icy look stopped her. "You mean being concerned about the lives of seven young girls is not enough? Maybe you need to quit assuming the world revolves around you."

Chapter Fifteen

She tried not to show how his words hurt her. "I'm going to take a shower."

Vanessa turned and walked out of the kitchen. Her voice didn't shake. She didn't cry. Her shoulders and head were high. Hell, she'd had enough years of being an Epperson to know how to look as though she was in control no matter what.

But inside she could actually feel her heart crack. Once she was around the corner, she began rubbing her chest as if that would ease a pain that wasn't physical.

Liam still thought of her as a selfish, self-centered person. He all but hated her.

She walked into the bathroom, shut the door behind her and peeled off yesterday's offensive clothes. The dried salt dragged across her skin like sandpaper as she removed them.

He didn't hate her. That was melodramatic. But he sure as hell wasn't interested in being close to her.

Liam Goetz hadn't been a part of her life in eight years. It shouldn't affect her at all if he wasn't interested in being a part of her life now.

But it did. She felt the tears she couldn't fight anymore well up in her eyes as she opened the door and stepped into the shower. His words had sliced at her.

Especially after the past twenty-four hours. She didn't

think their lovemaking had erased all the pain from their past—nothing could do that—but she hadn't thought it was just physical. It had been hot and passionate and something more.

At least it had been for her.

Evidently it had just been an opportunity too good to pass up for him. Just sex. Whatever anger he'd had for her eight years ago he obviously still had now.

As if he had the right to be angry. He hadn't lost everything.

She tried to hold on to that thought, to hold on to the anger and let it push out the pain, but she couldn't. The look in Liam's eyes in the kitchen was inescapable in her mind. More tears fell at the thought of it. He regretted last night. Maybe not the physical act itself, but he regretted their intimacy. And he still thought her selfish and self-centered.

Some things never changed.

She was startled to see the door to the shower stall open. Liam stood there, fully dressed. He reached over and shut off the water.

"I'm an idiot. I'm sorry," he said.

Vanessa stood there, dripping. He didn't look anywhere but at her face. In her eyes. She thought she could see actual anguish in his.

It was hard to look at him. "You said what you felt. You weren't very gentle about it, but you shouldn't apologize for saying what you think is the truth."

"But that's it. It's not what I think is the truth."

He took a towel hanging on the rack next to him. She expected him to hand it to her, but instead he wrapped it over her head and began to gently dry her hair.

"You've always thought I was spoiled, Liam. Self-entitled."

His fingers gripped the wet ends of her hair with the towel. "You were young. Your family had gobs of money.

You usually got what you wanted. But even then you weren't spoiled. Weren't ever mean."

He left that towel on her head and grabbed another one and began drying her body, starting with her neck and shoulders. Vanessa wasn't sure what to do so she just stood there.

"And you definitely aren't spoiled now. You are the opposite of self-centered."

"But in the kitchen—"

"In the kitchen I was a moron." She closed her eyes as he dried his way down her torso slowly and firmly. "I let frustration from the case, frustration from our past, bubble up into where we are now. I'm sorry."

"About last night—"

He crouched and began to dry her feet, slowly working his way up her legs. "Last night and this morning were incredible. I was just having a little difficulty separating the past from the present."

She gasped softly as he dried all the way up her thighs. *You need to tell him everything.*

She pushed the thought away as he stood and wrapped the towel around her waist, drying her back and buttocks. He grabbed the towel on both sides and wrapped the edges around his fists to drag her closer. He put his head down so his forehead touched hers.

"I'm an idiot. I'm sorry." He echoed the same words he'd started the conversation with. "Come to bed with me and let me make it up to you."

She tilted up her face to tell him his apology wasn't necessary, but he captured her lips in a kiss as he pulled her hips closer with the towel. The heat was there instantly, as always. As his tongue met hers, she forgot to breathe. Forgot everything but this feeling that had always existed between them. Eight years hadn't erased it.

He reached down and scooped her up, towels and all. He carried her to the bedroom and lay her down gently, reverently.

And proceeded to more than make up for it.

AFTERWARD THEY BOTH fell into an exhausted sleep. Their bodies didn't give them any other option. The pink light of dawn was creeping through her bedroom window when Vanessa finally peeled her eyes open.

Liam was lying on his side against her, face pressed to her neck, his arm and leg draped over her. She couldn't escape now if she wanted to.

She didn't want to.

She had never wanted to.

She needed to tell him the truth about eight years ago. It wouldn't change anything—nothing could change what had happened—but he deserved to know.

She felt him begin to stir. If she didn't tell him now, she'd never do it.

"I never chose my family, or my wealthy lifestyle, or whatever you want to call it, over you." Her voice was soft, husky with sleep, but she knew he heard her. As close as they were, she could feel the tension creep into his body.

"I don't understand. I came to your house. I heard you tell your family you didn't want to see anyone."

At least he was still lying against her. She just needed to get it out. "You asked me to marry you on September twelfth."

"I remember." His voice was strained.

"Do you? Do you really remember that day?" she asked.

They'd been on the beach walking. He'd gotten out of the army a few months prior and had started a job at the Drug Enforcement Agency—brought in as an agent because of his experience in Special Forces. He hadn't been exactly sure where they would be sending him, but he knew it would be Philadelphia, Chicago or Salt Lake City.

Wherever it was, he'd wanted Vanessa to come with him.

They'd been apart too much for the four years he was in the army, only seeing each other when he could make it home on leave. And even then they'd had to sneak around if they'd wanted any intimate time with each other. Vanessa had just barely turned twenty and still lived at home.

He'd asked her to marry him—to go to Vegas or a justice of the peace—so it could be done quickly. Both of them knew her parents would never give their blessing. So Vanessa and Liam wouldn't ask for their blessing. They would just do it.

He would come back for her a month later. She had agreed to be ready and to meet him there at the beach with whatever she needed to bring.

The relief Vanessa had felt that he'd asked her to marry him was high. She'd had news of her own to tell him but hadn't known how to say it. His proposal had taken off a lot of the pressure.

"Do you remember my reaction when you asked me to marry you?" she said.

More tension. "Joy, I thought," he said. "I thought you were as excited about it as I was."

"Anything else?"

He stayed against her for a long minute. "I don't know." He finally shrugged. "You seemed a little distracted or something, but I thought it had to do with all the planning and maybe fear about your parents. I definitely remember the fact that you wouldn't let me make love to you on the beach."

Vanessa closed her eyes and nodded. This was it. "Because I was young, and didn't know anything. And I was afraid having sex might hurt the baby," she whispered.

She knew the exact second her words sank in. He jerked away from her and was sitting up in less than a second flat.

"What?"

"That's why I was distracted that day. I had just found out I was pregnant the day before."

Myriad emotions crossed his face. "You were pregnant?"

"From when you had been home on leave six weeks before."

He still stared at her, mouth agape.

"I wasn't sure how to tell you," she continued. "I knew the job with the DEA was a big thing, and I wasn't sure exactly what our plans would be...if a baby would even fit into the plans."

She rushed on before he could say anything. "But then you asked me to marry you. You had to leave that night and things were crazy. I thought I would just tell you once you came back for me. We would figure it out together."

He blinked rapidly. "I don't understand."

Vanessa closed her eyes and took a deep breath. She had to get through this without breaking down.

"I went to a doctor to make sure everything was okay and someone at the office tipped off my parents." She opened her eyes. "They found out about the baby two days before you were supposed to come back. I told them I was leaving with you. That we were getting married."

Vanessa could feel the tears welling, but she forced them back. If she let herself start crying now, she'd never get through this. "My parents and I fought. I walked a few steps down our big staircase and then turned to yell some smart-aleck remark back up at them."

"Nessa—"

"I tripped. I fell all the way down."

Vanessa couldn't remember much about the fall. She remembered a sharp pain in her midsection before everything went black.

She looked over at Liam, who was staring at her as if he

could barely comprehend what she was saying. She knew this was a lot to take in.

"They took me to the hospital. I lost the baby." Her throat closed up and the words came out as barely more than a squeak.

"Oh, my God, Nessa." Liam ran a hand over his face. "Why didn't you tell me? Why didn't you call right away?"

"I was sedated at the hospital when they did an emergency D & C to keep anything from rupturing."

"Of course. I understand that. I would've understood it then, too. I would've been there."

"I came home the next day, but I was so out of it, Liam. I didn't know what day it was. I was distraught. My parents' doctor continued to keep me on drugs."

She saw realization dawn on his face. "When you didn't meet me at the beach like you were supposed to, I came to your parents' house. You were still under sedation when I got there."

"Yes. But, in their defense, I was hysterical. I wasn't handling anything well. Sobbing uncontrollably for hours."

Liam closed his eyes. Every nuance of his expression bespoke pain.

"When your father said you weren't going anywhere, that you'd changed your mind about everything, I didn't believe him. But when I heard you say you didn't want to see me, I thought he must have been telling the truth. You said you didn't want to see me—*to make me leave*."

She couldn't stop the tears. "It's all very blurry to me, but the one thought I kept having was that I didn't know how to tell you. I had miscarried our baby, Liam, from my own stupidity. I didn't want to tell you. So the words you heard were probably true."

He shook his head, wiping a hand across his face again, wearily.

"But I never meant I didn't want to marry you," Vanessa

continued. "My dad knew that and deliberately misled you. Once I began to come around, to realize I hadn't seen you, it was too late. It was days past when we were supposed to meet. My dad didn't tell me you'd come by, or what he'd said, until much later."

They both sat looking at each other in silence. The past lay between them like a canyon.

Vanessa finally spoke. "What my parents did was unforgivable. Once I found out, I walked away from them without looking back. But you had also walked away without looking back."

Chapter Sixteen

Liam felt as if he had been hit by a truck. The so-called facts that had shaped every detail of his life for the past eight years had just been proved false with one relatively brief conversation.

He couldn't sit on the bed any longer. Too much energy was coursing through him. He was still naked, so he grabbed his boxers from the floor and put them on.

He wanted to punch a wall, to fight an unseen foe, to howl out his pain. For a barely twenty-year-old Vanessa who had lost their baby. For himself at twenty-two thinking the love of his life had left him cold.

For all the years that had been lost. The pain both of them had lived through.

"Why didn't you tell me, Nessa?" he whispered, stopping his pacing. "Find me and make me understand?"

"After I left my parents I looked for you, but you were gone. I called that phone number you'd given me with the DEA, but they said you were unavailable. I tracked down your buddies here on the island a few days later, like I told you, hoping you were still on the Outer Banks. They told me what you'd said."

"Vanessa Epperson will never be anything but a selfish, spoiled brat who doesn't have it in her to care about another person." Liam remembered what he'd said. And at the time he had meant every word.

She shrugged. "That, combined with what had just happened, was too much for me. I pretty much shut down."

Liam walked over to the window and looked out. It was a terrible view of a parking lot and Dumpster, a testament of the modest rent of the apartment complex.

"Not that it makes a difference now, but when you called the DEA, I was on a deep undercover operation in Chicago. They didn't usually put someone so new under right away, but they'd needed someone young, rough around the edges and with nothing to lose, to go in immediate under pretty dire circumstances. I fit the bill to a tee."

He didn't tell her that he'd nearly died in that mission. He'd stayed in deep cover for six months, and when the DEA made its move against the drug ring he'd infiltrated, there had been such a shoot-out that he'd ended up in the hospital with two gunshot wounds.

He turned back to glance at her. "The DEA wouldn't have provided any info about me to you, of course. They didn't tell me of any messages."

"I didn't leave one," she whispered.

"And you've been away from your family ever since? Even though I know they didn't approve of me, I know you guys were so close."

She sat upright against the headboard of her bed and brought her knees to her chest under the sheet. She wrapped her arms around them. "I just couldn't stay there. I couldn't look at them the same ever again after that. I know the miscarriage wasn't their fault, but I just couldn't forgive them for chasing you away."

He pressed his forehead against the coolness of the window. "I should've come back to check on you. To fight for you. For us."

He hadn't been able to because of his mission.

But he wouldn't have anyway, even if his job at the DEA hadn't prohibited it. Because he'd always believed, deep inside, that the poor, orphaned kid—who'd been in trouble with the law—being raised by his grandmother, wasn't good enough for Vanessa Epperson, Princess of the Outer Banks.

Somewhere in his mind he'd always known it was just a matter of time before she figured it out, too. So when her parents had stood there and told him it had finally happened—that she'd come to her senses and realized he could never provide for her the way she would want to be provided for—it was just what he'd always expected.

And while he'd never really believed those harsh things he'd said to his friends—he'd been so angry and hurt at the time—he had to admit he had wondered, *worried*, if she could live without the pampering she'd been so used to.

How wrong he'd been. This tiny apartment—with a view of a Dumpster, for God's sake—was proof of that. That piece of junk car she drove, another. She not only could live without it, she had been choosing to live without it of her own accord for nearly a decade.

He shook his head. "I never should've said that to my friends. Whether I believed it or not, I never should have said it," he said without looking at her.

"I was spoiled."

Now he turned. "You were *loved*. Pampered, but not spoiled. You never thought of yourself as better than others or that your money entitled you to things other people couldn't have."

Her arms were still wrapped around her knees as if she were trying to keep the pieces from flying apart. That look, that sadness he'd recognized the first day he'd seen her, was back. At least now he understood what it meant.

She'd lost a child.

They'd lost a child.

Liam had no doubt it would've been loved—a little boy or girl. But having a child so early on would've changed the course of his life. He doubted he would be employed at Omega right now or would've shot so high in the ranks at the DEA.

Liam would've given the career stuff up in a heartbeat to have had Vanessa—and their child—healthy and happy and with him.

He was a man of action. A guy who got things done, often by any means necessary. It made him very effective at hostage rescue.

But there was no action he could take now, nothing that could ever be done, that would erase the desperate sadness that sometimes crept into Vanessa's eyes.

Too many years had passed, and even though they had just spent the night wrapped in each other's arms, the emotional chasm between them felt too large to ever be fully bridged.

Liam could never make up for the time lost. He felt a heavy weight on his shoulders. What could he do?

He, the man of action, couldn't figure out any action to take.

"Liam—"

A pounding on the front door stopped them.

Liam glanced at his watch. "Expecting anybody at seven o'clock on a Saturday morning?"

"No. Definitely not."

Liam snatched up his weapon from where he'd set the holster on the chair in the living room last night before going in to apologize to her in the shower.

He slipped on his jeans and she grabbed a robe. They walked to the front door. Vanessa cracked it open just the slightest bit.

It was Tommy Webb.

"Where's Liam Goetz?" the man asked without any sort of greeting. "He needs to come down to the sheriff's office to answer some questions."

Liam stuck his head in front of the crack so Webb could

see him. "I'm right here. What do you want?" He kept his weapon down at his leg where the assistant sheriff wouldn't notice it.

"Someone saw the two of you together and recognized you. I understand you had quite the run-ins with the law when you lived here before. I have some questions for you."

"Fine," Liam said. "I need a couple minutes to get dressed."

"Be warned, I have a man planted at the back of the complex, too. So don't try to run."

Liam rolled his eyes. "I'm not going to jump from a second-story balcony to get away from you just because you have *questions*. I'll be out in a few minutes."

"Hurry up."

Liam shut the door.

"What are we going to do?" Vanessa asked.

"I'm going to go with him."

"What?"

"He doesn't know that I'm law enforcement. At a cursory glance, because of some of the undercover work I've done, my employment with Omega or the DEA doesn't show up in a background check. I don't work undercover anymore, so my info is in all law-enforcement networks, but you have to dig a little further to find it."

"Are you sure?"

"He wouldn't be here like this if he knew I was law enforcement. He just thinks I'm a punk with a record who has shown up at a pretty inconvenient time."

Liam got dressed in fresh jeans and a black T-shirt.

"Why does he want to question you if he's the one involved with the trafficking ring?"

Liam wasn't sure about that. "I don't know. Maybe my connection to you. To see if there are holes in our story about Karine."

He slipped on his tennis shoes and sat to tie them. "I'm

going to text Derek and Joe. Stay here and don't go anywhere with anyone except them. One of them will be here within fifteen minutes."

Her face was worried. He wished he could reassure her.

"Should I call my dad and get him to send his lawyer?"

Liam knew how much it cost her to ask that. He sent his text to Derek and walked over to stand right in front of her. He tucked her hair behind both ears on either side of her face and left his hands on her cheeks.

"I'm going to be fine. This is actually a good thing," he said. "It gives me a chance to size up Webb. He thinks he's questioning me, but I'm going to be doing some delving of my own."

She nodded but didn't look too convinced. He reached down and kissed her gently. "I wish I could stay with you. I don't want to leave you now, especially not after our talk. Are you okay?"

Webb knocked on the door again. "Let's go, Goetz," he called.

Liam ignored him, all his focus on Vanessa.

She nodded. "Yeah, I'm okay. Just worried about you."

Liam's phone chirped with a message from Derek. Joe was only five minutes from Vanessa's apartment and would be there shortly.

That reassured Liam. After the near-drowning episode, he was loath to leave her alone. He kissed her again.

"Joe Matarazzo will be here any minute. He's an Omega agent, too. One of the best. Don't let him charm you into doing something stupid."

Vanessa raised one eyebrow. "I make no promises."

Liam chuckled and kissed her again. "I'll let you know as soon as I'm out."

"Be careful. You don't know who you can trust."

Liam turned and opened the door to Tommy Webb. He was very aware of that fact.

Chapter Seventeen

Webb started with the questions Liam had been expecting. How he knew Vanessa. His history with the police. Where he and Vanessa had been this week. If he knew anything about a teenage runaway sought for multiple crimes.

Webb showed him the footage of the break-in turned murder. Looking at it, knowing it couldn't possibly be Karine because she'd been with them on Tuesday night, Liam could easily see the setup.

Long brown hair evident throughout the clip. A slightly blurred image of Karine's face superimposed over whoever the person was in the video.

But it was a damn good job, Liam had to admit.

The questions took more than an hour. Webb would come at him from one angle and then another, hoping to catch Liam in a lie or a statement that contradicted what Vanessa had told them.

It was nothing more than a fishing expedition. Webb didn't have any real information about anything, partially because neither Liam nor Vanessa had done anything wrong.

But part of it was something else. As though Webb really was trying to get to the bottom of something he didn't quite understand. That he knew something was wrong but didn't know what.

Liam decided to take a chance.

Up until now Liam had been playing the bored hard-ass when answering Webb's questions—leaning back in his chair, focusing on his fingernails or an invisible spot on the leg of his jeans. But he stepped out of his role for a minute and really looked at the young assistant sheriff.

Webb was startled by Liam's sudden intensity as Liam leaned forward and put his weight on his forearms on the table between them.

"Webb, why are we here at this ungodly hour on a Saturday morning?"

Webb was taken aback by the question. "What do you mean? I'm trying to solve a murder. That's my job, Goetz. I'm the assistant sheriff of—"

Liam didn't let him finish his tirade. "And has there been anything odd about this particular murder, Webb? Stuff that just isn't adding up?"

Liam realized he was taking a pretty big chance. But if his instincts were correct, then they'd been wrong and Webb wasn't the person involved with the trafficking ring.

Webb looked at Liam for a long moment. "What sort of stuff?"

So the man *was* suspicious.

Liam shrugged. "I'm not sure exactly. Things just not adding up the way you think they should."

"Do you know something I need to know about?"

Liam turned and glanced at the two-way mirror behind him. He had no idea who was listening in on this conversation. Even if Webb wasn't their guy, it was someone from this office, and that person could be listening. Liam couldn't mention Karine or the girls.

On the other hand, if Webb was what Liam thought he was—an overzealous cop with political ambitions trying to make a name for himself and get some publicity by solving a murder—he could be an excellent ally.

"Webb, go see who's in the observation room."

"Why?"

"Just do it."

Webb shook his head but got up and left the interview room. A few moments later he was back.

"There's nobody in there," Webb said. "It's barely eight o'clock on a Saturday morning. Unless people have to be here, they're at home."

When Webb sat, Liam leaned forward and spoke as softly as he could.

"Somebody is going to figure out you have me here. I don't know who, but whoever that person is, you need to watch him, Webb. Carefully."

"What the hell are you talking about?"

"Did someone tell you to bring me in for questioning?"

"No. I figured out who you were and brought you in myself."

Liam leaned forward again. "Are you reporting directly to anyone about this case?"

"Why do you care?"

"Just answer."

Webb shrugged. "Nobody out of the ordinary. Just the sheriff."

"Is McBrien still the sheriff?"

Webb nodded. "How do you know that?"

"It's not my first time in this room, remember?"

"Yeah, I report to the sheriff—so what?"

"Has anybody else taken an unusual interest in the case? Asked questions about it? Followed very closely? Maybe offered to help?"

"This is a small place, Goetz. We don't get many murders, so, yeah, a lot of people in the office have been interested. Everybody has. Look," he continued, "I don't know what kind of game you're playing, but it's not going to work."

The man was confused, Liam knew, and irritated. Liam

didn't blame him for either feeling. But Liam was pretty sure that whoever was behind the trafficking ring was going to burst in here at any minute. They would be carefully monitoring who Webb brought in. If they were paranoid— and they would be—they would look further than the cursory glance Webb had given Liam's record.

Whether Liam was in town because of the human-trafficking ring or not, whoever was behind it would not want an active Omega Sector agent talking to the person they were using as their puppet.

"Anything about the video strike you as odd, Webb? A burglar leaving her long brown hair—an easily identifying feature—down for everyone to see? The fact that the burglar didn't turn and run when she could've easily made it to the door?"

He had Webb's full attention now. But Liam was running out of time and he knew it.

"Something's not right. I think you know that," Liam whispered, leaning closer. "Don't let it go."

"Who are you?" Webb asked just as softly.

The door to the interview room opened and an older man walked in.

"Goetz, it's been quite a long time," the man said. "Didn't expect to see you here again."

Sheriff McBrien. Was he the one behind all this? Did he know that Liam was law enforcement?

Webb looked surprised to see his boss. "Wasn't expecting you this morning, Sheriff."

"Well, when I heard my old friend Goetz was here, I thought I would stop by. What are you doing back around these parts?"

Liam still didn't know what McBrien knew, so he kept to his original story.

"I'm here visiting a friend."

"Vanessa Epperson?" McBrien asked.

"Yeah, we've sort of reconnected." Liam forced himself to relax in his chair. "You know, old flames and all that."

"It's been quite a long time, hasn't it?" McBrien cocked his head to the side. "Any particular reason why the flame has rekindled now?"

Liam shrugged with practiced nonchalance. "She called me out of the blue. Women. Hell if I understand them."

"I brought in Mr. Goetz to corroborate Ms. Epperson's story about her contact with the teenage runaway who may be our murder suspect." Webb was obviously trying to impress his boss with his thoroughness.

"And did you find out anything interesting?" Sheriff McBrien asked, coming to stand behind the seat next to Webb but not sitting.

Webb stared at Liam, but Liam didn't try to communicate anything. McBrien was too close, and too astute, for that. Liam willed the younger man to make the right decision and not say anything to McBrien about their hushed conversation a few moments ago.

"No, nothing particularly interesting," Webb muttered after a moment.

Liam forced himself not to breathe a sigh of relief.

"Mostly, I brought him in because of his past record," Webb continued.

The sheriff's eyes narrowed slightly. "Did Mr. Goetz say anything about his current occupation?"

Liam sat straighter in his seat.

Damn.

McBrien knew. *McBrien* was the one who had checked deeper into his record. And here he was, early on a weekend morning, checking on the situation personally rather than reading the report later.

Webb wasn't behind the trafficking ring. McBrien was.

"I probably shouldn't call you 'mister,' right, Goetz?"

McBrien said, watching him closely. "You probably prefer the title 'agent,' since you work for Omega Sector."

"What?" Webb fairly spewed. "That wasn't in his record."

"Yeah, you have to dig a little deeper to find it. But it's there," McBrien said.

Liam met Webb's eyes.

That, he tried to communicate to the other man. *That is an example of what I meant when I asked about things that bothered you around here.*

All he could do was hope Webb would see it for himself.

Liam shrugged. "I'm not here on any official business. So, no, I didn't mention it."

"Were you going to keep letting Webb treat you like a suspect? How long were you planning to keep the fact that you're law enforcement from him?"

Liam knew he had to tread carefully. He didn't have a good reason to keep his occupation a secret from Webb. Under normal circumstances he would've made it known immediately. Professional courtesy.

"Like I said, my reason for being here was completely nonprofessional." Liam winked at them. "I think that Officer Atwood who came to the hotel on Tuesday can attest to that."

McBrien didn't look convinced.

"Look, I haven't really mentioned to Vanessa that I'm law enforcement. I don't know how that's going to go over, so I'd like to keep it quiet from her and tried to keep it quiet from your assistant sheriff here." Liam shifted his weight in his chair. "Webb was questioning me about that teenage kid. I don't know anything, just like Vanessa didn't know anything. I just thought I would keep my Omega tie out of it. Easier for everyone."

He turned to Webb. "Besides, sometimes mentioning you're a federal agent makes some people nervous. Not that Webb here had anything to be nervous about. He was just doing his job. A routine follow-up with me, given my tie with Vanessa."

McBrien looked over at Webb. "Is that right?"

"Yes, sir."

Liam smiled. "See? No harm, no foul. But if you don't mind, I'd like to wrap this up. I've got a place a hell of a lot more interesting to be than this room." He winked at the two men. "I'll be staying at Vanessa Epperson's apartment if you need me. That's where Webb picked me up."

Liam stood. He'd done all he could do. He just hoped McBrien bought it.

"Well, I apologize for my mistake," Webb said. "I hope there are no hard feelings."

Liam stuck his hand out to shake the younger man's. "You were just doing your job." He squeezed Webb's hand just slightly. "I hope you'll keep doing your job."

Get the message, kid.

Webb nodded. Liam hoped he understood.

McBrien was largely silent during the exchange. Liam wasn't able to read him. Was he suspicious?

As they exited the room McBrien slapped Liam on the back. "Well, I may not be sure exactly what happened here this morning, but I am very glad to see you found yourself on the right side of the law. Happy to have you as one of the good guys, Goetz."

He stuck his hand out. Liam forced himself to shake it, although all he really wanted to do was to crush the man up against the wall and force him to tell where the girls were being held.

Liam had no doubt McBrien was behind this. He wanted to knock the smug look out of the other man's eyes and beat him until he fell to the floor.

"It's good to be one of the good guys, McBrien," he said instead.

Liam forced himself not to say anything further. Nothing sarcastic. Nothing that would give McBrien a hint that they were on to him. They walked the few steps to the lobby. Vanessa was there on the opposite side, looking in the other direction. She wasn't supposed to be here, but he was damn sure glad she was. Her presence gave added credibility to his lover story.

"But to be honest, I couldn't care less about good guys or bad guys," Liam murmured to the other men, gesturing to and all but leering at Vanessa. "I just care about *that*."

McBrien smirked. Webb pursed his lips in disapproval. Good, hopefully Liam wasn't wrong about the younger man and Webb would start really looking at what was going on around him. Liam had done all he could do to suggest there was a problem.

He knew both men were watching as he left them in the hallway and walked over to Vanessa. She was startled when she saw him, and stopped her worried shifting of her weight back and forth on her feet.

"I know I'm not supposed to be here—"

Liam kissed her.

He kissed her to stop her from accidentally saying anything that might go against his story. He kissed her to seal the story that he and Vanessa were lovers. He kissed her because…hell, for his entire life he'd never been in the same room as Vanessa and not wanted to kiss her.

But mostly he'd kissed her because he hadn't been able to this morning, after her news about all she'd lost—all they'd lost—eight years ago. He couldn't change the past, and didn't know what the future held, but right now he could kiss her.

He broke off the kiss a moment before it would've become uncomfortable for everyone.

"Thanks for coming to check on me," he said, leaning his forehead against hers. "I'm free to go."

But would he ever be free to leave Vanessa again? Liam had no idea.

Chapter Eighteen

"You weren't supposed to be here," Liam murmured to her as they walked across the parking lot together.

"I made Joe bring me," she said. "I wasn't sure what they were going to accuse you of, and I didn't want to leave you at Webb's mercy."

They made it to the car. Liam greeted Joe and they both got in the back. "Webb is not our guy."

"Really?" Vanessa stared at him. "What about all his questions and having a video clip that can't possibly be Karine?"

"I think he's being used to do someone else's dirty work. Webb's beginning to realize it, too."

"If the assistant sheriff isn't your guy, who do you think is?" Joe asked from the front seat.

Liam looked over at Vanessa. "Sheriff McBrien."

The sheriff. Vanessa could feel herself blanch. She and Liam had known the man most of their lives, although for Liam, not in a good way.

"*What?* Are you sure?" she asked.

"Webb may be a jerk with a political agenda, but he's not the one behind this. Webb can tell something is off about this entire investigation. He doesn't know what it is, but he knows something's not right."

"But *McBrien*?"

Marcus McBrien was an elected official, for heaven's

sake. Knowing that someone you'd known for years was capable of such crimes against girls was sickening on multiple levels. To think about how long it could've been going on, right under everyone's noses...?

Almost unbearable.

"I started thinking it wasn't Webb as soon as he brought me in for questioning and didn't know I was Omega. It wouldn't take much extra work to get that information. Someone who has something to hide—especially something as big as a trafficking ring with a missing girl—would check me out more thoroughly."

"And the sheriff was that person," Joe confirmed for him.

"Yep. And McBrien was determined not to leave Webb alone with me once he figured out I was Omega."

Vanessa didn't necessarily consider herself a violent person, but if McBrien was here right now she would pound him into the ground with a baseball bat. And wouldn't lose a moment's sleep over it.

After she found out where he was keeping the girls, of course.

"You certain?" Joe asked from the driver's seat. "Should we pull Derek off tailing Webb and put him on McBrien?"

"Yeah." Liam nodded. "Webb isn't our guy. I may never be besties with him, but he's just trying to do his job."

Joe snickered at *bestie* and took out his phone to text. "I'll let Derek know, then take you guys back to Vanessa's place." He made eye contact with Vanessa through the rearview mirror. "That good?"

Vanessa smiled. "Yeah."

"She wasn't supposed to be here at all," Liam told Joe. "Good job on that."

"Hey." Joe started the car then held both hands up. "Don't look at me. She was coming here with or without me. Unless you wanted me to sit on her, the best I could do was tag along."

"Couldn't you use your super powers?" Liam asked. "I don't think sitting on her would be necessary."

Vanessa imagined no red-blooded woman would consider having someone with the charm and good looks of Joe sitting on her a bad thing, although she didn't mention that to Liam.

"Super powers?" she asked.

"Yeah." Liam smiled as Joe drove out of the sheriff's office parking lot. "Joe is a hostage negotiator for Omega. He can pretty much talk anybody into doing anything. It's his super power—charming the pants off everyone."

Vanessa had been so worried about Liam and what was happening at the sheriff's office that she hadn't paid much attention to Joe beyond a cursory appreciation of his good looks. Now she really studied him.

"Normally, I just try to charm the pants off women," Joe muttered. "Guys, I prefer, leave their clothes on."

"Oh, my gosh, you're Joe *Matarazzo*." Realization dawned and she saw him wince in the rearview mirror at the recognition. "I think our families were both in Vail or Aspen a couple years at the same time. All the girls were gaga over you."

Of course, the Matarazzo family had made the Epperson family wealth look like chump change. They were wealthy with a capital *W*. Like, trace-their-family-back-to-the-*Mayflower* prestigious.

Joe was one of the Matarazzo sons and very much a playboy.

"So you work for Omega Sector?" she asked. She couldn't imagine anyone bearing the Matarazzo name would ever need a job.

"Yeah, I found a skill set I was good at or, as jackass over here calls it, my 'super powers.'" Their eyes met again in the rearview mirror. "Not that it helped me keep you at your place."

Joe looked over at Liam. "And you better shut up. I've got some secrets on you I'm sure you don't want shared, speaking of pants being off."

Vanessa studied scenery out the window at that. She knew Liam had had a life since they'd last seen each other. She'd even had a couple of relationships of her own since he'd left, however briefly. But she did not want to think about Liam with other women. Evidently, a *number* of other women.

Especially when she should've been the only woman in his life all this time. Would have been if they could've put their pride aside and fought for their relationship.

She should've tried harder to track him down. He should've come back and at least demanded to talk to her face to face.

They both should've handled it all so much differently.

Vanessa had never been too much of a romantic. Now, after years of being a social worker, she was even less so.

Eight years was a long time. The attraction was very definitely still there, but that wasn't enough. She was glad he now knew about the miscarriage, about what her parents had done—albeit to try to protect her—but ultimately that didn't change anything.

Vanessa looked at her hand that was linked with Liam's on his knee. They hadn't been able to figure out how to fight for their relationship when they were young and stupid and so in love with each other that it was tangible. How could they fight for it now when they were both so much more wary and wise?

And did they even want to fight for it?

Vanessa pushed all the questions out of her mind as they pulled up to her apartment complex. All that mattered right now was the safety of those girls. Whatever happened with Liam would happen. Vanessa wasn't going to worry about it now.

Joe—Joe *Matarazzo*, for heaven's sake—opened her door for her when they parked. It was still hard to believe the infamous playboy was now in law enforcement. He was one guy who would never be able to work undercover.

"I was just kidding about Liam with my comment," Joe said softly. "Just talking trash like team members do."

"Thanks." She raised an eyebrow at him. "But I think we both know there was quite a bit of truth to that jest."

"Just give him a chance," Joe said, his volume trailing off as they walked to the front of the car near Liam.

She glanced at both men. "The most important thing right now is to find those girls."

Joe nodded. "I'm heading back to Derek at the sheriff's office. If we need to follow McBrien, it will have to be a two-car job."

Liam nodded. "I'll use the laptop to see if any of McBrien's known associates sets off any alarms in the Omega system. I'm sure he probably keeps himself pretty clean, though."

"Derek and I will do the same from the car."

"We're going to need to move fast if we get any information. I'm not sure if McBrien bought my excuse for being here, although I think he did."

"What excuse was that?" she asked.

Liam turned fully toward her. "You."

Oh.

With Liam looking at her that way, every thought she'd just had about their relationship not working out vanished. With just one look she was completely enthralled with him again. She forced herself to look away.

Focus on the girls.

"We're ready for either a water or a land siege." Joe's words interrupted her thoughts. "We can get a full SWAT team in from Norfolk if you want, but I doubt there's any way McBrien wouldn't hear about that."

"And immediately kill all the girls," Liam finished for him. "No, we're going to have to handle this on our own."

Joe nodded. "That's how I prefer it anyway."

Vanessa looked back and forth between the two men. "You mean you guys are going to go onto the boat to get the girls?"

Liam cocked his head to the side and gave her that cocky smile she both loved and hated. "Hostage rescue. It's what I do, baby. Joe and Derek do the same thing, although Joe usually does a lot of talking with the perps beforehand."

Joe rolled his eyes. "It's not like I sit around and chat with them. But if there's any way of getting hostages out without using force in most situations, I try that. But not in this case. If we can get these girls out without being harmed, I don't give a damn whether those bastards are hurt in the process or not."

Liam looked at Vanessa. "If we can find out where the boat is, we can take it by stealth, or by more brutal means if necessary, as long as the girls won't be harmed. Or if they've moved to land, we're equipped for that, too."

Liam could handle himself. Even when they were younger, he'd had an awareness, a mental toughness that had gone way beyond someone of his teenage years. It had been one of the things that had drawn her to him.

But she still didn't like the thought of him risking his life. No amount of mental toughness could stop a bullet. The risks here were very real.

Liam took her hand. "Let's get some rest. You need a chance to regroup."

Vanessa nodded. Between talking about the miscarriage, Liam being taken in for questioning and thinking about the danger he'd be in trying to get the girls out, she felt as if her world was flying apart in a hundred different directions.

"Keep us posted," he told Joe as the man got back into his car.

LIAM CHECKED HER apartment again before he would let her inside. The thought of eating crossed her mind, but she pushed it away. She just wanted to sleep. She barely remembered making it to her bed and falling on it. But when she woke up the sun was much lower in the sky and she could smell…bacon?

Her shoes were off and she'd been covered up, obviously by Liam. She made her way out of bed and into the kitchen. She found Liam there making breakfast food with ease.

"You cook?" The Liam she had known years ago couldn't boil water. He'd never had to worry about cooking with his grandmother around. Vanessa made her way over to the table and sat.

He turned and smiled. "I do all right with breakfast."

"Breakfast is your specialty, huh?" She tried to keep her tone light but could tell it fell short. Joe's insinuation about Liam's sexual exploits came back to mind.

Liam looked over at her, jaw set. "I won't lie to you. There have been women since I left the Outer Banks."

"How many?" The words were out of her mouth before she could stop them. "Never mind. I really don't want to know."

She began playing with the napkin on the table. Did she want to know? No. She didn't want to think about Liam with one other woman, much less countless others. "I'm sure you've had other boyfriends."

"A couple, but never anything serious. And not for a pretty long while."

Liam didn't say anything, just finished cooking. He then

put the bacon, eggs and toast on plates and carried them over to where she sat. He didn't sit himself.

"There were a lot," he admitted finally. "A lot of women over a lot of years."

Vanessa couldn't make eye contact with him anymore. She felt stupid for asking. She hadn't expected him to be true to a relationship that didn't exist. It had never even occurred to her.

But to hear that she had meant so little to him that there had been *a lot* of women? She felt daggers flying into her heart. "I understand," she finally said, her food untouched. "You had freedom, had opportunity, had a chance to make up for time you'd lost just being with me for so many years."

He just stood in front of her for a long moment, then put both hands on the back of her chair, trapping her there as he leaned down so their faces were closer together.

"You know, I told myself those very words for years. *Years.*" His face inched closer. "And even more, I believed it. I believed that those women made me happy. Complete. A fun guy. That my freedom was the most important thing, and as long as I had that, I was golden. Had dodged a bullet by getting away from you. From us."

She couldn't breathe. She didn't want to hear this.

Liam dipped his head even lower so they were eye to eye. "It took me a long time to realize—"

His words were cut off by his phone ringing where it sat on the table.

"Damn it," he muttered. "It's Joe. I've got to take this."

He brought the phone to his ear. "Joe, this damn well better be the most important thing you've ever said."

Vanessa was close enough to hear Joe's response even though the phone was at Liam's ear.

Sheriff McBrien had somehow gotten away.

Chapter Nineteen

The conversation with Vanessa, as much as it needed to happen, would have to wait.

"Did you get made?" Liam asked Joe.

"No," Derek said, also on the line. "McBrien tricked us from the beginning. He sent someone out to his car around four o'clock. The guy had the same general build and coloring, so from our distance we thought it was him."

"Dude led us to a restaurant clear on the other side of the island," Joe continued. "We couldn't see inside, but we had both exits covered. When he came out an hour later, we realized we'd been set up."

Frustration knotted Liam's gut. He hadn't fooled McBrien this morning; the man was on to them.

"By the time we got back to the station, he had already left for real," Derek finished.

Liam walked out of the kitchen. He didn't want to have this conversation in front of Vanessa, although he knew there was really no help for that. No matter where he went in this tiny apartment, she'd still be able to hear him.

"Those girls are as good as dead," Liam mumbled. "McBrien is probably on his way out there right now to get rid of any evidence."

"Maybe not," Derek said. "He'll only do that as a very last resort because of all the money he stands to lose. Especially now that he's going to have to lie low for a while. If there's any way he can keep them alive, he'll try to."

Liam prayed that was true. But even if it was, it wouldn't matter. Unless they could pick up McBrien's trail again, they were no closer to knowing where the girls were than they had been days before.

"We're going to head back to you, formulate a plan," Joe said. "Maybe you should have Andrea try talking to Karine again. See if, now that a couple of days have gone by, she remembers anything."

"It's worth a shot. I'll call her. See you guys in a few minutes." He disconnected the call and turned to find Vanessa standing just a few feet behind him at the entrance of the living room, face pale.

"You heard?" he asked.

"I got the general gist. McBrien got away. Those girls are in even more trouble than before and we're back to square one."

Liam didn't even know how to soften that. "Yeah. Basically. But I have been running McBrien's known associates. Hopefully that will provide us with some info."

"What sort of people are you looking for?"

Liam shrugged a shoulder. "No any one characteristic in particular, but anything that might ring any bells. Maybe an old high school buddy he's known a long time and trusts implicitly. Or maybe a contact he's made more recently who might dabble in some illegal stuff on the side."

"It doesn't sound like something a computer can sort through."

"Definitely not. The Omega system can throw us info on people who have a criminal record, but McBrien won't have a lot. He's spent too many years keeping himself clean."

"So you're going through all this yourself."

Liam shrugged. "Me, the guys and Andrea. It's our best chance right now."

Liam knew it was a slim chance at best. Andrea was a hugely gifted profiler, even for her young age, but she couldn't pull something out of nothing. She would look for possible suspicious patterns with McBrien's associates—just as he, Joe and Derek would—but it was a time-consuming process and didn't guarantee results. If no one had ever seen McBrien with the men he was working with, there would be no possible link to them.

They could arrest McBrien, but it would be messy. No judge would allow them to hold him for long, and their only recourse would be to bring in Karine. Then it would be her word against the sheriff's. Traumatic for Karine and still wouldn't save the other girls.

If the worst possible scenario played out and they couldn't get the girls out safely, Liam would do his best to make sure McBrien went down for what he'd done to Karine at the very least. He would make sure the girl's story was told and her suffering wasn't in vain.

There was a knock on the door. Liam encouraged Vanessa to eat her food while he answered it, knowing it was Derek and Joe.

It wasn't. It was Assistant Sheriff Webb.

"You back to arrest me?" Liam asked.

"You should've told me from the very beginning you were Omega and almost all the questions could've been avoided," Webb replied.

Liam cocked one eyebrow. "You looking for an apology? Fine. Sorry I didn't tell you I was federal law enforcement."

Liam began to shut the door; he didn't have time to cater to the younger man's ego. Webb stopped him.

"No, I didn't come here for an apology. I came to tell you that you were right."

Those weren't the words Liam had been expecting.

Derek and Joe showed up behind Webb, both with their hands very close to their weapons.

"Guys, this is Assistant Sheriff Tommy Webb." He pointed to Derek and Joe. "Webb, these are my colleagues Agents Joe Matarazzo and Derek Waterman."

Webb nodded. "I guess you're not all here to see Vanessa Epperson. That seems to be the excuse de jour."

"No, we're not," Joe said. "But the real question is why are *you* here?"

"Let's at least get out of the hallway to have this conversation," Liam said, opening the door so everyone could enter. They all walked into the living room.

Vanessa joined them, coming to stand by Liam.

"Why is he here?" she asked.

"We were just asking him ourselves."

The younger man was uncomfortable, Liam could tell. He didn't blame Webb. There was a lot of animosity in the room and it was mostly pointed at him.

"You guys want to tell me exactly what the hell is going on?" Webb's frustration and confusion were evident.

"Why don't you tell us what you know and we'll work from there?" Liam said.

"Well, I know for sure that you're not in town to canoodle with Vanessa." He looked closer to where Liam's arm had wrapped around her waist and pulled her next to him. "Or not *just* to canoodle."

"Canoodle?" One of Joe's eyebrows popped up.

"Whatever. I know that's not why he's here. You're all not here for some sort of romantic venture."

"Okay, brilliant detective work, Webb," Derek interjected. "What else do you know?"

"I know there's something going on in the department. It involves Sheriff McBrien and Dwayne Anderson, the AV guy for the crime lab."

Finally a name. Liam looked over at Derek.

"I'm on it. Computer in the kitchen?"

"Yeah." Derek would run Anderson and they would

know anything there was to know about him within the hour. Hopefully it would be useful.

Webb watched Derek leave then turned back to Liam and the others. "I know it has something to do with that teenage runaway. The one accused of burglary and murder."

"Go on," Liam prompted.

"Well, I'd never heard anything about this girl at all, and then suddenly a week ago McBrien is asking me to personally find her. At first I didn't think anything of it. The sheriff's position is just as much political as it is law enforcement, so I thought maybe he was helping out a high-influence friend and trying to keep the situation under wraps. I honestly didn't think anything would come of it." He turned and pointed at Vanessa. "Until you showed up with her at the hospital.

"And then it got weird," Webb continued. "Girl wasn't at the hospital and McBrien got pretty stressed out when I told him she'd definitely been there but had run."

Webb began to pace.

"The next thing I know, we're doing car-to-car searches for some fugitive. We have a name but no real picture. The sheriff himself was searching cars. I've never seen that happen. Plus, he asks us to keep an eye out for the missing teenager while we're searching. Then the fugitive search stops as suddenly as it starts."

"Next thing I know, the teenage runaway we were searching for *discreetly* is a murder suspect and I'm supposed to question and perhaps even charge Vanessa Epperson for accessory."

Liam let him keep talking. It was important that Webb really understand for himself what was going on.

"So all the pressure to get this girl… Then, when I think I'm doing a good thing by bringing you in—" Webb turned to Liam "—the next thing I know, McBrien is letting you out. Just like you said he would. Because you're not only law enforcement, you're *elite* law enforcement. But Mc-Brien never even asked you one thing about the case or the girl. He should've asked you, regardless if you were Omega Sector or not."

Liam nodded. "He was trying not to draw attention back to the girl. In case I really was here for Vanessa and not on official Omega business. McBrien wasn't sure which."

Webb nodded. "When the sheriff left this afternoon, I went into his office. It's not unheard of. I've done it before. The fact that he lets others in there is either really gutsy or means he doesn't leave anything incriminating in there and is trying to give the appearance of an open-door policy."

Liam shrugged. "McBrien is definitely smart. I'd doubt he'd leave anything lying around his office."

"Yeah. Well, he came *back* into his office after he left. I ducked into his private bathroom, but was just about to announce myself when he got a phone call. Something weird."

Liam took a step closer. "Do you remember what was said?"

"I don't have to remember. I already had my phone out to take pictures if I found anything. So I recorded it."

Webb took his phone out. He'd made a video recording of the conversation. The video only showed the back of the bathroom door, but the audio was clear, at least Mc-Brien's side of it.

"Why are you calling me now, Anderson? I'm still at the office…Things are getting too complicated. We probably just need to get rid of the property and take the loss… Because there are people a lot smarter than Webb now involved. We just need to cut our losses…Fine, I'm listening. You have twenty seconds…

"Well, they certainly don't feel bad about taking advantage of our misfortune…I agree. Half is better than nothing. But it has to be tonight. If not, I'm going to get rid of it all personally...Okay, midnight, tonight. Harper's Cove. Don't call me again when you know I'm still at work."

Liam looked over at Joe. Midnight tonight at Harper's Cove. Liam knew where it was and knew it would be empty at this time of year.

The perfect place to sell the girls to some unknown buyer.

"So that's everything I have. You want to tell me what's going on?" Webb said.

Liam was willing to bet that Webb was a lot smarter than McBrien gave him credit for.

"Why don't you give me your best guess?" he said to the younger man.

"This missing teenager obviously has something on the sheriff. He was trying to find her quietly, through me and the bogus fugitive search. Then when that failed, he and Anderson killed some poor woman in her home and created some sort of phony murder video trying to frame or discredit the girl in case she came forward."

McBrien had definitely underestimated Tommy Webb.

"Human-trafficking ring," Liam told Webb. "One teenager—Karine—got away. There are seven more still on a boat somewhere."

Webb's curse was vile.

"We all agree with you," Vanessa said. "Liam and I have known the sheriff nearly two decades. It's inconceivable that he's capable of something like that."

Webb cursed again.

"Do you still have the girl? Is she somewhere safe?" he asked after a moment.

"Yes, she's with another Omega agent, someone not associated with either Vanessa or me," Liam told him. "Safe."

"It's already six o'clock," Joe said. "We don't have long to plan this rescue attempt. We'll need to be in position before their boat arrives in the cove. They won't be expecting anyone to already be out there."

"If you attack the boat, McBrien will kill those girls. I'm sure of it," Webb said.

Joe shook his head. "We're not going to use force unless there's no other option. Our plan is stealth. With any luck, we'll get the girls out before we even confront McBrien and whoever is with him."

"And by *confront*, Joe means take that son of a bitch down," Liam said. "I can guarantee that."

Chapter Twenty

Liam, Joe and Derek had done this before. It didn't take more than five minutes of hearing them plan for that fact to become obvious to Vanessa. They trusted each other. They respected each other.

They planned to get those girls out or to die trying.

Webb had helped them move an impressive amount of equipment, all in large black boxes, from Joe's and Derek's cars into her apartment. Then Webb left. He had his own role to play in this mission. He wouldn't be going out to the boat, but he would be making sure the buyers didn't escape after Liam and the guys got the girls out.

Vanessa just tried to stay out of the way as the men unpacked the boxes with certain things she recognized—guns, knives, some sort of dive skins—and many things she didn't. As they sorted and repacked what they would need, they discussed different possible scenarios.

"You're talking about a half dozen traumatized teenagers. They might try to fight us," Joe pointed out.

"Try to mention Karine's name if you can," Liam responded as he took a large duffel bag out of one of the boxes. "But we'll have to subdue them if necessary."

Vanessa hoped that wouldn't be necessary. She was sure the girls had been traumatized enough already.

They would be using some sort of watercraft they called a Zodiac, which was quiet and easy to maneuver. It was black and had no lights or reflective material on it, they explained. They would use an underwater trolling motor as long as they could then guide it the rest of the way manually.

The men themselves would also be in all black, using the cover of night to provide them with the stealth they needed to pull this off. A storm was brewing overhead. That would work to their advantage in masking sound.

Liam's background in Special Forces was obvious in everything he did as he situated himself for the operation. His placement of weapons, his ease with all the equipment, even the way he carried himself now that he was in full agent mode bespoke it.

"I wish there was something I could do," she said to him as the guys finished up with their final preparations. "Staying at the house with Karine doesn't seem like a very helpful position. What if we waited on the dock by the cove? That way when you guys got off the water she would be right there to reassure the girls."

Liam reached over and tucked a strand of her hair behind her ear, then cupped the back of her head with his large hand. "No. It leaves you too much out in the open. Knowing you're safe is the only way I can do this. It allows me to totally focus on those girls and getting them out. Besides, Andrea will be at the dock. Her presence will help the girls."

Andrea and Karine were on their way now to pick Vanessa up. Liam didn't want to take any chances on Vanessa being followed and Andrea would be able to spot and hopefully lose anyone tailing them.

"I don't like that you're the one taking all the chances."

"Risks are part of my job, but I've trained for them. Joe and Derek, too. This is what we do."

She hooked her hand around his arm, causing his elbow to bend and bring his face closer. "You just be careful."

"I will."

"And call me as soon as you've got them so I can bring Karine to see them."

"Yes, ma'am." Liam gave her a crooked smile and she felt her stomach do a little somersault.

She felt her phone buzz. Andrea was here to get her. It was just as well; Vanessa couldn't watch them prep any more. Every weapon she saw just reminded her of how much danger they would be in.

The sun was going down. They would be leaving soon. She said her goodbyes to Joe and Derek, and Liam walked her out to her car. He greeted Andrea and Karine.

"Tonight," he told Karine. "We're going to get the other girls out tonight. We know where they're going to be."

"Good," Karine said. "Thank you, Mr. Liam."

"Andrea will bring you as soon as we have them. We will probably need to meet at the hospital. That's the best place for them to go."

Karine flinched but nodded.

"It will be safe for them there. I promise."

"Okay."

Liam smiled at her. "Right now you and Vanessa are going to stay at the house. I'll call her first thing when you can see them."

He turned to Vanessa and opened the back door to the car for her. "Text me when you're at the house so I know you're okay."

She reached up and grabbed the center of his tight black shirt, pulling him closer. "Be. Careful."

She knew she had already said it, but she couldn't stop herself from saying it again.

"I will. Promise. This time tomorrow we'll be finishing up the conversation from the kitchen."

The one where he'd admitted to having been involved with *a lot* of women? She wasn't sure she wanted that. But she was willing to discuss darn near anything with him if it meant he was back safely.

"Deal," she whispered.

He kissed her softly. Sweetly.

Vanessa forced herself to step back. She had to leave now or she was never going to. She smiled at him and got in the car.

It was good that Andrea was driving, watching for anyone who might be following, because Vanessa was pretty much useless. Someone could've been directly behind them, high beams blazing, and Vanessa probably wouldn't have noticed. She was too busy thinking about Liam.

She just wanted this to be over. Wanted those girls to be safe. Wanted him and his friends to be safe, also.

Vanessa forced herself to focus. Liam and the team seemed more than prepared. They had all the equipment—under-water, above-water—they needed. When he had been in the army and she had waited at home, she'd never doubted his abilities. She wasn't going to start doubting them now.

The trip to the house Andrea had rented was made in silence, everyone focused on their own thoughts. It wasn't long before they pulled up there.

"You gals wait here while I secure the building," Andrea told them, leaving the car running. She took out her weapon—just as Liam had done every time they'd entered her apartment—and disappeared inside.

She was back in just over a minute.

"All clear," she said then smiled at Vanessa. "There's no reason to think this place has been compromised, and there definitely wasn't anybody tailing us, but precaution."

Vanessa smiled back. "I understand." She wasn't willing to take any chances with Karine's safety, either.

Andrea walked Vanessa and Karine in the front door.

The two women had obviously made themselves comfortable here. Karine immediately kicked off her shoes and headed straight for the fridge.

"I've basically been allowing her to eat whatever she wants, whenever she wants," Andrea whispered. "I figured, after everything, there couldn't be any real harm in that."

"Absolutely agree. Gallons of ice cream can probably help soothe any trauma. Or at least much more so than vegetables."

"She's been doing pretty well. Has woken up crying a few times and spends a lot of her time looking out at the water. But she's keeping it together. She's strong."

Vanessa nodded and watched Karine plop down on the couch, yogurt in hand—at least it wasn't ice cream—and turn on the television. "She's amazing."

"She'll have to heal on her own timetable. Nobody can set that for her," Andrea said, and then walked into the kitchen herself.

Sounded as though Andrea knew that from experience. She'd like to get to know the other woman better, but now wasn't the time.

"Okay, I'm going to meet Webb and help coordinate the Coast Guard's efforts." Andrea grabbed a water bottle from the fridge. "We want to catch McBrien and his buddies, but we also want the buyers, too. You guys stay here and wait for our call."

"How long do you think it will be?" Vanessa asked.

"It's hard to say. These types of ops have a lot of factors, and any one of them can affect the timetable. I would tell you to go to sleep, but I know you won't. But it will be after midnight, probably, before Karine will be able to see the girls."

If we can get the girls out alive. Andrea's eyes said it and Vanessa was glad she didn't say the actual words.

"After the call, someone will come get you to take you to them, okay?"

Vanessa watched as Andrea made her way over to Karine. She hugged the girl and whispered something to her. Karine nodded then sat back down.

"Follow behind me and lock the door," Andrea told Vanessa. "I know it doesn't have to be said, but don't decide to go for a walk or swim or anything. Just stay inside until we come for you."

Vanessa rolled her eyes. "Yeah, no worries. We'll binge watch some sitcoms or something if we can't sleep."

She knew she wouldn't sleep a wink. Not until she knew the girls were free and Liam was okay.

She locked and bolted the door behind Andrea then headed back into the living room. Karine was staring blankly ahead of her, yogurt still in her hand.

"You doing all right?" Vanessa asked as she sat slowly next to the girl on the couch.

"I hope everyone will be okay," Karine said.

"Liam is the very best, honey. His friends are, too. They'll get the girls out."

Karine nodded and scooted closer to Vanessa. "Okay, good."

"You'll need to be ready to see them and reassure them in the hospital. Do you want to go to sleep? Get some rest while you can?"

"No," the girl whispered. "I cannot sleep. It is hard to sleep always, but tonight I know I cannot."

Vanessa understood. "Then we'll just watch TV, okay? If we fall asleep, that's fine. If not, that's okay, too. What do you want to watch?"

Vanessa changed into shorts and a T-shirt before they searched through the channels until they found reruns of *The Brady Bunch*. When the channel promised they'd be playing the show all night, Vanessa and Karine settled back on the couch.

Vanessa lost count of how many episodes they'd watched—six? seven?—when she was about to ask Karine if they should turn to something else. No matter what decade the show was viewed, Jan was still so annoying.

Vanessa shot off the couch when she heard a voice behind them.

"It's so good to see young people watching something wholesome like *The Brady Bunch* rather than the smut normally found on television."

It was Sheriff McBrien. And he had his gun pointing right at them.

Chapter Twenty-One

Karine immediately began crying and cowering behind Vanessa. Vanessa put an arm around the girl and kept her pressed up to her back.

"You here to arrest me again, Sheriff? A gun isn't really necessary."

"I think we both know we're way past arresting. That's not really going to work at all."

Vanessa forced herself to look the older man in the eye without flinching. "How did you find us?"

"Webb."

Vanessa blanched; she couldn't help it. "Webb's working with you?"

McBrien rolled his eyes. "No. I can barely stand having that goodie-goodie around at the office, much less during personal business."

Vanessa tightened her arm around Karine. She wouldn't let this man hurt her again.

"Evidently he overheard a call today. Would've gotten away with it, too, if I hadn't had to go back into my office five minutes after the first time. Secretary asked if I had run into Webb, since evidently he'd been in there the first time."

Vanessa didn't say anything. She didn't want to confirm any details for McBrien.

"He was hiding in my private bathroom, I think. Normally that would just slightly annoy me." He gestured toward Karine behind Vanessa. "But with missy here getting away, and your Omega Sector boyfriend showing up, I couldn't just assume Webb was ignorant of what was going on."

He took a step toward Vanessa and she took a step back with Karine.

"I should just kill you now, but I'm too greedy. I want the money I can get for her." McBrien's face took on an ugly hue. "Plus, I might be able to get a bonus for you. You're pretty old as far as these things go, but I'm sure our buyers could find a use for you."

Karine began silently sobbing behind her. Vanessa had to force herself not to retch. She would not give in to fear. "Liam will stop you."

"You mean Special Agent Goetz, who is on his way to Harper's Cove? Yeah, sorry to tell you, once I knew Webb had heard me, I changed the location of the meeting with the buyers. Goetz can check the cove all he wants. We won't be there."

Vanessa had to figure out a way to get a message to Liam, but McBrien was having none of that.

"I'll need your phone, Miss Epperson."

Vanessa backed away again, but McBrien rushed forward, grabbed her by her shirt and threw her to the floor. Then he grabbed Karine.

The girl began sobbing louder.

"Shut up. You're the root of all my problems." He raised a fist in front of Karine. "Your phone, Vanessa, or the buyers will get one girl with quite a few bruises. Although I'm sure they'll be all right with that."

Karine's face was ghostly pale.

"No, don't hurt her." Vanessa scrambled to her feet. "Here's my phone. Here."

She thrust it at him and rushed to Karine, grabbing her away from him. She put her arms around the girl, trying to protect her even though Karine was almost as tall as she was.

McBrien threw her phone to the floor and stomped on it. It broke into pieces. Useless.

How would she contact Liam now?

McBrien pulled out handcuffs, cuffed both of them with their arms behind their backs, and pulled them to the front door.

He got right in Vanessa's face. "I'm here in uniform with a patrol car. If you scream, I will tell people you're on drugs and then I will make the next few hours of your life as miserable as humanly possible." He pointed to Karine. "I will make hers even worse. Got it?"

Vanessa nodded.

"Quiet," he said to Karine, who nodded. He obviously didn't know how well Karine spoke English.

There was no one around for them to yell to on the walk to the car anyway; not that Vanessa would've risked it. McBrien had real nerve showing up in an official sheriff's vehicle as if he wasn't committing some of the most heinous crimes possible. But he was smart; it was the perfect cover.

If he could get Vanessa and Karine and the other girls to the buyers, they'd be gone forever and the only bit of evidence against McBrien would be a convoluted recording that didn't directly mention any crimes.

If he couldn't get Vanessa and Karine to the buyers, all he'd need to do was shoot them and say they'd come at him in a life-threatening manner and he had to defend himself. After all, there was already a recording of Karine killing someone else.

They were in trouble and Vanessa could not figure out how to get out of this. The only option she could see was to try to tackle McBrien herself while Karine ran. It wasn't a great plan. McBrien probably had six inches and seventy-five pounds on her, not to mention the added handicap of both her and Karine having their hands cuffed behind their backs.

But she knew if she let McBrien get them on whatever boat he was taking them to, she'd never be able to get Karine safely off again.

Vanessa didn't even let herself think about the other girls. There was nothing she could do to help them now. All she could do was try to save Karine's life.

She felt the girl push closer to her where they sat in the back of the squad car and wished she could put her arm around her. Not that it would be much comfort in this situation.

Karine pushed up against her again and Vanessa looked over at her.

"I'm sorry, honey. I know you're scared," she whispered.

Karine pushed up against her again and whispered something, but Vanessa didn't know what.

"Just be ready to run when I make my move," Vanessa said in the lowest voice possible. "Run as fast as you can."

Vanessa doubted it would be enough. But it was their only option.

Karine shook her head and brushed up against her again.

"Hey, shut up back there," McBrien told them. "Or I can break your jaws and make you shut up."

Vanessa looked over at Karine. Hopefully the girl had heard her and understood the plan. Despite McBrien's threats, she seemed to be keeping it together, although she kept pressing against Vanessa.

Then Vanessa felt Karine's hand touch hers from behind them. She had to hold her arms at an awkward angle to make the contact, and Vanessa knew she must be terrified to want human contact enough to hurt herself for it.

She felt Karine press something into her hand. Karine wasn't looking for contact at all.

She was giving Vanessa her phone.

McBrien had assumed Karine didn't have one. Heck, Vanessa had even forgotten about it in the chaos.

There were only so many numbers programmed into the phone Liam had given the girl. Hers. Andrea's. Liam's. It was a cheap, prepaid flip phone and Vanessa wasn't entirely sure about the buttons. She felt out the number pad as carefully as she could with her fingers and then pressed what she thought was the 2 and Send.

She didn't know if they were the right buttons. She didn't know if it was even the right phone being called. She didn't know if Liam would even have his phone on, since he was in the middle of a mission where silence was important.

Those were a lot of ifs.

But it was their only chance.

Sitting in the middle of Harper's Cove, low in the Zodiac, everyone wearing night-vision goggles to see in case the boat with the girls also wasn't using any lights, Liam knew something was wrong.

"There should've been movement by now. From somewhere," he muttered.

There was no sign of the boat with the girls; no sign of the buyers. No sign of *anyone* out here.

"Even with the storm we've got pretty good visual, Liam," Derek said. "If there was someone out here, we'd be able to see them."

"Maybe something got changed. Time. Place," Joe said.

Maybe McBrien and his buddies had reconsidered and decided to just cut their losses and kill the girls.

Nobody said it, but all three men were thinking it.

Liam got out his phone. "I'm going to call Andrea. Maybe she's heard something from Webb."

Liam got his phone out of the waterproof casing attached to his specialized wet suit. As he reached to press

Andrea's stored number, he was surprised when his phone buzzed in his hand.

Karine.

Why was she calling him?

He brought the phone to his ear. "Karine?"

Nothing.

"Karine?" he said again.

They were safe at the house. Maybe she butt-dialed him by accident, but Liam wasn't taking any chances.

Both Derek and Joe were watching him. "Call Vanessa," he told Joe. "I don't want to hang up here in case this is a problem."

He turned to Derek. "Get Andrea or Webb or someone to go to the house."

Both men were already ripping out their phones to make the calls.

"Karine?" Liam said again, keeping his voice quiet, since he wasn't sure of the situation. If this was just an accidental call, she would realize it soon.

But the fact that they were sitting in an empty cove, with no missing girls in sight, made Liam believe this was not just an accidental call. He kept his ear to the phone as the other men made their contacts. Derek was soon talking to Andrea, but Joe almost immediately had his phone back down.

"Vanessa's went straight to voice mail."

Damn it.

"I had a tracker app put on Karine's phone, just in case she went out somewhere and got lost." He gave Joe the information. "Find out where she is."

Joe started running the phone-finding app on his own device. Derek disconnected his call.

"Andrea is on her way to the house now. She should be there in less than ten minutes," Derek reported.

"Has she been able to contact Vanessa or Karine?"

"No. She's going to keep trying."

"I've got a ping on Karine's phone," Joe said. "She's not at the house, that's for sure."

Liam muttered a curse under his breath.

"They're in a moving vehicle heading toward the water," Joe said.

Derek started the engine on the Zodiac. Not the silent one, the big one. Built for speed.

"Which direction?" he asked.

"Looks like, based on your report, near that island where your car was pushed off the bridge."

"That's not too far from here by water," Liam said, pointing to the direction they needed to go. "It's around the inlet."

It was also an ideal place for some sort of shady deal to go down. There wouldn't be any car traffic at this time of year, and boats could get to it easily.

Liam muted his end of the phone so the noise wouldn't come through the other side, but kept his ear to it in case Karine or Vanessa said anything.

The situation had just gone from bad to nearly impossible.

Chapter Twenty-Two

Vanessa recognized their location as McBrien drove over the bridge. This was the place where she and Liam had almost died two nights ago. Although it was on the other side of Nags Head, by boat it wasn't all that far from where Liam and the team were.

If she could just let him know her location… She had no idea if the phone was even working.

McBrien parked the car and dragged them out of the backseat and toward a boat. Karine did her best to help hide the phone by walking as close behind Vanessa as possible.

The sheriff moved in front of them as they walked out to the small dock where the boat was tied off. Vanessa pressed the phone into Karine's hands.

"Put it in my pocket," she whispered. There was no way Vanessa could maneuver her arms to slide it into the front pocket of the loose shorts she was wearing.

"Shut up back there," McBrien barked.

"She's scared, McBrien. Just chill out."

The sheriff turned to glare at them. "She should be scared."

Let him glower. Karine had gotten the phone into Vanessa's pocket. It was still open and still running, as far as Vanessa knew. She had heard something at the beginning of the call that she was pretty sure was Liam, but there was only silence now. She was going to keep the call open in case that would help him.

McBrien dragged them onto the boat. The same one that held the girls. Vanessa looked at Karine. The girl's face held no color whatsoever. Vanessa couldn't imagine what a nightmare it must be for her to be coming back here.

As the boat pulled away, McBrien unlocked their handcuffs. "I don't think there is any need for those, but they can go right back on if there is any sort of problem."

Vanessa nodded and immediately put her arms around Karine. She wouldn't give McBrien any reason to use the cuffs again. If they jumped overboard—*when* they jumped overboard—it would be critical for their arms not to be locked behind their backs.

The girls were nowhere to be seen, probably still captive below. Vanessa saw two men besides McBrien. One was driving the boat and the other made his way over to the sheriff.

"I thought you said you were going to kill them," the man said to McBrien.

Vanessa's arms tightened around Karine.

McBrien rolled his eyes. "Relax, Anderson, we can still get rid of them if we need to. But I thought it was better to see if we could get more money for them from the buyers. Especially since we're going to have to lie low on shipments for a while. The heat is too high. Going to be too high for a long time."

So this was Anderson, the guy Webb had mentioned. Karine refused to look at him, huddled into Vanessa. If Vanessa had a gun right now, she would probably kill all the men on this boat.

But she didn't have a gun; she only had her wits, a terrified teenager attached to her side and more traumatized girls in the hull of the boat.

She prayed Liam was on the open line of the phone in her

pocket. She had to try to help him. Get McBrien talking so hopefully Liam would have a clue as to where they were.

"It must have made you pretty nervous when Liam and I were out here so close to the action the other night. Was it you who rammed the car off the bridge?" she ask the sheriff.

"No." He actually chuckled. "That was Anderson here. He didn't know who you were at the time, just knew you were snooping around where you didn't belong."

"What about Webb? He was out there, too. You didn't try to kill him."

Anderson finally spoke up. "Webb always checks out Riker's Island after he goes to Sally's diner on Thursday nights. He's nothing if not a creature of habit. We knew about Webb, expected him. We just didn't know about you. Were you following Webb or on to the location?"

"We were following Webb, actually. We thought he was behind this."

"See, Anderson, all that for naught." McBrien slapped the other man on his back. "I told you drowning them was overkill. They were after Webb the whole time. As if he is intelligent enough to get away with something like this."

"So he's not in on this with you?" Vanessa figured her best bet was still to play as dumb as possible. Not give away any clues about what they knew or didn't know, or where Liam was.

"Really, he didn't come blubbering to you in his normal Boy Scout way? I'm surprised. I would've thought he'd report back to you as soon as possible once he heard me on the phone."

"I don't know." Vanessa shrugged. "Liam was going into Norfolk to tell them his theory. Get backup or whatever. I haven't seen him or Webb since we were at the sheriff's office."

"Do you hear that, McBrien? This place is going to be swarming with cops soon." Anderson was pacing, agitated.

McBrien frowned, narrowing his eyes. "They know nothing. Have nothing. Nobody can tie us to anything that has happened."

"But what about Webb? And her boyfriend, the Omega agent guy?"

"They can't prove anything. As long as you don't say anything or do anything stupid, we'll be fine. I've got measures in place to cover us."

Anderson looked ready to crack right now. Vanessa knew he'd never be able to hold up against Liam once questioning began. Liam would uncover the truth.

Vanessa and Karine might not be around to see it, but Liam would make sure these men paid for their crimes. That was comforting. Not much, but a little.

The boat slowed. They had to be close to where McBrien planned to meet the buyers.

"How did you find us at the house?" Vanessa asked him. In part to stall but also because she was interested.

"Once I figured out your boyfriend was an Omega agent, I figured there was no way he was here just to see you." McBrien shrugged. "No offense."

Vanessa didn't respond.

"I figured if this one—" he pointed at Karine "—was anywhere, it must be with you guys. It's off season, not a lot of rentals. Easy enough to find one rented by Andrea Gordon, who just happens to also be an Omega agent. It would be quite a coincidence to have two Omega agents vacationing here on the same weekend."

"That Omega agent we were staying with just went out to get some groceries. She'll be back. Soon. And will be looking for us."

McBrien didn't look concerned. "I guess she'll wonder where you guys went."

"It will seem very suspicious."

"Not with the footage Anderson has concocted. We'll just add a little clip of you in there in the doctored footage of the burglary-murder. Then basically it will look like you waited for your chance and then you ran."

Vanessa had to admit, McBrien seemed to have thought everything through. His job as sheriff already gave him a platform from which to declare his innocence. Without Vanessa and Karine around to directly accuse him of anything, all evidence against him would be circumstantial at best.

"I see the buyers, boss." The big man behind the wheel spoke for the first time.

McBrien looked down at his watch. "Good. Right on time. Pull up. I'll bring them on here to look at the merchandise." He turned to Anderson. "You and Paul get the girls ready below. I'll keep these two with me.

He grabbed Vanessa with one arm and Karine with the other, separating them. Vanessa struggled and McBrien backhanded her. She felt blood pool in her mouth.

McBrien smiled. "The buyers might like a little appetizer before the main meal."

"I've got two boats in my sight, Liam," Derek said.

Liam had hooked the phone to his ear via an earbud so he could hear what was going on at the other end over the motor of the Zodiac.

Vanessa and Karine were still alive. The relief Liam had felt at hearing Vanessa's voice had overwhelmed him. He couldn't hear her well, but he realized she was trying to give them clues as to where McBrien was holding them. She didn't realize he could track Karine's phone.

Damn McBrien. The man was smart. And he was right; without Vanessa and Karine's testimony, they didn't have very much on him. Even the call Liam was overhearing would probably prove worthless in court. There were too many factors distorting the sound. Any good lawyer would argue that what Liam thought he heard was actually something else.

But that didn't matter because Liam very much planned to have Vanessa and Karine alive and well to testify against McBrien.

Joe had slowed the Zodiac and was now using the quieter trolling motor. About a hundred yards from both boats, they stopped completely. This was as close as they could get without being heard, even with the choppy waves from the storm coming up. They were already pushing it.

They watched with their night-vision goggles as the two boats moved next to each other. Liam disconnected the call and took his earpiece out. He couldn't take the phone into the water with him, although he hated to lose the connection. Now was the time for action.

Rage boiled through him as he saw McBrien roughly separate Vanessa and Karine, then hit Vanessa in the face for some reason. She staggered but didn't fall.

Liam took a step toward them on the Zodiac, unable to help himself. "I'm going to kill that son of a bitch," he said.

"Keep focused, Liam," Derek muttered, having seen what happened. "If you don't, you won't be able to make the smart decisions. The decisions that are going to get everyone out of here safely."

"He just backhanded her." Liam could barely get the words out around his clenched jaw. "You have no idea—"

"I have no idea?" Derek cut him off. Even in the dark Liam could see the other man's raised eyebrow. Derek did know. He knew exactly what Liam was going through. Just six months ago a drug lord had held Derek's wife, Molly, at gunpoint and had hurt her without Derek being able to do anything about it. Had hurt her worse than just a backhand.

"I'm sorry. I just—" Liam bit off the words. "It's hard to not rush in there guns blazing."

Derek nodded. "I know. But we get Vanessa out just like we got Molly out. By being smart."

"Um, just want to remind you that Liam also drove a vehicle through Molly's front door. Not sure exactly how *smart* that was," Joe commented.

"Shut up, Joe." Liam's words held no sting. "We got the job done. That's what counts."

And they would get the job done now. Liam took a deep breath and pushed his rage deep down. He'd pull it back out if and when he needed it. "We infiltrate from the back. Get the girls out. Maybe seeing us pound on their captors might help them trust us a little. Once we've secured the area, gotten the girls in the water, I'm going to go up to the front. I'll handle that. Remember, quiet until there are no other options."

"Roger that," Joe responded.

The men readied themselves and their weapons, knowing this was the perfect time to move with the chaos of both boats coming together. It would be loud and rocky. And since their Zodiac was nearly impossible to detect in the darkness of the water—thank God for a moonless, stormy night—McBrien and his men would have no reason to be suspicious.

All three men entered the water with no sound and swam quietly toward the rear of McBrien's boat. Liam and Joe silently treaded water, weapons raised, as Derek made it up the ladder. He then took out his weapon and covered Liam then Joe as they followed.

Liam could hear McBrien talking in the front of the boat. The thought of Vanessa there with him, with people who were here to buy and sell other humans, made him sick.

Derek communicated via hand signal that he was about to open the door leading to the galley. This was it. They had to get down there quietly and take out the two men before either of them could alert McBrien.

At the slightest crack of the door, they could hear girls crying. Joe's faced hardened as Liam gave him the nod to go forward. Liam followed, with Derek bringing up the rear, facing the back door so no one could sneak up on them.

The smell of unwashed flesh and human waste was overpowering as they moved farther into the galley. This hull was meant for two people for a couple days at most, not seven girls for nearly a week.

Joe rounded a corner—a tiny hall that housed probably a restroom and closet—and kept his weapon and eyes focused in front of him, giving a signal with his hand that what he could see was clear. In standard procedure, Liam moved past Joe into the forward-most position. He took a few more steps up to the corner.

He brought his head around and then back in an instant.

The two men weren't paying any attention to the back of the room. They were too busy scoffing and gawking at the girls as they threw clothes at them and told them to change. The girls didn't understand and most were crying.

The youngest one—good Lord, she could only be eight or nine—was far in the back, obviously being protected by the other older girls. From where she sat on the floor, she could see Liam. She stared at him with big, dark eyes.

Liam gestured for her to be quiet, but had no idea if she knew what he meant. She just kept staring.

It was time for the attack. Every moment they wasted, they could lose the element of surprise. He felt Joe and Derek flank him. With hand signals he told them he would take the man furthest away and Joe was to take the one closest. Derek would continue to guard the door behind them.

This had to be quiet and fast. Anything else would probably cost Vanessa and Karine their lives.

On his count Liam and Joe flew around the corner. Both kidnappers had weapons they reached for but never even got close to getting them out.

From the corner of his eye Liam could see Joe take down Anderson. A quick uppercut to the jaw, followed by a hard right, had the man dropping to the floor. A third hit to the face knocked Anderson completely out.

Liam's target was much bigger. Liam shot a modified karate chop to the guy's throat, in essence rendering him voiceless. With him unable to warn anyone, Liam completed the process of taking the perp out. He couldn't deny that every blow felt good. Even when the man was on the floor, Liam kept punching him. When he thought about what this guy had done to Karine, to these girls—

"Liam, enough, man." Joe's hand on his shoulder stopped him. Liam looked over, almost startled to see him there.

"He's out," Joe continued. "Let's get the girls off the boat."

Yes, that was the most important thing. Focus, Goetz. "Yeah, secure these two and let's get going."

He turned to face the girls, who were all staring at him with terrified eyes.

Chapter Twenty-Three

Watching him pound someone into the floor, even one of their captors, probably had not helped him establish any trust with the girls. But Liam couldn't do anything about that now.

"We help," he said slowly, softly. He wanted to use the shortest sentence possible, since he wasn't sure how much English anyone knew, if any.

None of them was crying or screaming, but none of them ran in his direction, either.

"Karine sent us."

He had their attention.

"Karine?" one of the oldest girls said. "She is alive?"

"Yes," Liam said, smiling as gently as he could. "But we need to get out of here now."

He waited while the girl explained what was going on in their native tongue.

"We must go. Swim to our boat," he told them.

"No, too far?" the same girl said. "Sharks. The man told us there were sharks."

They didn't have time for this, but the last thing Liam wanted was seven hysterical girls on his hands. They were barely holding it together as it was.

"What's your name?" Liam asked the older girl.

"Julia," she responded softly, the *j* sounding like a *hoo*.

"Julia, no sharks," Liam said. "I promise." He was telling the truth. There might be some out in the ocean, but there wouldn't be any in the bay.

Julia spoke to the other girls again. After a few seconds they nodded. All except for the little one, who began crying.

"What's wrong?" Liam asked.

"Liam, we've got to go. McBrien is going to be looking for these guys any minute," Derek said softly from the doorway.

Joe stood from tying and gagging the two men. "I'm ready. They're secure."

"Why is she crying?" Liam asked about the little girl.

"She doesn't know how swim."

Liam met Joe's eyes. "Can you carry the little one? Derek can lead the others. I have to get to Vanessa and Karine."

"No problem," Joe said, making his way toward the little girl.

She immediately jumped back and began sobbing.

"No, no. Shh," Joe said, backing up.

"Can you tell her he's going to carry her in the water, to the safe boat?" Liam asked Julia. "Joe is very strong and very kind. He will not let anything happen to her."

Julia crouched near the little girl and obviously tried to explain, but the girl just cried harder. She kept pointing to Liam.

Joe walked over to Liam, putting more distance between him and the little girl, since his nearness seemed to upset her.

"Liam, we're going to have to subdue her if she doesn't calm down," Joe said. "I hate to do that, but it might be the only way."

"I agree, Liam. We need to move. *Now*," Derek chimed in.

"Julia, we've got to go. Make her understand."

"I'm sorry." Julia looked up at Liam from where she was crouched. "She only wants to go with you."

"Me?" That wasn't what he had been expecting.

"There's no accounting for women's taste, man. Just do it, Liam," Joe murmured. "Let's get out of here."

Liam reached down and scooped up the little girl. She immediately stopped crying and put her arms around his neck.

"Okay, let's go." He led them up the stairs. The girls followed behind him, with Joe and Derek bringing up the rear.

Out of the bottom cabin they made it to the back of the boat. Liam immediately made his way down the ladder into the water, the little girl's arms still trustingly wrapped around his neck. He had no idea why she trusted him, but he was glad to get her out of that hell.

It occurred to Liam that had he and Vanessa's child lived, he or she would've been just about the age of this child now. Somewhere a mother and father were distraught about their missing daughter. Liam vowed he would see their family reunited.

He heard her gasp at the cold water, but she didn't cry or do anything else. The water was pretty chilly and the girl wasn't wearing much clothing.

"Okay, sweetie, I need you around on my back," he whispered once they were fully in the water. He knew she didn't understand, but when he shifted her weight around to his back, she went easily. He could still feel her little arms around his neck.

Liam glanced back to see that Derek and Joe were successfully getting the other girls into the water and began swimming when he saw that they were down. He swam fast, not waiting for the girls to keep up. He needed to get back to the boat to help Vanessa and Karine.

The girl held tightly to his neck, giving him free range of movement. It only took a few minutes to get her to the Zodiac. He tossed her light body over the side and she giggled just the slightest bit.

"You stay here. Okay?" He held his hand out in a stop gesture then pointed inside the Zodiac.

The girl nodded. Liam touched her cheek softly then was gone, swimming silently back toward McBrien's boat. He passed Joe and Derek on the way with the other girls.

"Get them to safety," he told Joe. The girls seemed to be doing okay, but all of them were cold.

"Be careful, Liam." Joe swam on, leading the way to the Zodiac.

VANESSA WAS HUDDLED at the side of the boat with Karine, watching McBrien have a beer with two men at the table.

They had touched her; groped her through her clothes. Laughed as she'd kept Karine behind her and away from their disgusting hands. When she had spit at them, McBrien had hit her again. This time the blow had knocked her to the deck.

"This one has some fire to her," one of the grotesque buyers had said.

"I'm sure we can find someone who will have a lot of fun finding a way to put that fire out," the other buyer had said.

All three men had laughed as if they'd just heard the funniest joke on the planet.

Vanessa had just stayed down on the deck. Karine had joined her, huddling against her side. The rain began to fall.

Out of the corner of her eye, she saw movement at the back of the boat. At first she thought it was Anderson and the big guy, Paul, bringing the girls out to be paraded in front of the buyers.

But then she realized it was people scurrying the other way, toward the back from the hull. Someone dressed all in black caught her eye.

Liam. Or maybe Joe or Derek. *They were here on the boat.*

"Dwayne, Paul, hurry up!" McBrien yelled. "What's taking so long?"

Vanessa knew what was taking so long: Liam was getting those girls off the boat.

"Karine," Vanessa whispered directly into the girl's ear. "It's very important that you don't make any sudden moves or look over there, but Liam and his team are on board. They're getting the girls out."

Karine stopped crying. She nodded.

"I'm going to try to give them more time, if I can. Keep these guys distracted."

"No, Vanessa. They hurt you," Karine implored.

Vanessa didn't reply, just held the girl close to her. The men at the table kept drinking their beer and laughing at their own stupid jokes as if they were at a barbecue rather than in the process of destroying lives.

"Anderson, what the hell is going on? Hurry up!" McBrien yelled again when he'd finished his beer. Then he turned to the buyers. "I'm sorry. I'll go check on them myself."

Had Liam gotten the girls off the boat? Were they safe? Had he had enough time? Vanessa didn't know.

She stood and walked toward the sheriff. "McBrien, I've got to go to the bathroom."

"Shut up, Vanessa. Sit back down."

She grabbed his arm. "Really, it's an emergency."

McBrien's eyes narrowed as he looked at Vanessa then toward the stern of the boat. He pushed off her hand and began rushing toward the back.

"What is going on?" he snarled.

Vanessa tried to grab him again, but couldn't. McBrien only made it a couple of steps before he fell to the deck in a flying tackle from Karine. He immediately punched the girl and she flew off him and against the side of the boat. Vanessa also tried to stop him, but he just shrugged her off.

"McBrien, what the hell is going on?" one of the buyers asked, sitting more stiffly in his chair.

"Yeah, why don't you tell the man what's going on?" The voice came from the other side of the boat.

Liam.

He was here and he had a gun pointed right at the sheriff. Thank God.

McBrien stopped his walk toward the stern and turned around to face Liam.

"Ah, Agent Goetz. I have to admit, I'm a little surprised to see you here. I thought you'd be out somewhere in Harper's Cove."

Liam just grinned as if he had nothing better to do than talk to McBrien. "I heard the party was here. Couldn't resist."

He turned his head just slightly toward the buyers, who had stood and had a panicked look in their eyes.

"You two just keep your hands far away from your body. I have no beef with you, just with him." Liam jerked his chin toward McBrien. "I think we can avoid any unnecessary hard feelings between us if you'll just leave now."

Vanessa wanted to howl her anger at the thought of those men—those men who had groped and humiliated her, who had obviously bought children from McBrien before, given their level of comfort with him—getting away. But she forced it down. Liam had a plan, and for whatever reason, that plan involved letting these guys go.

Maybe Webb was around nearby to pick them up. Maybe Liam just knew that the safety of the girls outweighed arresting these bastards right now. Whatever his plan, Vanessa would trust him.

"Yeah, we don't have any beef with you, either, man," one of the guys said as they turned, arms far from their torsos, toward their boat.

Liam nodded. "Glad we understand each other. Get out. Now."

The men walked full speed to their boat. Within a moment they had tossed the metal gangway that connected their boat to McBrien's and were pulling away.

"That had to have hurt, Mr. Super Agent," McBrien mocked. "Letting them go like that."

Liam now had the gun trained directly at the sheriff.

"I have no doubt you—or one of your two partners—will roll on them in an attempt to reduce your sentence. We'll get them."

Vanessa got herself off the deck and helped Karine to her feet. She backed them to the side of the boat, far from the line of fire between Liam and McBrien. She didn't want to take a chance on Karine getting hurt.

And she was very, very worried that McBrien did not look the least bit concerned that Liam was pointing a gun at him. That he was about to be arrested on some pretty hefty charges.

"McBrien, put your hands on your head. You're under arrest." Liam took a step closer. "Anything you say can and will be used against you in a court of law—"

"Let me stop you right there. I have something that might change your feelings on this whole situation," McBrien interrupted.

Liam rolled his eyes. "I'm pretty sure nothing is going to change my feelings about arresting your ass."

Something at the stern of the boat caught Vanessa's attention. It was Joe coming up the ladder they'd used to take the girls out. Good, now Liam had backup.

"If you think I'm going to let you reach for anything near your body, you can think again, McBrien," Liam continued. "I don't care what you have to show me. If you make a sudden move, you're dead."

"No, it's right here in my hand." McBrien's smile was

chilling. He opened his hand to show a small mechanical device in his palm.

"Yeah, what's that?" Liam asked.

"It's a detonator for the explosives I rigged to this boat."

Chapter Twenty-Four

From the edge of his peripheral vision, Liam saw Vanessa blanch and pull Karine closer to her, but he kept his focus on McBrien. They had tried to account for as many scenarios as they could when they'd planned this rescue op.

McBrien being willing to blow himself and everyone else on the boat straight to hell hadn't been one of them.

"You probably don't want to shoot me, because it's a pressure detonator and I just armed it. If I let pressure off this lever, everything goes boom. Your precious Vanessa. That brat. All the girls below deck…"

"You," Liam finished for him.

"Me, too, that's true." McBrien shrugged. "It's a chance I'm willing to take."

Liam saw Joe walk silently behind McBrien. He knew Joe could hear everything McBrien was saying, and would know not to take the man out. It wasn't worth the risk if they had any other options.

Joe began moving toward Karine and Vanessa. If he could get them off the boat, it would be completely clear.

Thunder cracked immediately over them and rain began to fall in earnest. The noise might work to their advantage. Liam needed to keep McBrien's attention on him while Joe got Vanessa and Karine to safety.

"Really? What about your partners? You going to take them out as well as yourself? Seems a little overkill, if you'll pardon the pun," Liam said, relaxing his posture slightly and shifting a little more to the side so McBrien's focus was away from where Joe was joining the women.

"We both know what happens to me if I go to prison. Previous law-enforcement officers doing time in a maximum-security facility? I won't last long and my life would be a living hell while I do."

That sounded just fine to Liam, but he forced himself not to say so.

"It doesn't have to be that way," Liam said instead. "We can talk to a judge, make it so you aren't put in with the general population. There are other options. Don't do anything rash."

It was an empty promise and McBrien knew it.

"No!" He took a step forward, waving his arm. "There are only two options. You let me go or everyone on board dies."

The older man was turning to look at the other side of the boat.

"McBrien, what the hell do you want me to do?" Liam shouted through the rain to bring the man's attention back to him. "Am I just going to swim with a bunch of girls? I can't let you go. This is the only boat."

McBrien didn't know the girls were gone. Let him keep thinking he had the upper hand. Liam saw Joe begin to lower Karine into the water. Good. As soon as she and Vanessa were off, he and Joe had more options.

None of them were particularly good options, but they were options.

"I know you have a boat out there somewhere, Goetz. Even if you were idiotic enough to think you could swim all the way here, you had to have something to take the girls back in."

"The plan was to take the girls in this boat. To arrest

you and whoever you were working with and bring the boat back to shore." The lie came easily from Liam's lips.

"You always were a pain in the ass, Goetz," McBrien said. "Even when you were a no-good teenager just looking for trouble. No one could believe it when you scored the princess of the island.

"I know your daddy had a fit when you first brought Goetz ho—" McBrien turned toward Vanessa as he said it, just in time to see Joe help her over the side and into the water.

"What the—"

Joe and Liam both immediately took action.

Joe threw Vanessa into the water.

Liam flew forward to tackle McBrien.

Joe was running toward them.

But it was too late.

As Liam tackled him, McBrien began to laugh hysterically.

"I'm glad to take you with me if I have to go," McBrien whispered. Madness lingered in his eyes as he lifted his hand to show Liam the lever that was now no longer compressed.

The boat was going to blow.

Liam bounced to his feet knowing he wouldn't make it off in time. But then Joe hit him in the hardest flying tackle he'd ever felt. They both flew over the side of the boat as fire and unbearable pressure suddenly surrounded them, accelerating them through the air.

Liam felt heat burn his body, sear his lungs, before they hit the water.

Then he felt and saw nothing but blackness.

VANESSA HADN'T BEEN prepared for Joe's help over the side of the boat to turn into a sudden, painful shove, but she'd known what it meant.

McBrien was going to blow up the boat.

She grabbed Karine and they began to swim as hard and fast as they could.

They were still close enough to feel the searing heat from the blast, to feel the momentum as it pushed them what seemed like a very far distance in the water.

Vanessa grabbed for Karine again, called for her, as debris flew all around them. For one terrified moment she couldn't find the girl in the darkness and rain, but then she broke through the surface a few yards from Vanessa, sputtering.

Vanessa swam to Karine and got beneath her, trying to support her weight so she could catch her breath.

"Are you okay?" Vanessa asked. "Are you hurt anywhere?"

"No, I'm okay," Karine murmured between breaths.

A piece of the boat, obviously buoyant from how it bobbed merrily in the water, drifted toward them. Still supporting Karine as best she could, Vanessa kicked out her leg to try to grab it. She succeeded in getting it to float directly in front of them and deposited Karine's weight on it. The girl grabbed and held on.

The rain was pouring. Vanessa could hardly figure out where the boat—now in small pieces all around them—had once been. How far had the momentum pushed them? Which way should they swim? Which direction was land or the Zodiac?

And, oh, God, had Liam gotten off the boat before it exploded? Vanessa had no idea.

The water was rough from the storm and the explosion. Vanessa tried yelling, but received no response. She tamped down the panic that threatened to overwhelm her. Her life, Karine's life, depended on her not panicking.

But looking around the dark, choppy waters with no one around and no land in sight? It was tough not to panic.

Vanessa wasn't sure what to do. Were they better off picking a direction and swimming toward it? Was it better to wait here in case someone brought rescue vehicles?

Karine was resting, exhausted, on the boat plank Vanessa had grabbed. She didn't blame the girl. Every bone in her own body ached. And the water was cold.

It was only October, so the cold at least wasn't life-threatening. But that didn't mean it wasn't uncomfortable. And the rain certainly wasn't helping.

Vanessa hoisted herself up on the floating boat piece as far as she could to look around. All she needed was one glimpse of a light or one sound from a location she could pinpoint and it would give her somewhere to go.

She couldn't see or hear anything. She sank back down in the water.

Karine was shivering against the plank. They would swim, or at least kick while holding the plank. That would help generate body heat. They would move in the direction of the explosion.

Or at least what Vanessa hoped was that direction.

"Let's kick, Karine," Vanessa said. "It will help us stay warm. We'll go toward where Liam and the other girls are."

"O-okay." Karine's voice was weak. "Are they dead?"

"No, sweetie." Vanessa touched her shoulder with hands that weren't very steady because of cold or fear or both. "They're alive. Everyone is alive. Liam and Joe and Derek got the girls off the boat long before the bad man blew it up. They're okay. They're all okay."

Vanessa prayed it was true.

They swam in silence, in the rain. Both of them held on to the plank and kicked. They swam for five minutes, ten minutes, longer. Vanessa lost track.

They had to have passed where the boat had been; it couldn't have been this far. Vanessa couldn't see anything.

She couldn't hear anything. The storm was drowning everything out.

What time was it? Was it anywhere near dawn? It had been after midnight when McBrien had taken them from the house, so maybe it was about 3:00 a.m. now. Still a couple of hours before the sun would start to rise and she could hopefully see where land was.

She felt a sting against one of her legs, then another one. Jellyfish. The Roanoke Sound was famous for them in the late summer and early fall. They weren't dangerous or their sting even terribly painful, just uncomfortable.

Karine was falling asleep on the plank. Both had long since stopped kicking.

"Karine, let's see if we can get our weights totally on the plank. See if it will support us both, okay? Then we can rest."

Karine nodded weakly then shifted her weight more onto the float. Almost immediately upon finding herself in a horizontal position, she closed her eyes, drawing her legs up to her chest for warmth.

Vanessa pulled her weight onto the floating plank, too, but as soon as she did it began to sink. It wasn't buoyant enough to hold both of them. She slid back off to keep Karine from going under.

"Should I get off?" Karine murmured, barely lifting her head.

Vanessa felt another sting. There was no way she would subject Karine to this; she'd been through enough. Vanessa could survive a few jellyfish stings. It would soon be morning. All Vanessa had to do was to hang on. Literally and figuratively. This wasn't the *Titanic*. Vanessa wouldn't freeze.

She lost track of time as she was stung over and over. No one sting was unbearable but, taken altogether, her legs began to feel as if they were on fire. Tears rolled down her cheeks at first but eventually dried up, too.

She just wanted to sleep yet knew she couldn't. If she did, she would fall off the board and drown. She had to hang on.

But it became harder, more agonizing. She whimpered as she tried to move her legs. They felt stiff and awkward. And incredibly painful.

She laid her head to rest on the board, long past caring about the temperature of the water. She could see the subtle change of texture in the darkness furthest away.

The sun was beginning to rise.

Soon Vanessa would be able to get her bearings, to know which way to find the shore. Unfortunately she wasn't going to be able to do anything once she knew. There was no way she could swim or kick. She could barely move at all. The stings were unbearable now.

She kept her head where it lay, close to Karine in case the girl woke up. Vanessa just tried to hold on but didn't know how long she would be able to.

Chapter Twenty-Five

Liam had never known fear like this. All-encompassing, wrapping him from head to toe.

They couldn't find Vanessa and Karine.

Liam would be dead if it wasn't for Joe. His tackle momentum had gotten them both off the boat before the detonation. And although the protective material from their specialty wet suits had shielded them from the worst of the blast, Joe had still been injured. He was on his way to the hospital right now with burns and a puncture wound. But he was conscious and had assured Liam he would be fine.

Derek and the girls were all right—they were scared and wanted to see Karine—but none of them had been hurt in the blast. They, also, were on their way to the hospital, Derek in charge of their custody for the time being.

Now Liam was out on the water, along with Webb and the Coast Guard, looking for Vanessa and Karine. This storm was making everything more complicated, especially since they couldn't use helicopters for the search effort.

"Sir, this will be much more effective during the day. The sun should be up in just a couple hours."

But Liam couldn't stand the thought of them out here, maybe hurt, definitely scared, for even a minute longer than they had to be.

"The water temperature, even with prolonged exposure,

should not be life-threatening. Barring injury, of course," the man continued.

Liam set his jaw. "It's still damn cold, I'm sure, especially with their lack of body mass. We keep looking."

"Yes, sir."

Liam kept searching for anything that might catch his attention in the night. Any changes in texture in the darkness or items that might reflect light. Once every thirty seconds or so, they blew a whistle, although it was probably pretty muffled by the storm.

"Do you know how far they were from the boat when the blast occurred?" another rescue team member asked.

"They were far enough. They're still alive."

"I'm sure that's true," the man muttered.

"They were farther than Joe or I were."

Everyone was wise enough not to mention that Joe was currently in the hospital, despite the protective layer his wet suit had provided. Vanessa and Karine hadn't had that protection.

They hadn't had Liam and Joe's strength or their survival training.

Liam refused to admit that at some point this might become a body recovery effort rather than a search and rescue mission.

Vanessa Epperson was alive. Nothing else was acceptable. And when he found her, he wasn't sure he was ever going to be able to let her out of his sight again.

They began to make wider sweeps as the night went on. If Vanessa had swum in the right direction, where the boat had exploded was less than a mile off shore... But on a stormy night, in rough seas, finding that direction might have been difficult. If she had swum in the wrong direction, she could be headed out of the cove and toward the open water of the Atlantic. That could prove deadly.

How long could they swim and which direction had they

gone? Those were the questions everyone tried to answer to direct their attention in the search.

The sun had just pinkened the sky the slightest bit when something caught Liam's eye through his binoculars. He threw his focus to whatever it was he'd seen in the water.

"Southwest about five hundred yards," he called out. "I'm not sure it's them, but there's definitely something in the water."

Liam didn't let his hopes get too high. They had found various pieces of wreckage in the water throughout the evening. But this was definitely a good-sized chunk.

The boat operator turned and sped in the direction Liam had indicated. A few moments later Liam's hands clenched on the binoculars.

It was them.

Karine was curled up on a plank of some sort—obviously a piece of the boat—mostly out of the water. Vanessa had evidently dragged the top half of her body over the plank when she'd become too exhausted to do anything else.

But even from several yards away, he could see that their faces were out of the water. That was at least promising.

Although their lack of movement was not.

The Coast Guard's boat was able to pull directly up beside them. Liam didn't even wait for permission or instruction; he just lowered himself into the water so he could be directly beside Vanessa.

"Vanessa?" He shook her softly but she didn't move. "Vanessa, wake up, honey."

Nightmares from the other night when Vanessa hadn't been breathing in the water flashed through Liam's mind. He tried to find a pulse.

"Mr. Liam?" Karine lifted her head weakly and looked at him.

"Hey, Karine. Are you okay?" He asked the question

while moving Vanessa's thick hair out of the way so he could find her pulse.

"Miss Vanessa hasn't talked in a long time."

Liam swallowed his panic. There were a lot of reasons Vanessa might not have spoken. Exhaustion being one of them.

When he couldn't seem to find a pulse at her throat, he moved his hand to her wrist.

C'mon, baby.

It had been the same words he had used when he'd needed her to breathe before.

And it seemed to work again. He found her pulse beating in her wrist. Thank God.

"She's still breathing, Karine. Okay? We need to get her on the boat and back to the hospital. You, too."

Karine nodded. Two more men from the rescue team had joined them in the water.

"These guys are going to help you onto the boat. Is it okay if they touch you? I'll be right here, but I've got to help Vanessa, too."

Karine nodded again, although Liam could see her stiffen.

"Good girl."

They hoisted Vanessa onto the vessel and Liam climbed up the ladder. The men assisted Karine but tried to touch her as little as possible, aware of her situation.

They laid Vanessa on a small cot in the section of the boat that wasn't exposed to the elements. One of the men wrapped a blanket around Karine as she sat on the floor.

Liam turned all his attention toward Vanessa as the boat sped toward shore. She still hadn't moved, hadn't made a sound. He, along with the ship's medic, peeled her out of her wet clothes, checking her for injuries while wrapping her in a blanket.

Liam saw the tiny wounds on Vanessa's legs at the same time the medic did. Dozens and dozens of tiny welts.

"Sea nettle stings," the medic said. "Sound is full of them this time of year."

Anybody growing up in the Outer Banks knew about this type of jellyfish. They were a nuisance but generally not life-threatening.

Of course, Liam had never seen this many stings before. And he couldn't imagine how painful sting after sting would be. "Is there anything we can do for her?"

"She's probably in a sort of toxic shock," the man replied. "We'll radio ahead to the ambulance and hospital to notify them of the situation. They'll have a specialist standing by."

The man turned to go make the radio contact.

"She's still breathing. Still here," he said, turning to look back from the steps leading up to the control room. "That's the most important thing."

Liam nodded, then sat on the cot and gathered Vanessa up in his arms. Her body was cold to the touch.

A few moments later Karine scurried over from her spot on the floor to a place on the floor closer to the cot. "Will she be okay?" Karine's voice was hoarse.

Liam didn't know if it was from emotion or from what she'd been through. He reached down and touched the girl's head. "Vanessa is strong. She's a fighter."

He pulled Vanessa closer to him as if to will her to do just that. "Did you get stung by anything, Karine?"

"No. I was on top of floating board." Karine began to cry. "I should have let Vanessa up, too. I did not know fish were hurting her."

Liam stroked the girl's head again. "I know, honey. Vanessa is sometimes too stubborn for her own good. But she wanted you to be safe. I'm so glad you're safe."

"But Vanessa—"

"Shh. Vanessa will be fine, you just watch."

Liam prayed it would be true. The longer she lay so still in his arms, the more he worried.

"We got the other girls out, too," he told Karine. "You'll be able to see them as soon as we get to the hospital."

That at least helped clear up the tears. Liam moved his hand back to Vanessa to move strands of wet hair from her face and to wrap her more securely in the blanket.

"C'mon, baby, wake up," he whispered against her temple, bringing her closer to him. At least her skin wasn't as cold now.

Once they reached the dock, an ambulance was waiting to take them to the hospital. The EMT looked as if he was going to question Liam's right to be in the ambulance, but quickly put his questions to rest with one look at Liam's face. There was no way in hell Liam wasn't riding in the vehicle with Vanessa.

"She's coming with us, too." He pointed to Karine, who jumped in the ambulance with them. The EMT quickly closed the door before anyone else got in.

Vanessa didn't move the entire way, although her pulse and breathing remained steady.

Liam stayed with her as long as he could once they got to the hospital before a doctor told him he would have to wait in the waiting room. They would provide an update as soon as they could.

Liam let the nurse know where he could be found for the next few minutes in case anyone came out with an update about Vanessa, then took Karine to see the rest of the girls. They were all being kept together, guarded by Derek and a whole slew of kind-faced nurses and social workers.

The girls were ecstatic to see Karine. They all hugged and sobbed and held on to each other. These girls were bonded together in ways that no one else would ever be able to completely understand.

As Liam watched from the doorway, touched but anxious to get back to the waiting area in case Vanessa needed him, Derek joined him.

"Vanessa?"

"Unconscious. Multiple sea nettle stings, prolonged exposure to the elements…who knows what else? But she's breathing. I'll take that for now. I need to get back for when the doctor comes out with a report."

"I'll stay here with the girls. I just want to double-check that everything is in order with them before I release them from my custody."

"Thanks, Derek. Does everything seem all right with them medically, all things considered?"

"All are suffering from dehydration." Derek grimaced. "And they've all been assaulted, except for the youngest one."

Liam looked over at the little girl who had clung to him while they swam. She was looking at him. Thank God she had been spared that trauma, at least. The rest was bad enough.

"But it looks like all of them are going to be okay. We've already made contact with the Estonian embassy to figure out how we can make sure the girls are returned to their parents. If the parents aren't the ones who sold them to the traffickers in the first place."

It was difficult to think of parents doing that to their own children, but Liam knew it happened more than people expected, especially in situations where the rest of the family was starving.

Liam nodded. "Let's stay on top of that. I want to make sure none of those girls is sent back if it's just going to result in the same thing happening."

"Oh, believe me," Derek said. "Molly would have my head if I sent even one of those girls home to a bad family situation. I just hope I'm not about to become the adoptive father to seven teenage girls."

Liam chuckled. "Nothing less than you deserve. Speaking of…how's Joe?"

"Fine. Already flirting with the nurses. I think they'll release him tomorrow. Burns on his back and a puncture wound from some debris, but nothing serious."

"Thank God for the Kevlar wet suits."

"Absolutely. Would've been much worse otherwise." Derek slapped him on the back. "Get back to Vanessa. I can tell that's where you want to be. I've got everything covered here. I'll keep you posted if something changes. You do the same about her."

Liam nodded and jogged out of the room and down the hall to the emergency waiting area. He checked with the nurse, just in case, but found he hadn't missed any updates from the doctor. He settled in to wait, hoping it wouldn't be too long.

The longer he waited, the more worried he became. That many jellyfish stings…could they be toxic? Was she having an allergic reaction? Did she have a head trauma they didn't know about?

There were so many possibilities. Many of them terrifying.

Vanessa's parents were rushing through the Emergency entrance just as the doctor came through the waiting room door to provide an update.

"What's going on, Doctor?" George Epperson demanded. "What's happening with our daughter?"

"I'm Dr. Turner. Who are you?" the doctor asked Liam.

"Her fiancé." Liam told the lie without batting an eye. There was no way he was going to be kept out of information loop when it came to Vanessa.

Both her parents turned to stare at him but neither said anything.

"Is your name Liam?"

"Yes."

"Good, I'm glad you're here," the doctor said. "Miss Epperson has been asking for you in her sleep. I think she will find your presence comforting."

"I'm going back there right now."

The doctor touched his arm. "They're moving her to a private room and need a little while. You can go back there in just a minute. Let me give you an update first."

Vanessa was calling for him. That was really the only update Liam needed. But he forced himself to listen. Maybe there was a complication he needed to know about.

He turned back to the doctor. "Okay."

"Well, first…" the doctor said, "let me assure you that Vanessa is going to be fine. And at this point it does not look like her pregnancy was jeopardized by last night's events."

Chapter Twenty-Six

Liam grabbed the counter next to him, trying not to be obvious in his need for support. Vanessa's parents had no such reservations. Her mother, Rhonda, swayed into George, grabbing his arm.

"Pregnancy?" Rhonda asked.

"Did you know about this?" George asked Liam.

"No. Not this time, either." His eyes narrowed at the older man.

George had the good grace to at least look away.

Liam turned toward Dr. Turner. "Are you sure, Doctor? I don't know much about pregnancy tests and hospitals, but if Vanessa's pregnant, it would not be by much—only a few days."

"Interesting." Dr. Turner looked at the chart again. "Vanessa definitely has traces of hCG—the pregnancy hormone—in her bloodstream, enough for a viable pregnancy. We had to test for it when deciding the best course for treating the stings. There's no chance she could've been pregnant, say, roughly ten days?"

Liam remembered what Vanessa had told him about not having any other lovers for so long. "Not a chance. Does that mean your test could be wrong and she's not pregnant?"

The doctor looked at his chart again. "No, the opposite, in fact."

What the hell did that even mean? The opposite of

not pregnant was pregnant, right? But it was too early to tell that.

"Let me make sure these hCG numbers are right and I'll get back to you."

"What about her other injuries?" Liam asked. "Is she going to be okay?"

"Yes. Although painful, the stings of the *chrysaora quinquecirrha*, or what we know around here as a sea nettle, aren't fatal unless you have an allergic reaction. She shouldn't have any permanent damage from the stings."

Liam released a breath he didn't even know he had been holding.

"It was actually just bad luck on Ms. Epperson's part that she was even exposed to them. Given another two weeks, it would be too cold for them to be in the water." Dr. Turner shrugged. "Of course, given another two weeks, the water might have been cold enough to do Vanessa much greater harm."

"So why is she still unconscious?" Liam asked.

"Mind protecting itself. We estimate she was stung over four dozen times—the pain was immense, I'm sure. Coupled with the elements she'd been exposed to, not to mention she'd been kidnapped, right?"

Liam could see George and Rhonda's shocked looks from the corners of his eyes.

"Let's just say she'd had a pretty traumatic night. Her body needed a break and her mind gave it to her. Now that she's warm, hydrated and not in pain, she's starting to wake up."

And Liam needed to get in there.

"I'll be back with the hCG numbers after we run the test again. I don't want to confuse the situation for anyone."

She was either pregnant or she wasn't pregnant. It wasn't too confusing, as far as Liam was concerned. He just wanted to know which. Actually, right now he didn't even care about that. He just wanted to see Vanessa.

As he turned to walk down the hall, Rhonda Epperson grabbed his arm.

"I know Vanessa doesn't want to see us," she said. "And we're not going to force ourselves in there and upset her even more. It sounds like she's been through enough."

Liam nodded. "I'll tell her you're here. Tell her you're worried. She's not heartless. Just stubborn."

"I suppose she told you about what happened eight years ago. The miscarriage...how I mislead you," George said. "For what it's worth, I am sorry. I honestly thought both of you would just get over it."

Tears welled in Rhonda's eyes. "But Vanessa never did."

"If it helps, I never did, either," Liam said.

"I was wrong to interfere like that," George said. "I was just trying to protect my only daughter from someone I thought might be of questionable repute."

Liam could understand that. He didn't agree with Epperson's measures, but he could definitely understand his motivation. "I'll talk to Vanessa once she's awake. Explain. Maybe it's time for all of us to put the past behind us and just concentrate on the future."

"Do you really think it's possible she's pregnant?" Rhonda asked.

"It could be possible, just not likely that she's far enough along for them to detect it. So I think it's probably an error."

Both George and Rhonda looked crestfallen. Evidently it didn't bother them anymore that Vanessa could be permanently linked to Liam through having a child.

That didn't matter because, child or not, he planned to be permanently linked to Vanessa for the rest of his life. All he had to do was convince Vanessa. Which he planned to do starting right now.

EVERYTHING FELT FUZZY as Vanessa awoke. Thoughts seemed to process slowly, almost one at a time.

She wasn't in the water anymore. She didn't have to swim. Those jellyfish weren't stinging her anymore. Karine was safe. All the girls were safe. Liam was right here next to her.

How did she know all this? She opened her eyes just the slightest bit.

She knew it because Liam was lying next to her on her hospital bed whispering these facts over and over in her ear.

She turned toward him. "Hey," she whispered.

She felt his lips move against the side of her face. "There you are."

"How long have I been out?"

"We're not sure how long you were in the water. But you've been in the hospital a couple of hours."

"Have you been with me the whole time?"

Liam pulled her closer. "As soon as they would let me in. You were stung a lot of times and there were some... considerations when treating you."

"What sort of considerations?"

Liam shifted. "I didn't really understand it. I'll let the doctor explain."

That didn't sound promising, but Vanessa let it go.

"And the girls really are all safe?"

"Yes, we got them out safely. I had a tracker app on Karine's phone, so once we knew how to use it, we were able to get to you."

Vanessa explained how McBrien had found them at the house, using Andrea's name.

"McBrien was smart. If we hadn't already gotten the girls out, he probably would've been able to get away. He definitely had no plan to go to prison, that's for sure."

The doctor came into the room. Liam didn't even shift except to pull Vanessa closer.

"I'm Dr. Turner, Vanessa. I see your fiancé found you."

Fiancé? Vanessa looked at Liam. He just shrugged.

"Thanks, Doc," Liam said. "I had no problems finding her at all."

"How are you feeling?"

"Nothing hurts, so that's good, right?"

"We have you on some pain medication through your IV, nothing too strong, given the situation, but it's good you're not in any discomfort. Given the nature of sea nettle stings, all pain should be completely gone by tomorrow anyway."

"Great, but given what *situation*?" She looked from Dr. Turner to Liam. What weren't they telling her?

"We double-checked those numbers I was telling you about before," the doctor said to Liam.

Vanessa sat all the way up. "What numbers? What's going on?"

Dr. Turner took a step closer. "Treating the sea nettle stings was complicated by the fact that we found traces of hCG in your bloodstream."

She looked at Liam again then back at Dr. Turner. "What is hCG? Is that bad?"

"No." Dr. Turner shook his head. "It's the pregnancy hormone. Every pregnant woman has it in her blood."

"The pregnancy hormone…" Vanessa's voice trailed off, not sure she was actually understanding.

"Your fiancé thought it might be an incorrect test reading, since you couldn't be more than a few days pregnant."

"Yes, that's true. Is it even possible to tell this early?"

Dr. Turner nodded. "Yes, especially with a blood sample like we used. But what was even more interesting was the relatively high levels of hCG in your blood. That's what made us think you were further along in the pregnancy than you are."

"Is that bad?" Liam asked. "Dangerous?"

"No." Dr. Turner smiled. "High levels of hCG is usually indicative of a mis-estimated conception date or, as in your case, it means you're pregnant with multiples."

Vanessa couldn't seem to process what the doctor was saying. She looked at Liam again but he looked just as dumbfounded.

"What?" she finally asked.

The doctor patted her on the shoulder. "We won't know for sure for a while yet, so everyone should be sure to take that into consideration, but it's highly likely that you're pregnant with twins."

Vanessa turned and stared at Liam, who was staring back at her. As if from a distance she heard the doctor excuse himself and walk out, closing the door behind him.

"You're pregnant," Liam whispered.

"I can't believe it."

"With *twins*."

Vanessa shook her head and put a hand over her stomach. "What does this mean?" It was almost too much to process, given everything that had happened in the past twenty-four hours.

"It means we need to finish that conversation we started the other day at your apartment."

Vanessa tried to pull away. She didn't want to talk about Liam with other women. "Liam, look—"

"No, I want you to hear what I have to say, Nessa. I should've said it years ago, and I would've said it now anyway, even if the doctor hadn't just come in here and told us we're going to be tied to each other's lives forever with the baby—babies—you have inside you."

He cupped her face. "I'm not going to let our pride, or

miscommunication, or well-meaning family keep us apart any longer. We lost eight years of our life together, and I don't want to lose a minute more."

He brought his lips to hers and kissed her. Softly. Full of tenderness. The passion, for once, took a backseat. "Yes, there were other women. Too many. But none of them was you, Nessa. I thought I was being a playboy, enjoying my freedom. But really I was just killing time until I finally grew enough brains to come back and get you."

"Liam—"

He kissed her again. "And I was coming for you, Nessa. I just didn't know it yet. Your call gave me the excuse I needed. I love you. I've never stopped loving you. I should've fought for you then."

"I should've fought for you, too," she whispered. He wasn't solely to blame in this.

"I will spend the rest of my life fighting for our family. If there is one thing the past twenty-four hours has showed me, it's that I have no desire to live without you."

"But what about our jobs? You live in—"

"I. Don't. Care." He punctuated each word with another kiss. "I will quit my job and work at a convenience store before I will be separated from you again. Baby, babies, or just you and me—I don't care. I'm not leaving your side again, unless I hear the words directly from you for me to go. And even then I don't think I can do it."

These were the words Vanessa had dreamed of hearing for eight years. "Well, I don't think you have to worry about that because I don't plan to say them."

"Good."

There was a soft tap on the door. Derek peeked his head in. "Sorry to interrupt. We heard you were awake and someone was very interested in seeing you."

Karine flew in from behind Derek. "Vanessa!"

Vanessa opened her arms and the girl ran into them. Liam got up from the bed to allow the girls to embrace.

"I was so worried. I am so sorry I did not help more with swimming."

Vanessa smoothed Karine's hair. "No, no. Don't say that. We made it. Everybody made it. That's what counts."

Vanessa looked over at the doorway, where a little girl was standing next to Derek. "Who's that?" She smiled at the little girl.

"That's Tallinn. She's one of the girls from the boat. The youngest one I told you about."

"Tallinn demanded to see Liam," Derek said. "Especially when she found out Karine was coming here."

Liam made his way around the bed and knelt in front of Tallinn so they were close to the same height. "Hey, sweetie, how are you doing?"

The little girl looked down at the floor. Vanessa's heart melted as Liam put a finger under Tallinn's chin and smiled at her.

"I'm glad you're here," he said. "Want to come sit over here with me?"

Vanessa didn't know if the girl understood what Liam was saying, but she definitely understood the kindness in his voice. Liam sat on Vanessa's hospital bed and reached down to hoist Tallinn so she was sitting up there with them. A few moments later Liam was showing the girl how to make the bed move up and down. Soon the girl was giggling softly and playing with the buttons.

Liam would make a great father. Vanessa had no doubt about it.

He caught her looking at him.

"We've got to get these girls back to their families. Make sure they're safe. Then we're getting married," he said softly to her.

"Better late than never," she whispered back. "And in case you were wondering, I love you, too. Always have."

He winked. "I know."

One Year Later

VANESSA AND LIAM stood in the judge's chambers, the beautiful Rocky Mountains of Colorado Springs visible outside the window.

Vanessa hadn't made Liam go through on his promise to work at a convenience store so they could be together, although she honestly believed he would have if she had demanded to stay in the Outer Banks. But she knew his work at Omega Sector Critical Response Division was too important to him—too important in general—for him to quit. They'd bought a house here six months ago, since one look at Liam's bachelor pad had her decreeing she would never live there, nor allow any of her children to.

Liam had readily agreed.

It had taken two months of cutting through bureaucracy and red tape before they had been able to get the girls back to their families in Estonia. Vanessa had sworn she would never touch her parents' money, but she'd been wrong. When proper channels weren't working quickly enough to get the girls home, Vanessa found that her parents' money helped things work much faster. She'd had no qualms about using it for the girls.

Liam had helped her work through a lot of the anger with her parents. They had wanted to protect her, he'd explained to her more than once. Anything they'd done, as wrong as it might have been, had been done out of love. Vanessa would always mourn the years—and life—lost, but she could at least see his point and had begun to let them back into her life.

When she'd found out that her parents had set up funds to pay for all the girls' medical bills, had made sure they had one of the best therapists in Estonia to help them, and had set up college funds for all of them, she had given up the last hardness she'd held against them. These were her children's grandparents.

Her parents were here with them now in the judge's chamber, each holding one of their grandsons. Twins. Born four months ago. Healthy and perfect.

"Weren't you just in here a few months ago?" the judge asked.

"Yes, Your Honor," Liam replied. "Since you had made our marriage official, we were hoping you'd make our family official, too."

The older man raised one eyebrow at them. "I'm glad to see you don't have half of Colorado Springs here with you today like last time."

They had wanted to get married before the babies came, but between getting the girls back home, moving across the country and everything else that had been going on, neither of them had had the time or inclination to plan a wedding.

They had decided to just get married in the judge's chambers: simple and to the point.

Vanessa had invited her parents, who had come. Liam had invited a couple of the guys from Omega Sector.

The next thing they knew, so many people had come to witness their nuptials that the judge's chamber had been completely filled. The judge had ordered them all downstairs to the courtroom, and had performed the ceremony there.

Vanessa and Liam had both been touched by how many people had wanted to show their support. And especially touched by the fact that George and Rhonda had flown Karine and her parents over for the ceremony.

Karine had stood as Vanessa's maid of honor. Derek as Liam's best man.

"No, sir," Vanessa answered the judge. "Just family today."

They had found the families of all the girls—had personally witnessed that they were good family situations with parents that had been distraught by their daughters' abductions—and had returned them all to loving homes.

All except little Tallinn.

She'd been an orphan, had been one before she'd been kidnapped, and had no family to return to.

When Vanessa found out, she hadn't known what to do. The thought of putting her back in an orphanage where the same thing could happen to her again... Vanessa hadn't been able to even stomach it.

"She'll stay with us. We'll adopt her," Liam had said.

It had taken money and time. And a special visa that had allowed Tallinn into the US because of the trafficking situation.

She now stood between Vanessa and Liam, holding each of their hands, having picked up English in the way only a child could, and smiled at the judge.

"I am happy to sign this final adoption decree for you to join this family, Miss Tallinn." The judge smiled at the little girl. "Are you sure that's what you want? For them to become your mommy and daddy?"

Tallinn's grin was from ear to ear. "Yes, sir. Then I want ice cream. Baby brothers can't have any because they too little."

The judge chuckled. "Well, let me sign this so we can get on to other important things."

He signed the paper and handed it to Liam, who thanked him.

Tallinn ran off to see her mimi and granddad and baby brothers.

Liam wrapped an arm around Vanessa's waist and pulled her closer as they walked out of the chambers. "It wasn't the way we'd planned it, but we have a beautiful family, Mrs. Goetz."

Vanessa kissed him.

"Forever."

* * * * *

Janie Crouch's
OMEGA SECTOR: CRITICAL RESPONSE
series continues next month with
MAN OF ACTION.
Look for it wherever Intrigue books
and ebooks are sold!

Lynne Graham has sold 35 million books!

To settle a debt, she'll have to become his mistress...

Nikolai Drakos is determined to have his revenge against the man who destroyed his sister. So stealing his enemy's intended fiancé seems like the perfect solution! Until Nikolai discovers that woman is Ella Davies...

Read on for a tantalising excerpt from Lynne Graham's 100th book,

BOUGHT FOR THE GREEK'S REVENGE

'Mistress,' Nikolai slotted in cool as ice.

Shock had welded Ella's tongue to the roof of her mouth because he was sexually propositioning her and nothing could have prepared her for that. She wasn't drop-dead gorgeous... *he* was! Male heads didn't swivel when Ella walked down the street because she had neither the length of leg nor the curves usually deemed necessary to attract such attention. Why on earth could he be making *her* such an offer?

'But we don't even know each other,' she framed dazedly. 'You're a stranger...'

'If you live with me I won't be a stranger for long,' Nikolai pointed out with monumental calm. And the very sound of that inhuman calm and cool forced her to flip round and settle distraught eyes on his lean darkly handsome face.

'You can't be serious about this!'

'I assure you that I am deadly serious. Move in and I'll forget your family's debts.'

'But it's a *crazy* idea!' she gasped.

'It's not crazy to me,' Nikolai asserted. 'When I want anything, I go after it hard and fast.'

Her lashes dipped. Did he want her like that? Enough to track her down, buy up her father's debts, and try and buy rights to her and her body along with those debts? The very idea of that made her dizzy and plunged her brain into even greater turmoil. 'It's immoral… it's blackmail.'

'It's definitely *not* blackmail. I'm giving you the benefit of a choice you didn't have before I came through that door,' Nikolai Drakos fielded with a glittering cool. 'That choice is yours to make.'

'Like hell it is!' Ella fired back. 'It's a complete cheat of a supposed offer!'

Nikolai sent her a gleaming sideways glance. 'No the real cheat was you kissing me the way you did last year and then saying no and acting as if I had grossly insulted you,' he murmured with lethal quietness.

'You *did* insult me!' Ella flung back, her cheeks hot as fire while she wondered if her refusal that night had started off his whole chain reaction. What else could possibly be driving him?

Nikolai straightened lazily as he opened the door. 'If you take offence that easily, maybe it's just as well that the answer is no.'

Visit **www.millsandboon.co.uk/lynnegraham**
to order yours!

MILLS & BOON®

MILLS & BOON®

Mills & Boon have been at the heart of romance since 1908... and while the fashions may have changed, one thing remains the same: from pulse-pounding passion to the gentlest caress, we're always known how to bring romance alive.

Now, we're delighted to present you with these irresistible illustrations, inspired by the vintage glamour of our covers. So indulge your wildest dreams and unleash your imagination as we present the most iconic Mills & Boon moments of the last century.

Visit **www.millsandboon.co.uk/ArtofRomance** to order yours!